# TEXAS LOVING

Leisha parted the shirt to expose the colorful wealth of bruising upon Kenitay's chest and middle. "This looks awful!" she cried in distress. "Are you sure nothing's—"

Her words broke off as his fingers cupped her chin, lifting her head. "Nothing," he repeated softly, "except my heart."

Leisha closed her eyes and leaned into the gentle possession of his kiss.

"Thank you," he whispered against her lips.

"For the kiss?"

"For my life."

"I'm afraid that poor life's not worth much right now."

"If it were possible, I would pledge it to you."

Leisha took a shaky breath and tried to laugh. "What would I do with it?"

"Whatever you like." His eyes were open, a brilliant emerald color and full of glittering promise as he teased more kisses along her jaw and down her neck. "I have committed my future to my father's memory, but for now, I am yours."

A slight tremor passed through Leisha, a combination of warm lips moving upon sensitive skin and hot suggestion taking over weakening will. "Mine," she mused as her hands came up to hold his head and her torso arched to greet the brush of his mouth at the moist vee of her shirt opening . . .

Books by Dana Ransom

THE PIRATE'S CAPTIVE
REBEL VIXEN
LOVE'S GLORIOUS GAMBLE
ALEXANDRA'S ECSTASY
LIAR'S PROMISE
WILD, SAVAGE LOVE
WILD WYOMING LOVE
DAKOTA DAWN
DAKOTA DESIRE
DAKOTA DESTINY
DAKOTA PROMISES
TEMPTATION'S TRAIL
TEXAS DESTINY
WILD TEXAS BRIDE
TEXAS RENEGADE

Coming in December 1996:
SWEET TEXAS DREAMS

Published by Zebra Books

# TEXAS RENEGADE

## DANA RANSOM

**ZEBRA BOOKS**
**KENSINGTON PUBLISHING CORP.**

ZEBRA BOOKS are published by

Kensington Publishing Corp.
850 Third Avenue
New York, NY 10022

First Printing: March, 1996

Printed in the United States of America
10 9 8 7 6 5 4 3 2 1

*For Audrey Stancil and
Nancy and Mary Scott:
fans who have become friends
and make it all worthwhile.*

# Prologue

"Stay put."

Hard words for a boy of ten to obey when anxiety and anxiousness had him fidgeting right down to the soles of his new boots. But the soft, authoritative tones of his stepfather's voice had never been questioned before and wouldn't be now. His features solemn, the half-breed boy nodded up at the man behind the Texas Ranger star. And the man smiled down at him, a reassuring gesture further reinforced by the light knock of his knuckles beneath the boy's determined chin.

Kenitay returned to his impatient vigil, leaning against the peeled bark porch rail. Beneath the shading tip of his Stetson, watchful green eyes missed little of what went on in the dusty surround of Arizona's Fort Apache. He wanted to believe his adopted father could make his wish come true. It would be too cruel to come so far only to fail. It could well be his last chance to see his true father; anticipation swelled amid a bittersweet sorrow for the circumstances.

His father was a proud Apache warrior. For Kenitay's first five years, he and his white mother had lived with him, enjoying the nomadic life of the fierce and free people in the savage beauty of the West Texas Bend. Then the rangers had come and a great price of horses had been paid to return his mother to her own kind. He had gone with her and, while he had done his best to learn the ways

of the whites, his soul still stirred with the age-old rhythm
of his father's clan.

And now those proud people were no more. People who
had ruled the plains and known no master had been conquered by vast numbers of invading whites unwilling to
share a harsh land of plenty with those who had been there
first. The only way to survive was to surrender—and a people who had lived off an ungiving land for centuries knew
all about the price of survival. It was often bitter but it had
to be paid. And pay, they had. The cost was their freedom.
The cost was their homeland. In order to satisfy the white
government's greed and fear, they would be banished from
the mountains and plains they loved to return in two years
from some foreign place called Florida. A place of hills
and water and timber and grass, they'd been told. A place
where they could all live together in safety, not as prisoners.
Perhaps it would not be so bad, this place, Florida.

Then why had his adopted uncle's gaze gone so dark
with shadows when they talked of it?

Kenitay hadn't seen his father since he'd taken a Chiricahua wife and followed her people to Arizona, as was
the Apache custom. It was distance, not his new family's
dictates, that kept them apart. And now, in this final hour
of the Apache people, he'd been brought across those arid
miles to say good-bye. And his heart was breaking.

It was big enough news to reach them in the sleepy
town of Terlingua, Texas. After another year of leading
the U.S. Army on a futile chase, Geronimo, their last great
leader, was making his terms of surrender. Kodene, Kenitay's father, was one of those last fearless holdouts shun-
ning U.S. government rule even though his Chiricahua
wife and remaining family were residing peacefully on the
Arizona reservation. Kodene's spirit had been too restless
to confine amid the stale smells of camp life and reluctant
charity. But now that the time of fighting was at an end,
this once-legendary warrior was ready to lay down his

arms in hopes of finding peace amongst his family. When news had come that these last brave rebels would come through Fort Apache before following the rest of the renegades to Florida, Kenitay had begged an opportunity to see him, to speak with him. Because his own young spirit was troubled. He had to hear with his own ears that his father forgave him for remaining behind in their homeland while the rest of his people were sent away.

It wasn't that he didn't care for his adopted family. He did. He'd found a place amongst them, close to their hearts. His stepfather was a deep-souled man with a quiet strength, an unshakable sense of honor, and a love great enough to accept a half-caste child along with the two he'd fathered. And though Kenitay dressed in the white man's stiff-soled boots and cotton cloth, he'd never lost touch with his Apache roots—his uncle had seen to that—nor had he ever been made to feel ashamed of them. That respect his new family held for the part of his past they didn't share caused his stepfather to bring him all the way from Texas in the faint hope that a few words could ease a burdened mind.

Kenitay leaned on his elbows and studied the dusty, blue-coated soldiers with interest. There was a time in his not-so-distant past when such a sight would have filled him with hatred. They had been his enemy, a threat to his people. Now, they were just men, like his stepfather and the Rangers he commanded. And he hoped these men would listen to the request of a Texas Ranger captain: the plea of a son to say farewell to his father.

Something was happening outside the gates. From where he stood on the porch outside the army commander's office, he couldn't quite see what it was. He glanced over his shoulder at the forbidding door that was firmly closed to him. Behind it, Ranger Jack would be arguing his case. His stepfather had said to trust him and he did, implicitly. He'd also said to stay put, but that was made more difficult once a ten-year-old's curiosity was aroused. He could see the soldiers gathering outside the gates and he could see the reservation Apache gathering— men, women, and children. And there were guns. A furrow of concern lined his brow. Why would the soldiers bring guns to bear upon a peaceful people?

He was off the porch before a conscious decision was made to disobey and once he started toward the commotion, his own circumstances were easily forgotten. His step quickened and soon he was running, caught up in the confusion and chaos of the moment.

It was the fear he saw on the faces of the Apache people that woke a panic in his heart. It was a timeless response to yet another betrayal, and though Kenitay was too young to remember such things, still he was shaken to the core. The Chiricahua and Warm Springs people living on the reservation had taken no part in the recent uprisings. They had been living content with their lot, causing no trouble, believing themselves wards of a benevolent government. So why were guns being pointed at them? Why were they being separated, the women and children from the men? The wariness inbred in them bespoke a treachery they were helpless to protest. And then the word they feared was finally spoken . . . *Florida.* An exile not only for the rebellious but for the obedient as well. Kenitay watched it all, not understanding the connotations.

A sudden shove sent him stumbling forward, out from under his new Stetson and in the way of a stern-featured sergeant. Before he could scuttle to his feet, the soldier had him by the shirt collar and was slinging him toward the weeping group of Apache women.

"Git on over there with the rest a yer kind, ya sneakin' little savage."

"But I'm not—"

A sharp kick to the ribs knocked the rest of his objection from his lungs.

"Hey, Sarge. Go easy. He's just a kid."

"Kid, nothin'. Nits make lice. You ain't never seen what their kind does when a decent white man turns his back on 'em. Go on, boy. Quit draggin' yer feet. The train ain't gonna wait on ya." That was followed by gritty laughter as Kenitay was hurled to his hands and knees amongst the huddled gathering. In an instant of stark clarity, Kenitay realized the man's mistake. Without a hat to cover his straight black hair, he didn't look like the son of a Texas Ranger captain. He looked like an Apache.

His fright was overwhelming and the distance to that safe porch seemed miles away. Kenitay regained his feet and started to walk back toward the fort. He tried to make his steps sure and unafraid but one glimpse to the side told him his progress was noticed.

"Hey, you!"

And he began to run.

Before he'd gone ten feet, rough hands got hold of him and wrestled him around, away from where he never should have left. His heart was pumping wildly, his thoughts were frozen. He screamed aloud in terror as they pushed him back toward where the others cowered.

"I'm not a reservation Indian! I'm not an Apache!"

The words denying his heritage were out of his mouth before he could stop them, words born of fear and desperation. His wide eyes were fastened on that far building that held his stepfather as he struggled wildly to get free.

"Ranger Ja—!"

His cry was halted by the smashing force of a rifle stock against his jaw. His world went black and the taste of his own blood was as thick as his terror as he pitched face-first onto the hard Arizona ground, sinking into nothingness.

"Kenitay?"

Jack Bass searched the abandoned porch, concern

mounting to overtake the disappointment of the news he carried. His familiarity with the U.S. Army hadn't inspired much hope in him but he'd been willing to try, just to give ease to the desolation in his son's eyes. And now he had nothing good to tell him.

But where had he gone?

"Kenny?"

Surely he wouldn't have wandered off, not after the danger had been impressed upon him. The men in this fort were not the rangers who had accepted him amongst them. These men were hardened Indian fighters, frustrated by long patrols chasing a ghostlike enemy. They wouldn't much care that the soft-spoken boy was half white and lived tame with his mother's family. The army commander hadn't. There was little sympathy for the Apache here in Arizona, not on this triumphant eve of their destruction. There would be no visit with one of their renegade leaders. There was nothing left to do but go home and try as best he could to comfort the boy he thought of as his own.

But where was he?

" 'Scuse me, Private. Have you seen a boy hanging around where he doesn't belong? He was here waiting for me just a minute ago."

"Sorry, Ranger. Ain't seen one."

"What's going on?" He nodded toward the congestion of soldiers and Indians on the other side of the gate.

"Order just come down that all of 'em was to go to Florida."

Jack frowned. He had no great love for the Apache but they had earned his respect as an enemy of unequalled ferocity, daring, and endurance. He wasn't ashamed to claim a trace of their proud blood in his own veins. And he wasn't ashamed to raise one of their kin under his own roof.

"I thought these folks were under your protection. I hadn't heard they'd been giving you any trouble."

"An Injun's an Injun. Good riddance to all of 'em, I say. Then maybe a man can rest easy in his hair at night."

A particularly bad feeling came over Jack just then. He stepped down off the porch and started toward the front gates. The private was quick to put himself in front of him.

"Sorry, Ranger. Yer gonna have to steer clear of that. Army business."

"But my son might have wandered down there."

"Don't you worry. The men will shoo him away. Probably jus' prowlin' around like young boys are wont to. Be back as soon as he figures he's been missed."

Then Jack spoke it plain. "He's part Apache." The glaze that came over the private's eyes instilled a terror deep down in his heart. "I'd better go look for him."

"No. Can't let you do that. I'll pass the word around for you. What's the kid's name?"

"Kenitay."

That sheen of hostility grew more intense.

"He's not part of this," Jack was pressed to explain. "His people are Mescalero. I want him brought back to me unharmed."

The private's hard gaze said clearly that the loss of one half-breed boy was not a big priority. "I'll do what I can, Ranger."

Jack was still waiting for him to do it as the day stretched into heavy evening shadow. The fort was alive with activity. It was hard to gain a second of anyone's time—they all made it known that his interference would be unappreciated. He was a Texan and a ranger, not of the Arizona military. He had no pull here, just whatever courtesy they thought to extend. And none of them was feeling very courteous. Finally, he breached professional protocol to push his way back into the colonel's office to ask in a tightly controlled voice what they were doing about finding his son.

"Cap'n," the officer said with a clinical cool, "has it occurred to you that the boy might not want to be found? That just maybe he wants to go with his own people?"

"*I'm* his people! Me and his mama and his brother and sister! He didn't come here to run away. He came to say good-bye to his father."

"And perhaps that's what he's decided to do. Cap'n Bass, I wouldn't presume to tell you what to do, but were I you, I'd just head back for Texas. The boy knows where you live and he'll find his way back there if he's a mind to."

"We're not talking about a lost dog, here. That boy is only ten years old," Jack ground out.

"He's an Apache, isn't he?"

"And that's that?"

"Yessir, I'm afraid it is."

Seething with frustration, Jack growled, "Guess I'll just have to go look for myself."

"I wouldn't advise that, Ranger. You go stirring things up and I'll have you clapped in irons until the lot of them are moved out tomorrow."

They were at a momentary impasse, eyes locked, wills grappling, when there was a tap at the door.

"In!"

"You wanted to see me, sir?"

"Yes, Sergeant, step in. Cap'n Bass, here, says his boy, a ten-year-old half-breed, might have got mixed up with our reservation Apaches by mistake. Do you know anything about that?"

"Nossir." The sergeant's features never so much as flickered as he spoke that bold lie. He was seeing the fall of his career along with that of his rifle butt. "Ain't nobody under guard that don't belong there, sir."

The colonel made a self-absolving gesture. "There you

go, Cap'n Bass. He's not with them. I suggest you check around to see if any horses have come up missing. Your boy could well have lit out to meet up with his daddy."

Jack clapped on his hat and set it square. "Not without telling me, he wouldn't."

"Be glad to put you up for the night, Ranger Bass. If the sentries get wind of the boy, I'll see you're sent for."

"I'd appreciate it," came his dry-as-Texas-dust drawl.

Out in the lonesome darkness of the porch, Jack's steely bravado gave way to a parent's anxiety and pain. His unsteady hands scrubbed over the taut angles of his face. What could have happened to the boy? Dear God, there was no way he was going back to his wife to tell her he'd lost another one of her children.

"Ranger!"

The call hissed from the hidden passageway between the board and batten buildings. Jack approached with caution, his palm nestling against the stock of his .45 until he could make out the shape of a slight figure hanging back in the shadows.

"Who's there?"

"I have news of the boy."

At that point, Jack abandoned care. He hopped off the porch and strode back into the deeper hues of the night. "What do you know?"

The man came forward, not much more than a boy himself. Jack could tell by his manner of dress that he was one of the Army scouts, an Apache used to track down his own kind. He wore the four-button blue tunic over white army-issue underwear, a Hardie hat, and a red headband to identify him as a "friendly." Furtive eyes flashed about, then he extended a small garment. Jack took it and his whole world fell away in an instant.

It was Kenitay's jacket. It was black with crusted blood.

* * *

Awareness came and went in feverish waves. At first, Kenitay thought the rocking motion was a part of that delirious dream. It went on and on without ceasing, that side-to-side shift, causing pain with every jostle. He was lying down but the position was cramped, forcing his knees to an odd, uncomfortable angle. His head was cradled in softness to cushion the movement that brought such agony to bear. Over the pounding of his misery, he heard gently tittered words phrased in his father's tongue. And that's when it came to him.

He was amongst the Apache.

He was on a train.

The train bound for Florida.

Sitting up nearly cost him his fragile consciousness. His first glimpse out cloudy windows confronted him with a strange, lush landscape as foreign and frightening as the pain in his face. He tried to cry out but protests were sealed behind the massive swelling to his cheek and jaw. A tiny bleating sound of panic was all he could manage.

The woman who held him began a flow of soothing sentiments to persuade him to lie back down and rest. Fretfully, he obeyed, blinking back his distraught tears. He would be brave. Surely, Ranger Jack would come for him. How far away could Florida be? On the other side of Texas, closer to home than even Arizona.

Ranger Jack would come.

All he had to do was wait.

# One

They squatted over their small cookfire in dirty drover coats like desert predators sharing carrion. There was no talk. Tension and weariness were telegraphed by scarcity of movement and in features cut as sharply as the wind-ravaged buttes around them. A saddlebag sat in their midst, an indifferent distance from each of them but very much the focus of their thoughts. It held their future, be it long with luxury or violently short. Knowing it could go either way made for uneasy trail companions who trusted each other about as much as they did the world around them.

They never heard a sound of warning, no jingle of tack, no shush of hooves. The figure just appeared at the edge of their fire, as sudden and silent as a ghost of one of the Apaches who used to haunt the West Texas plains. All hands grabbed for lanterns as a soft voice drawled out, "Mind if I approach your fire?"

Something in the quality of that voice made them hesitate.

Taking no objection as permission, the figure moved in closer. The spill of firelight moved up from the curled toes of Apache-style moccasins to the loose trousers tucked in at the knees. A buckskin shirt hung to mid-thigh and was cinched at the waist by a pistol belt. A very small waist. Beneath the intimidating tilt of a Stetson, only the finely cut jawline was visible, that and the uncompromising line of a mouth too ripe to belong to any man.

"You boys look mighty edgy. Expecting trouble?"

"Don't hurt to be prepared for it," one of the men replied. "Where you hail from, friend?"

"Blue Creek."

The hard cases exchanged a look. Blue Creek was a close cousin to Terlingua.

"Got a name?"

"Bass."

There was a collective gasp as trouble suddenly took on more meaning than they were prepared for.

"Harm Bass?" one of them whispered with an almost religious reverence.

"If it was, you'd all be dead by now. Happens the sheriff you shot during that robbery was a right good friend of the family. You'd be smart to let me take you in alive or my father will make you long for the mercy of a quick drop on a short rope."

No one moved.

In that moment of gathering intensity, the presence of three men and four coffee tins took on significance just a tad too late as a large shadow separated from the night to deliver a felling blow with his revolver butt. Their challenger went down without a sound.

"You boys are about as sloppy as a batch of cheap whores, " growled the motley group's leader as he stepped in from the night. Good thing he'd been out relieving himself when danger had come calling. "Letting somebody get the drop on you like you was a bunch of schoolkids."

"We never heard nothing, Drake. Came up outta nowheres. Said the name was Bass."

That was added as if it would excuse everything. But Drake Collier was unconvinced. He hunkered down and gripped the intruder's shoulder, flopping the limp figure over. Then he stared as the Stetson came loose to reveal a fan of long blond hair.

"Goldarnit, Drake! That there's a woman!"

But Collier didn't reply. His mouth had gone suddenly dry. His anger with his men was replaced by something much uglier as he studied the way soft buckskin molded to a tempting swell of bosom. An unexpected bonus. His lips curled up into what might have been a smile.

"What are we gonna do with her?"

Collier's laugh was incredibly cruel. "You can't be that stupid."

"Drake, she's a Bass!"

"Tell you what. I'll save you all from him by keeping her to myself. How'd that be?"

No one had anything to say. The name *Bass* had spooked them plenty. They'd heard things . . .

With a sneer of contempt for his compadres' timidity, Collier hooked his hand beneath the young woman's underarm and dragged her away from their campfire. Knowing him like they did, the others would never think to interfere so they stayed put and sweated the fact that his lusts gave them more to fear than just a hangman's noose.

What a stupid mistake, a possibly fatal mistake.

That fact swam back into her throbbing head on a swell of sickness. Pin dots of pain engulfed her vision as she tried to open her eyes. A large shadow loomed over her, the threat of it vague to a mind dazed beyond comprehension.

She was on the ground. The hard-packed Texas soil made for a rocky resting place. She should get up. She should do something about protecting herself. But these, too, were vague concepts. Movement was impossible. The thunder in her head overwhelmed all else.

The shadow grew nearer, enveloping her, settling to become a crushing weight on top of her. Sour scents assaulted her nose but when she tried to turn her head to the side, agony exploded through her temples. Then a brutal pressure took hold of her jaw, trapping her face, holding it immobile as lips ground into hers. A sound of objection gurgled up but was easily smothered. She was gasping raggedly when the smashing kiss finally lifted. A harsher breathing, louder than her own, rasped above. Then the weight was gone and she knew a moment of confused relief.

Until she felt a tugging at her clothes.

Struggle was useless. Her limbs wouldn't obey her. A heavy fog numbed her responses, the dizziness making her too lethargic to fend off hands that pulled at her with hasty purpose. A purpose unknown to her. Until her knees were wrenched wide apart. Until a pain that far surpassed the one in her head tore up inside her.

Leisha Bass's mind was suddenly, frightfully clear. This man—this smelly, vicious, beast of a man—was raping her of her innocence. And she could either lie there and wait until it was over and let him kill her to cover up her shame . . . or she could stop him.

She gritted her teeth against a scream as he slammed into her again, streaking her insides with a violating agony. Fury replaced fright. He wasn't paying any attention to her now, too focused on his filthy pleasure. And that was his mistake. Leisha's hand groped downward, seeking the top of her boot and the knife she kept there. Grasping it with a firm hold, she jammed it between his ribs with the same force he'd used to invade her.

As she tottered back into the circle of firelight, she could tell that not one of the men had ever expected to see her again. Especially not with their dead leader's gun in her hand. She took a grim satisfaction in their disbelief. It almost made up for what she'd suffered due to her earlier carelessness. Well, she wouldn't be so careless again.

"Taste dirt, *cabrones!*"

All three flopped belly-down without a word.

Shock was shaking up through her. Only outrage had gotten her this far. She wanted to kill them for what they, in their cowardice, were willing to let the other do to her. But she forced those purely female thoughts aside in lieu of a better, colder revenge. She would take them in as her prisoners. She'd tie their hands and herd them in front of her horse like the animals they were. And the accolades she received would numb the horror and disgrace of what had been done to her. How dare they assume she would be so easy to dismiss!

Then the gun in her hand began to waver wildly and her knees, wobbly at best, started to give way. As she tried desperately to brace herself, the trauma her body sustained betrayed her efforts. The darkness was back, flooding upward in an inevitable tide. But as she sank into it, she was aware of a strong support beneath her elbows. Thoughts of the dead man, Collier, surged up to bring one last frantic resistance. Then, the words stopped her fight. Soft-spoken Apache words that whispered all was well.

She twisted around, battling the encroaching blackness, to get a glimpse of her rescuer. His features bobbed in an indistinguishable blur. Green eyes. She remembered green eyes as all else faded away.

Thirteen years was a long time yet he knew her immediately. There was no way to disguise that arrogant Bass posture or the cold ferociousness of her low growl. Leisha Bass. Lovely. Lethal.

He wasn't sure what he'd stumbled into. He recognized the signs of outlaws on the run. And he could see the signs of abuse in Leisha's blood-streaked yellow hair and in the red flecks on her bared thighs. Explosive anger rose swiftly in him. He'd been angry for thirteen years but that couldn't top this sudden horrendous fury.

He didn't have much time to reflect because she was starting to go down, swooning even as he reached her. Her beautiful blue eyes darted up to his—eyes like her father's, but he couldn't say he saw any recognition there. Then she was gone, hanging slack in his embrace.

The three on the ground were casting nervous looks behind them as he shifted her weight so she wouldn't interfere with the free use of the gun in his hand. They were scared and he could feel no danger from them. This wasn't his business. He had no interest in them but he didn't want to be looking over his shoulder all night either.

"It's like this, boys," he murmured in a crisply spoken English that was almost conversational. "I've got no time for you. Now that means either I can let you go and you can run like hell into the next county or . . . I can kill you. Makes no difference to me but thought it might to you."

"We had no part in what happened to the woman," one of them yelped frantically. "We be thieves, mister. That's it. An' we don't want to die. I'm a fast runner, mister. Could be I'd make Mexico by morning."

He cocked the gun he'd taken from Leisha's hand. "All three of you of that same mind?"

They stammered that they were.

"Get up slow and drop your hardware." They scrambled to do so, a little of their confidence returning now that death didn't seem to be staring down that single bore with so much certainty. Crafty eyes darted to the saddlebag. Seeing that furtive shift of attention, he growled, "Leave it. And the horses."

"But mister, we're a long way from nowhere—"

"I could send you straight to hell if you were looking for a shorter trip."

Suddenly, the long walk didn't seem to bother them as

much. The three of them shuffled off into the darkness and after listening for a while, he eased the hammer down on the revolver. He understood the nature of men too well to fear they'd be back. None of them was a leader capable of organizing an attack on him to regain what was theirs. They'd run like the coyotes they were and would count themselves lucky. Maybe they would make Mexico by morning.

Leisha became his prime concern. Gently, he lowered her down on top of one of the men's bedrolls. She lay there, sprawled and seemingly boneless, unaware of the sight she presented in her half-clad state. He tried not to pay it any attention, either. He sifted his fingers back through her matted hair, feeling the beginnings of an impressive lump where the skin was split and discolored. Rummaging through the bandits' belongings, he found a clean neckerchief, wet it, and bound it snugly about her brow. She never stirred. Fearing that the Mountain Spirits might already be luring her soul away, he loosened the bag of *hoddentin* he carried on his ammunition belt and placed a pinch of those precious powders upon her tongue. His White Man's wisdom told him it was only the yellow pollen of the cattail rush but his Indian ancestry toted the miraculous power of the sacred offering. And in times of trouble, he always relied on the whisperings of his Apache soul over the shallow truths he'd learned in mission schools. They hadn't been able to beat that out of him.

Having done all he could for the more serious of her injuries, he let his attention shift to the other personal and perhaps deeper wound. A dire oath moved silently upon his lips as he eased his palm along one sleek thigh. He'd seen what she'd done to the pig who'd taken her and he applauded her bravery. But that wouldn't make the act itself any easier to live with.

With a touch that was whisper-soft and as reverent as if he was handling a child, he bathed her and tugged up the baggy trousers he'd found discarded near the dead man. Though the initial damage had been done, he couldn't see any sign of the dead man's seed. She would be broken but not breeding. That was good. A small consolation.

"Your spirit is strong, *silah*," he murmured with a degree of tough admiration. "You will survive this." Unable to help himself, he stroked a callused hand along one still cheek.

With one sudden move, as quick and unexpected as a snake strike, she nearly had his heart on her knife tip before he could react.

She was snarling like a wild thing when he caught her wrist and compressed it until the blade fell from numbed fingers. Her body thrashed beneath his, all taut, hard muscle and supple strength as he pressed her down to keep her from harming herself. She was a strong woman. Excitingly so—if he could have forgotten the circumstances.

"*Enjuh, silah.* All is well. I won't hurt you. I'm not one of them. They're gone. I'm not one of them."

She went still except for the way her chest was heaving with frantic and furious breaths. Her gaze was cloudy, unfocused by the blow she'd taken to the head, but the quiet calm of his voice seemed to reach her. There were tears on her face. However, fearing he would alarm her further, he fought the desire to brush them away.

"It's all right, *silah.* I'm taking you home to your family. You're safe now."

That news agitated when it should have reassured. Her head began to toss restlessly.

"Don't . . . don't . . ."

"Don't what?"

"Don't tell them how you found me. Don't tell them . . ."

"I won't."

She relaxed then, her confused gaze flickering, easing

down into a more natural peace. He waited, retaining her wrists until he felt her go loose-limbed and vulnerable. Then he backed away, troubled by the depth of tender feeling stirring in a heart that should have been impervious to such betrayal.

She was a Bass.

He should have let them kill her. It was better than she and her family deserved from him. After what they'd done.

Too upset to remain in watch over her, he squatted down beside the saddlebag, figuring it would give him some clue as to what he'd stumbled upon. And looking inside, there was no doubt. It was stuffed with money. The men were bank robbers, and fearless, foolish Leisha had thought to take them in single-handedly. Like father, like daughter. That much hadn't changed. He fingered the bank notes pensively. There was a lot of currency in the bag, enough for him to escape the territory and live in splendor. Perhaps in California. Somewhere he could shake off and lose the stigma of *renegade*. He'd lived in the White world before. He'd have no difficulty convincing them he was of their kind. If that was what he wanted to do. But it wasn't. Other things held a priority in his life.

Getting even with the Basses was one of them.

They might have turned their backs on him but he hadn't forgotten them. Not by a long shot.

He flung down the bulging leather pouch and dropped into a cross-legged position before the fire, opposite Leisha. He studied her through narrowed eyes while his mouth worked into a thin curl of retribution. If he was any kind of man, he would make use of this opportunity. Instead, what was he doing? Coddling the enemy, allowing tender memory to geld the righteous anger burning for expression. Tension and traitorous affection warred within him.

*Yusn*, she was beautiful. She'd been a fiery child, more arrogant and self-sure than any female had a right to be.

She'd never backed down before anything, not even then. Oh, how that had angered a young boy trying to establish his fledgling manhood. She'd refused him the slightest dignity. She'd been the better rider, the better tracker, the better runner, the better aim. And she'd shown a cool contempt for his tantrums and brash assertions of superiority. He'd known she was his equal and it galled him that she knew it, too.

Until he'd kissed her.

It had been a rough mashing of mouths, an impulsive gesture by an angry boy determined to prove his mastery. And he had. She'd backed away from him in a confused wobble. He'd expected her to hit him. But oddly enough, her expression had gone all stiff and funny and her eyes welled up with tears. Tears! That had shocked him to the soul for he'd never seen her cry about anything. Then she'd run from him without a word and instead of feeling proud of himself, he'd felt somehow much smaller.

Staring across the fire with a dark intensity, he wondered how it would feel to kiss her now. Then he chided himself severely for having that curiosity. He'd as soon trust a scorpion than believe in a Bass again. He'd had thirteen hard years to come to that conclusion and he wasn't about to change it now just because his childhood nemesis had grown up to be startlingly lovely and all his mindless male glands were responding. Appearances were deceiving. Her father had taught him that. An ironic lesson.

It was then she started making soft, plaintive sounds in her sleep. He tried to ignore them. He couldn't be expected to give her comfort. Who'd been there for him? He glared into the flames, his face pulling into disagreeable lines. Let her fight her own demons. But his gaze kept sneaking up for a glimpse of her and the hard angles of his expression wouldn't hold.

Muttering a curse, he went to settle in next to her. He murmured her name and she surprised him by sitting up to entangle her arms about his neck. He could feel the dampness of her cheek pressed into the hollow of his throat. He swallowed jerkily.

"Don't cry," he heard himself saying in a strangely tight voice.

"Daddy?" Her cry wavered pitifully.

"It's all right." Daddy, indeed! But his hand was stroking her hair in a soothing rhythm and the atonal melody of an old Apache chant came back to him, moving his chest in a calming vibration as he softly hummed and rocked her in his arms. Her hold on him didn't lessen as her panic stilled. He'd hoped it would even as he nudged the golden tangle of her hair and let his lips move over it in a brief caress. His eyes closed and he was lost.

They stayed like that for some time, each dependent upon the solace found within the other.

"I hate you," he mumbled finally. "I hate all of you. That's not going to change." But contrarily, he was mouthing kisses against her uninjured brow and his heart was beating with a crazy, bittersweet distress. Words spilled out in helpless abandon. "I love you, Leisha. I've always loved you. How could you have abandoned me so easily?"

Then there was nothing but melancholy night sounds to form a reply.


He awoke with the clank of gun metal against his teeth. "Who are you?"

Careful not to move anything beyond his eyelids, he looked up to see Leisha kneeling beside him. She looked bad, face flushed and damp with fever, her eyes all glassy and vague, her breathing coming in uneven gasps. But the barrel of the gun she'd jammed into his mouth was fatally steady.

Slowly, he moved the gun aside with a non-threatening

sweep of his hand. "I'm the man who saved your life last night."

She blinked in confusion, then looked impossibly haughty. "I didn't need your help."

A smile quirked his lips. "No, of course you didn't."

"The money—"

"It's right over there. I didn't touch it."

"I mean to take it back. I'm not sharing the reward with you. I tracked them down. I had them under my gun."

"It's all yours."

"The man I killed—"

"I buried him."

"The others?"

"They took off."

"You let them go?" Even dazed, she managed to sound accusing.

"I couldn't watch them and see to you. They were nothing. Not worth the waste of a bullet."

She nodded then, an awkward movement that brought a furrow of pain to her brow. She was struggling with alertness. "You were speaking to me in Apache. Who are your people?"

"It doesn't matter now. They're all dead."

She seemed to consider that for a time, her expression softening with a sympathy he didn't want from her. She lifted a trembling hand to her forehead. It was a fragile gesture, defying the growl of her tone. "I suppose you're waiting for me to thank you."

"You don't need to thank me. In fact, I'd rather you didn't. I don't want us to be beholden to one another."

She picked that moment to slump forward, right into his arms as he was sitting up to catch her. She mumbled a few incoherent words that blew warm and electric against the skin of his bared throat. Then a soft, surrendering sigh breathed out of her and he found he was the one trembling.

It was time to get her to her own people.

He made short work of quitting the crude camp. He saddled her horse. They'd ride together. He strung the other four behind them. He'd take those with him and use them and their tack for barter. He tied the saddlebag down behind the saddle skirt. He kicked out the remaining ashes of their fire and loaded Leisha up in front of him. Then he started out for the base of the Chisos, the place his heart still called home no matter how he might deny it.

She didn't wake again and that made the ride easier. As easy as it could be to hold a woman like Leisha Bass without improper thoughts. Her head was resting upon his shoulder, providing a constant torment as her yellow hair tickled beneath his chin with every rocking movement. Bad temper increased in tandem with bodily tension and by midmorning, his jaw ached with it. He was tempted to shove her out of the saddle and never look back, to take her down to the ground and never look ahead. It was a miserable morning, full of chafing emotions.

He stopped at midday to let the horses blow and to take in some water. When he tilted the canteen up to Leisha's mouth, she drank greedily then murmured a surprisingly docile, "Thank you." That low, submissive tone had his heart doing flip-flops within an ever-tightening chest. *Yusn,* he couldn't wait to unload her upon her family so he could put as much distance between them as possible.

Why was he beginning to fear there weren't enough miles in the entire territory?

It was a deep purplish dusk when he came to the Basses' side yard. He purposefully didn't linger. He didn't want to invite any reminiscing. He didn't want to be seen. He climbed down and arranged Leisha so she wouldn't tumble from the saddle. Then, holding the other horses, he swatted hers and sent it forward toward the house. He didn't wait to see if she got there safely. He couldn't afford to. He vaulted up onto the first horse and wheeled it away.

Running from what he could never escape.

# Two

Leisha could hear them arguing outside her door. The words were inevitable, considering how she returned home the night before during the family's dinner hour, slumped in the saddle and insensible. She woke up in her own bed with only scant snatches of memory of how she'd gotten there. Her mother was leaning close in the lamplight, her touch gentle against the pulsing bruise on her temple. Leisha recalled wondering in a moment of awful anguish if there was something her mother could do to ease the other pain, the one that wasn't so noticeable where it scarred her heart and mind. But, of course, she'd said nothing and all had faded into a vague, wandering slumber until she'd awakened with a clearer head and aching conscience to those tense voices out in the hall.

"She's what you made her, Harmon. I don't see how you can expect any different."

"So you think it's all right what she did?"

"No, of course not! All I'm saying is that she's not going to listen to me. You talk to her."

A pause. "She's a daughter."

"She's your child, Harmon. She always has been. I'm just the woman you married. You're her sun, moon, and stars."

"Ammy—"

"Talk to her, Harmon, before she gets herself killed."

Leisha closed her eyes to feign sleep the instant the

door opened. She didn't actually hear her father cross over to the bed. He moved with the softness of the wind; she felt the stir of his passing even when no sound betrayed him. She knew when he came to a stop and after a long second passed, knew there was no use pretending. Or hiding. She looked up at him.

In her eyes, he'd always be the most handsome man alive. If she was what he'd made her, he was what Texas had made him: hard, spare, shaped by the cruelties of its savage past. His slightness of stance, his softness of step, the dramatic angles of his face, his bronzed skin and black hair, those things spoke of his Apache lineage. But the pure blue of his gaze and the hint of a smile contrasted that tough facade, adding an extra dimension to the legendary West Texas tracker that would never be shown to those who'd read his dime novel exploits or shivered uneasily at the mention of his name. They'd never see or be able to understand what he became under this roof: devoted husband, doting father, and content with those two things.

"How do you feel?"

"Better." A lie, considering the way the speaking of that single word awoke a volley of thunder through her head.

"Up to telling me what you got tangled up in?"

She wasn't. "How's Sheriff Lowe?"

His eyelids drooped down to shutter the emotion in his gaze. An infinitesimal movement most would never catch but one that spoke volumes to those who knew how to read the subtle shadings of his mood. "He'll be all right. They got the bullet out but it's the bed rest that will probably kill him. Gives him too much time to wonder if he's getting too old to be toting that badge. He's mad at himself for letting them get away with the town's money. Is that what you're carrying in that saddlebag?"

She tried to nod but discomfort speared between her temples. She settled for a quiet, "Yes."

Then, there was no more avoiding the issue.

"What happened?"

"I got the money back." Beyond that, she wasn't quite sure.

"You ride up with a knot on your head bigger than most foothills, toting bank notes and four sets of pistol belts. I'd say there's a sight more to it than that."

Leisha was suddenly all sharp awareness. He didn't know anything about the man who'd helped her! That much was clear or he'd have made a big deal out of it. She was silent for a long minute, trying to force her thoughts to wade through a muddled mind. He didn't know. He thought she did it all on her own.

Was there any reason for him to believe different?

For in telling a partial truth, she would be trapped into telling all. That she'd lost her chastity in a moment of overconfidence. That she failed miserably and had to rely on a stranger to salvage her honor. That she was just a daughter after all and not worthy of his respect. Pride clotted up inside her, forcing a fierce barrier against a total, face-reducing honesty.

Then she heard herself saying with a crisp brevity, "I tracked them to their camp but one of them managed to get a drop on me. Hit me upside the head. I had to kill him but the others slipped me."

It was the first time she'd had to confront that truth and the enormity of it trembled through her. She'd never taken a life before. She was surprised that it would act so strangely upon her. Then there was an all-too-perfect recall of the scorch of rank breath upon her face, the scent of stale clothing, the feel of his rough hands and brutal intrusion. The horror of that replay surged to its dramatic conclusion. The frozen image of the man's dead eyes brought an unaccustomed roil to her stomach but she fought it down and held staunchly to an emotionless facade. Her father saw right through it, even if he couldn't guess the full extent of her distress.

His palm cupped beneath her chin and it quivered in that compassionate well. "I'm sorry." And he bent down to touch an absolving kiss to her brow.

"Oh, Daddy." That moaned from her, from a soul embittered by its first taste of darkness. Her arms stole about him and then it was better. She couldn't remember when he'd stopped holding her the way he had when she was a child, only that she'd missed it. His embrace felt good around her now—solid, supportive, surrounding. As if he could keep the whole world at bay. Along with a few stark memories.

"It's all right, *shijii.*"

*It's all right, silah.* The remembered tones of an unfamiliar voice intruded into her peace. Who had said that to her? Who had comforted her and called her the Apache endearment for sister or cousin?

Who knew her secret shame?

Anxiety had her clutching tighter at her father's shoulders. She felt the change in him immediately, that sudden uncomfortable stillness followed by a gentle separation. He took her arms and unwound them, pushing her away at the same time. Though she longed to stay close, she was too weak to struggle against that purposeful distance he levered between them. Left to the indifferent embrace of her bedcovers, Leisha grabbed for a cool gruffness to camouflage a deeper hurt.

"I want to ride into Terlingua to claim the reward for Collier."

"You're lucky to be riding anywhere, girl. You'll stay put until we tell you different. If you'd listened to what you were told, you wouldn't be flat on your back with artillery fire going off in your head."

"I did what you would have done."

He ignored that bit of logic. "You should have let me

handle it. Finding the man who shot Cal was my business. What made you think you were up to the task?"

"I brought back the money, didn't I?"

"Almost at the cost of your life. And you were forced to take the life of one man while the others got away. Leisha, I can take no pride in what you've done."

Those words couldn't have wounded deeper if he'd delivered them at knifepoint. She sucked a stabilizing breath around a heart that was aching. "I'm sorry, Daddy. I'll do better next time."

"There won't be a next time! Leisha, you're not hearing what I'm telling you." He shook his head in exasperation. "I don't want you out chasing down desperadoes, dragging home half dead, killing folks . . ." His gaze grew distant behind a glaze of personal pain. Then he blinked and the steely quality of his stare returned. "Your mama was right. You're too much like me and I can't let that go on. I should have seen it sooner. Things are gonna have to change."

"What things? Daddy, don't talk to me like I'm a child. I know the life I want to live."

"What kind of life? Alone? Living out of bedrolls on hard ground, feeding off fear and danger?"

"It was good enough for you!"

"It's not what I want for my daughter."

She went all squinty-eyed and reproachful. It was as if he looked into a mirror. "And just what *do* you want for me?"

"The things your mama has. A nice house, kids to raise—"

"A man to call my master? No, thank you. That might be fine and good for a soft Eastern woman like Mama who needs it made easy for her but not for me. I'm not going to sell off part of my pride to have a man support me. I can take care of myself."

Harm stared at her for a long moment, displaying a rare

anger and clearly at a loss for words. Then he rose up and paced to the window. "Girl, you got it all wrong. Don't ever speak about your mama 'less you're using a tone of respect. That woman is just as tough as I am and twice as stubborn. We've stood off a gang of outlaws and a passel of Apaches side by side. You've forgotten that 'cause we've had things so easy lately. She's put up with me all these years and I don't know where she gets that kind of courage. There's nothing soft about your mama except her heart where you're concerned and her head where I'm concerned. She's the one supporting this family. If there's a master in this house, she's it. And I wouldn't have it any other way."

Leisha snorted in disbelief. "You come and go as you please—"

"Because she lets me. You don't know nothing about how it is between me and your mama or between men and women. It's high time you learned."

Leisha froze up inside. She knew all she needed to know. She knew men ran the Texas plains and arranged their world to suit themselves. It was a place where they could escape from a new century right around the corner; from doilies and pillow shams, stiff collars and derby hats, store-bought shoes and satin-backed vests, chintz curtains and civilized manners. They wanted their women at home tending those things that they secretly abhorred and Leisha shared their disgust for all things proper. She refused to become one of those docile ladies storming the streets in useless protest against bad language and Demon Drink. She didn't want to be looked at as an object of annoyance. Or a receptacle for lusts. That was one lesson just recently and most cruelly learned. She'd never give a man the liberty to take from her what had already been stolen. She knew what awaited her in the life her father was describing. And she wanted no part of it.

She didn't say those things to him because suddenly,

her head began to pound and she was too weary for further argument. She would just have to prove in fact what her father refused to hear in words. She'd have to make him believe that she was just as capable as any man.

That she wouldn't be pushed aside in his affection in favor of her brother.

Seeing her silence as an avenue of escape, Harm returned to the bedside and touched another brief kiss to her brow. "You rest now, little girl. When you get to feeling stronger, we'll see about getting you civilized. It's my fault for letting you run wild, playing at being a boy. It's time I turned the reins over to your mama and let you follow her lead."

Nothing could have possibly sounded worse to Leisha Bass.

"Sheriff, there's trouble brewing over at the Midas. You'd best come take a look-see."

Billy Cooper set down his nice warm cup of coffee. "Oh, hell." The last thing he wanted to do on this chill night was wade into a saloon brawl and knock a few empty heads together. He wanted to be home tucked in next to his cozy, loving wife or even out under the stars with the rest of the ranger boys. Anything was preferable to baby sitting a town full of farmers and mischief makers. That wasn't his idea of a good time at all. Dang Jack Bass anyway for volunteering him to sit in for Calvin Lowe. He hoped it wouldn't take the lawman too long to mend.

Checking the chambers of his Colt, Billy crossed the street in his long-legged stride and pushed through the batwings of the Midas. At once, he knew the source of the trouble and he cursed under his breath. He knew that belligerent voice, even slurred as it was by whiskey. It was his nephew, Jed. He'd taken the boy and his sister,

Jessie, in after their mama died some ten years back from the wasting effects of the hard life she'd led. And it broke his heart to admit he hadn't been able to turn either of them off the wicked pathway they'd already learned from his late sister, Julie. One that was repeated from his own parents. A cycle of abuse and indifferent neglect he'd managed to escape with the help of a young hellion by the name of Sarah Bass.

"Uncle Billy, you got to do something 'fore Jed gets himself hurt."

He looked down upon the overly painted face he could scarcely recognize as Jessie's. She'd been working the Midas, serving drinks for the last few months. He had no problem with that. It was an honest, if not an easy, wage and she was of age. As long as she didn't start earning extra on her back. He and Sarah had made that crystal clear. They wouldn't watch while she repeated her mama's mistakes.

"What's your brother up to this time?" he asked and sighed wearily. Though Jed still had his clothes under his and Sarah's roof, they rarely saw the boy unless it was to bail him out of trouble. It was penny-ante things so far: drunk and disorderly, brawling, reckless discharge of firearms. But Billy feared it would escalate into more than harmless hell-raising if someone didn't take a firm hand. And as much as he didn't like to consider it, that firm hand was going to have to be his.

Especially when he heard what his nephew was up to.

"He was slapping around Brenda. Oh, I know he didn't mean nothing by it, he's just drunk an' all."

Billy's mood seized up. That was the excuse he used to give when his own father was sleeping it off and his and Julie's hides were covered with welts. He'd learned since then that there was no excuse good enough for raising a hand to children. And none at all for abusing a woman. It was time Jed found that out, too.

"I'm gonna have to kick that boy's butt."

"You're too late. Some stranger stepped in and done it already. They's over there."

Billy waded impatiently through the crowd of gawkers to observe the scene for himself. It was a tense one. Leather had been cleared and dying was in the air as the two foes squared off at the corner of the bar. The girl, Brenda, was weeping, a bloodied bar towel held to her lip. Jed was all drink-glazed and battered, none too sure of his footing. The gun he held was a sobering threat. The other man was part Indian, also armed, and that was enough to put the inhabitants of the Midas into an uproar. Even if he was in the right.

"Put 'em down, boys. I'm in no mood to miss my supper 'cause I'm seeing the both of you to the undertaker's."

Jed bristled up and blustered, "It ain't my doing, Uncle Billy. This here breed got to stickin' his nose in my business. I had to show him who's boss."

"Looks like he done showed you, son. And since when is it respectable business to be knocking around a woman?"

"Hell, she's just a working gal. Part of what she gets paid for."

Ignoring the fully cocked pistol, Billy grabbed himself a handful of Jed's shirt and jerked him up for a rough shake and an even rougher growl. "Nobody gets paid to take pain off anyone else. Do you hear me? I don't care what she does for a living, you got no right, no right at all, to treat her bad."

Jed's jaw firmed up into a truculent block and he glared resentfully, not saying anything more.

"Gimme that gun afore it goes off and I end up hanging you."

The .45 was surrendered peacefully enough.

"You know where the jail is. March to it."

"Uncle Billy—"

"Don't make me escort you."

Sullenly, Jed Cooper slunk out of the bar, then Billy turned his attention to the second party involved. He was big for an Apache and obviously able to handle himself, for he sported no sign of meeting Jed's fists. He regarded Billy with a stoic expression out from under the downward angle of his Stetson and offered no excuses.

"You'd best hand over your piece, too."

"I didn't do anything wrong, Sheriff."

A soft statement of fact, not an argument. Billy believed him but he also believed it was in the fellow's best interest to make a fast exit from the saloon. He could read discontent on the faces of the cowboys around them. They didn't like to see one of their own taken down by an Indian, no matter what the circumstances. That part of their past was still a raw wound to many who held grudges from the '60s well into the '90s.

Billy extended his hand. "Be smart, son."

The pistol did a slow loop on the man's finger, coming to a stop butt first. Billy took it, then gripped the man's arm for good measure. He could feel muscles bunch in objection and said a silent prayer that he wouldn't make a verbal protest here in this unfriendly setting.

Apparently, the young man was no fool. He gave way graciously and allowed the law to lead him outside. There, he balked.

"You'd better come on with me."

"Why are you taking me to jail?"

"Jus' consider it a free night's room and board on the good citizens of Terlingua. You'll get a safer rest there than anyplace else." He nodded back toward the doors of the saloon where a few glowering patrons had gathered. "I'll turn you out first thing in the morning when tempers have had a chance to cool."

"I didn't do anything wrong," he restated with great dignity.

"Didn't say you did."

When he had made both of his overnight guests comfortable in back, Billy kicked his boots up on the desktop and stared into his cup of cold coffee. What was he going to do about Jed? It was partly his fault. He hadn't been strict enough. He couldn't force himself to lift a disciplining hand. Sarah handled the trips to the woodshed for their own kids but Jed and Jessie had been allowed too much freedom and too little restraint to make up for the harshness they'd experienced in earlier years. He couldn't believe that loving them wasn't enough. And he did love them, just like they were his own. What was he going to do?

There was a tap on the door and the sound of a sultry voice. "Sheriff, you up for something warm on a cold night?"

He grinned wide, his troubles forgotten for the moment. "Why, whatever do you have in mind?"

"Oh, some fried chicken and biscuits with hot gravy and maybe I could be convinced to serve up something special for dessert."

"Are you trying to corrupt this here officer of the law from doing his appointed duty?"

"Think there's a chance of it?"

"Oh, baby, I'm easy. Try me."

Setting her basket aside, the enticing female settled on his lap and down upon his lips for a long, languid kiss. Then he sighed deeply and held her tight. After having four of the half-dozen kids they'd once agreed upon, Sarah Cooper was no longer that skinny little Bass girl who'd demanded he surrender up his heart in order to have her kisses. She was a lush, pleasing handful of woman and he loved having his hands full of her.

"What's wrong?"

He should have known he couldn't keep it to himself. "Got company in the back." He didn't need to explain who that was. His wife leaned back to study his face. She touched one lean cheek with a tender stroke.

"Are you all right with that?"

"Can't seem to do anything about it. How'd I go so wrong with them?"

"You didn't. You know that. They were already bent to the hard life when they came to us. You couldn't have given them a better chance to make good. Now you've got to let them make their own choices."

"What if they choose wrong?"

She responded to the anguish in his voice with another lengthy kiss, then whispered, "I love you, Billy Cooper. Your dinner's getting cold."

"It can wait a minute," he murmured as he drew her back into his arms. After a time, he asked, "What are you doing in town this late? Who's watching the kids?" Their housekeeper, Chonita, had taken a husband and spent her nights with him in their small place on the edge of town.

"Elena and Cal. I brought them in with me. I wanted to spend some time with my handsome lawman husband."

"Well, here I am, a prisoner to your will."

"I was hoping we could have the back to ourselves. I miss having you in my bed."

He grinned wider. "You're a naughty girl, Sarah Cooper."

"Yeah, but you like me that way, don't you?"

He responded to her saucy challenge with a smoldery look and a husky, "Oh, yeah, I like it just fine."

She was rubbing his shoulders, working him into a weak-will compliance. "Billy?"

His eyes were closing. "Ummm?"

"Billy, would you ever consider taking over this job permanently?"

He looked up at her in surprise. "Sheriff, you mean?"

She nodded.

"You mean I should quit ranging? I thought that was okay with you?"

"It is . . . I mean it always has been. There didn't seem to be any other options. But I was talking to Calvin and Elena and he's sounding real serious about hanging up his star and he thought maybe you—"

"I'm a ranger, not no out-of-a-town's-pocket tin star. Did Jack say something to you? He got some problem with me he's not telling?"

"No. No, of course not. It would grieve my brother something fierce to lose you as his second. But Billy, I've been doing some thinking, too. And I kind of like having you in town, close by. When you're out on patrol for weeks on end, I—well, I worry some."

"Why didn't you say something?"

"Because I come from a ranging family and we don't cry about things like that. And I'm so proud of you wearing a star, I could burst." She fingered the badge he had pinned on his shirt that said "SHERIFF" instead of a big, bold "TEXAS."

"But you'd have me trade it off to run folks in for spittin' on the sidewalk and lettin' their dogs run loose?"

"Will you at least think about it?"

She sounded so anxious and looked so damned hopeful, he said, "I'll think on it."

And he did, long after the hot supper was gone and she'd returned to the Lowes' with a sweet promise to bring his breakfast over in the morning. Taking on the sheriff's spot would mean he could keep a closer rein on Jed. It would keep him home at night. And he did like sleeping in his own bed with Sarah curled around him.

Sunup came with him still pondering. Billy strolled back into the cellblock where Jed was snoring up an unholy ruckus. His other boarder was seated on his unmussed bunk, waiting in immobile silence for his release. Billy fit the key in his door.

"Sorry if all that noise kept you up. You're free to go, jus' like I promised. I wouldn't try for a drink at the Midas for a while, if I were you. No hard feelings, I hope," he added as he held out the man's hardware.

The young Apache came to reclaim his belongings and as he started out the door, he turned to his amiable jailor and murmured, "No hard feelings, Ranger Bill." Then he was gone.

It took Billy a while to remember how to breathe around the emotion clogging up his throat. *Ranger Bill.* He could only recall one person ever referring to him that way.

But that was impossible.


Going into the saloon and being drawn into a fight was foolish but looking down upon the place he'd once called home was the greater folly. But sometimes the heart demanded foolish things of a man and he'd as soon get over it now so he could get on with what had to be done.

It looked good, that small adobe house his mother had made into a home. How wrong he'd been to think it was meant to include him. Memories came flooding back: playing in the yard with his half-brother while a column of rangers headed out, most likely toward another confrontation with his father's people. And as he watched through a misty haze of years gone by, he saw the man he'd once called Father stride out into the early morning light. Sunlight glinted off his ranger star as he turned to embrace a spritely auburn-haired girl. Could that be Katie? She'd been a toddler when he'd last seen her. Now she was a pretty young woman. The sense of time's passage hit him cruelly. How easily they'd all gone on without him.

He'd wanted to wait long enough to see his mama but suddenly, he couldn't bear the thought of seeing her and knowing she'd given him up for the sake of this new family. He saw the door open and the sweep of a long skirt upon the porch boards. Panic overcame the swell of longing and before he could stop himself, he was wheeling his horse away, riding blind from the image he'd purged from his broken heart. After several miles, that bitter anguish turned to anger, the anger that had been his constant companion since a train had left for Florida thirteen years ago.

Nothing could ever make up for that pain.

Except revenge.

# *Three*

Leisha bore the indignity of being carted to town in a wagon wedged between her mother and sister as best she could. It was her part of a compromise after a long morning of argument. Her mother hadn't thought her strong enough to make the trip but she'd proven her wrong by getting dressed and joining them at the breakfast table with news that she was riding in on her own. That started up more protests. She couldn't go alone. What if she weakened on the ride and swooned out of her saddle? All the bluster in the world couldn't shake her mother from that possible scenario. They'd all go, her father had finally declared. They'd use the trip to visit with the Lowes and with Jack and his family. And Leisha would ride in the wagon with the other women. He'd delivered that in a no-nonsense tone that would brook no further discussion. Leisha reluctantly submitted.

Then her mother suggested she change into something more fitting for town, something like a dress. It was as if a tornado touched down at the breakfast table.

For the sake of familial harmony, the dress issue was abandoned and Leisha rode in sullen victory in her buckskins. With a Stetson to cover the bandage at her temple, she glared at her brother from beneath its shading brim as he sat a saddle at their father's side. A cocky eighteen, Rand was an almost perfect replication of his father in all but temperament. He and Leisha had enjoyed a covertly hostile rivalry ever since Harm had held the former aloft to proudly proclaim he had a son. In Leisha's mind, what he had was a vain and boastful brat who took great pains displacing her as her father's favorite. And she despised him.

Contrarily, she felt only affection for her younger sister. Becca was no threat to her. She was dainty and intellectual, at home behind a book and terrified by the vast outdoors. That was a secret Leisha helped her keep. It wouldn't do for a Bass to admit to being afraid of anything. By her timidity, Becca had won her sister's protection and Rand liked her simply because she was sweet-tempered and never filleted him with a sharp tongue the way Leisha did. Harm was happily ignorant of all this sibling dissension and Amanda did her best to keep things calm under their roof.

But when Rand cast a baiting look toward a seething Leisha, a blow-up was sure to follow. She bent to pick up a pebble from the wagon boot and after pensively weighing it in her palm, flung it discreetly. Unexpectedly stung by the tiny missile, Rand's horse bolted, nearly unseating its rider.

Harmon glanced around to see his son struggling to control his mount. "That horse too much for you, boy?"

"Nossir," Rand insisted as he fought to bring the animal back into line.

"Maybe he ought to ride in the wagon with us, Daddy," Leisha drawled out with a drip of sugary venom.

Having seen it all, Becca stared straight ahead and wisely said nothing.

Calvin Lowe's place on the edge of Terlingua was one of sentimental value to the Basses. It was there that Harm proposed to and married Amanda Duncan, the rich Eastern schoolgirl who'd hired him to find her missing brother. Cal had the distinction of being the only man Harm trusted like family. He'd been sheriff of the dusty border town for better than twenty-five years and before that, a

Texas Ranger alongside Harm's brother-in-law, Will. He'd
been responsible for bringing Sarah's brother, Jack, into
the rangers and for keeping young Billy on a straight line
when he was prone to wander. When he'd taken a bullet,
his first in a quarter-century of public service, trying to
thwart a bank robbery, it was considered a personal attack
to the Basses. And no one with a lick of sense messed
with one of the Basses.

Cal was sitting like pampered royalty on his front porch
swing entertaining Billy and Sarah while his pretty Mexi-
can wife, Elena, fussed over him. He looked well, much
better than the first time Harm had knelt down at his
bloodied bedside to vow he'd see to the men who'd shot
him. Only the extra bulk of bandages beneath his shirt
told of the ordeal he'd barely survived.

"Howdy, Harm, all. Nothing can bring you out across
a desert like the smell of Elena's cooking."

Loosing one of his rare wide smiles, Harm swung
down, drawling, "All this spoiling making you think of
retirement, Calvin?"

"Thinkin' on it, Harm, if I can put the town in good
hands." That's when he looked meaningfully toward Billy.

Harm didn't miss the exchange. "You thinking of trad-
ing in your star, boy?"

"Thinkin' on it, Uncle Harmon. Sarah's pushing me
thataway."

Sarah came to fling her arms about the tough Apache
tracker, peppering his reddening cheeks with kisses. "You
talk to him, Uncle Harm. Get him to see the settled life
isn't so bad."

"Stand down, little girl. If you want to butter me up
good, fetch me some of Elena's coffee."

Leisha watched the affectionate play with a glower. It
would seem her father had no trouble accepting his niece's
enthusiastic hugs. Her glare followed her cousin into the
house. Married life had changed Sarah Bass. She'd once

been a fiery free spirit, at home in the saddle with ambitions to be a tracker like her uncle. Then the handsome young Billy Cooper had gotten hold of her, filling her with four kids and keeping her at home where she'd gotten soft, plump, and domestic. Even now she was courting Harm's favor by scurrying to cater to him. A servile female. Just what her mama wanted her to become.

"Rand, help your mama and sisters down," Harm instructed as he accepted the coffee from Sarah and let his arm curve fondly about her waist.

Amanda and Becca were handed down with careful deference. Then Randall Bass looked up at his eldest sister and extended his hands in a great show of courtesy. She skewered him with an icy look and turned to angle down on her own, except he caught her and swung her around deftly. To struggle would have invited undue attention but as soon as her feet touched down, she was lunging back. And was abruptly beset by dizziness.

"Easy." Rand cuffed her upper arms to steady her. "You all right?"

"Fine," she gritted out, brushing his supporting hands away along with the consideration his soft tone implied. He stepped back and waved her grandly toward the porch.

"What brings you out here, Harm?" Calvin was asking. "Just curious on how I was spending my idle time?"

"Partly that, but we got some business to attend first." His cool gaze cut over to Leisha. "Seems we got some bank money to return and some reward money to claim."

Cal blinked. "Harm, when did you have time—"

"Not me. Leisha."

"That so! Well, I'll be. Another Bass to keep the legend alive."

Leisha stepped forward, basking in the glorious praise that managed to offset her niggling conscience whispering she didn't deserve it. "A finder's fee for the bank notes and the bounty on Drake Collier."

Cal hesitated. "That bounty specified *dead.*"

"I know."

"Well, I'll be," he muttered more quietly. "All right. I'll wire for it. You want it put in your family's account or cash in hand?"

"The account is fine."

"I'll see to it then. I'm right proud of you, girl."

Leisha's gaze canted to Harm, hoping to see some of that pride there as well. But his stare was fixed and opaque, revealing nothing of what he was feeling. And some of her elation faded.

Sarah slipped her uncle's arm. "Amanda, why don't you come on inside and help me serve up some pie."

"You didn't make it, did you, baby?"

Sarah pinched her husband's dimpled cheeks in passing. "If you weren't so sweet-faced, I'd never put up with your sass, Billy Cooper."

Once the two women were inside, Sarah dropped her jovial tone. "She killed a man? How's she handling it?" It was a subject they both could empathize with. Each had been forced by circumstance to take a life: Amanda had accidentally shot the man who'd killed her brother and Sarah had quite purposefully disposed of an outlaw threatening Billy and Jack. They understood the ramifications of such an act and had suffered them. Now Leisha had joined that grim sisterhood and they were justifiably concerned.

Amanda gave a heavy sigh. "From what I can tell, she feels no remorse. I'm worried about her, Sarah. I know the path Harmon walked too well and I don't want her to follow him. She won't talk to me. She looks at me like I'm something foreign to her. Harm's tried but he's not very good at that sort of thing."

"She needs a husband."

Amanda smiled. "Do you have one handy? One she wouldn't gut out in the first five minutes?"

"Jed's always shown an interest in your girls but I'm afraid that'd be marrying into a trouble I wouldn't want to wish on either of them."

"I'd considered sending her East to stay with my relatives in New York for a while. Harm thought that was a fine idea. I think he was hoping she'd slaughter them all and save him the trouble of traveling up there someday to do it himself." His animosity toward her greedy family was well established, which made them Leisha's enemies, too, and Amanda was too kind of heart to turn husband or daughter loose upon them. "The problem is, she's of an age where we can't force her to do anything. She seems content to stay at home and idolize her father."

Sarah grinned. "I probably never told you, but there was a time when I had quite a fancy for Uncle Harmon, myself."

"But you grew out of it and found yourself a husband. By her age, we'd both married and had children. She's not interested in even looking. I don't know what to do."

"Have you thought of sending her to Austin to stay with Sid? He's got his law practice well in hand and could introduce her to some fine young men."

"Did any of those fine young men impress you when you were there?"

"No," she admitted ruefully. "Nothing can compare to a good West Texas man."

Amanda nodded in agreement. There was just something about those tough, independent Texans bred in the Bend. "What we'll have to do is find her one that'll hang on to her whether she likes it or not."

But both realized their plan was a lot easier to conceive than to accomplish.

It was after lunch before Billy could manage to get Harm off to one side for a private talk. Jack and Emily had arrived with their two children and the place was positively swarming with Basses. Elena was delighted, for she and Calvin hadn't been able to have children of their own. Something to do with what had happened when she was held captive by the Apache and Harm had rescued her for a fifty-dollar fee offered by an anxious young ranger looking to marry her. The Lowes considered themselves godparents for all the Basses, from Harmon all the way down to Billy's five-year-old, Julie, and they welcomed the noisy, ever-growing clan without reservation.

"Something on your mind, Cooper?"

"Maybe nothing but I wanted to run it by you just the same."

Harm paused, gauging the sudden seriousness of the man he'd come to like and respect within their tightly knit family circle. It must have been something delicate for Billy to have pulled him away for private counsel and to have put a pattern of horizontal concern upon the young ranger's brow. "I'm listening. It have to do with taking over for Calvin?"

"No. Sarah'll coax me over to her way of thinking. I think I'll let her work on it for a while." He grinned. "I enjoy the benefits when she's of a persuasive mind."

Harm returned his smile, then waited. It was something big or the boy wouldn't be so edgy about bringing it up. He let Billy toe the ground with the tip of his boot and work up to it gradually.

"This about your sister's kid?" Harm suggested, trying to make it easier.

"Jed? No—well, sort of, in a way. Had to pull him out of a bad spot over at the Midas last night. He'd been laying rough hands on an upstairs girl and another fellow took exception to it. They almost come to gunplay by the time I stepped in and toted them off to jail." He fell silent again, looking so uncomfortable Harm began to feel nervous.

"You want me to teach the boy some manners, that it?"

Billy glanced at him, startled. "No, that's not it. Though it'd be grand if you could work some miracle there. This ain't about Jed. It's the other fellow that's got me spooked. Part Apache in his early twenties." He hesitated, then gave Harm an intense look. "Do you remember Emily's boy?"

Harm did. "Billy, that's impossible."

"He called me Ranger Bill, Harmon," he continued with a mounting anxiousness. "He's the only one who ever called me that."

"Billy—"

"I know it's crazy. I know it can't be him but my God, Harmon, I knew that boy real well. I was right fond of him. And looking at that kid this morning gave me a chill I can't shake."

And from where she stood at the edge of the porch just out of sight, Leisha experienced a chill, too.

In a slightly harsh voice, Harm asked, "You say anything to Jack about this?"

"What could I say?" Billy raked his hands through his mane of blond hair. "Harm, you know I'd never ever bring Jack and Emily any pain. Something like this would—would—well, I wouldn't do such a thing to them. Unless I was sure."

"And you want me to make sure for you."

"Would you? If there's some chance—"

"After I see my family home, I'll circle around and see if I can pick up his track."

Billy sighed in relief. "I'd be real obliged to you, Harmon. I know it makes no kind of sense but until I find out for certain, my mind won't leave it alone."

But to Leisha, it made perfect sense.

Of course.

Kenitay.

She remembered those vivid green eyes. Eyes like Emily

Bass. *Silah,* he'd called her, because though they weren't related by blood, they were linked by ties of family.

It had to be.

But she had to be sure.

She returned to the gathering inside and after a few moments of calculated thought, approached Amanda wearing her most pathetic expression.

"Mama?" She allowed the slightest quiver to shake through her words. Just the signal mothers listened for when concerned about the health of their children.

"Leisha, are you all right?"

"It's just all the noise and such. I'd feel better if I could lie down for a bit, someplace quiet. I thought maybe I'd go on over to Jack's and stretch out there for a while. I'll come back over if I get to feeling better or you can just stop to pick me up on your way back home."

And loving, trusting Amanda believed every word. "Do you want me to take you over there? Or I could ask your brother—"

"No. I can make it on my own. It's just across town. Don't worry about me. Enjoy your visit with everyone."

When her mother leaned forward to gently kiss her cheek, a pang of guilt twisted right down to Leisha's toes. But she refused to recognize it. Not when her mind was flying ahead to other things.

Selecting Rand's deep-chested black, she rode straight and fast, right past Jack's house near the Ranger barracks. Out into the scrub of the Texas Bend.

Because she had to be sure.

It was an easy trail to pick up. He was still riding one of the bank robbers' horses and she was all too familiar with the irregular shape of its "good enough" shoes fashioned from a blacksmith's barrel of old stuff. The day was cool but a persistent touch of fever made for an uncomfortable inner warmth. She should have gone to Jack's to lie down and given her body a chance to recover but time was against that plan. She had to find Kenitay—if it was Kenitay—before her father did. Just to make sure certain things would remain unsaid.

Aside from that urgency, there was the anticipation to drive her onward. Kenitay had always meant more to her than just another cousin or a childhood friend. He'd been a kindred spirit. He'd understood her passion for their shared Apache past and he was a wonderful challenge to her formative warrior skills. Not that he approved of her as a warrior-in-training. That was strictly for men. But she'd cheerfully flaunted convention with her father's encouragement and she thought her half-Apache cousin liked her for doing it. He always seemed to see beyond the reserve she maintained before all the others, to be attuned to things that mattered to her. Things like heritage, things like pride and honor, things like independence.

And then there was the kiss.

She wasn't romance-minded, not like her sister Becca, who spent dreamy hours immersed in their mother's old love stories or sighing over their family history. She wasn't going to wait for some hero to come rescue her from her lot. She'd do her own rescuing, thank you very much, and if she didn't like her lot, she could take care of that herself, too. Growing up, boys provided an irresistible physical challenge. She could run with the best of them and enjoyed her victories. Looking to them with any kind of emotional dependency seemed foolish to her. Why do less than she was capable of just to flatter some fellow's sense of importance? Why spend her days waiting for some maiden's dream to come along when she preferred the doing to the dreaming? Why hang her heart upon the whims of another?

She knew from the start that she wasn't the kind boys fancied. They liked fluffy girls who giggled and squealed and fainted at the sight of a spider, girls who made them feel bigger and stronger and protective. They didn't harbor tender feelings for girls who looked them straight in the eye and advised them on how to core out a rifle barrel. They liked females who oohed and ahhed at their daring exploits, not the ones who bested them. Leisha could be their chum, their buddy, but she would never be considered for arm dressing or courting. And she told herself that suited her just fine. She didn't want a bunch of gawky boys hanging around the porch, blushing and stammering the way they did around Becca and her friends. She preferred a direct conversation to that nonsense they spouted hoping to engage a girl's affections. She didn't want to be an object to be won. She wanted to be an individual who was respected. And if that didn't sit well with the menfolk of West Texas, so be it.

But Kenitay's rough kiss made her realize what a bluff she was hiding behind. Because she'd liked it. Because it had made her feel all weak and warm inside and as helpless as one of those females she despised. He was the only one who'd ever touched upon that inner softness despite all the years that followed. When she'd lost him, a door had closed upon those possibilities and she'd continued firm in the belief that no other could tempt her to open it again. That knowledge had been part relief, part regret, but she'd gone on and she'd forgotten that a half-Apache boy had once made her feel giddy and defenseless. She'd shored up her heart lest that kind of foolishness sneak in again. Because when he'd gone, she thought she'd die from the ache of it. She didn't want to experience that stripped-down-raw-to-the-emotions feeling again because it left her without control, without strength. Afraid. No one had been able to take that pain away. Time had finally soothed the sharpness teething on her heart. She'd vowed never to expose herself to that kind of agony over any other man.

And she wanted to see him again just to convince herself that she was no longer vulnerable.

One track on the ground became two and Leisha realized that the man she followed had been joined by another. They didn't ride side by side the way companionable Texans did but one before the other in the way of the Indians who always sought to disguise their number by riding in each other's tracks. And she grew cautious. If it was not Kenitay, she could be confronting two renegades bent on trouble and that, she wanted no part of.

They were cold camped on the edge of an arroyo with their backs to open ground. Smart. Wary. As if they knew they were being hunted. She rode up slowly and soundlessly, wanting to get a good look at them before they saw her. But Apaches were singularly hard to sneak up on, even for one as well trained in stealth as Leisha had been. They both came up out of their crouches, ready to meet anything, friend or foe—probably foe from the deadly way they both went grabbing for guns. She met their surprised stares and quick reflexes with the greeting end of her carbine, just to buy herself enough time to see who it was she was intruding upon.

The man closest to her was a full-blooded Apache. He was small and wiry, wearing a mix of traditional and white man's garb. He was very well armed and looked anxious to bury her quick.

The other man was taller, heavier through the body with fairer skin and an Anglo softness to his features that made him handsome in a way no true Apache could claim. He wore cowboy trail dress, Indian spirit jewelry, and sported the long, loose-flowing hair of the Mountain people. The gaze that fixed her so intently was as green as prairie grasses and there was no doubt that he knew her.

Just as she knew him.

It was Kenitay. And he wasn't pleased to see her.

# *Four*

"You look like you've seen a ghost, *silah*."

Leisha sat her saddle, staring through an odd paralysis. It *was* Kenitay. She thought she'd convinced herself to believe in the possibility but seeing him standing there before her was a shock of incredible proportion. She couldn't speak. She couldn't move in her own defense as the smaller Apache darted forward to grab her reins and wrench the rifle from her hands. He'd gripped her arm and was about to jerk her down as well when Kenitay interceded.

"Gently, Eenah. She's family."

His voice was a soft sneer of contempt without a trace of the fondness his words might imply.

The Indian coaxed her to dismount with a rough tug. Leisha settled to the ground on legs none too steady. She wasn't sure what weakened them—the frailty of body or heart. The latter was beating like a mad thing, making it difficult for her to think, let alone act.

"So surprised," Kenitay continued in that searing drawl. "Why's that? You didn't think I'd be back to pay my respects?"

She finally found speech. "H-how could I think that?"

"Guess all of you were hoping I'd just stay quietly out of your lives forever. Sorry to disappoint you."

His words made no sense but the fact that he was speaking them—that he was here at all!—made Leisha abandon her attempt at understanding his anger. She understood only one thing: an empty part of her had suddenly been filled. In two quick strides, she had her arms around him, hugging him fiercely. And for a moment, he hugged her back.

He hadn't meant to. He didn't want any part of this woman and her family but when she pressed close and snuggled in tight, he forgot the resentment. In fact, he forgot all reason. There was just Leisha, a child no longer. His every boyish fantasy grown up into a young man's dream. And she felt better than anything he could remember out of the last thirteen harsh years. After all that depressive futility, she was a fresh wind of hope and he clung to her, breathing it in with a desperation. His hands were buried in the golden luxury of her hair that felt like silk and spun sunlight. He could feel the ways time's passage had matured her as she pressed against his chest and nestled between his thighs, creating a dramatic stir in both places. And he wanted to hold onto her because of the past she represented and then, that same reason had him thrusting her away.

"How touching."

Unable to tolerate her feigned look of confusion, he spun away and struggled to hang onto the saving strength of his hate. It was hard to do with her fragrance up inside his nose and the fluid curve of her still warm upon him. He had to remember what weakness had brought him before. He had to hold firm against it.

"Kenitay, you can't know how good it is to see you."

When she said his name, it was like a stroke of fiery longing coursing through every fiber of his being. And when her tone softened an extra degree, the heat was followed by a feverish chill. He shook it off.

"Is it? One would almost believe you were sincere."

"How could you think I was not?"

That she would even ask such a question solidified his

fury. How, indeed! He whirled back to confront her with a gaze as severing as a pull of good steel. "Because it's thirteen years too late, that's why."

Leisha was at a loss with his brittle temper and the seething hostility that defied the questions she was bursting to ask. Questions like where he had been and why he hadn't tried to contact them before this. The fact that he was calling her a liar impugned the tenderness of her emotions. And it made her angry at herself for so blatantly expressing them. She wasn't one to make false demonstrations and he should have remembered that. Then she smelled the heavy swirl of liquor surrounding him and she retreated behind a cautious regard.

"You're drunk."

Her flat summation made him wince but he couldn't deny it. Yes, he was drunk. He'd been rushing with headlong purpose to get to that point since they'd made camp that morning. Alcohol was a familiar balm for the pain of life learned upon the reservation, one he shunned as best he could but the anguish of confronting his past was an agony too great to endure. It was either numb it or do something about it and he wasn't ready to take on his tormentors yet. And he refused to betray the reason for his sorry state to one of its causes.

"A common condition for my kind," he drawled out. "Some would call it the only freedom allowed us."

"Drunkenness isn't freedom. It's a trap for fools."

He chuckled wryly. "And it's caught greater fools than me." His tone and his glare grew colder. "Why are you here?"

Leisha cast a hesitant glance toward the stoic Eenah. She didn't want to air things of such a private nature in front of him but necessity blunted her embarrassment. She looked back to Kenitay. "It was you who took me home to my family."

Not a flicker of movement would answer yes or no so she pursued the question more forcefully.

"You were the one who stepped in and drove those bank robbers off and took care of me."

"If you've come to thank me for it, I already told you that wasn't necessary."

"Billy Cooper recognized you."

"So?"

"So, my father is coming to find you."

"Thanks for the warning. I'll make sure I'm gone before he gets here."

Leisha stared at him in frustration. "What's wrong with you? Don't you care that your family wants to see you? Just to know that you're alive?"

"If they cared if I was alive, they would have checked years ago." Before she could say anything more, he interrupted with a curt impatience. "You wasted your time coming here. Go home. I've nothing to say to you or your family."

When he started to walk away, she placed herself in front of him, becoming a barrier to his physical and emotional escape. "Where have you been? What's happened to make you so hard?"

"I've been in hell. Where you and your loving family sent me."

She was so startled by his reply that she let him slip around her to stalk off toward the edge of the arroyo. "Kenitay!"

He froze up, then faced her slowly, an unpleasant smirk marring his handsome features. "Oh, I get it now. You're here to make sure I don't say anything to your father."

She wasn't quite skillful enough to keep the color from leaving her cheeks. Because that was part of the reason, the one she had difficulty speaking. She'd come hoping she would find the gentleness of the man who'd tended her with such sensitivity, who'd allowed her the dignity of her lies. But that man was not here before her. She didn't know this man with his hard, gemlike eyes and cynical smile.

He gave a harsh cough of laughter. "Oh, don't worry, *silah,* I won't tarnish your honor with something as ugly as the truth."

Her pallor became a flush of fury. Without a word, she strode back to where Eenah was still holding her horse. She snatched the reins from him and began a tug of war for possession of her rifle. The Indian glanced to his companion. Kenitay gave a slight nod so he released the Winchester. Leisha vaulted up into the saddle with a lithe grace and with one last stabbing glare at his insolent expression, she applied her heels and was gone.

Kenitay watched her go. At his sides, his hands worked in agitated fists. He cursed, once quietly and regretfully, then again with a deep, pulsing rage. Who did she think she was, riding in here to extract a favor from him? As if he cared a damn about her pride! As if he was worried about her recovery from the blow to her head and the loss of her honor. He wouldn't allow himself to fret over how unstable her health appeared. And he absolutely refused to care if news of her defilement ruined her future. He wouldn't.

He wouldn't!

Not for a Bass.

"She is one of those who turned you out." Eenah spoke up softly and Kenitay gave a start, having forgotten he wasn't alone.

"Yes."

"And yet you let her ride away without tasting your scorn. Your thirst for justice is not what I had expected. I had not thought you would go weak at the first minor conflict."

Kenitay glared at the smaller man. "You don't know anything about what is in my heart."

"No?" Eenah's slight smile mocked him. "I, too, have

lain awake nights hungering for the day when I could return some of the pain I suffered. I have seen those of my family die, and now wait in torment until the time when I can avenge myself against those who slew them. I don't know what is in your heart? Darkness is there. Darkness and righteousness. And until you answer for those things, your life will know no harmony."

"What should I have done?" Kenitay challenged hotly, then regretted doing so as the answer formed cold and clear in his companion's black eyes. He saw death there. Kenitay spun away and returned to their gear. He grabbed up the bottle of whiskey and took a long pull from it. Its harshness brought no calm, only a more maddening loss of focus. He didn't need to question Eenah. He knew in his Apache soul what he should have done. What he should have done when he came upon her the first time. But perhaps Eenah was right. He was too soft. He had the blood of the whites to weaken that which beat rich and red for retribution.

"They treat you the way all whites treat the Apache— like a dog who can be tempted to become a pet with the offer of scraps then be chased away when they grow tired of it. Can you deny this is so?"

Kenitay said nothing. The emptiness of his belly was churning on the liquor, working on his rage.

"What do you owe these uncaring people who pretend to invite you in, then drive you away with sticks and stones? Can you hold affection for your enemy? Do you forgive them like a foolish woman or a weak child or would you take the revenge of a man?" Then his voice became a silky provocation. "What would your father do?"

That softly asked question played upon all the anguish and struggle of his past. No other words could have incited such a black response.

"My father would have retaliated for the hurts done to

him and his by inflicting injury upon those who wronged
him. He would have shown no mercy."

"Because he was Apache. What are you?"

Kenitay faced him with features carved of native stone.
"I am my father's son."


A kindred spirit.

What a fool she was to think that's what she'd find.

Leisha struck the dampness from her cheeks and
blinked hard to concentrate upon the wavering terrain
ahead. She was angry with herself because she'd gone
chasing dreams. She was angry with him because he was
not what she was hoping to find. Instead of a linked soul,
she'd discovered one twisted beyond all recognition.

For all her trouble, she'd found only one answer. It had
nothing to do with Kenitay's past or her own uncertain
future. It had to do with the way her heart started beating
with an unsettled rhythm the minute he'd straightened to
his full-grown height to give her an eyeful of the man
he'd become. It had to do with the way the years had
shaped his features upon the mold she remembered of the
boy. And the way he'd felt against her when he'd forgotten
himself and held her close: strong, hard, yet momentarily
yielding. The kinship she'd felt for the boy had matured
into a powerful attraction for the man.

Then he'd pushed her away with his rude manner and
harsh words and she didn't know what to make of him
or her own confused emotions.

A sound like restless thunder rumbled through her consciousness. At first, Leisha thought it was an echo of her
pulse beats, amplified by the pain in her head. Then the
tempo grew louder and she realized it was the pattern of
hoofbeats approaching rapidly from behind. Glancing over
her shoulder, she got the impression of a rider bent low,
coming up on her fast. Something in that aggressive

crouch set off a self-preserving alarm inside her that screamed, *Run! Protect yourself!*

Lashing back with her heels, she startled Rand's stallion into a surging gallop. But, although the black was strong and fleet of foot, there wasn't enough time to build the momentum needed to escape the man and animal already bearing down at full speed. She grabbed for her carbine and at the same moment, the pursuing horse drew up alongside. Steely fingers closed about her wrist and the resulting push-pull cost Leisha her balance. As she started to slide, her gaze flew to the face of her attacker. The instant of relief she felt when she saw it was Kenitay was quickly destroyed with her recognition of the show-no-mercy glaze hardening his features.

They both went down, slipping off the heaving flanks of their mounts, tumbling together toward the sudden, solid impact of Texas earth. Then they were rolling through the dusty wake of the racing horses, momentarily stunned yet forced by circumstances to make a quick recovery.

Her every instinct shouting danger, Leisha fought against him. She tried to kick but he wrapped his legs about hers to still their thrashing. It was like trying to escape bands of iron. He had her wrists imprisoned and when they came to rest upon the hot, arid ground, his greater mass pinned her flat. Panic exploded with that sense of helplessness and overwhelming threat. She tried to hit him but her arms were rendered useless at her side. She tried to throw him off but the bucking and twisting of her body accomplished nothing except to prove his mastery. Her spinning mind couldn't fix upon a reason for his actions, though knowing why wouldn't matter much. Visions of Drake Collier brought the wildness of terror to her futile struggles when Kenitay wedged himself up hard to force a reluctant spreading of her thighs but even those frantic movements were efficiently tamed. Fi-

nally, her own weakness led to a fearful resignation of
what was going to happen but her spirit refused to be
quelled. He could take her body by force because he was
stronger; however, she'd leave no doubt in his mind of
how contemptible she thought him.

Leisha opened her eyes and looked fearlessly up into
the dark rawness of his expression. And she spat in his
face.

His head jerked to one side but he didn't free her hands
to wipe the spittle from his cheek. There was no change
in the stark, emotionless chill of the gaze that terrorized
her. Unwilling to submit meekly to what she couldn't prevent, she cursed him fiercely in the three languages she
spoke. When she'd exhausted every slur she knew, she lay
panting beneath him, clenching her teeth against the
frightened part of her that would beg for some nonexistent
mercy. If nothing else could penetrate the blackness that
moved him to do this despicable thing, he would remember that she was brave.

*Do it now!* came the Apache cry for retribution up from
his tortured soul. *Punish them for what they've done!* It
was his right. It was his duty! The spirits of his loved
ones wailed for this violent retaliation. His beautiful half-
sister Cathy, cut down in a hail of Ranger bullets. His
father, beaten beyond his ability to endure. His people,
lied to, cheated, left to die in a hostile foreign clime. The
pain of his own disillusionment and the misery he lived
in because of misplaced faith. They owed him! It was the
Apache way to go for evens. It was inbred in his soul.
He tried to still his frantic breathing into a calm, calculated rhythm. He tried to focus on the woman prone beneath him as a meaningless vessel for his vengeance, to
use, to break, to rend as viciously as her family had the
trusting heart of an innocent boy. To take her with all the
indifferent hatred festering in those shattered dreams. His
arousal was full and hard enough to split rock, making

him capable of inflicting indescribable hurt and incredible suffering to the soul of this woman who already had experienced enough to fear what he could do.

Yet in that face, shielding the fright and frailty, was a courage of humbling strength.

His breath seethed between gritted teeth. Anger and hatred swelled to volcanic proportion, encouraged by the confusion of liquor and Eenah's prodding words. Thirteen years of pain was distilled into a fury so intense it scorched away all vestiges of what had once been kind or gentle.

But it wasn't enough.

Because he wasn't detached or emotionally uninvolved. Because he couldn't in the heart of him believe that raping, torturing, and ultimately killing Leisha Bass was going to lessen the anguish he carried inside. He couldn't believe that doing this wrong would right the wrongs done to him. And realizing that flaw of character enraged him all the more.

She was glaring up at him, damning him with her eyes, daring him with the narrow set of her lips. And she wouldn't back down, not an inch. Not Leisha Bass. He could feel her trembling but there wasn't a speck of timidity in her bold stare. That look said it would be harder to tame her than break her.

His mouth dropped down upon hers in a hard, hurtful crush, bruising her lips in retaliation for the way his weakness for her bruised his pride. She didn't move. She didn't make a sound. And when he lifted his mouth, the defiant fire still blazed in her eyes. The hatred he saw there stung deeper than her earlier curses.

Before he could consider his motives, Kenitay lowered his face once more. This time, she anticipated him and tossed her head to one side. Undaunted, he let his mouth move softly along the curve of one cheek. Her body went tense as if expecting some sudden betrayal. He heard her breathing shiver then catch as he eased down to taste the tender flutter of her pulse point. He rode out her frantic swallow.

When he came up on his elbows a second time, she was staring up through eyes wide and guilelessly blue. The wariness was still there and the uncertainty. But another kind of fire had replaced the resistance of moments ago. A beckoning fire. One that could consume as well as warm, if he wasn't careful.

He didn't feel like being careful.

They met in the middle for their next kiss, Leisha rising to it with an unpredictable urgency. Her mouth opened to invite a deeper union, which he was eager to provide. A rough, hungry mating of tongues followed, waking low, needy moans from the back of her throat. And then, she was straining up against him.

He couldn't breathe. He couldn't stop himself from taking more and more from that lush, willing cavern. This wasn't what he'd had in mind at all. His wasn't supposed to be the will that broke under pressure.

He pulled back, panting hard. She was very still, her eyes open, watching him. Gradually, he released her hands. Now, he thought, now she'll hit me and things will revert to a safer challenge, one I can win.

But her angry blows never fell. Instead, she looked at his mouth, studying its sensuous shape while tasting her own with the tip of her tongue. Then, without a trace of shyness, she reached up and filled both palms with his face, bringing him back down for a wild feasting pleasure that stunned him and left them both gasping.

He'd been chaste too long. The anxious ache in his groin told him explicitly how long it had been. He moved himself over her, rubbing insistently, seeking a sign of receptiveness but instead she went stiff.

"Leisha," he whispered in husky encouragement then went after her kisses once more. He was thinking about the supple feel of her strong legs around him. About the heat and magic they could make together. About making her sleek body dance beneath him with passion instead of protest. But she was fighting to bring her knees together even as he was asking with the rock of his hips that she become pliant. Her fists braced against his shoulders. Her mouth moved beneath his in an expression of tightly restrained panic.

"No . . . please, don't."

He could feel her agitation mount in every hurried breath and he knew she had to be thinking about the time before, outside the glow of the outlaws' fire. Just remembering her anguish as he held her in that savage aftermath brought an inexplicable cooling to his desire for her. Such was the power she held over him. He didn't understand it and yet, he couldn't resist it.

And as he kissed her face all over and murmured, "I won't. I won't hurt you, *silah*," the incredible irony of it struck him: he was soothing away her fear of an assault when he'd pulled her down with that very intention; he was quieting the very horror he'd planned to cause in her for the sake of his revenge.

Some Apache he was.

How ashamed his father must be of him right now, as ashamed as if he had heard him as a young boy disclaiming his Indian heritage.

With one last, fleeting brush of Leisha's lips, Kenitay rolled off her and onto his back at her side. They both stayed like that for a time, staring at the searing blue of the West Texas sky, struggling to recover their breathing.

Finally, Leisha turned her head slightly so she could regard him with a cautious glance.

"So?"

"So?"

"What now?"

He wasn't sure of her now. She was in control of her

emotions, masking them well, even as the swelling of her mouth said otherwise about what had happened minutes ago. He wasn't sure of himself, either. He'd already surrendered too much of himself to her to feel comfortable about it. She was supposed to be his enemy. He couldn't seem to remember that.

Leisha gave a slight start when he surged up to his feet. He was a big man, broad through the shoulders, built like sturdy steel. She'd felt his power and wisely respected it but she felt no threat from him now. Just that same wariness she hid behind.

He reached his hand downward and said gruffly, "Now I take you home where you belong."

She slipped her hand into his and let him lift her to her feet. Then she refused to let him go.

"It's where you belong, too."

He recoiled from her words as if they were poisonous. "No," he stated flatly, and began to tug within her grasp. She hung on tenaciously.

"It's your home, your family."

"No!"

"Kenitay—"

His fingertips pressed upon her lips.

"Don't ask them," was his quiet request.

And what she would ask and what he wouldn't say weighed heavily between them, secrets overshadowing even the flare of passion. Leisha wasn't one to give up easily.

"Talk to me."

"I can't. Not to you."

"To my father then. There's precious little in this world he doesn't understand."

Kenitay crooked a smile at her naivete. "And what would I say to him? That after I was unable to rape and murder his daughter, she suggested that I seek his counsel? I'm sure he'd be very responsive to that."

She refused to smile and continued to stare at him until he felt uncomfortable within his own skin. He took a step back.

"We'd better go."

They found his horse, but Rand's black had probably returned to Blue Creek and was muzzle-deep in feed by now. At least her family wouldn't be alarmed by the arrival of an empty saddle. Kenitay swung up with a quick Apache grace, then reached down for her. Leisha gripped his forearm and he pulled her effortlessly up behind him. When her arms inched hesitantly about his waist, he nudged their mount into an easy lope.

After several miles passed in tense silence, Leisha began to relax by slow degrees. She wouldn't think about what had happened. She would only look ahead. Her thoughts were too frazzled to contemplate the complexity of what Kenitay was about. She knew he was on the run from something. She knew he hated her family enough to wish her unspeakable harm. And that he cared for her, or for the memory of her, enough to keep him from carrying out the vengeance he sought. There was no use prying for answers. There was nothing as stoic as an Apache male. She was used to her father's silences. She'd have better luck forcing words from a rock than getting him to give away something he didn't plan to share. Kenitay would be no different.

She moistened her chafed lips and thought back to his kisses. He'd learned a lot in thirteen years.

Where?

With whom?

Unbidden, her hold on him tightened and he responded with a slight intake of breath and a gradual tightening of his muscles. Hands that had been clasped in front of him now pressed palms-down to his shirtfront, contouring to the firm plane of his abdomen. She nudged up closer so her knees tucked up under his to support the hard swell of his thighs atop hers and her breasts flattened against his back. Then she leaned into him by slow degrees until her cheek rested upon one rigid shoulder and her eyes closed contentedly. Just for one unguarded moment, she would let herself enjoy him. She would absorb the feel of him, the masculine scents of horse and dust and drink that clung not unpleasantly to him. And she moved her palms, letting them slide leisurely up his chest until one fit over the steady thunder of his heart. It was a nice moment. One she would never forget. The feel of boy grown into man. A man she'd kissed with a reckless abandon. A man she didn't know and couldn't understand. A dangerous man.

But she was no stranger to dangerous things.

She glanced over his shoulder, then stiffened and exclaimed, "Not to Blue Creek! My family'll be waiting for me in Terlingua."

Kenitay went rigid. "I won't take you there." His family was there, too.

"But you must. Otherwise, they'll come looking and sometimes my father doesn't stop to ask a lot of questions first."

"I can handle your father."

Leisha didn't disagree but her silence doubted him.

"All right. Terlingua. But only because you're weak and need your family's care."

"I'm not—"

But he kicked the horse into a jarring canter to effectively silence her complaint. She hung on tight and gripped her mouth shut, stewing on her annoyance until they reached the edge of the dusty little border town.

"Take me to Jack's. My family's supposed to meet me there." Then she circumvented his protest by saying, "No one will be there. They're all over at the Lowes'."

So he brought her up to the adobe house where he'd spent the happiest five years of his life. Just thinking of it brought his resentment back to its dangerous simmer.

"Get down," he ordered, catching Leisha's wrist to pull her off. She slid down, then captured his hand between hers.

"Wait with me."

"No."

"Kenitay—"

"These people mean nothing to me." But there was a bit too much denial in his tone for her to believe him.

"If they mean nothing, it should cost you nothing to see them."

His jaw squared and his eyes took on the brilliant bottle-glass sheen that was both hard and opaque. "Let me go."

"Coward," she challenged softly.

With a jerk, he freed his hand. He looked as though he might say more but instead wheeled the horse away, leaving her to his dust and her own disappointment.

# Five

Leisha was dozing fitfully when Jack, Emily, and their two children returned. She'd always liked her cousin and his family. He was sober and straightforward with steel-clad honor and a gentle heart. He was Harm's favorite of his sister's four children. Emily was the perfect mate for him. She'd led a hard, hurtful life, from what Leisha had learned of it, and then had blossomed beautifully under Jack's tender care. She'd borne a daughter, Cathy, with Neil Marcus, her first husband and Jack's former Ranger captain, and Kenitay with the Apache Kodene. She'd taken him as a second husband when she thought Neil had been killed in the same raid that saw her and her small daughter captured. Jack rescued her from the Mescalero, winning her and Kenitay in a barter. Emily's daughter had been accidentally killed in a botched Ranger raid upon Kodene's camp. When Marcus died in the line of duty, Jack and Emily married and had Carson and Katie.

There were a lot of hushed-up stories surrounding the facts she'd been told. Becca hinted at some grand and scandalous romance but Leisha ignored her. She accepted what she saw and didn't care to speculate beyond it. Emily was a fine woman deserving of Jack's love, and their two children were hard-working and decent like the both of them. They were good, solid-souled Texans who'd built upon a tragic past they preferred to keep behind them.

And now Leisha was about to bring that painful past back to their door. And she was wondering if she should.

"Leisha, how are you feeling?" Emily was immediately all maternal care. When Leisha claimed she was better for the rest, Emily headed for the kitchen, calling back, "Your mother said to tell you they'd be by after supper. Harm and the sheriff had some things they wanted to talk over, so you might as well join us." She then brushed aside Leisha's half-hearted offer to help for which Leisha was grateful. She, like her own mother, had no talent for or interest in cooking unless it was necessary for survival. So while Katie helped her mother, Leisha sat back and listened to Carson petition his father.

He was a good-looking boy with his father's clean features, auburn hair, and pale blue eyes that evaluated everything around him with a somber fairness. He wore a sidearm and was well-versed in its use, like all West Texans over the age of ten, and had his father's even temper to regulate it. He and Rand were great friends and Carson was a stabilizing influence upon her reckless brother.

"Daddy, I been giving thought to what I plan to do for a living."

"Thought you were interested in ranging, son."

"Well, I toyed with that idea some, and I wouldn't say it's not something I might try."

"But . . . ?"

"But I was thinking if Billy takes on the sheriffing job, I might offer to back him up as his deputy."

Jack was silent for a long moment, giving careful consideration to the boy's words. He was a thinking man, not given to rashness in speech or action. He'd learned the hard way what impulse could lead to. He spoke quietly, with a measuring tone of reason. "You're seventeen, Carson, and you're talking about biting off a man's job."

"I know, Daddy. You don't think I'm up to it?" It wasn't a challenge but an honest question.

Jack sighed, trying hard to separate his protective feelings from what was fair. "I started ranging when I was sixteen and I can't say you're any less of a man then I was then."

Carson started to smile.

Then Jack added, "I'll see what your mama thinks."

The smile faded. "Okay, Daddy. Guess that's only right."

Emily and Katie started setting things around the table and further discussion ended with the call to supper. Leisha ate in pensive silence. She was wondering what her parents would have to say if she announced she had any plans for the future other than finding a husband and setting up house. She glanced up at Carson Bass, judging him critically on the basis of ability, and had to admit she was as qualified for the position of deputy as he was. If not more so. Carson had never killed a man. But who would think of taking her on for such a job, even if her father didn't nail her down to the floor first? That was a woman's lot in West Texas—hell, in all of Texas and most of the country! And she was far from happy with it.

There was a light tap on the back door and Katie excused herself to answer it. She returned wearing a perplexed expression.

"Somebody looking for you, Mama."

"Who is it?" Emily asked as she rose.

"No one I know."

Jack started up from his chair but was stilled by the soothing stroke of his wife's palm along his shoulder.

"I'll see who it is. You go on and finish."

Jack watched her disappear into the kitchen, then was about to return his attention to his plate when he heard Emily's cry and the crash of the coffee cup she'd been carrying. He was up, grabbing his .45 from his pistol belt hanging on the back of his chair, then dashing toward the back of the house with a look so lean and fierce it would have sent any sensible intruder running for cover.

He skidded into the kitchen, colliding with Emily as she stepped in front to block him. She grasped his gun hand, wrestling it down. Her face was as white as the apron she was wearing.

"Em, what is it? What's wrong?"

She was turning back toward the open door, at the same time leaning against him for support. When his arm spanned her middle, he was alarmed by the hard tremors shaking through her.

"Oh, Jack," she whimpered in a voice so frail and strained, he was immediately in a ferociously protective panic.

"Emily, what the hell—" Then he took note of where she was staring. He could just make out the shape of a man standing on the back porch in early evening shadow. His features toughened into an angular study that was far from friendly. "Step on in here, mister," came his deep, commanding growl.

He entered through the back door, moving slowly, unsure of his reception. He watched the tense Ranger's pistol, gauging the possible threat. Then, once in full light, he lifted that cautious gaze up to the face of the man himself. He watched as the dark, dangerous lines buckled with confusion. Then Jack Bass's icy glare underwent an instantaneous meltdown that welled up in eyes gone round with surprise as his mouth moved soundlessly.

He looked from the stunned Ranger to the woman clutched up at his side. His own voice was painfully soft and uncertain.

"Mama?"

The breath left Emily Bass as that one word overcame her disbelief. With a quavering sob, she tore away from Jack and launched herself across the kitchen, her arms enveloping the unfamiliar figure of a man who'd called to her with the beseeching voice of a child long lost.

"Oh, my God! Oh, my God! Kenitay!" She was weeping too hard to say more than that. She clung to him with a desperate strength, nearly rending his shirt from his broad, stiffly squared shoulders as if she feared if her grasp lessened he'd slip away again.

Very gradually, his arms came up to form a loose curl about her.

Jack walked forward until the two men were eye to eye. Kenitay experienced a strange chill looking at him from an equal height. They stared at each other for a few heartbeats. Then, in a tone so gruff it rumbled, Jack said, "Next time I tell you to stay put, goddammit, you stay put!"

Then Jack's big hand caught the back of his head and he pulled Kenitay into an embrace so tight he could barely draw a breath—not that he could manage one through the emotion squeezing his chest. This wasn't at all the welcome he'd expected . . . but it was the one he'd dreamed of on those lonely nights when the emptiness got so big it seemed to swallow his soul. His stepfather's grasp, his mother's tears. He'd pictured it a million times and each time, painful reality cut like a fresh blade. If he was holding onto a lie, it felt so good he couldn't make himself release it. He soaked up the warmth of his mother's hug and let his head rest briefly against the familiar comfort of Jack's shoulder. And his spirit wept with the joy of their reunion even as his mind was struggling to explain it.

Why the tears thirteen years too late?

From over Jack's shoulder, he saw Leisha in the doorway with a restraining arm about his half brother and sister. She wasn't smiling but he sensed a deep satisfaction in her stillness. Katie was clearly confused. There was no way she could have remembered him but Carson's grin was like a homing beacon even as he was wiping the streams of wetness from his face. Leisha gave them both a tug, hauling them back out of the kitchen to allow the three some privacy.

That's when Jack's fingers meshed in his hair, pulling his head up and holding him firm so there was no way to avoid his piercing stare. His eyes glittered like damp steel.

"You'd better have one powerful good reason for staying away and letting your mama nurse a broken heart."

That soft accusation was what Kenitay needed to bring his scattered emotions in check. He levered back, his features taking on a hard, impassive mask. He couldn't look down at his mother. That would have been too hard. Finally, he said with a tint of disbelief, "You want a reason from me?"

"Right now," Jack demanded in a terse voice.

"I don't owe you anything."

"After you tore this family in two, I think you do!"

"Jack!" Emily was hanging on his arm, begging him with her teary gaze to back down but he was hearing her wails and moans of grief. He was remembering the nights when he'd sat up rocking her as she wept herself into an exhausted sleep. And then he'd sit dry-eyed until dawn blaming himself until the sorrow of it drove him close to collapse. No, he wouldn't back down. Not after all that. Not after he'd had to make that trip home alone clutching an empty jacket to do what no man should ever have to do twice in one lifetime.

Kenitay jerked free and stumbled backward, seeking to gain perspective with distance. But he couldn't. In a harsh tone that held the bitter tears of more than a decade, he cried, "I trusted you! I thought of you like a father!"

The look of bewilderment that came into Jack's eyes set the fuse of his long-impotent fury. And then Jack began, so soft and sincere, "Son, I don't know what—"

"I'm not your son!" He struck off the hand that Jack reached out to him. "No father would so betray a son.

And *you!*" He finally glared at Emily, his anger and pain exploding with horrific force. "How could you let him do it? Did you want an easy life so bad that you would trade me for it? *Puta!*" And he spat on her clean kitchen floor.

The sound of Emily's wounded cry brought Jack's hand flashing out, his palm connecting with a jarring force. As Kenitay recovered his balance, the furious Ranger seethed, "Don't you ever speak like that in my house!"

Rubbing his jaw, feeling the sting of that slap as if it was an exclamation point to all his years of misery, Kenitay was able to do what he'd never been able to do before: sever his ties to these people to whom he'd mistakenly given his heart.

"I was a fool to come here," he growled. With one last scathing look at his mother's tear-streaked face and Jack's rigid expression, he whirled away and stalked toward the door, turning his back on their treachery for the last time.

"Kenitay!" Emily took a step to follow but Jack's arms wrapped tight about her, holding her at his side. Her frantic gaze rose up to his unyielding features then flew after the retreating figure of her son, her love feeling the terrible pull between them. In anguished decision, she flung off her husband's grasp to race after the child she'd lost. She wound her arms through his elbows, pulling him to a stop. "No! I won't lose you again!" And she pressed her cheek between the wide spread of his shoulder blades, refusing to surrender the tangible evidence that his return was not a dream.

"Let me go. You never wanted me here."

"How could you say that?" Emily cried, holding on even tighter when she felt his bodily denial. "You know Jack nearly gave his life so I could have you—so we both could have you. How could you doubt how much we love you?"

"Then why did you let them take me away?"

His voice cracked with the tremendous importance of

that one question. Not knowing the answer had tortured him day and night, poisoning his heart, tarnishing his soul to a point of near-total darkness. And once he'd touched upon that horrendous hurt, he couldn't keep the rest inside.

"If you loved me, why didn't you come for me? I waited—" Again, the strength of his voice failed him.

"Who took you?" Jack's words were so low and raw, they were almost indistinguishable.

"The soldiers at the fort. I went down to see what was going on and they snatched me up, thinking I was one of the reservation Apaches. When I tried to tell them different, they hit me and when I woke up I was halfway to Florida. I always believed in my heart that you would come for me. But you never did. You never did."

There was a long silence, then Jack's reply. "Because they told me you were dead."

It was so simple. It made perfect sense. And yet it had never occurred to Kenitay until just this minute. Then he could see it clearly even before Jack went on to explain.

"No one would tell me anything at first. It was like you'd just disappeared. They tried convincing me that you'd run off but I wouldn't believe that. Then an Apache scout brought me your bloody jacket and told me that an Army sergeant had struck you with his rifle and killed you and was trying to cover it up. Even when the man admitted to the deed, I didn't want to believe it. Not until I saw for myself. But the Apaches, they wouldn't give up your body for the burying. They said they had already taken care of their own."

*They'd thought they were protecting him!* Kenitay realized that at once. Protecting a helpless boy from those who had injured him. Of course they would have lied and hidden him from further persecution. They had no way of knowing they were concealing him from family.

Jack had come up behind Emily and was touching his

forehead to the back of her head. "I still didn't want to
believe it. I didn't want to go back home without—without
something. I made a fuss, wanting to force the issue, and
the fort's commander had me slung in the brig overnight.
The Apaches were gone by the time they let me loose
and I was told in no uncertain terms that if I followed,
they had orders to shoot me down. So I—I came on home
without you, to let Emily know I'd lost another one of
her children."

Emily turned to envelop Jack in a tender embrace. Kenitay looked back over his shoulder to watch them in silence.
Then his mother looked up at him and asked, "How could
you ever think we'd give you up without a fight?"

How indeed? It had been easy. He'd found himself among
a suspicious, embittered people who trusted nothing to do
with the whites—from experience. It hadn't taken them long
to wear down the hopes of a frightened young boy, to turn
him against the very deliverance he sought. But just the
same, he should have known better. He should have trusted
in the man he knew Jack Bass to be. He should have believed in the love his mother always showered upon him.
But he hadn't. He'd given up on them. He was the one
who'd done the betraying in thought if not in deed. And he
suddenly didn't know how to deal with that reversal.

"I have to go."

Emily's hand was instantly gripping his sleeve. "No!"

He couldn't look at her, not with so much guilt and
confusion threatening his composure. "I need to think—
about things. I'll be back when my head clears."

"Kenitay!"

But he was already gone, slipping out through the back
door like a shadow.

"Let him go, Em," Jack advised gently.

"But Jack—"

"Let him go. He's his own man now, Emily. A man we
don't even know."

"He's our son!"

"And he'll be back when he gets to remembering that."

Her teary gaze lifted. "How can you be so sure?"

"Because this is where his home is. And we're the family who loves him."

Leisha found him at the edge of Terlingua where the town shaded off into deep desert. He was sitting on the edge of the stone well the Mexicans used for watering livestock, waiting there for his horse to drink its fill. She gave a sigh of relief. She was afraid he had slipped her and she wasn't feeling fit enough to trail him again.

She'd overheard most of what was said. It hadn't been intentional—their conversation had been too intense for such a small house. She wasn't sure what Kenitay needed right now. Maybe it was to be left alone. She wasn't terribly sensitive to the moods of others, having never learned the softness of compassion, so she didn't know if he would welcome her. But she knew pain when she heard it and his voice had been ripe with agony. She didn't want him to ride off without doing—something. Anything.

He must have heard her approach and recognized her step because he didn't look up. He wouldn't have been so trusting with anyone else. He didn't move at all until she was standing so close their knees were almost touching. He did look up then. She was very good at seeing past a stoic front. And what she read of what he didn't want her to see knocked a hole in her heart.

She didn't think about it. She just did it. Her hand cupped under his chin, lifting it, holding it steady as she bent to place a kiss on his mouth. His response wasn't much, just a slight give beneath the pressure of her lips. But when she began to straighten, feeling a bit embarrassed by what she'd done and wondering if she'd made a fool of herself and how she was ever going to meet his eyes, his arms went

about her waist. He locked them tight, drawing her up close
between the spraddle of his thighs. When they were as snug
as they could get without her climbing onto his lap, Kenitay
rested his head against the slight swell of her bosom. She
waited, tense and uncertain, but he didn't move, nor would
the strength of his embrace lessen. She had no idea what
a woman should say at such a moment so she stayed silent,
letting the slow caress of her fingers through his hair convey
what words could not. It seemed to be enough, for he lingered like that for a long while and she let herself enjoy
the feel of him with a cautious sort of exhilaration, thinking
perhaps this was what he'd needed after all.

The sound of a wagon approaching Jack's, only a long
stone's throw down the street, brought the two of them
apart. Kenitay was instantly on his feet and Leisha snatched
up his hand impulsively.

"Come home with me."

He gave her a flat, fixed stare that said nothing about
what was moving behind it but he didn't try to pull away.
She tried to be more convincing.

"Talk to my father. Sleep in a good bed. Then you can
ride off in the morning if you want to."

He didn't answer but his hand opened, easing out of
hers with a slow slide of their fingertips. Pride wouldn't
allow her to ask again. If he didn't want anything from
her, so be it. She wouldn't go begging if leaving was what
he had in his mind.

Without another word or even a good-bye, Leisha turned
away and trotted back toward her cousin's. She refused to
recognize her desperate wish that he would follow. But
when she was rounding the corner of Jack's adobe and cast
a casual glance back, she saw to her disappointment that
he was already gone.

"Where's my horse?"

Rand's curt demand greeted her as she stepped up onto
the porch. Her brother was seated in the back of the buck-

board, looking very grim indeed. It was hard to hang onto her smile but she did to remark blandly, "Must have slipped my knot. Not very well trained for one of our animals."

Rand glowered. He'd taken great pride in breaking the black and teaching him manners. His sister's cool remark was a slap in the face.

"Come on, little girl," her father called. "It's late and we got to get a move on."

"I've already said good-bye to Jack and his family so there's no need to go in."

Harm was obviously impatient to leave so he accepted that with a nod. "Climb on up in back and let's go."

She took in the space next to Rand with a jaundiced eye but did as she was told. When they were sitting stiffly side by side and she'd answered her mother's concerns about how she was feeling, they got underway, pulling out of Terlingua on the road home.

Facing backward, she was able to watch the dark strip of trail behind them but no one followed. After several miles, she gave up trying to peer through the shadows and closed her eyes to ease the throb in her head. Before long, she was nodding off into an exhausted slumber, the one she was supposed to have gotten at Jack's. She was unaware of her brother angling slightly to make his shoulder into a convenient pillow nor did she see his glum scowl become a faint smile. She was next to dead until they rolled up in front of their big frame house; their mansion, Harm called it.

Her first thought was to go right up to her room but she was distracted when Harm lingered outside, his horse still wearing tack after the wagon was put away and the others were inside.

"Daddy? You coming in?"

His smile was smooth and evasive. "Not just yet, little

girl. I've got me a couple of miles of riding to do. A favor for that Cooper kid."

Then she remembered his promise to track down the man Billy thought he'd recognized as Kenitay.

"Daddy, you don't have to go."

"Gave my word I would, so I guess I do. Tell your mama I'll tuck in with her before morning.

"Daddy—" How exactly was she going to tell him? He was waiting, one foot up in stirrup iron, the other anxious to swing over saddle leather.

Then she heard the sound of a rider's cautious approach and she released a small smile.

"Daddy, you don't have to go now."

# Six

If Harm Bass thought he was looking at a ghost in his front yard, he never betrayed his alarm. He stared impassively up at Jack's adopted son, then sent that probing glance sliding to his daughter.

"You knew of this."

"I wasn't sure until just today," Leisha answered.

That sketchy reply was enough for the moment. Harm came around to catch the bridle of Kenitay's horse. "Step on down, son. You must have a story to tell. I'll have Amanda put on coffee." Figuring that was all that needed to be said, Harm headed for the house, expecting to be followed.

Kenitay hesitated, casting a glance over his shoulder at the freedom of the desert then ahead toward the welcoming lights inside the Basses' house. Seeing his indecision, Leisha spoke up.

"Mama can't claim to be any kind of a cook but she does make a tolerable cup of coffee."

He swung his leg over the pommel of his saddle and slid to the ground in one fluid move. Leisha was impressed by his strong grace but she didn't let that show in her expression. Instead, she turned and started for the porch, not waiting for him or offering any further invitation. She didn't take a full breath until she heard the sound of his light tread on the front steps behind her.

Harm was waiting in the hall, giving a curious Rand

instructions for the care of the horses. When Leisha and
Kenitay entered, the elder Bass spoke to the latter in a
low Apache greeting, directing him with those same gutturals into the parlor then steering him there with an easy
hand upon his shoulder. Rand caught Leisha's arm, drawing her aside. He was staring warily after the strange
Apache who claimed such a familiarity with his father.

"Who is that?"

She gave him a bland smile. "Family," was all she
would say, then turned to brush off his suspicious questions. "Aren't you supposed to see to the horses?"

Rand scowled at her, resenting her inclusion into something he knew nothing about. But he went to do as he
was told.

In the parlor, Kenitay felt the memories of the house
soothing away his uneasiness. This was the first white
homestead he'd ever been inside. When he was five, Harm
had brought him here from his father's camp to where his
mama was waiting. He didn't know the white language then
and much that followed remained a confusion to him even
now. Harm and Leisha spoke Apache and made him feel
less fearful of the strange place and odd customs. He remembered his mama bringing a half-dead Ranger into the
front yard and his father's warriors riding in on their heels,
toting Harmon over one of their saddles.

What happened then could have been a full-scale mas-
sacre but the respect the Mescalero had for Harm and the
sheer pluck and quick intelligence of his then-pregnant
wife turned bloodshed to barter and the Apache had ridden
away with a huge herd of Bass horseflesh in exchange for
one white woman and her half-Apache child. Amanda had
borne Rand that day and Kenitay found himself part of a
new world as well. He wasn't sure of much but he knew
a great price in property and pain had been paid for him
and his mother.

Beneath this roof, Jack had taught him his first words

of English and he'd come to trust the man behind the dreaded Ranger star. Upstairs, he'd sat on Jack's bed, the one he was sharing with his mama, and he was asked what he thought of the three of them being a family. After Jack promised he would become Kenitay's second father, not a replacement for the first, the young boy thought it a fine idea. He'd liked the thought of being one of the Basses—so much so, it was an almost irresistible lure to him even now.

"Harmon, I thought I heard—"

Amanda's voice trailed off as she stared, recognizing but not understanding what she was seeing.

"Ammy, you remember Jack and Emily's boy."

"I seem to remember that he was dead," she answered with her typical bluntness.

"We were fixing to get to that as soon as we got some coffee."

"I-I'll put some on," she said and backed from the room in a rare state of speechlessness.

Before they could get comfortable, a flushed Becca hurried in, rambling, "Mama just told me that—Oh! It's true!" And with a rustle of petticoats, she raced up to wrap her arms around Kenitay's neck, planting an impulsive kiss upon one sun-bronzed cheek. She stepped back, blushing hot at her own boldness but smiling happily to offset it. "Oh, my, you're not at all the little boy I remember anymore. I seem to recall you paddling Leisha for putting a lizard down the back of my dress."

A slow, genuine smile spread across Kenitay's face. "I'd forgotten that." He took up one of Becca's soft hands and gave her a twirl for his inspection. "And I seem to remember a sweet little freckled-face girl. Why Becca Bass, you've grown up to be a beauty."

Becca giggled and grinned with pleasure.

Across the room, Leisha ground her teeth and glowered at the way her sister's silly flirtations won a smile and a compliment when Kenitay hadn't yet given her the benefit of either.

At the opposite doorway, Amanda was stunned to recognize the passions moving on her eldest daughter's face in a brief, betraying flicker. She looked to Kenitay, seeing what a strong, handsome young man he'd become with that exotic blend of white and Apache lending the same wildness that had so attracted her to Harm. She was smiling as she swept up behind her husband. He caught the hand she sent curving across his chest and gave her a questioning glance.

"I'll tell you later," she murmured next to his ear with a warm kiss. "The coffee'll take a few minutes to heat but my curiosity won't. Welcome home, Kenitay. Where have you been?"

"Now that was right subtle," Harm drawled.

"What? You don't want to know?" she chided, settling on the arm of his chair.

"I would have been polite enough to let the man make himself comfortable."

"Kenitay, sit down. Make yourself comfortable. Then tell us everything."

"Ammy, I swear you make me squirm in my own home."

"I'm just getting to what's on everybody's mind without a lot of awkward hemming and hawing. I was raised to be practical."

"You was raised to be rude."

Amanda arched a slender brow and readied a retort when Kenitay figured he might as well get to it.

"It's all right. Mrs. Bass has cause to ask."

"Mrs. Bass? I used to be Amanda. I still am."

Kenitay smiled faintly. "Amanda." He took a seat on her expensive imported sofa and, much to Leisha's chagrin, Becca scooched up beside him to slip her hand over his, familiar as you please. Worse yet, he didn't seem to mind.

"Since my wife has ruled out manners," Harm began, ignoring Amanda's frown, "suppose you start in on that story. Where you been, son?"

"Places you never want to see," Kenitay told him quietly.

Rand slipped back in and came to stand next to Leisha. The two of them were unwittingly united as they both glared at the couple on the couch: Rand at the interloper who claimed his father's attention and Leisha at her sister for claiming the spot she longed to hold.

Quietly, without emotion, Kenitay filled them in on what had transpired that day at Fort Apache, adding what Jack had told him to what he already knew. Then he continued.

"The government's lies destroyed the Apache people when its army could not. While Geronimo negotiated peace with Gatewood, who was liked and respected by our people, General Miles was already planning to send all the reservation Apaches, as well as the scouts who had served the soldiers faithfully, to Florida with the last renegades. This was in complete violation of the terms of surrender—and treachery to those who believed that words on paper protected them.

"The last warriors were told they would be in the East for only two years and that this Florida was much like our beloved mountains. That it would be a place where all could live together safely, not as prisoners but on our own reservation lands where we could exist in comfort. More lies. No reservation was waiting. We were considered prisoners of war. Our people weren't allowed to be together as one. We were separated and sent to three different army camps: Chihuahua's band to Fort Marion; Geronimo, my father, and his warriors to Fort Pickens; and me, along with the women and children, to St. Augustine. You could not imagine a world more different from our own or more unkind to our people. You can't know how it felt to have no freedom, no hope, to be confined against your will with only death and despair around you."

"I know."

Harm said that with a soft intensity as Amanda's arms went tight about him and she kissed his brow. And from the shadowed look in his eyes, Kenitay thought perhaps he did.

He went on to briefly describe the year spent in the humid hell of Florida, where, even after his broken jaw healed to allow him to voice his protest, no one listened. There, he lived with Kodene's second wife and her family. So many sickened and died that public outcry forced the government to move them to the Mount Vernon Barracks in Alabama, which was an improvement in conditions and where, at last, they could all be reunited. He didn't speak of his shock at seeing his father again. Kodene had been wasted by disease, drink, and desolation to a skeletal caricature of his former self. He'd been both pleased and devastated to find his son living among the government's prisoners and for a while, things were easier to bear. Until the burden of having his son watch a once-proud man crumble to pathetic ruins forced Kodene to withdraw and become resentful even with those who loved him.

Five years later, Kenitay went on, they were moved again, this time to Fort Sill in Indian Territory, which again was better but the temptation of having their homeland so close yet still out of reach was a constant torment. They were able to build houses of their own at the military reservation and farm small patches of ground but the promised allotment of land for each and all never materialized—another in a long history of lies.

"Then after my father died, I decided I'd had enough of living tame and another brave and I slipped off the reservation to head home."

He glossed over it so quickly, they knew there had to be more he wasn't saying.

"What happened to your father, Kenitay?" Becca asked with a compassionate innocence.

"He was taken from our home at night by one of the soldiers. This often happened when my father drank too much and trouble followed, so I wasn't too concerned. Until he didn't return in the morning. I went to ask what had happened and was told that he had tried to stab one of the guards and was shot and killed."

"And was this the truth?" Harm queried.

Kenitay shrugged. "It might have been. It was no secret that my father hated all white men and especially soldiers. The bottle made him believe he once again had the pride of a warrior and when he'd wake from that dream and find it was not true, it would make him—upset. He might have tried to kill a guard. But if that was what had happened, they would have let me see his body to make an example of him. I would have been allowed to prepare his burial. I never saw him. They wouldn't allow it. I heard later that some had seen him and that his body was covered with marks of a beating, a beating harsh enough to cause his death. The two who know that truth were the men who'd asked to speak with him. Civilians, not soldiers. Men from the Bureau of Indian Affairs, Agents Beech and Westfall."

Harm went suddenly still. Then he asked in a strangely taut voice, "This man, Westfall, what did he look like?"

"A big man with black hair and a bushy beard. He had a different accent, like the kind we heard in Alabama, very thick and slow. Do you know him?"

Harm skipped over that question to ask, "And are you after these two men for answers? Is that why you left the reservation?"

"Why would you think that?"

"Because that's what I would do."

"I don't know where to look, Mr. Bass, and if I did,

I'm not sure I'd want to risk being caught and sent back to Fort Sill. I like the smell of free air. I thought you said you understood."

"I do. And you are wise to stay clear of trouble. Now, it's late. Becca, show Kenitay where he can wash up and bunk for the night. We'll see you at breakfast."

"I appreciate the hospitality," Kenitay said as he was rising.

"You're family," Harm summed up.

Becca took hold of Kenitay's hand and tugged him up. She led him past the two cold-eyed sentinels at the doorway, Leisha and Rand, whom he walked by with an exchange of curt nods before disappearing up the twist of the stairway. Rand waited a few seconds, then slipped up after them like a silent shadow. As much as she would have liked to follow, Leisha hung back. There was more to discover here.

Leisha could tell that her parents wanted to have a private word together but if those words concerned Kenitay, she wanted to hear them. She murmured a good night, which they both answered distractedly, and she was forgotten before she even passed through the door. In the quiet hall, she leaned back against the wall to listen. Her father had taught her the best defense came from never being taken by surprise. And sometimes the only way to learn the things she needed to know came from being where she wasn't supposed to be, hearing things she wasn't meant to hear.

At least that's how she excused her eavesdropping.

"What do you think of him, Harmon?" Amanda asked as she slid off the arm of the chair onto her husband's knees. His arms went around her, cinching up in a tight circle. She broached the question casually but her mind was racing ahead, building upon that quicksilver attraction she'd seen in her daughter's eyes. She didn't think this was the time to mention that she thought Kenitay might be the perfect answer to their problem with Leisha. She wanted to do a little more observing before she brought Harm into that picture. And she wanted to know his unbiased opinion before she tossed in the variable of their daughter's future.

"I think there's a whole 'nother story between the lines."

"You don't believe him?" That wasn't a good sign, she thought.

"I don't think he told us any lies, if that's what you mean."

"What do you mean?" Amanda leaned back to study the pensive pucker of his brow and the unpromising thinning of his mouth.

"I think that boy's been through more of a hell than he's telling. He's hiding something big behind his eyes. I just don't know what it is."

"Something bad?"

"I don't know. He's good at covering up what's on his mind."

Then Harm fell silent and Amanda starting paying closer attention to what was working behind his fixed stare. Over the years, she'd learned to interpret her husband's silences.

"Harmon, what's wrong?"

He didn't try to tell her it was nothing. Nor did he answer her. She watched him for a moment, reading signs she hadn't seen for a long time.

"Do you know this man, Westfall? The name seems familiar."

Harm's reply was slick as black ice. "We were never formally introduced."

And Amanda knew right then. "He's the last of McAllister's men, isn't he?"

Again, Harm said nothing but his features firmed into angles as sharp and taut as the wind-sculpted desert.

"And what is it you're planning to do about it, Harmon?" There was no way to disguise the shake of alarm in her voice. He glanced up at her through opaque blue eyes and she could see he was already far away from this home they'd made together.

"I don't know that I plan to do anything."

His reply brought no comfort.

"Just like Kenitay plans to do nothing about finding out what happened to his father." Amanda snorted impatiently. "I've lived with you too long to believe that."

His callused hand fit to her cheek. "I love you, Amanda."

And terror leapt in her heart.

"Don't do anything, Harmon. Just let it go. It's been so long, so many years."

"A wound such as mine does not heal with time," he stated with a sudden fierceness. "The only way it can mend is if it is lanced first. This man, Westfall, is a poison in my blood, Ammy. Even if I choose not to act on it, it will act on me. He owes me. What he took from me can never be replaced. I must demand an accounting. It's the Apache way. My way."

She shivered at the implication, then hugged him tight. With her fingers threaded through his straight black hair, she pressed a hard kiss to his brow, to the ridge of his cheek, finally upon his narrowed mouth. Gradually, under the relentless persuasion of her lips, his softened and parted to allow a deeper union. After a time, Amanda leaned back just far enough so their gazes could mate as intently as their mouths had. Hers was troubled.

And that bothered him more than just a little.

"Ammy, I'm sorry to have brought such sorrow into your heart. I never meant to."

She caressed his upturned face between her hands. "I have no regrets, Harmon. None at all. All of it's been worth it to have you. I don't want to lose you now. I need you. Don't go after him. Please. Put that part of your past behind us. I know you can. I'll help you to be strong. Justice will find him even if it's not by your hand."

"But I want it to be by my hand! It's a vengeance that should be mine!"

"Let it go, Harmon. For me."

Leisha listened to the ensuing silence. Her mother was winning him over with her kisses. His will couldn't stand against them. It was no surprise that when he spoke again, it was to make a soft concession.

"Don't cry, *shijii*. You are my life. I made you that promise. I won't give you cause for tears. You've shed too many over me already."

"I love you, Harmon," came Amanda's reply. It was weak with relief.

Leisha scowled. How predictable of her mother to play the helpless female to curb her father's pride. It was a shameless device he never seemed to catch on to. Probably because he wouldn't expect such tricks from the woman he loved.

The sound of movement from within the room alerted Leisha.

"I'm going out for a while," Harm announced as he set Amanda from him.

"Don't go far or stay long."

"I won't.

"I'll wait up for you."

"You don't have to."

"I want to. Then you can make it worth the wait."

His soft chuckle was followed by a sigh. "I would be nothing without you, little girl."

"Don't keep me waiting too long, Harmon."

Leisha dodged back to avoid her father's detection as he strode for the front door and out into the cool nighttime breezes. She thought about following him but reconsidered. There were easier answers to be had.

Her mother was wiping at her eyes with the edge of a linen hanky.

"Mama?"

Amanda looked up in surprise. "I thought you'd gone to bed."

"Who is this man, Westfall?"

Amanda's expression closed up tight. "He's someone from your father's past. I'd rather you didn't bring up his name again. It upsets your father."

"Why? What did he do?"

"Things you needn't know about unless your father chooses to tell you."

Leisha bristled at the idea of secrets shared between man and wife that excluded her. "I'm not a child, Mama. If it's about Daddy—"

"It's none of your concern. And you are a child, our child. One who is ready to drop from exhaustion. March upstairs, young lady. And forget anything you might have heard. It's a past that should be buried. Don't dig it up."

Such words started a fire of curiosity.

Leisha climbed the stairs slowly. Every inch of her felt as though it had been beaten with a stout stick. Her head throbbed with every pulse beat. She was too weary for the thoughts that consumed her and was unprepared for the sight that battered her senses when she turned upon the upper hall.

Kenitay was coming out of the far bathroom. He'd just finished washing up and was bared to the waist with his shirt draped around the broad spread of his shoulders. His damp hair was sleek as black silk and lamplight gleamed along the bronze contours of his powerful upper body. She'd guessed he would look like that—graceful and muscular, like Rand's stud horse. It was an exciting combination in a man. There was that same sense of proud command and fluid strength in every movement. He saw her and stopped. She could almost imagine his nostrils flaring as his eyes narrowed into veiled slits. He was every inch a wary male animal.

It grew impossible to breathe. She could feel the tender wildness of his kisses in possession of her heart and soul. And she could hear and feel his urgency as he asked for more than kisses. And she wondered how much encouragement it would take from her for him to ask again. Something hot and dangerous had sparked between them that afternoon and she'd been sensible to pull away. Staring at him now, vibrating with that awareness, she didn't feel all that sensible anymore. She was confused by the power he held over her emotions. And because she was who she was, she resented it and sought a way to shake that hold. Because it also scared her. She took a guarded step back.

Kenitay smiled grimly and gave her a brief nod before turning into one of their many bedrooms. Almost at once, Leisha was gasping, starving for the taste of air and trembling inside.

"He's handsome, isn't he?"

Leisha gave her sister a quick, suspicious look. But Becca was leaning against her doorjamb, gazing dreamily down the hall.

"I suppose," Leisha growled, following the direction of her stare. She didn't see the way her sister looked at her in surprise. Or the way she smiled almost in sympathy.

"Kinda scary looking though, don't you think?"

Leisha scowled at her. "Only to you who is afraid of everything."

The flicker of hurt passing through Becca's docile dark eyes made her immediately regret her harsh words. Her own unfamiliar jealousy was not her sister's fault. Why would he treat her with the same deference he had Becca when she'd made it very clear in action and word that it was not appreciated?

"He's not the same person you remember, Becca," she

said by way of an apology. "His soul is heavy with secrets."

"You sound like Daddy."

"Daddy's a good judge of character."

Becca kept her smile to herself, wondering what their daddy would think if he knew Leisha had lost her heart over their furtive guest. She, of course, had no plans to enlighten him.

"Here."

Leisha took the length of muslin Becca extended. "What's this?"

"One of my nightdresses. Since we have company, I thought you might like to wear a little more than usual to bed."

Leisha liked the feel of clean sheets against her bare skin and both of them knew their mother would have a fit if she found out. Amanda was sometimes annoyingly proper.

"It's not like I plan to walk in my sleep," Leisha grumbled. Then she was heartily shocked by the lift of her sister's brows that suggested maybe Kenitay walked in his.

As she stripped gingerly out of her buckskins, Leisha rubbed the abused portions of her anatomy that were bruised by her fall from Rand's horse and as she did, she considered the danger she'd invited beneath their roof. Now that she knew Kenitay's reasonings, she could excuse his attack upon her. He'd thought himself justified to take revenge against the Bass family. It was part of a code her father had taught her. Now that he and Jack had cleared up all misunderstandings, she didn't think he was a threat to any of them. He was family. And he'd been so desolate when she'd found him sitting at the well in Terlingua. She couldn't just ignore his pain. She'd thought if anyone could exorcise personal demons it was her father. She hadn't intended to wake those out of his own past.

She slipped on the frilly nightgown and frowned down

at the rows of lace and ribbons. Not exactly her style of dress. Yet she remembered well the dress her mother's relatives in New York had sent her when she was just a girl. It had been like this one, all flouncy and feminine. And wearing it at her father's coaxing had made her feel—different. Uncomfortable and yet content. She'd known she was pretty. She could tell by the softening in her father's eyes. It was the way he always looked at Becca. She'd liked it and at the same time rebelled against it. Because she wasn't like Becca and those stuffy parasites in New York. She was her father's child and she didn't need fancy dresses or soft female stirrings to complicate her life.

And she didn't need to consider Kenitay with such fluttery anticipation. After all, it wasn't likely she'd be yielding to his persuasive touch again. He would be riding out of her life again soon.

The sooner the better.


She couldn't move.

Leisha woke with a quickly stifled cry. Panic had her heart banging against her ribs in a hurtful rhythm. Her skin was damp and she was panting from the intensity of her nocturnal struggles. When she tried to sit up, she realized what she'd been fighting against. Not the shadow of Drake Collier pinning her helpless beneath him. It was Becca's nightdress tangled about her legs, restricting their freedom.

It was no easy task suppressing the terror trembling through her. The rush of memory clouded her mind on the last vestiges of sleep. She swore she could feel those sweaty, groping hands upon her skin. For a moment, she feared she was going to be sick but a sense of anger and revulsion overcame the urge. Clean. She needed to feel clean.

Leisha stumbled down the hall on tottery legs. She set

to scrubbing off the film of Collier's memory with an anxious fervor, so obsessed with the task she wasn't aware of the soft sobs wrenching up from her throat until there was a light tap on the door.

"Leisha? You all right?"

Then before she could respond, the door opened.

A moment's silence, then a booming, "What the hell happened to you?"

# Seven

Leisha grabbed a handful of Rand's shirtfront and jerked him into the bathroom with her, shutting the door with her heel as she shoved him up against the wall.

"You shut up about this! Don't you dare say a word to anyone! You go blabbing to Daddy and I'll cut you off at the knees!"

But her brother was more concerned with her tears than her threats. "Lemme see."

"What? No! Stop it! What do you think you're doing?" She slapped at his hands when he reached for the hem of her nightgown and was dismayed when he reversed their positions, clutching her hands and holding them harmless in one of his while using that forearm to press her back against their mama's fancy French wallpaper. "Let me go! I hate you!"

"I know you do," was his casual reply. He had the muslin gown hiked up nearly to the top of her thighs, then went very still, studying the marks impressed upon her flesh. Discolorations in the shape of a man's hands. Leisha let her head drop back against the wall. She was panting softly, not fighting him anymore. Very slowly, his gaze rose to meet hers. His eyes were as lethal as a freshly blued gun barrel.

"Who did this?"

"It doesn't mat—"

He ripped off a fierce oath and asked again, his voice so low it was nearly a growl. "Who did this to you?"

Leisha sucked in her breath and met his stare with a cold directness. "I took care of it already. I killed him."

Rand muttered another curse and released his hold on her. He was agitated and at a loss. "Did you tell Mama?"

"No. Are you going to?"

"I don't guess I will."

He looked awkward and angry, not knowing what to do, admiring her so much he had to bite down hard to keep the praise inside. He knew she didn't care a bit for his approval.

"Are you all right?" he asked at last. He'd never heard her cry before and the sound had shaken him.

"I'm fine," she lied. But her teeth were chattering as if she were suffering from the same chill icing over her stare.

"Do you want me to—"

"I don't want you to do anything. I can take care of myself."

He gave her a faint smile. "I know you can." And with a nod, he started to withdraw.

"Randall?"

He glanced her way.

"Thanks."

"Sure."

"Rand?"

"What?"

"Would—would you have gone after him for me?"

He gave her a slow, thin smile that was Harm Bass all over. "Oh, yeah. And *dead* would be too quick a word to describe what I'd do to him when I got him."

Then he left her there alone, surprised to discover after eighteen years that her brother was someone she liked.

But she had lied to him. She wasn't fine and she

couldn't take care of herself. And she was in desperate need of rectifying both those things.

And one thing came to mind—one act that would restore her pride, if not her honor.

Leisha wasn't the only one awake and restless. Amanda lay in bed beside her husband, watching, waiting. The frenzied lovemaking they'd shared earlier should have exhausted her. It had taken the edge off Harm and he'd fallen right to sleep. But his was a fitful slumber so she stayed alert and ready should he need her, knowing he would.

He gave a sudden jerk in the throes of a familiar dream. His breathing quickened, growing light and fast, and his knees tucked up tight against his chest. Amanda had left the bedside light burning so it wouldn't be dark if he awoke. It glimmered upon the tears tracking his face. Soft, despairing cries worked up through him, expressing the pain and fear he never would allow to escape him when awake. He wouldn't have whimpered if they were tearing off strips of his skin.

And they had, hadn't they?

She eased her arms around him, holding him still, absorbing his shivers. And in her mind, she damned them, every one of the eight who were dead and gone and the one who still remained to tease back these wretched memories with just the mention of his name.

"No . . ."

"Shhh. Harmon, it's all right."

"Don't . . ."

"No one's going to hurt you, Harmon. you're safe here. Safe with me."

"Becky—*Mama!*"

"Shhh! It's just a dream. Dreams can't hurt you." But

how could she believe that when he cringed and twisted in her embrace, reliving the horror, the madness.

He gasped sharply and his eyes flew open, wild, glazed with panic.

"Harmon?"

He took a wavering breath. "Ammy?"

"I'm here. It's all right. I'm here. Go back to sleep, Harmon."

"Don't let go."

"I won't."

"Don't let them hurt me."

"I won't."

Slowly, his eyes closed and he relaxed against her. Amanda gave a sigh of relief. It hadn't been so bad. This time. But it would get worse. As long as Westfall was out there roaming free while Harm was a prisoner of the past.


Kenitay stretched out on the bed and let his hands rub over the bottom sheet. It was smooth as silk. He hadn't been on sheets like this for—for a long time. He closed his eyes, not wanting to think about anything, especially not about making love to Leisha Bass on sheets as fine as these. If his mind had to chew on something, he'd rather it be something else.

He thought instead about the thirteen years of festering hate hinged upon a mistake. For thirteen years he'd had a loving family waiting. And he hadn't even known. They'd thought he was dead and had mourned him while he was sweating away in the army's prison stewing for revenge. They loved him and wanted him back amongst them.

They didn't know him.

How could he pretend that one instant of truth would change thirteen hard, formative years? He wasn't the man Jack Bass could have made of him, a man like Carson.

It was too late to try to step back into those shoes. He wasn't the son of a respected white Texas Ranger. He was the son of an Apache warrior who had taught him honor above all else, pride above personal pleasures. He could not linger on fine sheets when he knew he had work to finish. Work that would forever separate him from this family and a future amongst them.

He wondered what Harm Bass would do if he knew how close his daughter had come to defilement and murder at his hands? Instead of enjoying the sheets, he'd be lying cold under them. Harmon understood Apache reasoning. Touch something of mine, pay for it with something of yours. And pay dearly. Leisha had almost paid that price.

Why had she kissed him back?

She'd gone from panic to passion in an instant. It had to be more than the fact that they'd known each other as kids. There was a power in her response that had him helpless. He'd kissed women before. He'd been something of a novelty on the reservation because Apaches didn't go in for kissing. He'd learned it from living with Jack and his mama and watching their strange white mating rituals. And the Indian women, once they'd gotten over their shock, had liked it just fine. He'd never bedded any of them, though several had let him know they wouldn't object. He'd had too much respect for them and their families to casually take what should be given in tribute. He'd had his carnal affairs with white women who'd been excited about the idea of doing it with an Indian. They'd been women of social stature and whorish morals. It hadn't meant anything to him.

But Leisha—oh, she'd pulled a different kind of tension through him. One that still twisted and turned inside in a restless need for release. A need for her. She'd spat in his face. What tremendous spirit she had. A warrior's defiance in a female form. If only he had the time to explore that intriguing combination. To what end? What was the point? Would her fancy mama from the East with her silky sheets and big house approve of her daughter running off into the desert with the likes of him? He had enough to worry about without the shadow of Harm Bass hanging over his head.

A few hungry kisses did not mean commitment. Leisha was a hard woman to figure. She scorned things female and what he desired from her was the essence of the form. He was asking for what she might never be willing or able to give. The ordeal with Collier had scarred her deeper than she would ever admit. His suggestion that they head toward intimacy had thrown her into a terrible panic. Maybe it was best he leave it alone. Give her time to heal. She needed someone to be there for her, to show her the pleasurable steps passion could take when she was ready. She didn't want to take those steps with him now.

Then why had she kissed him at the well?

Was he supposed to believe that meant anything? Well, it had. More than it should have. Probably more than she meant it to. Because it was the first touch of tenderness he'd known for far too long and it had unstrung all his defenses.

Leisha Bass was not meant to be in his future. He had no future to give.

And he had no more time to languish under this roof pining for the life he might have led.

He finally drifted off but he was a necessarily light sleeper, used to rousing with the slightest sound. He was somewhat surprised to feel the mattress give on one side. He hadn't heard the door open or the approach of footsteps.

Leisha.

"Kenitay?"

Her whisper woke a flurry of expectation from which one thing surfaced: she'd come to him.

He opened his eyes to find her leaning over him. Her hair was loose, a golden kiss highlighting sun-bronzed features. She was wearing something white and surprisingly feminine. That she would go to such effort to seduce his senses added to the enticement. Not that he needed much encouragement.

She only had time for a soft squeak of alarm. He had her by the forearms and was quick to roll her beneath him, his mouth coming down over hers in that same movement to stifle any further sound. Leisha lay stiff for a moment, her eyes wide open, her mind too stunned to demand a reaction. A noise escaped her. It could have been a protest. It didn't sound like one.

He shifted so that his body leveled over hers, pressing her to the sheets. His mouth opened and came down hard, forcing hers to part. The sudden plunge of his tongue stabbed through her shock. Her body responded where her thoughts had been slow to, becoming molten beneath his galvanizing touch. His fingers bunched in her hair, making fists against her temples, anchoring her head while his tongue thrust deep, again and again. She opened her mouth wider to accommodate him, wanting that wild shock of passion flamed by his kiss. Heat ran through her, coursing to embarrassing places, places that ached to feel him moving hard and forcefully against them; her straining breasts, the smooth concave of her belly, and moist apex of her thighs. All were shamefully eager for him.

Yet the moment his attention shifted from the devouring kisses to the caress of his palms along those sensitive spots, the desire fled. A resistance just as urgent made her thrash against him.

He felt her reluctance and was quick to croon, "I won't hurt you, *shijii.* I promise." He said the warm Apache endearment the way her father said it to her mother, with tenderness, with care. And she almost gave in. Until his hand moved up her thigh. Over the painful bruising, waking a remembered sense of degradation and helpless shame.

"Get off me!"

"Leisha—"

"Stop! I didn't come here for this!"

He paused, lifting up, his green eyes gleaming. "Then why did you come?"

"To talk to you. Dammit, get off!"

"My mistake."

He rolled onto his side. Once freed from his oppressive weight, Leisha was able to draw a decent breath. She floundered a moment, struggling to gather up the scatter of her dazed defenses. She couldn't let him know how badly she was rattled.

"So, what was so important that you'd come to have a midnight chat in my bed dressed like this?" He fingered one of the bodice ribbons, then lifted it up to brush the white satin against his lips. Leisha shuddered inside.

"I didn't want to be overheard." She snatched the ribbon out of his hand. Hers was shaking. "And what's wrong with the way I'm dressed?"

His eyes dropped down for a scorching assessment. "Nothing. Not what I expected, is all."

"I haven't given you the right to expect anything."

*Then why were you sucking my tongue down your throat?* he could have asked most reasonably. But he didn't. There was an odd vulnerability to her bravado. It made him want to protect her and he was sure she wouldn't like knowing that.

"So, talk."

He was leaning up on one elbow, his features impenetrable, the sheet falling away to pool at his waist so that she was confronted with all those sleek contours of skin over muscle. She couldn't focus there but when she lifted her gaze, it settled on the immobile set of his mouth. The shape of his lips was sensual suggestion, all lofty upper

arcs and pouty lower swell. She didn't want to dwell on
kissing him. That was too dangerous. She raised her sights
a notch, studying the bridge of his nose. Constant expo-
sure to the sun cast the crest of his cheekbones in a deeper
amber hue, warming his complexion with a hint of rosy
burn. It made her think of a sunrise sparking off the distant mesas, waking heat and fire within weathered stone.
And her fingertips itched to soothe along that bold bone
structure seeking inner flame.

She blinked hard, disrupting the direction of her
thoughts. *Yusn,* wasn't there an unappealing inch upon the
man that wouldn't invite a lusty speculation?

"Well?"

She cleared her throat gruffly and stared fiercely at the
ridge of his brows. "What do you know about this man,
Westfall?"

"What's your interest?"

"Personal."

"Then there's nothing to tell." His bland refusal brought
her temper into play.

"What do you mean *nothing?*"

"Westfall and his partner are *my* business. I don't want
you intruding."

"I'm planning to go after him. You can share what you
know or I'll find out on my own."

Several deep vertical lines grooved the bridge of his
nose. His voice was a threatening rumble. "You're not
going anywhere. You will stay here where you belong,
where your father and brother can look out for you."

"I don't need anyone to look out for me!"

Very softly, he said, "You forget I know different."

*"Cabron!"* She swung her fist at his head but he intercepted it easily and she found herself once again flat
on her back. She panted angrily and squirmed with all
her might but couldn't slip him.

"Vengeance is a man's right, Leisha. Don't get in my way. I wouldn't want you to get hurt."

"You arrogant, bullying—"

He silenced her with a voracious kiss, intentionally proving her weakness and his own superior strength. It wasn't a kind thing to do but it was necessary. He didn't want to come upon her the way he had in that outlaw camp. He didn't want to find her in a worse situation.

When he lifted up, he found her all spitting fury.

"My father and brother will kill you for that!"

"Tell them," he challenged. "But then I'd have to tell them everything I know."

She gripped her molars together. What a hateful man! "Maybe I'll just have to kill you myself." She tugged hard and he released her. She had to crawl over him to escape the bed and in passing, was distressed to find he wore nothing beneath the sheet. That knowledge had her knees knocking and her heart pounding. Her intention of stalking for the door was more a desperate reel.

Let him laugh, she thought with a frantic anger. Let him think of her as helpless, a victim just waiting to fall into trouble. She'd prove him wrong. She'd find Westfall first, then see if he felt like making a joke at her expense!

He'd forgotten who he was dealing with. Her last name was Bass. And he wasn't going to get in the way of her tribute to her father. Nor was he going to keep her from restoring her sense of self-worth.


"Running out without saying your good-byes?"

Kenitay glanced over the back of his saddled horse to see Leisha's slender figure silhouetted against the glare of daybreak. "Told you I was leaving today." He went back to tightening the double girt.

"Guess that excuses the rudeness then. My mama's not

the best cook so I can see wanting to avoid breakfast but a cup of coffee wouldn't have killed you."

"Thank your family for their hospitality."

"You should do that yourself."

He gave a savage sigh and leaned his forearms upon the smooth saddle skirt. "I don't want to drag this out, Leisha. I've no place here. I did what you asked. I came and saw them. Now, I've got to go."

"What are you running from?"

He hesitated just a second too long. "I'm not running from anything."

"When I came up on you and your friend, you looked like rabbits looking for a hole. Who's after you?"

"You're pretty set on getting into my business, aren't you, *silah?* No matter what I tell you, it won't be enough."

"Try the truth."

He gave her a bland smile. "You wouldn't believe it."

"Try me."

"Tempting," he murmured as his gaze skimmed down the mannish garb she wore, insinuating another interest, "but I don't have the time." He grabbed his bridle and started to lead his horse out of the barn. He stopped when he came up alongside her and flashed a provocative grin. "Maybe I could stop in to see you again sometime, if you like."

Her eyes went all flinty. "I *don't* like."

He laughed softly, then before she could second-guess his intentions, he hooked an arm about her shoulders and jerked her up tight against his chest. His kiss was hot as a brand. His brand. She stumbled back, gasping, then as he watched with a mocking smile, she wiped the taste of him off her mouth with her sleeve.

Kenitay rolled up into the saddle and gathered his reins. He gave her a brief look. "I'll be seeing you, Leisha

Bass." Then he kicked back his heels and cantered off toward the dusty plains.

Leisha sighed and slumped back against the planked door. Her mouth was pulsing from the hard possession of his. Her temper was riled by his dismissive words and cock-sure attitude. But a soft smile sketched her lips as she whispered after him in a confident tone, "Sooner than you think, Kenitay. Sooner than you think."

# Eight

Harm Bass was getting ready to go manhunting.

His family knew the signs. He came downstairs toting a change of clothes rolled up and ready to store behind his saddle. He wore tough-soled Apache moccasins with his big knife sheathed where they turned down at the knee; the binoculars Amanda had bought him for Christmas years back hung around his neck. His expression was all business and already as far away as that high powered focus. And when he grabbed Amanda up in the kitchen, it took the scent of burning eggs to pull him off her lips.

The five of them gathered at the table, Kenitay's chair conspicuously empty.

"The boy lit out already?"

"Said he was in a hurry, Daddy," Leisha supplied, not looking up. She was afraid of what he might be able to read in her eyes. "And he said to thank everyone for the hospitality."

"At least he remembered that much of his manners. How 'bout some coffee, Ammy?"

As she filled his cup, Amanda rubbed his back with her other hand. "Looks like you're getting ready to ride out, too."

"Soon as I'm done here. Pass the biscuits, Becca. Rand, you hogging that all for yourself, boy, or you fixing to share it out?"

"Sorry, Daddy." He set the platter of ham in motion.

Amanda lingered behind her husband's chair until he looked up in question.

"Something on your mind, little girl?"

"Just this."

She captured his chin in her palm, keeping its upward tilt so she could claim a long, lavish kiss. It took a moment for his eyes to blink open after she moved away.

"What was that for?"

"To last me until you get back because I don't think you'd let me drag you back upstairs for what I'd really like to do to you."

"Ammy!" His gaze flashed toward his children in embarrassment. "That's not exactly table talk."

"We're all adults here, Daddy," Rand remarked casually. He was trying not to grin.

"Some of us are," Leisha corrected, giving her brother a haughty look.

Amanda ignored them as her palm caressed the lean angles of her husband's face. "Where are you off to, Harmon?" As careful as she was to sound nonchalant, he caught the slight edge of worry in her tone.

"I promised Calvin I'd go after those other three bank robbers," he said as he started cutting up his ham.

Amanda looked relieved but Leisha was immediately all attention. "I could help you out there, Daddy. I got a good look at all three of them and—"

"And you can identify them when Rand and me bring 'em back."

Leisha's shocked and angry gaze darted across the table at her brother. Rand was staring fixedly into his plate. He said nothing.

"I should be the one riding with you, Daddy," came her quick protest.

He gave her a long, steady look before turning back to finish up his eggs. "I want you here at home, mending."

She read between the lines; she'd had her chance—now he was cleaning up after her.

Without a sound, she rose from the table and strode out of the house.

Rand cleared his throat diplomatically. "Daddy, she'd probably be more use to you on this than me."

"If you don't want to go with me, boy, jus' say so."

" 'Course I do but—"

"Then quit your gabbing and grab up your gear."

"Yessir." He snatched up a handful of biscuits before striding to the stairs.

"I'll clear the table for you, Mama," Becca offered, seeing the way her mother was gazing down upon her father's dark head. She scooted to the kitchen fast with an armload of plates.

Harm was swallowing down the last of his coffee when he became aware of the tickle of Amanda's fingertips at the nape of his neck and around his ear. Then it was more than the potent coffee waking him up. She was leaning up against the back of him, her breasts cushioning his head, her lips nibbling along his brow.

"Harmon?" she purred.

"Ummm?" he managed to mumble.

"About that trip upstairs . . ."

He gripped her wrist, practically dragging her with him around the bend in the stairway. She was at the waistband of his jeans, the bodice of her dress already open, before they even got to their room. He turned her inside it and slammed the door, meeting her urgent, opened-mouth kisses as she was tugging denim down over his hips. They were still a room away from the bed.

"Oh, hell," he mumbled into her hurried breaths and shoved her back against the wall. He tucked up her dress, made short work of tossing off her drawers. With his hands cupping her bare buttocks, he lifted her up then down upon his rock-hard arousal. Then he was pounding into her, letting her know in this most primitive way that it was hell to leave her. With her legs wrapped around his waist and her hands buried in his hair, she released her shout of satisfaction into the silencing crush of his mouth.

Figuring he'd make her wait while he took his own sweet time, Harm carried her to the bed, stumbling over the tangle of his jeans and falling with her. They took an awkward bounce and Amanda gave a startled little gasp as the movement drove him up even farther inside. She seized his flanks and held him there, her eyes rolling with a luxurious delight.

"Oh, Harmon!"

"Shame on you, Mrs. Bass! A woman your age, married for more than half your lifetime, carrying on so in front of impressionable youngsters." He was nuzzling her neck and she arched it in a sensual bow.

"They weren't the ones I was trying to impress."

"Well, you still impress me plenty."

"Are you planning to finish this or can you wait until after lunch to leave?"

"I've got to go. Ammy, you drive me crazy. You know that, don't you?"

But she couldn't answer because he'd started to move in a rough, pleasing rhythm, carrying her well on her way to a second shattering climax.

When they were both limp and contentedly sated, Amanda smoothed back the hair that had fallen across his brow. "Harmon?"

"Ummm?" He didn't attempt to move or open his eyes.

"I love you."

"Ummmhmmm."

"You're just going after those three outlaws, right?"

He turned his head slightly so he could meet her stare. "That's what I said."

"You're sure?"

"I gave you my promise, didn't I?"

"So those robbers are the only reason you're riding out?"

"No."

She waited for him to finish.

"I need to get outside for a while. Someplace—safe."

She understood without him saying more. He needed to get out beneath the hot sun and clear sky, where the need to concentrate on survival would overcome the chance for too much thought. He'd be all right out there in the desert with their son, doing what he did best—living off the land and running a trail. Someplace where constant thoughts of Westfall wouldn't drive him to madness. "You and Randall be careful."

"They're dead men."

"Harmon, you don't have to kill them."

"They shot Cal."

"Did he ask you to kill them for him?"

"No. He wants 'em brought back for trial." He sighed heavily. "Guess I'll have to bring 'em in."

"I love you."

"Does that mean I can leave now or do I have to prove it to you some more?"

"Would you?"

"Sassy girl. You trying to kill me? I'm not a young man anymore."

"Who wants a young man?" she murmured, going for his lips again and lingering there to the limit of their breath. "I like what I have. Bring it back in one piece."

"Yes, ma'am."


Harm strode across the yard with a particularly strutty walk. He carried his carbine and his wife's hot kisses and was ready to be gone. Rand had the horses tacked up and set to go and that's where he was heading when he saw Leisha moping by the corral.

"Leisha?" When she didn't respond to his call, he repeated it. "Leisha, *shijii,* aren't you going to see me off?"

"Good-bye, Daddy," she muttered.

He detoured over to where she stood, waiting in front of her until she glanced up through misty eyes.

"Are you going to see to things for me while I'm gone?"

She blinked hard and her eyes took on a gleam of polished silver. "Yessir, I am."

"I always depend on you. You know that, don't you?"

"Yessir, Daddy," she mumbled faintly.

"And if you don't give me a hug, I'm gonna swat you but good."

Her arms twined about his neck in a near-choking hold. He held her for a long moment, then said, "You're just like your mama. You drive me crazy, the both of you. And I love you. All of you. You're my world."

"I love you, Daddy. And don't you worry," she promised fervently. "I'll take care of everything."

Leisha set off to do just that the minute he and Rand rode out of the yard.

"Mama, I'm going into town."

There was a flurry of movement behind her parents' closed bedroom door, then Amanda appeared with her gown buttoned up crooked, her hair coming down out of its pins, and her mouth all passion-bruised. In the middle of the morning. Leisha raised a scandalized brow. Then she noticed the pinch of worry around her mother's eyes that was always there when Harmon rode out.

"To town? What do you need there?"

"I wanted to check and see if my reward money got to the bank."

"If you need some money—"

"I want to see about my *own* money," Leisha corrected and her mother was taken aback by the tone of her voice.

"I see. Well, I don't suppose it would do any good to tell you I don't think you're fit enough to make that long trip."

"No, I don't suppose it would."

Amanda sighed. "Be home before dark."

Leisha didn't reply. She was buckling on her sidearms and expertly checking the loads as she headed for the front door. It wouldn't do to be caught unprepared.

Becca was standing out on the front porch, her cheeks becoming flush of color.

"Are you going after him?"

"Who?" Leisha asked impatiently.

"Kenitay."

Leisha gave her a long, startled look. "Why would I want to do that?"

"Just thought you might. Anything you want me to tell Mama when you don't show up for supper? Just in case you change your mind."

"You read too many books, Becca."

"And you don't read enough. I think he's worth running after."

Leisha glared at her. "You don't know anything about him."

"Maybe I know more than you think." And with a haughty tip of her head, she turned toward the house.

"Becca? Tell Mama not to worry. Make up something. You're better at that than I am."

"Leisha? Is he a good kisser?"

"W-what?" Then when her sister waited patiently for a reply, she scowled and said, "Yes."

Becca beamed. "I thought he would be. Happy hunting. Don't bring him home over your saddle."

Leisha rolled her eyes heavenward as if unable to believe her sibling's lunacy. But even as she strode down to get her horse, she was feeling the contours of Kenitay's mouth on hers.

* * *

The Terlingua jail was hot and airless in the lull of afternoon. Billy Cooper was propped up behind Cal Lowe's desk, dozing beneath the tip of his hat.

"Working hard, Sheriff?"

He thumbed up his brim and grinned at Leisha. "Hardly working. If I sit here much longer, I'm gonna start collecting calluses on my butt—beggin' your pardon."

Leisha glanced to the side, frowning at the sight of Jed Cooper sweeping out the cells in back. She had no liking for the shifty, hungry-eyed coyote. She admired Billy and Sarah for what they were trying to do, bringing up his sister's kids and all, but they should have been smart and cut their losses with this one.

"What can I do for you, Leisha? Got any more outlaws in tow?"

She stiffened up at his good-natured teasing. "No. Daddy and Rand went after the other three robbers so you'd better get a room ready."

"Or three boxes. I'll warn the undertaker so we'll be ready in either case. Happens I know your daddy pretty well."

"Seems it would make your job easier if he brought 'em in facedown."

"That it would." He chuckled, then looked over at Jed. "Get 'em good and clean, Jed. We're expecting company. You're about halfway to working off your bail." Then he returned his attention to the dusty young woman before him. "You was saying?"

"How would I go about finding someone who works for the Bureau of Indian Affairs?"

"This just a question or business?"

"Business."

"Where's this fellow out of?"

"Fort Sill, the Oklahoma Territory."

"Got a name?"

"Westfall."

"Guess I could send a wire over there and ask. This something you're doing for your daddy?"

"It's a surprise so I'd appreciate it if you wouldn't say anything."

"I didn't know ole Harmon liked surprises."

"He'll like this one."

"If you say so." He unwound his long legs from behind the desk. "Speakin' of surprises, heard tell Emily's boy, Kenny, turned up bold as brass. Had him in my jail the other night and didn't even know him. Knocked the stuffin's outta Jed."

Leisha slid a look over at the gangly Jed. It wouldn't take much, she said to herself.

"Always liked that boy," Billy was musing. "Clear head, deep thinker. Like Jack. Always wondered what kinda man he'd have turned out to be. Right fine one, I reckon. You get a chance to see him?"

"He stayed the night at our place before movin' on."

"Movin' on? After all this time and he can't even stay around long enough to say more than howdy? He say where he'd been all this time?"

"Locked up at Fort Sill with the rest of the Apaches."

"Bad piece of luck. He say what he was up to?"

"Said he had some business to take care of. Can we get to mine anytime soon."

"Sure thing. Take a walk with me over to the telegraph office."

Once the wire was sent, there was nothing to do but wait for a reply. Too restless to sit around at the jail, Leisha prowled the streets of Terlingua. Business was picking up and there were a lot of new faces due to a rumor that companies were coming in to start mining for cinnabar. If mines opened, Billy Cooper wouldn't have much time for sitting on his butt. Progress would come to their sleepy little town whether they liked it or not, dragging them toward the new century with the rest of the country. And with progress came trouble. She smiled to herself. Maybe she'd offer to be Billy's deputy alongside Carson.

She found herself loitering outside the mercantile, staring in through the cloudy glass window. It took her a minute to figure out just what she was staring at and then she was surprised. What caught her eye was a red dress. Not just red but that deep-textured scarlet that streaked the mountains in the morning in such vivid strokes. It was of a heavy silk, its full sleeves gathered in elaborate pleating that ended in a band of gold brocade and a thick spill of scarlet lace. The same gold formed a high collar and contained the richly puckered material of the bodice in bands below the bosom and at the waist where the fabric was released in stylish folds that swept to the floor. There were tassels aplenty and ordinarily, Leisha would have cynically thought of curtains but she stood there, hating to admit she was admiring the impractical creation. Her eyes lingered along the full gathers of the bodice that would lend an ample shape to even the flattest form, then her gaze moved down to that tiny waist. A waist to fit the span of a man's hands. She drew a constricted breath, imagining the warmth of Kenitay's palms burning through that glossy scarlet silk.

"Show you that new Smith and Wesson, Miss Bass?"

Leisha gave a start and looked almost guiltily toward the store's proprietor.

"Fine-looking handpiece. Would look mighty fine in that rig you're wearing," he coaxed.

Leisha studied her reflection in the glass. With her hair pulled back and hat set square, her figure roughly clad in men's clothing, she looked more like a spindly boy. Like someone who *would* be admiring a revolver instead of a frilly red dress. She stepped away from the window, muttering, "Jus' looking."

"Tell your family howdy for me."

"I'll do that." And she walked briskly away from that red-tasseled daydream.

Billy wasn't at the jail. His sullen-faced nephew was plopped behind the desk, reading one of the "WANTED" dodgers cluttering the spur-marred wood top. When he saw her, an unpleasant smile curved up and his eyes glittered.

"Well, howdy there, Miss Leisha. Billy ain't back yet. But I'd be right happy to keep you company."

Leisha gave him a chill smile in return. "I can amuse myself. You go on with what you're doing."

He folded up the poster and tucked it into his pocket with a smug chuckle. "You say you did some talking to that renegade boy of Jack's?"

"Yes. Thought you had a run-in with him, too. Or were you too busy picking up your teeth to do much talking?"

His smile never faltered but his eyes thinned into hard slits. "He blindsided me. Dirty fighter, like all them Injuns.

"The bottle was probably what blindsided you. Did Billy say how long he was going to be?"

"Said he was waitin' on your reply so you might as well make yourself at home." He went back to his leering at the snug fit of her buckskin trousers. "Ain't seen that pretty little sister of yours in town lately. Where's she been hiding?"

"If I told you that, she'd have to find another place to hide."

Jed laughed. "Damn, but you're a prickly one. But slap a corset on you and some dangly earbobs and I betcha you'd be just as fetching as your baby sister. Could probably get yourself a good-paying job over at the Midas. They like their girls tough over there. I like 'em that way, too."

Leisha ignored him. But even if the compliment *had* come from the scummy Jed Cooper, it got her thinking.

*Just as fetching as her baby sister.* She wondered if that was the truth or just Jed's way of getting a rise out of her.

"Say, Leisha-honey, did that redskin boy happen to say where he was heading?"

"Why? Were you looking to go another round with him?"

Another narrow smile. "Just thought I'd be smart and stay outta his way."

"That would be smart. And no, he didn't tell me where he was going."

"He tell you anything else? Whisper sweet nothings in your ear maybe? Seem to recall you being mighty friendly with him when we was kids."

Leisha's glare was pure ice. "You recall wrong."

Jed gave another hoot of laughter. "That right? Then why are all your feathers up? You an' him planning on meeting up somewheres maybe?"

"Hey, Leisha. Got that information for you," Billy said as he strode in. Jed came vaulting out of his chair, and Leisha instantly forgot all about him. "This what you was wanting to know?"

She took the telegram and scanned the contents. Her bland smile gave no hint of her inner excitement. "Yes. This is just what I wanted. Thanks, Billy. And remember, don't say anything about this to my daddy."

"I know. Big surprise. I won't."

Then she surprised him with the quick fling of an arm about his neck, dragging him down so she could press a kiss on one tanned cheek. He recovered fast enough to envelop her in a big bear hug that was warm as a woolly robe and lifted her right off her feet. Crushed up close, Leisha caught the scent of soap-scrubbed man and leather from his vest and she had a pretty good idea why Sarah was so crazy about him. He felt good wrapped around her. For someone else's man.

"Well, you just feel free to ask a favor any ole time," he told her, settling her back to her feet. "Don't you go getting into no trouble. Your daddy and me are at peace for now and I'd like to keep it that way. Pity the fellas who come courtin' you girls and having to face up to his squinty-eyed stare. Was hard enough sneaking Sarah away from him, him being her uncle and all. He saw us married at gunpoint, you know."

No, she didn't know.

But Billy was grinning fondly. "I owe him a big one for that. Made me see the error of my wild and foolish ways, you might say. This Westfall ain't some beau you're chasing down, is he?"

"No. Nothing like that. I've never met him. He's a— friend of my father's."

"You an' your family stop on over for supper real soon. Chonita likes to show off her cooking and Sarah and the kids love the company."

Leisha promised that they would as she headed for the door. Jed was languishing there, his legs crossed at the ankles, making a barrier across the opening. She paused, waiting for him to move, which he did after giving her another leer. She still had to pass uncomfortably close and as she did, his hand caught the curve of her rump, squeezing familiarly.

"Jus' checking to see if there was woman under them cowboy clothes," he drawled with a smirky grin.

She held his stare unblinkingly and gripped the crotch of his denims, twisting hard. His face went alarmingly pale. "Jus' checking to see if there was any kind of man under all that bragging," she returned. His breath gushed out shakily when she let go and stalked away.

He was still bent double when he heard Billy's chuckle.

"Boy, a word to the wise. Don't be riling one of them Basses if you want to keep your pieces and parts intact."

"Bitch," Jed gasped harshly as his hard glare followed Leisha's lithe step as she crossed the street.

"That she might be, but she just outmanned you."

He straightened slowly, fighting the urge to grimace. He scowled at his uncle with no trace of affection. "Figures you'd stick up for them instead of your own family."

"Son, they are my family and I'm right proud that they'd lay claim to me. So don't go shaming me in front of them. If you're finished lolligagging, pick up that broom and get back to work."

"To hell with that and to hell with you. I got me things to do. Things that'll bring me some real money and respect around here." He stormed out the door and down the boardwalk without looking back.

Billy threw up his hands in resignation. What was he going to do with a boy so determined to go wrong? Maybe he would call on Harmon and let his uncle beat some sense into the surly fool. Harm Bass had sure scared him toward the straight and narrow.

He forgot about his nephew as he was called upon to break up a fight between the blacksmith and a disgruntled customer. By the time he returned to his office, sporting a beaut of a black eye for stepping in at the wrong time, he didn't want to hear about anyone else's problems. Pouring a cup of bitter reheated coffee, he dropped down in his chair and went to poking through the stack of "WANTED" posters he'd picked up while sending off Leisha's telegraph. He tossed out those he'd already seen and added the others one by one to the pile he had yet to peruse. Then, he stopped and stared, reading one of them over and over.

"Oh, sonofabitch," he whispered, reaching for his hat.

"Hiya, Uncle Billy. That's a right nice shiner! You're just in time for supper. Come on in."

"Can't right now, Carson. Is your daddy here?"

Carson read the signs of serious business on Billy Cooper's face and he grew somber. "Sure. I'll get him for you."

Billy fidgeted on the porch, hating like hell what he was about to do but not knowing any way around it. He stiffened his resolve when Jack came to the door with an amiable, "Hey, Sheriff. Coming to beg your way back into a real job?"

"Jack, can you come out here for a minute?"

Jack's smile faded. "What's up?"

"Something I need to show you. Dammit, I feel mighty bad about this but I figured you ought to know."

Jack stepped out, his brow crowded with concern. He put out his hand and Billy passed him the dodger with obvious reluctance. Jack gave it a curious glance then stared hard, all sharp concentration.

"What do you want me to do about it, Jack? It's your call."

"I'll take care of it. Thanks, Billy."

"Whatcha meaning to do?"

"Find him."

"You going as a Ranger or as his daddy?"

"Both." He looked again at the paper in his hand. There was a crude likeness penned on it but there was no mistaking the chiseled features and finely shaped mouth. Or the description.

Half-Apache, green eyes.

Kenitay.

Wanted for the murder of a federal officer at Fort Sill, Oklahoma Territory.

# Nine

Leisha rode without any specific plan in mind until she realized she'd crossed a particular set of tracks several times on her way out of the Chisos toward Shafter. She told herself she wasn't following Kenitay. In fact, it was her plan to get ahead of him. If he didn't want her to interfere in his business, that suited her fine; she didn't want him intruding on hers, either. West Texas covered a lot of empty miles. There was no need to bump into each other. But that didn't stop it from happening.

She picked up the faint cadence of another set of hoof-beats shortly after noon. Her hand was resting easy on her pistol grip when a horse and rider finally took shape off to her left. There was no mistaking an Apache in the saddle. There was no better horseman on the Texas plains. Except her father. And her cousin Sarah before she'd decided to repopulate the Bend with Billy Cooper.

She looked without appearing to and recognized Kenitay's companion, Eenah. He didn't approach her but rather shadowed her from a distance for better than an hour. Finally, she got tired of it and jerked the reins of her mount in his direction. He greeted her with a stoic face but no outward threat.

"Why are you following me?" she demanded.

"I was going to ask you the same thing."

"Perhaps it's because we're going after the same thing." That broke through his Apache reserve. He glared.

"This does not concern you. Go back home. Do not interfere with us."

"What concerns me is my own business. And I have as much right to travel this trail as you do."

He reached out to snag her reins and Leisha reacted quickly, kicking at his hand. She maneuvered her horse back to a safe distance. Her hand was once again on her pistol.

"Don't mess with me," she growled. "You'll be jumping into more trouble than you're ready for."

"Says who?"

"Says me. I'm my father's daughter and if you know the name Bass, you'll know enough to stay outta my way."

Eenah sat his saddle like a statue. Then he asked, "Who is your father?"

"Harmon Bass of the Mescalero Apache." She said it proudly, flinging it like a challenge, knowing there wasn't an Apache alive who didn't know his name. And reputation.

Eenah was no exception. He knew the name. But it wasn't respect she saw in his black stare. For a moment, she could swear she saw hatred. Then the blaze was gone and his gaze was once more opaque.

"Come," he commanded. "I will take you to our camp. Then we will decide what to do with you."

She started to gather up her reins. He anticipated her.

"Run and I will chase you down. For one of such a noble name, I would not think you'd choose to flee like a rabbit."

His words had the desired effect. She stiffened in the saddle and nodded. He steered his animal ahead, never looking back to see if she was there. He knew she would be.


Kenitay rose from where he'd been sitting on his heels in the partial shade of a giant yucca, using the sun at his back to conceal him. He was able to observe the two riders before they actually saw him. He was glad they couldn't see what worked upon his face when he recognized the one with Eenah as Leisha Bass. It wasn't the anger that flashed to his head but rather the longing that stabbed through his heart he feared would betray him. He was cursing her for her foolishness in following even as a slight smile moved his lips when he considered her bravery. They'd been riding steadily since Eenah had met up with him just beyond the boundaries of the Bass ranch so she must have been pushing hard to overtake them. He had to give her credit for grit. And he'd like to give her the flat of his hand where she should be wearing a bustle instead of britches.

He stepped forward and knew the moment she saw him. Her head shot back and her hat brim tipped down to shade her eyes. Wary and ready. Just like her daddy had probably taught her. Harm Bass should have known better than to give such knowledge to his girls. Vengeance was a man's path and he didn't like the idea of her walking on his heels. But he did like the idea of seeing her again so soon. Too much.

"You don't listen, do you?"

She gave her chin an arrogant little hike. "I haven't heard anything worth heeding."

"I thought I made myself real clear."

"You thought yourself someone important enough for me to pay attention to. You were wrong."

He must have been crazy to have actually been glad to see her! She sat her saddle fearlessly when he stalked toward her but when he grabbed her wrist, she was all mean motion. Her moccasined foot planted square in the center of his chest and hit hard, driving the air out and forcing him backward. But she hadn't counted on him not releasing her. She was jerked from the saddle to fall with him, hitting the ground hard in a spread-eagle on top of him. When she started to struggle up, he swept her legs out from under her, dropping her down on her rump beside him. He was instantly covering her, grappling for her hands, meaning to show her who was boss until he felt the sharp prick of her blade beneath his chin.

"Let me up."

He didn't move for a moment, using his weight to press her flat, their faces only inches apart. She was panting, her heart fluttering against his chest like that of a captured sparrow. He was frightening her, yet the blaze in her eyes was fiercely defiant. She gave an upward nudge with her knife and he felt a warm well of blood where it nicked him.

"Get off."

It wasn't the threat of the blade that got him to move. It was the sudden tremor shivering through her limbs. But he would never let her know that as he backed up slowly until he was balancing on the balls of his feet, crouching over her buckskin-clad thighs. She came up quickly on her elbows, knife poised to make another defensive move should he be foolish enough to try anything.

"I wasn't following you."

"Here you are."

"Like I told your friend, we're going after the same thing." She scooted backward until her legs were clear of him then drew her knees up protectively. "I don't want to be in your camp anymore than you want me here so don't pretend that you have any right to dictate to me. You're not the reason I'm here."

That said, she glared at him, hoping he would believe it. It was true. Mostly.

"So," he murmured softly. "What are we supposed to do with you?"

"If we let her go, she'll just get in our way again," Eenah stated. "I don't trust her out there running loose."

Leisha's eyes narrowed. "You can't stop me."

Eenah's dark gaze slid over to his companion. "Not as long as she's able to ride."

Kenitay's features were immobile.

"Meaning?" Leisha prodded with a gruff bravado meant to cover the way her insides were shaking. They could take her horse and leave her afoot and helpless. They could use her and give her over to the merciless desert predators. They could kill her themselves. She wouldn't be able to stop them. Because she didn't think she could force herself to take Kenitay's life in her own defense.

She stared at him, trying to penetrate the cool green glass of his gaze. She couldn't tell what he was thinking. She didn't know the man he'd become. Maybe he did see her as an annoyance worth crushing. Maybe he wouldn't blink an eye at slitting her throat. She couldn't be sure. And that scared her plenty. Just because he'd kissed her didn't mean he wouldn't kill her if provoked.

"Meaning you don't leave us much choice," he drawled at last, still giving nothing away.

He moved toward her and Leisha instinctively shrank back, her eyes growing round and dark-centered. But he was only reaching for her hands to help her up to her feet. She prayed he didn't read her fear in that instant of weakness. He brought her up and let her step back to an impersonal distance without commenting. Then came his conclusion.

"You'll have to ride with us."

She could have made a big fuss right then but she was still shaken by the panic he'd made her feel. That helplessness that wouldn't go away. Suddenly, she didn't want to be alone and left to deal with that black void of terror again. Once Kenitay had given her breathing room, reason returned and she knew she had nothing to fear. He wasn't going to harm her. He'd protected her before and would do so again. And she was grateful even as she chafed with resentment.

"That would seem the logical thing to do."

Kenitay raised one brow, surprised by her surrender to common sense. He'd expected her to hold out with a little more bluster. He liked the fact that she knew when to give up.

But giving up wasn't what she had in mind.

"We can ride together but I'm not letting you slow me down," Leisha stated to earn both men's incredulous stares. "This is a union of convenience, nothing more. I'm not going to watch over you and I don't expect you to watch over me. But when we catch up to them, Westfall is mine."

Kenitay regarded her suspiciously. "What do you want with him?"

"That's my business, just like what you mean to do with Beech is none of mine. Agreed?"

Kenitay looked to Eenah, who returned his gaze impassively. He was an Apache to whom logic was all. It was better to have an enemy close where he—or she—could be watched. He didn't argue. Then Kenitay said to Leisha, "All right."

"I found out where they'll be—"

"On their way to Shafter," Kenitay cut in. "We already know."

"Oh." She blinked, her sense of importance somewhat deflated.

"We'll need you to ride in ahead of us to scout around. They both know us so it wouldn't be to our advantage to get spotted before we grab them. You find out where they'll be and we'll take them."

Leisha nodded. That sounded fair. "I want Westfall alive. I don't care about the other one."

"Agreed."

"Then what are we waiting for? We're wasting daylight."

* * *

They stopped for the night out in the middle of nowhere. Both men dismounted and saw to their horses, then waited. Leisha was busy with her own mount so she didn't catch on right away. And when she did, she was plenty mad.

They were waiting for her to set up their camp.

Cursing the superior thinking of Apache men, she flung her saddle down and dropped down on it with her saddlebags in hand. Kenitay and Eenah exchanged a puzzled look but she ignored them.

"A fire would be nice," Kenitay said at last.

"Yes, it would," she agreed. "It would break the chill." She looked up at him patiently.

"Fetch the wood, woman," Eenah demanded and that's all Leisha needed to go down his throat with both feet.

"I'm not here to see that you're nice and warm, not before or after dinner. If you want a fire, get your own wood. If you want a meal, cook it. If you're interested in anything else, find that elsewhere, too. I'm not along for your comfort and convenience so get used to the idea right quick. I'm not your woman and even if I was, I wouldn't jump at the snap of your fingers. If you're hungry, I suggest you go looking for something to eat."

Then she reached into her pack of supplies for a tin of canned meat, opened the top, and dug in. She'd had the time and money to stock well for the trip, something neither of the men had. So while she dined with relative ease, they were forced to scavenge for wood and after having no success in finding their own chuck, sat before the fire munching jerky.

Leisha sat staring into the flames because if she didn't concentrate her gaze somewhere, it would stray to Kenitay. That would be foolishness and not at all what either of them wanted. He'd ridden away, hadn't he? She had a goal of her own, didn't she? And yet . . . thinking about it teased her mind and tormented her body.

He was the only man she'd ever kissed on the mouth with a woman's passion. She supposed Becca would attach some sentimental meaning to that. All she knew was that she'd liked it. If only she didn't know what followed.

She'd never been interested in men-women things. Her parents indulged in them freely and frequently and with obvious anticipation so she had to conclude that these things were enjoyed by both parties. She remembered the soothing stroke of Kenitay's hand upon her hair, the agitation of his lips moving along her neck. The yearning waking inside her then was evidence that she could take pleasure in his touch. But overshadowing the idea was the dark menace of memory and that crowded out all else.

Restless with the direction of her thoughts, she rose up and walked the perimeters of darkness under the pretext of checking on her horse. The animal was a fine chestnut gelding but then all of the horses her mother raised as a hobby were exceptional creatures. Her mount greeted her with a soft whicker and the nudge of its velvety nose. Pensive of mood and distracted of mind, she leaned into the animal's powerful shoulder, absorbing the welcome warmth of its hide to chase away the chill inside her.

"It's no crime to pitch in, you know."

Kenitay's voice, sounding so deep and close behind her, shot a shock of alarm through Leisha. She spun, at the same time lunging back. The bump of her body sent her horse dancing with a nervous snort.

If he noticed her startlement, he didn't let on. "We usually all do our share on the trail. Things seem to work better that way than if we each tend our own business.".

She swallowed her panic to preserve her pride then took an arrogant Bass stance. "I didn't get the feeling I was being *asked* to contribute. I'm not playing squaw for you. We're here on equal footing and I won't be treated as less than a partner."

His gaze lowered slightly. "I've never partnered with anyone who looked so good in pants."

She said nothing but her gaze shot sparks like steel on flint. She smiled wryly.

"But then you don't want to hear that kind of stuff, do you? You want a man to admire you only for the way you sit a horse and draw a bead and hold your own in a fight."

"That's right."

His voice lowered a notch. "You don't want to be told that your hair is like sunlight spilling over the mountains on a clear day or that your mouth makes a man think of making crazy promises he can't keep."

She wet her lips in agitation. "No, I don't."

"But it sure riled you plenty when I said those kind of things to your sister. I thought maybe it was because you wanted me to say them to you."

"Don't be ridiculous," she snapped, casting a wary eye toward the distant fire where Eenah sat out of earshot. "Why would I want you to lie to me?"

"Is that what you think they are?" He took a step closer. "Lies? You don't think I look at those tight pants and your yellow hair and your ripe mouth and think all sorts of hungry things?"

"Why would you?" Her heart was beating furiously and her mind was spinning with wanting to believe him yet knowing he was not speaking truth.

"Because I think you're the most desirable woman I've ever seen."

"W-Why are you saying these things to me?" She started backing up, feeling crowded by the intensity of his mood and the direction of his conversation.

"Because they're the truth. And because I want to kiss you and I don't want you to pull away."

"Don't—"

But his hand was already skimming the line of her jaw, his fingers curling beneath her chin to lift it. She stood motionless and let him come down to her. It was just a whisper of movement upon her parted lips, the brevity of it making her anxious for more.

"I want to make love to you and I don't want you to be afraid."

But she was already stiffening in resistance.

His mouth flirted with hers again, quieting her panic.

"But not now. Not yet. You let me know when it's the right time."

"There won't be a—"

"Yes, there will. Oh, yes, there will. I want you, Leisha."

"But I don't—"

"Yes, you do."

She jerked her head to the side, struggling for clarity of thought so she could make a rational argument. "Quit telling me what I want."

"I'm not. I'm just repeating what you tell me with your eyes." His arm had eased behind her shoulders and was exerting a steady pressure to close the distance between them. She resisted and wondered why she wanted so desperately to yield. "I won't hurt you, Leisha. Don't be afraid."

"I'm not afraid of you," she stated boldly, then was forced to prove it was true when he said simply, "Good." She reached up to palm the hard angles of his face. His eyes blazed with emerald fire, a heat that struck like lightning. She rose, intending a rough demonstration to conquer his questions as well as her fears, but he had no intention of allowing her to salvage her pride at his expense. He wanted her to surrender it.

His hand caught in the heavy weave of her golden hair, using that anchoring grip to maintain control. When he tugged to one side, the friction scorched her senses. But she refused to be mastered. Her fingers clenched in his long, straight hair. Her tongue thrust past the tempting barrier of his lips, plunging right to the cavern of his soul.

He made a raw sound of surprise and satisfaction and began dueling fiercely with that silken invader. And while he'd promised *not yet,* his body was saying *yes now* as he crushed her against him with a strength that intimidated the fragile thread of her bravery. Her hands became fists, pushing at his shoulders. Her head shook him off and tucked into the safe harbor beneath his chin.

"Leisha—"

"I don't want complications in my life."

"This doesn't have to be complicated."

Those were the wrong words. No, sex wasn't complicated. Emotions were. What a clear-cut statement of what he wanted from her. She shoved him back angrily. "It doesn't because nothing's going to happen. No more pretty lies, *silah.* I don't want to hear them."

He watched her stalk back to the fire while he struggled to get his passions reined in. What had he said? She was the most confusing female he'd ever met. None of her subtle actions were reinforced by overly hostile reaction. Her yes-no games with his emotions had him tense and aggravated. He couldn't push because he sensed her genuine fear. He couldn't retreat because there was the occasional mingling of their moods that hinted at heaven. But she was right. Now was not the time. Here was not the place.

But she was wrong about one thing. Something was going to happen between them.

Soon.

# *Ten*

The uphill terrain was a relief from the heat of the Chihuahua Desert. The West Texas town of Shafter appeared in the early afternoon like an oasis in the vast region of mountains and rolling plains. Its population had been steadily growing along with the prosperity of its silver mines. To Leisha, it meant a hot meal, a cool drink, and a chance to redeem herself.

Westfall was there waiting.

"Ride on in and see what you can find out," Kenitay was saying. He'd been distant and reserved since she'd walked away the night before. She didn't want to concern herself with him now. She had business to concentrate on. "Don't try to take them on your own. Leisha, you hear me?"

"I'm not going to take any chances," was her cool reply.

"We'll camp here and you get on back as soon as you have some news."

She nodded once and kicked her horse into a brisk canter, never once looking back.

"You are foolish to trust her."

Kenitay gave Eenah a sharp look. "What do you mean?"

"She is one of them, not one of us. What makes you think she will come back?"

"She said so."

"Did she?" Eenah shook his head sadly, as if feeling

sorry for Kenitay's deluded state. He trusted none of the white race.

There were times when Kenitay wondered if his companion was holding his own mixed blood against him. But he and Eenah came from the same people. He had been of the Mescalero before his family was killed. Eenah never spoke of them but that was the Apache way. It was bad to speak of the dead and it would have been unforgivable to ask questions. Kenitay simply accepted what was. He and Eenah met in Alabama where they had formed a tentative friendship. Then at Fort Sill, Eenah had proven himself by aiding in Kenitay's escape from the reservation. He didn't say much. He didn't like much of anything. He wasn't the best of companions but he'd been there when he was needed. He had his own grudge with Beech and Westfall so they rode together with a single purpose. They didn't talk about it. Men didn't do such things. But from time to time, Kenitay wondered what moved behind the Apache's black stare and emotionless smile.

And then he found himself staring after the trim figure on horseback through narrowed eyes and a matching suspicion.

She'd better come back.


It was the same in every hotel. The desk clerk took one look at her trail-worn men's attire and their lips clamped up tight. Leisha was fresh out of good will when she stopped at the registry of the Claymore to be received with the same disapproving stare.

"Do you have a Westfall or Beech on your books?"

"I'm sorry—Miss. I'm not allowed to give out guest information. Hotel policy, you understand."

"I understand that I asked a civil question and I expect an answer. All you have to do is glance down at that book right under your nose and tell me yes or no."

"I'm sorry. Like I said, we can't give out that information to just anyone who walks in asking."

Leisha smacked twenty dollars on the polished desktop and picked up the registration pen. She spun the book toward her and aggressively scrawled her name. Then she turned it back toward the clerk. "There. Now I'm not just anyone."

The clerk glanced at the name and then went bug-eyed. His Adam's apple bobbed up and down above the confines of his tight collar and his hand shook as he reached for the key board. "I'll put you up in room 12, if that's all right with you, Miss B-Bass."

"That's fine."

"How long will you be staying with us?"

"Until my business is finished."

"That would be day after tomorrow. The parties you were asking after will be checking in on Thursday."

Leisha palmed the key with a thin smile. "You've been very kind."

"If you want to find out more about your friends, there are a couple of soldiers that checked in just before you who will be traveling with them."

"Would you happen to know where I can find these soldiers?"

He pointed out the front door. "Over across the street in the Call to Glory."

Leisha followed the direction of his hand. The Call to Glory was a saloon.

"Can I take your bags up for you, Miss Bass?"

"I'm traveling light," she murmured, already starting for the front door.

The saloon was a fine one with a long mahogany bar and gleaming brass footrail. A large, clear mirror hung above it and lush, colorful nudes adorned the other walls. Even at the early pre-dinner hour there were a few intense-looking men at the tables of chance and the footrail hosted a long line of spurred boots from those just passing through. Including a fine pair of glossy Army blacks. Leisha headed down the length of the bar to where the two soldiers stood bending their elbows and nudged in between them with a softly murmured "Excuse me." While they were both glaring in annoyance, she took off her hat and gave her head a shake, sending a cascade of heavy blond hair about her shoulders. One of the men gave her a contemptuous glance and returned to his drink. The other, a young corporal, went round-eyed in surprise and was suddenly all smiles. She focused on him with a coy cant of her eyes and a small smile.

"Might I be so bold as to buy you a drink, ma'am?"

"Why I'd like that, Corporal. Thank you kindly."

"What'll you have?"

"What you've got is fine."

He looked with raised brows at the harsh liquor in his glass, then at the curve of her bosom made apparent as she leaned against the bar on her forearms. And he grinned wide. "Yes, ma'am." He ordered her one. "My name's Johnny Wonderly outta Fort Sill."

"You're a long way from home, soldier."

"Escort duty, ma'am."

"Someone important?"

"Naw. Just some government paper pushers."

"That's no kind of job for a man like you." She let her gaze linger down the line of shiny buttons on his uniform jacket. She watched the fabric expand as he drew a proud breath. Her drink came and she took it down with a casual toss. That was one thing she could thank Jed Cooper for. He taught her how to drink without grimacing behind her cousin's barn when she was fourteen. She'd liked the taste and snuck it on occasions. Her father disapproved of strong liquor; he was strictly a one-beer man. The corporal smiled at her zest and ordered another for each of them.

"Might I ask your name, ma'am?"

"Bass. Leisha Bass."

He blinked. "Bass? Not as in—"

"My father."

His mouth framed a silent "O" as Leisha reached for her second glass. She was smiling.

"Careful there, Johnny. Are you sure your friend isn't going to miss you?"

Johnny Wonderly rounded the corner of the stairwell, weaving grandly from side to side. He couldn't seem to negotiate the rest of the hallway so Leisha towed him while he slurred, "Naw. Price is a fine fella. He'll be hip-deep in card play for the rest of the night."

"Good. Which one is yours?"

"Six. End of the hall." He started fishing in his pants for the key. It clattered to the floor out of his fumbling fingers. Leisha bent down for it, propping the drunken soldier up with her shoulder. "You sure got pretty hair," he murmured groggily.

Leisha held onto her scowl and toted her heavy burden the rest of the way. After unlocking the door, she muscled him inside the room, then closed it for privacy. There were two single beds on either side of an open window facing the rear of the hotel. She could see the slanting roofline of the story below and the darkness of the sky. Then all she could see was shiny buttons and blue wool as Johnny Wonderly got his second wind.

He took her clumsily into his arms and tried to coax her into a kiss. It took all her willpower to appear willing while at the same time discouraging his immediate intentions. She rubbed his sleeves and purred, "Did you bring the bottle?"

"Gots it right—right here." He pulled it from the pocket of his coat. "You ain't still thirsty, are you?"

"I thought we'd share a little toast. To what's to come."

He grinned foolishly. "I like that idea. Ain't never seen a female who can hold her liquor like you can."

"Now, Corporal Wonderly, you wouldn't be trying to get me pie-eyed so you can take advantage of me, would you?"

"Oh, yes, ma'am—I mean, no, ma'am."

She pushed out of his awkward embrace and claimed the bottle. "Got any glasses?"

He patted his jacket pockets. "Seem to have forgot them."

She tipped up the bottle, drinking directly from it. The liquor had long since ceased to burn. It slid down warm and pooled with a heavy heat in her belly. She passed the whiskey to her drinking companion and he took a long, sloppy swallow.

"You were telling me about these men you're escorting," she crooned as she reached for the buttons on his tunic.

"Coupla would-be politickers with enough money and backing to pull strings with my commanding officer. They're here to negotiate for some cattle for the reservation and do some private business with the mines."

"And then?"

"Then we're to pack 'em off to Austin. They got some fancy dinners and such to attend and want to flash us around like whores on their arms just to show that they're big men. Beggin' your pardon for puttin' it so bold."

Leisha shrugged off his apology, her thoughts spinning ahead. "That's why they asked for an Army escort? Just to look important?"

"Said something about their lives being threatened. Guess that could be true, seeing as what they do for a living, being government men and all. We're not supposed to let anyone within twenty yards of them 'lessin' it's with their invite."

Then he abruptly lost interest in talk.

"I been wondering all night what's under them buckskins."

His voice had gone all deep and husky and the sound had Leisha instantly on a wary edge. She was standing too close to him and the drink had blurred her reaction time. He had his arm snaked about her middle and her body bent back over it with the force of his kiss before she could think to step away. His mouth was hard and hungry. Any liking she'd had for the amiable Johnny Wonderly vanished. She could feel his aggressive arousal pressing against her as his other hand rose to capture one of her breasts. He was rough in his handling and she squirmed her protest, fighting him and her own fright. He wasn't as drunk as she'd believed. He was strong. And he was determined.

The curl of his arm had pinned hers in tight against her sides. There was no way to reach for a weapon or to effect any kind of an attack. She couldn't breathe. His kiss continued until her head was swimming and sickness started swelling up inside her on icy waves of panic.

Then, abruptly, he groaned and went slack against her, nearly dragging her down with him before she could shed his lax embrace. She stumbled to catch herself, staring down at the awkward way he fell to the floor. Then she lifted her stare to see Kenitay holding the pistol he'd used to club the amorous corporal senseless.

Her first reaction was overwhelming relief and gladness. She was one second from casting herself into his arms when his cutting words stopped her.

"I hope I'm not interrupting something."

His tone was the sobering shock it took to wrench her back in control. "What are you doing here? How did you get in?"

"Man shouldn't leave his window open 'less he wants company. As for what I'm doing, I'm saving you from the benefit of what he had in mind."

"Who asked you to? I was doing just fine by myself!"

His eyes narrowed as he returned his revolver to the belt slung low on his hip. "Yeah, it looked like it." He grabbed her wrist. "C'mon. Let's make tracks before he wakes up."

Leisha tugged back. "No. We can't leave him like that."

"You want me to tuck him in all nice and cozy?"

"Yes, that's exactly what I want you to do."

He stared at her blankly and she sighed in aggravation.

"Better he wake up thinking what was supposed to happen, happened, and he was just too drunk to enjoy it. Otherwise he'd be looking for whoever cold-cocked him."

Kenitay gave her a faint smile. Nice piece of reckoning. He could smell the liquor on her but apparently it hadn't affected her cleverness. Just like a woman. Men got slow and stupid when they'd had too much. Women got crafty. "Wait for me in the hall—"

"I have a room. Number 12."

"All right. I'll tuck Romeo in and be there in a minute. I want to know what he had to tell you. Or didn't you do any talking?"

His cool tone had her hackles up. "That's why I let him bring me up here. Why else?"

"Should have figured that, knowing you. Go on. Unless you want to help me strip him."

She scowled and left.

He was acting like an idiot. Kenitay knew it but he couldn't seem to stop himself. He'd been fine until he'd seen Leisha cross to the hotel on the arm of her incapacitated soldier friend. They'd been laughing together, looking mighty friendly. An explosion of jealousy all but drove him to madness. Instead of trusting her, he'd followed at a safe distance. Then when they went upstairs instead of into the dining room, which was where he'd hoped they were headed, he'd been ready to pounce upon the man with his blade bared. There was no sense of reason to his emotions. They just were and it took all his restraint not to act on them.

It was the height of insanity to go creeping around on the roof of the hotel. If he'd been seen, there'd be no explaining his way out of it. It was a stupid thing to do. Leisha hadn't invited him to be her guardian and she sure as hell hadn't intimated that she wanted him as anything else. But he'd been possessed by the need to know what was going on in that soldier's room. And when he'd peered in, things seemed harmless enough. At first. Then Leisha had touched the fellow in an encouraging manner and was opening his tunic.

He should have left right then, figuring she had other business in mind. But he'd lingered, arguing between wildness of heart and coldness of mind. Should he tend his own affairs or burst in and kill the soldier? Or slay both of them? He'd been trying to decide when the soldier made his move. The sight of Leisha in another man's embrace had his blood beating like primal drums. He'd decided he'd at least kill the man who had managed to win over her affection when he saw Leisha stiffen and begin to struggle. Then there was no question of staying out of it.

But did she thank him?

Hell, no!

"C'mon, Blue Boy, let's get you in bed," Kenitay growled as he lifted the slack figure off the floor and slung him unceremoniously onto one of the mattresses. He gripped one of the glossy boots and wrestled it off, then the other. "Looks like neither of us is going to get anything worthwhile tonight but at least you'll have the pleasure of thinking you did." He stripped the man down to skin, then for the finishing touch, ripped the sheets and blankets loose from the foot of the bed and tossed them partially over him, muttering, "Sweet dreams."

* * *

Once in the hall, Leisha staggered suddenly as the full brunt of the liquor hit home. She had to lean back against the wall for a moment to get her bearings as her perception of the world took on a strange rippling effect. As soon as it subsided, she continued to her room, keeping one hand on the textured wallpaper to guide the way.

Damn him for his arrogant interference!

She shut the door behind her and was tempted to latch it. She didn't need his help. She was doing just fine. Wonderly had told her everything she needed to know. He'd been about to exact payment for that information when Kenitay arrived. And once again, he'd been her rescuer.

Damn him!

She paced and suddenly saw things more clearly. She wasn't angry with him. He had saved her from a nightmarish situation. What made her furious was that she hadn't been able to save herself. She'd been paralyzed by her own mental weakness. Her own fear was the enemy and until she could conquer it, she would never feel confident in her ability to protect herself. All men wielded that intimate weapon of humbling consequence and pain. As long as she feared it, she was inferior to them. She had to overcome the feeling of helplessness or it would always keep her a victim of Drake Collier's crime. His single act had stripped her of her sense of independence and it was time she reclaimed it.

The door to her room opened and Kenitay slipped in from the hall.

"All put to bed," he whispered as he checked the hall before turning toward her.

Leisha's gaze ran a calculating survey from top to toe while he stood near the door wearing a suspicious frown. There was no denying she liked looking at him. And liked his kisses. He could be the answer to her dilemma.

"So," he began, watching her watch him. "What did you learn about Beech and Westfall?"

"They'll be here day after tomorrow. That boy and his friend are among a group assigned to guard them, apparently due to threats on their lives. Do you know anything about that?"

"No."

She wasn't sure she believed him. She came closer and his wariness increased. "They'll be staying here in the hotel so I thought I'd keep this room so I can be close."

"And you thought that soldier-boy would get you closer still." There was a tang to his words that she couldn't identify. Not anger. Not exactly sarcasm. Something else.

"He could still prove useful. The soldiers are supposed to keep all strangers at bay." Leisha was standing right in front of him, toe to toe. He didn't retreat but he was cautious.

"And you're not a stranger anymore, are you?"

"No." Her hand rose so that her fingertips could follow the dramatic peaks of his upper lip and return in a glide along the full lower swell. He was very still. "I can use him to find out their schedule."

"And you'll get word to us?"

Her knuckles rubbed up along his jaw and across the high ridge of his cheekbone. "I said I would, didn't I?"

"And what are you going to tell your soldier when he asks what happened tonight?" He closed his eyes briefly as the pad of her thumb stroked beneath the arch of his dark brow.

"I'll tell him it was memorable."

"And if he wants a repeat performance?" There was that growl to his voice again, that possessive agitation that made her both annoyed and excited.

"I want you."

His eyes popped open. "What?"

"I want you to make love to me."

She was caressing his face. He caught her hand and pulled it down rather roughly. "Why?" he demanded.

"Does it matter?"

He stared at her with an intense scrutiny. "It might. I don't know."

"Don't you want to?" Her other hand started pushing up his shirtfront, coming to a rest over where his heart was banging a savage tempo. There was no way he could deny it, not with the way his pulse was pounding. Then he gripped that hand and pulled it away, too.

"That's not what I asked, Leisha."

"You told me to let you know when the time was right." She leaned against the front of him, letting her body go all liquid. "The time's right."

He frowned in the face of her seduction. "I don't believe you."

Leisha groaned in irritation and shoved away from him. *"Cabron!* First you say yes, then you say no. Well, I say to hell with you!" But when she tried to spin away, he had her about the waist to bring her back up against the hard surface of him. His head lowered and the kiss he pressed upon her was hard and hurtful. When he eased back, his stare was penetrating.

"Still want me?"

She was panting and her answer was like a snarl. "Yes."

His reply was no friendlier. "Let's get to it then."

His tone was a dare. She could see he didn't think she was serious. Little did he realize just how serious she was. Determinedly, she undid her pistol belt, letting the weight of her .45 carry it to the floor. Then she shrugged off her loose-fitting buckskin shirt, leaving just buttoned-down cotton over bare skin. She reached for the top button and released it, moving steadily downward. The alcohol helped keep her hands from shaking.

Then his were there to take over the task after gently brushing hers aside. He moved slowly, as if expecting her to stop him at any second but she stood her ground, holding his gaze as fearlessly as she could, watching the way his eyes seemed to change in intensity from jade to brilliant emerald.

When the last button gave way, his palms swept the chemise from her shoulders and it fell, baring her to the waist. After a long beat, he lowered his gaze and she could almost feel the heat of it detailing her small, taut breasts.

*"Yusn."*

He breathed the oath reverently.

His hands eased up along the curve of her torso, skimming supple flesh, molding the scant bounty of her bosom within his rough palms. Leisha fought to keep her breathing slow and regular. He couldn't know how terrified she was. If he did, he would stop and her goal would go unrealized. The crutch of drunkenness suddenly deserted her. Her teeth clenched against the need to chatter. Her eyes shut so he wouldn't see her fear reflected back.

*Trust him, trust him,* her mind repeated in a soothing litany. He'd said he wouldn't hurt her. She felt his mouth come down upon hers and let him part her lips with the exploring probe of his tongue.

She would do this thing. She had to. It was face her fear or go home and hide from it forever. She couldn't let it have control over her any longer.

And Kenitay was going to help her get over it.

# Eleven

Feeling drugged by the reality of holding Leisha in his arms, Kenitay reminded himself to court her passions slowly, to let them build gradually, strongly, lest she lose her nerve.

She was afraid and doing her best to hide it. He wasn't sure what her motive was for pursuing intimacy with him— and he wasn't about to risk spoiling it by asking a second time. She said she wanted him. He wanted to believe that. Because it did matter to him. He could couple with any woman.

He wanted to make love to Leisha.

He moved away from her lips, puzzled by her passivity. Her eyes opened slowly and she looked up at him through a maddeningly impenetrable gaze. She didn't flinch when he palmed her cheek. Nor did she simmer with expectation. If she didn't want him, why had she allowed things to go this far?

Was it some kind of game?

Then Leisha caught his hand and led him over to the bed. She paused long enough to shinny out of her trousers before sinking down upon the mattress. Spread there upon those white sheets for his inspection, his for the taking, Kenitay got an uncomfortable image of a sacrificial virgin, opening herself for the pleasure of some wrathful god. And he hesitated.

Then she reached up for him.

Her fingertips framed his face, coaxing him down to where her moistened mouth was waiting. This time she joined in the union, flirting coquettishly with his tongue, then drawing it in with a wicked suction. At that point, he crossed the line of caution. Why she wanted him no longer mattered. Having her was all.

Leisha couldn't deny she liked kissing him. It was a delicious give and take of challenge and submission, playful and yet at the same time so intense it made her breathing labor. She could have spent the entire evening feasting upon his mouth but she'd invited him to do more and she knew he wouldn't be satisfied with this first level of carnal knowledge.

All too soon, he was shifting his focus from her lips. He continued to kiss her in soft, teasing little nibbles all over her face then finally trailed down her neck where he chained them around the delicate ridge of her collarbone. Leisha held her alarm in cautious check. She didn't dislike what he was doing. It was but an overture to what she knew awaited.

His hand had come up to cup one of her breasts. It wasn't a greedy movement the way the soldier's had been or painful like Collier's before that. He eased over the natural contour as if studying the gently sloping terrain. And she was surprised by her response. An achy sensitivity awakened beneath his touch, becoming a hard peak at the encouragement of his fingers. Then his head dipped down and before she knew what he was doing, he'd taken that turgid nipple into his mouth, sucking hotly, laving with the slick rough of his tongue until a helpless sound escaped her.

"Don't . . . stop." The words came out in a broken moan and he paused, forcing her to concentrate long enough to put them together. "Don't stop."

She felt his smile against her flushed skin and the warmth of his breath as he murmured, "Wasn't planning to." Then he turned his attention to the other side and she was arching up in an undulating pleasure.

Her hands came up to clasp his head between them, her fingers restlessly plying the sleekness of his hair. It came to her then in this passion-drenched state that this was what her parents had in mind when their gazes locked across the supper table as their conversation got heavy with innuendo and their hands began to wander. Now she knew why her mother was in such a hurry to get them tucked into bed some nights or her father seemed distracted enough to walk into walls. It was knowing these sensations waited behind their closed door.

As encouraged as he was by her soft cries, Kenitay knew she'd resist him when she anticipated his next move. His hand stroked down the supple curve of her hip and he could feel tension trailing behind it. The only thing to do was throw off her suspicions with the unexpected.

He gripped her knee and urged it up into a tented position. Though her eyes were closed, he knew she was alert and alarmed, just waiting for him to cover her with his greater weight. So he didn't. Instead, he slid down farther on the bed and because she had no idea where he was going, she was completely unprepared for his sudden, explicit kiss upon her golden nest of curls. He heard her gasp and her body shook. It was a sweet surface quiver, not a deep shudder, so he continued.

Using his thumbs to open the way, he tasted her, treating her to the same insistent teasing he'd showered upon her breasts. He sampled the salty succulence with the slow stroke of his tongue, then feasted at that hot center until he unleashed an incredible flow. Her breath came in raw pulls, fast, faster. As he plunged hungrily inside her, he could feel the tremors building. When it came, her release was of volcanic proportions; and he continued to provoke shattering aftershocks until she grabbed a handful of his hair to pull him up to meet the needy wildness of her kiss.

She quieted at last, her breathing still ragged, her eyes open and dazed as her gaze was lost in his. Her lips parted. She gave him a shaky smile and his control was gone.

He kissed her with all his pent-up passion, struggling as he did to strip off his shirt and his pants. Her palms slid up on the bare flesh of his back and arms, a repetitive, anxious motion, stroking his desire higher. He eased over her, settling between the wanton spraddle of her relaxed thighs and then sank himself deep and sure inside her before she had any time to think about it. He gave a shudder of intense delight. She was hot and wet and well prepared. She clung to him like hot butter in a closed fist. He shouldn't have hurt her.

But suddenly she went stiff beneath him. Her welcoming softness became all denying angles. She tore away from his kiss, her breath coming in rapid, panicked snatches. And all the pleasure he brought her was swallowed up by the pain that had come before him.

"No!" Her cry escaped her not as an objection but as a whimper of distress. Her palms pounded against his ribs and shoulders and finally fell limply to the mattress.

"Leisha," he whispered against her mouth, trying to coax her back toward passion. But her eyes stared right through him, stark with fright, blank with anxiety. He was throbbing with the need to continue, a hard, hurtful urgency. "Leisha, I won't—oh, damn!"

He rolled off her and instantly she turned so her back was to him and her knees were tucked up in a protective knot. She was crying and he was shaking. After swallowing down several deep breaths, Kenitay managed to get his raging desires under a loose sort of control. He leaned over Leisha's shoulder, saying her name softly.

"I can't," she sobbed. "I can't do it. I just can't go through with it. I'm sorry. I'm sorry."

He kissed the cap of her shoulder and rubbed her arm with a gentle friction. "It's all right, *shijii.*"

"No, it's not all right!" He was startled because she sounded angry. Then she thrust off his hand and glared up at him and he realized she was mad. No, furious. "It's not all right. I've got to master this—this weakness. I thought with you—"

His expression went blank. "You thought what?" When she didn't answer, he drew his own conclusions. They weren't pleasant ones. "You were using me, is that it?"

She didn't lie to him.

"You let me think—" He broke off and rephrased it tightly. "No, I wanted to think it was something else."

"Kenitay."

Her voice held a pleading note, a pitying tone that unstrung him. "My fault," he ground out. "I should have known better."

"You don't know anything," Leisha countered fiercely. "I have never in my life been afraid of anything except this one thing and you. I couldn't go on being a slave to it—"

"Me? Why would you be afraid of me?"

"I'm not. That's not what I said."

"It is, too."

"It's not."

"Why are you afraid of me?"

"That's not what I meant to say."

"But it is what you said."

"Stop being so difficult. I'm trying to apologize!"

His look went all tender. "You don't have anything to apologize for."

She blinked, her fury derailed. Feeling the threat of tears mounting again, she looked away from him. "I didn't mean to disappoint you. I know you were expecting—more."

His hand curved around her face, forcing her to turn back to him. His words were intense. "You didn't. You were—wonderful, beautiful. You gave me more than anyone else ever has."

She looked wary and at the same time so painfully vulnerable. "Really?"

He leaned in to kiss her brow. "You are an exceptional woman, Leisha Bass," he vowed as he began to gather her up in his arms. She was at once aware of his hot nakedness pressing against her own.

"I think we should get dressed."

"I don't," he stated, hugging her tight. "This is nicer." Without releasing her, he reached down to snag the covers, pulling them up over the both of them. He blew out the lamp and settled down with her in the darkness. She was tense against his side but not struggling. That was good enough. "Good night, *silah*. You've nothing to fear from me and you might as well learn that now 'cause I'm not going away any time soon."

She lay still and thoughtful for a long moment. He could hear her soft breathing.

"Kenitay?"

"Ummm?"

"What you did—" He didn't need to see her to know she was blushing.

"What about it?"

"Thank you."

He was smiling up at the ceiling. "My pleasure."


Leisha awoke with a throbbing headache and a warm weight draped across her. Her eyes shot open to the nose-to-nose sight of Kenitay asleep beside her. It was the curl of his arm about her waist anchoring her snug against him. Neither of them had a stitch of clothing on. For a moment she was totally blank on the events of the pre-

vious evening. She remembered trying to drink that young
corporal, Wonderly, under the table then dragging him up
to his room to coax information from him. Then he'd
grabbed her up for an unwanted kiss and some heavy-
handed groping. And then . . .

And then she remembered everything.

She'd asked Kenitay to make love to her. What had
begun as a coolly calculated plan had been lost somewhere
in the magic of his kisses. She'd undressed for him. She'd
let him put his hands, his mouth on her, letting him do
things she'd never have imagined a man doing . . . and
she'd liked it. She hadn't guessed pleasure could be felt
as intensely as pain until it scalded the senses.

And then she remembered the feel of him, all hot and
huge, crowded up inside her private place, impaling her
like a helpless wild thing. And the smothering fear that
followed. A form of madness had taken hold of her then.
She couldn't seem to focus on the fact that it was Kenitay,
or realize that he wasn't hurting her. The only thing possessing her mind was the need to escape the source of
torment, the sense of shame.

And he'd let her go, without hesitation, without recrimi-
nations.

Leisha stared at his relaxed features. What kind of man
was he? How was it possible that after all the hardships
he'd endured, he'd managed to retain so much tenderness
and care?

He'd called her *wonderful, beautiful.*

Did he mean those things?

And why should it matter to her if he did?

It wasn't as if she was looking for a man.

But if she was looking, her gaze would certainly stop
here. He was very handsome. She'd always thought so. He
exuded strength and character even in repose, with all those
intriguing angles carved by both experience and heritage.
The furrows in his brow were offset by the sweeping soft-

ness of his mouth. One of the thin braids he'd woven from plaits of his long hair made a negligent curve across one weathered cheek and she found herself stroking it back behind his ear. And once she'd touched him, she couldn't pull away.

His cheek was rough with morning stubble. The frictions against her palm was an odd enticement. She hadn't found simple masculinity to be an attraction before, but his was.

She'd told him she was afraid of him. But not in the way he'd assume. It was horror and disgust that made her fear Drake Collier. It was the power of his appeal that made her fear Kenitay. It was a dangerous and futile attraction that could never know fruition. Not when their goals were so different. Not when she couldn't partner him in the one way he wanted.

His eyes came open and she found herself captivated. He showed no surprise at seeing her. A slight smile curved his mouth.

"Good morning. How's your head?"

"My head?" She stared at him blankly.

He lifted his hand from her waist and pantomimed tossing back a shot of rye.

"Oh. Fine. I've never had a problem holding my liquor."

His smile took a wry bend. "Such a weary voice of experience.

"Unlike yours, which was won so nobly."

His expression firmed and in a tight tone, he asked, "Are we going to start fighting before we even get out of bed?"

His reference to their position flustered Leisha. She'd almost forgotten that they were skin-to-skin under the covers. To distract him from that fact, she murmured, "My mama says some of her best days start with an argument before breakfast."

Kenitay's look softened. "Your mother and father are very much in love. It's easy for them to dismiss harsh words. They live in an enviable state."

Leisha was silent for a moment. Her mind was picturing waking up each morning to the warm glow of green eyes and warmth of a bristled chin. An odd fluttering stirred in her belly. It must be hunger, she decided. It *was* breakfast time.

Then his palm eased along the curve of her cheek and back through the tousle of her hair. Everything stilled in an instant as awareness perked like a full-bodied morning brew.

Leisha's eyes sank shut as he drew her up close. She was expecting his kiss but his face nuzzled into her hair, his mouth then touching her temple, her cheek, the arch of her throat.

"There are better things to do than argue," he murmured as he tasted the passion hurrying her pulse beats.

She placed a tentative hand upon his shoulder, surprised by how sleek and hot it was beneath her palm. He lifted himself to seek her lips, pressing a long kiss on them. She could have stopped it by turning her head to the side. Instead, she parted her lips in invitation and he groaned as he sank inside.

On some distant periphery, she felt his groin begin to swell and push against her. That did force her retreat.

Realizing why she pulled away, Kenitay smiled almost apologetically. "I can't help that but I don't have to do anything about it, either. You can't expect a man not to stand up and take notice with a woman like you curled up in his bed. I'll behave myself." His smile grew more engaging. "It's a shame to let a good morning go to waste. Can I at least kiss you some more?"

Her eyes were narrowed warily but her answer was the one he wanted to hear. "I guess I wouldn't mind that so much." And she was fixed upon his lips before he had a chance to respond.

What followed was a lot of slanting and sliding and seeking while Kenitay fought to remind the heavy ache in his groin that it was just kissing. Just kissing. Rushing would earn a quick retreat. He believed in a slow, steady capturing of ground, inch by inch, foot by foot until the objective was conquered. It was ground worth securing for his claim. And when she was ready, he meant to stake it deep and file it forever under his name alone. Those were the thoughts moving behind the passion of the moment. He didn't dwell on them. He didn't stop to consider what he was mentally forming while he was feeding upon the willing sweetness of her lips. If the conclusion had come to him then, he would have pulled away in shock and denial.

He was thinking about a permanent bond.

He was thinking about a lifetime with Leisha Bass.

He was thinking about a wife.

But because he wasn't ready or able to commit to any of those things, he stuck to what he could keep within his anxious grasp. That was her own burgeoning desire. He vowed to shape her innocent passion to his will, spoiling it for any who thought to follow.

He wanted her wild for him.

She made a throaty sound of encouragement as his hand moved to her breast. Nimble fingers tugged and tormented it into a tingling rosette, tempting him down to provoke an even sharper pleasure with the rough attention of his mouth and teeth. She was clutching at his head, moaning his name. Emboldened by her reaction, his hand moved down to slip between her thighs. He was greeted by a moment of tense denial then by a cautious relaxation. He let his fingers stroke her, probing through the guardian folds of flesh to the vulnerable core of her femininity. She made a low, incoherent noise as her face pressed to his shoulder. He could feel the hot pulse of her breath matching the throb of her body as he rubbed her slick and fast. Her cry of completion was muffled as she convulsed against him. And that left him unbearably aroused.

"Say you want me, Leisha. Say you want me," he urged, tipping her face up for more frantic kisses. But she said nothing, returning his kisses languidly as her body melted along his in a satisfied liquefaction. He ground his teeth and held her tight, his breath sawing harshly until he could find some degree of control. He remembered his arrogant idea to tame rather than take her. God, if he'd only known what a torture that was going to be.

He'd told her to trust him. He hadn't known how difficult it was going to be to trust himself. With a heavy sigh, he kissed her brow and leaned back to observe the sated loveliness of her features. That was close to his undoing. She looked like a voluptuous angel, all kiss-bruised and passion-ripe. And she was denying him the same splendor.

Her eyes opened slowly and a chiding smile shaped her lips. "That was more than kissing."

"I got carried away. It's easy to do with you in my arms. Do you mind?"

"Are you crazy?"

And she was smiling, a temptation meant to carve a man's heart like initials on a tree. *Kenitay loves Leisha.* But was the feeling mutual?

"We'd better get dressed. You're too distracting." His voice sounded like a growl and Leisha liked it. Boldly, she pulled him to her for another wet kiss. This time the momentum was broken by a tap on the door.

Leisha had time to clutch the sheet up to her shoulders as Kenitay turned to look over his. Both their guns were a world away.

The door pushed open and Jed Cooper stood framed within it. He stared for a moment, his wide eyes registering shock, then narrowing into something much more unpleasant.

"Well, lookee here. Ain't this something. And here I was beginning to think you didn't like men, Leisha-honey. What's your daddy gonna say about this, you all buck naked and bedded down with the likes of him?"

"You breathe a word, Jed Cooper, and I'll rip out your gizzard with my bare hands."

He laughed, enjoying their helplessness as he lifted the bore of his rifle. Then his expression chilled. "Didn't think you'd be seeing me again so soon, did you, Breed? Looks like I got the upper hand this time, don't it?"

"What do you want?" Kenitay demanded coldly. He angled so that Leisha was protected behind him. He wouldn't have her exposed to the ogling stare of a man like this.

"What I want, you're gonna get for me." He laughed again. "I'm gonna be a rich man at your expense."

"What are you talking about, Jed?" Leisha spat, impatient with his prattle and with the untimely interruption.

"I'm gonna give you to the count of five to get out of that bed and get dressed. Then I'm gonna march you on over to the marshal's office to collect me a tidy reward."

Kenitay went very still but Leisha was seething.

"Reward? Reward for what?"

"Murder, Leisha-honey. You're bedded down with a cold-blooded killer. Your daddy'd be so proud."

Leisha waited a long beat for Kenitay to deny it.

He didn't.

So she did, loudly, angrily. "You're a liar, Jed!"

"Am I? Ask him. Ask him what else he's been into other than your tight little—"

"Watch your mouth," Kenitay warned with a lethal quiet.

Jed sneered at the threat. "Ask him about that soldier he kilt back at Fort Sill."

Again, Leisha waited but instead of arguing his case,

Kenitay sat up and reached for his pants, saying, "Don't involve her in this. She doesn't know anything."

Leisha stared at him, confusion and disbelief giving way to a terrible truth. *He was guilty.*

"Looks like you wasted a ride on the wrong stud horse, darlin'. Maybe if you ask real nice, I'll use some of the money I get for him to show you a good time before I take you on home to Mama."

Kenitay was off the bed without warning. He had Jed by the throat in a heartbeat, putting a good scare into a man who still remembered all too well the impact of the Apache's fists on his face. Jed managed to wedge his rifle muzzle up under Kenitay's chin, regaining control of the situation.

"Back off, stud. She ain't gonna want you with your brains splattered all over the ceiling. 'Course, if they don't hang you right off, she ain't gonna want what's left of you after you get outta prison, anyway." He jabbed hard with the barrel. "I said get back."

Kenitay eased backward and the minute he did, Jed drove the gun barrel into his midsection with all his might, doubling him. A quick swipe of the stock brought it around to slam into the side of his head, dropping Kenitay to his hands and knees in a daze of pain.

"You bastard!" Leisha scrambled off the bed in a co-coon of sheets and dropped down beside the wobbling man. Her arms went protectively about his shoulders as she glared up at Jed, warning him with the fierce stare not to try any more cruelty. Kenitay stirred back to full awareness and then he looked up at her, surprised, an intense question framed by his expression.

Hers was just as serious. "Tell me he's lying."

Again, he let the opportunity pass and Leisha frowned, starting to draw away. His hand came up to clamp the back of her head, holding her firm for the hard plunder of his kiss. It was rough with passion and the taste of good-bye. Leisha jerked away, her eyes tearing up with anger, with betrayal, with loss. He spoke just once in a low, somber tone but it wasn't to deny Jed Cooper's claim. It was to strike his own.

"I love you, Leisha."

She was so stunned, she let Jed pull him up right out of her arms and march him half-dressed and reeling off to jail.

# Twelve

The inside of the rock and adobe Lajitas saloon was thick with smoke and rank with the scent of the unwashed. No breeze drifted in through the batwing doors to stir lazy, late-afternoon air where shadows hung heavy over men crouched at cards. An old toothless whore brought a new round of drinks using the top of a water barrel as a tray. She cackled when one of the drunker patrons made a grab at her bony flanks. She slapped his hand away, crying, "Pay first, *Yanquee.*"

Two figures pushed open the doors, causing a ripple of movement through the stale haze. One or two indifferent faces glanced up in idle question. Just a little cowboy and a kid. Nothing worth their notice.

"Beer," the small Texan ordered. Then, after a pause, "Make that two."

The barkeep brought the drinks, sloshing most of the amber brew out onto the top of the ancient bar. He pocketed the coin and went back to chasing cockroaches with his near-bristleless broom.

The boy and the man drank down their beers. The elder had his back comfortably to the room but the younger was nervous, casting frequent glances over his shoulder until the other pressed a brief hand to it, calming him without a word. His beer gone, the older man ambled easily over to a table of chance to linger behind one of the players' shoulders. He tucked in the cards defensively and lifted a surly gaze.

"Do you mind, mister? You're in my light."

Then he went rigid in his chair and cards fluttered every which way. His Adam's apple bobbed over the broad blade niched in against his throat.

"Hell, go on an' stand there! I don't care!"

"I'm looking for a trio of *hombres* who did some banking up in Terlingua."

There was a mumble of curses and some not-too-discreet movements toward gun leather.

"Back me, Rand."

A big bore carbine came up into play, quieting things at the table real quick.

"Now, as I was saying, these would-be robbers shot a friend of mine and led my little girl on quite a chase before she had to kill one of them."

The man under the knife took a hasty breath. "What's your name, friend?"

"It's Bass and I'm not your friend."

"God's my witness, I never laid a hand on your daughter! It was Collier. He's the one what took her. None of the rest of us would be fool enough to mess with one of yours. You got to believe me!"

There was a long silence, then a soft, deadly drawl. "Just what exactly are you saying?"

"It wasn't me! It was Collier what clubbed her and laid her down. Honest to God! You ain't got no beef with us. Collier's dead. She done him, her and that breed what showed up."

Harm's free hand tangled in the man's hair, jerking back hard enough to bring the fellow up on his heels in a painful backward arch. "And you expect me to believe that? That the only one of you who laid a hand on her was the dead one?"

"Yessir, Mr. Bass!" He was weeping frantically.

"I don't think I believe you."

"Oh, God—"

"He's telling the truth, Daddy."

Harm canted a glance toward his son. That stabbing look demanded an immediate explanation.

"Leisha told me. She said she killed the one who—him."

"She told *you.*"

"Yessir."

Harm fell silent again. The sound of his breathing was like steel upon a whetstone. Then he eased off the man and said, "You and your *compadres* get up real slow."

"What're you gonna do?" the man whimpered.

"We're gonna take a ride."

"The hell you say," one of the others spoke up for the first time. He was pale and sweating but there was a sharp desperation to his stare. "I ain't gonna let you take me out into no desert for butchering. You gonna kill me, kill me here."

With that, he jumped up from his chair, grabbing for his gun. Rand's carbine boomed and the fellow dropped back into his seat, his face reduced to blood and bone before he tipped over backward in a loud clatter.

"I ain't gonna cause no trouble!" the man under Harm's knife yelped.

"Me neither!" cried a second.

"Then let's move it out of here," Harm said.

"Them's my winnings."

"You won't be needing them." Harm nodded to the man behind the bar. "Take 'em for your trouble."

The barkeeper didn't move. "You want I should bury that one?"

"Do whatever you like. He's beyond caring."

The two bank robbers marched docilely out of the saloon to where their horses were tied. Harm made quick work of lashing them to their saddlehorns and putting their

animals on a lead behind his. They'd ridden about a mile
out of town when Rand began to weave.

"You all right, son? Whoa. Easy now." Harm caught
the back of his shirt as he leaned out of the saddle to
spew his lunch.

"I'm sorry, Daddy," he managed to groan before another bout of sickness hit him.

"Nothing to apologize for."

"I-I just never seen anything like that before."

"Next time aim for the midsection. Stops just as fast
and is less—messy."

That grim visual brought on another round of heaving.
Finally, Rand straightened in the saddle. His features were
grey, his expression firm. "I'm sorry to go all weak-
livered on you."

"You were there when it counted. I'd be a mite concerned if it didn't bother you some."

Rand gave him a direct look. "It didn't bother you?"

"Son, things like that stopped bothering me when I was
ten years old."

Rand swallowed hard, then glanced back at the men
trailing them. "What do you mean to do with them?"

Harm was studying him carefully. "What do you think
we should do?"

"They didn't really do nothing but rob the bank and
run."

"No, they didn't do nothing. They didn't stop their
leader from shooting Cal or—or from hurting your sister.
That makes 'em cowards and no less guilty."

"What would you do with them?"

Harm's smile was thin and scary. "I don't think you're
up to hearing about it right now. It's your call, Rand. What
do you think your sister would want?"

Rand looked at the frightened men again. "I don't
know, Daddy. I think she'd say torturing them wouldn't
change anything that happened."

"Might make her and me feel better, though. So you want to take 'em back to Terlingua?"

Rand's expression went suddenly savage. "I want to rip their bowels out with my bare hands." He took a breath. "But I think we ought to take 'em in and let the law handle them."

"That what you think?"

Rand firmed up behind that decision with a strong, "Yessir."

"You're a better man than I am, son. Let's get a move on. I got me some talking to do to your sister."

*He loved her.*

What a hell of a time to say so, just before he was being toted off to jail for murder!

Leisha dressed in a hurry, so angry and upset she couldn't seem to get things on straight.

He'd lied to her. Well, not exactly lied but that was a whole lot of truth to leave unspoken. She should have guessed it was something like that. She'd known he was on the run from something.

But *murder!*

How dare he go and profess his love when there wasn't the least chance she could tell him how she felt before he was stepping into air wearing a custom-fitted noose! As if she knew what she was feeling. She wanted to pull the trap door out from under him herself!

*Oh, God, what if they hung him?*

She was chewing on that bit of anxiety when she exited her room and ran smack into Johnny Wonderly. He looked ashen and far from steady as he swept off his hat to offer up a weak smile.

"Morning, ma'am."

It was all Leisha could do not to shove him out of her

way. But then reason prevailed and she gave him an enticing smile.

"Good morning, Corporal. I trust you're feeling better. You dropped off so sudden and sound last night I didn't have the heart to wake you."

He blushed deeply, afraid to admit when he'd awakened to find her gone, the first thing he'd done was grab for his money belt. She hadn't touched a penny. "I think I need to apologize for not . . . um, living up to your expectations."

He looked so sheepish, Leisha could almost forgive his rough handling. Almost. But business was business and Wonderly could still be of use so she touched his tunic front with a slight stroke of her fingertips.

"Why, Johnny, how can you say that? You were everything I expected . . . and more."

He looked flustered and pleased, finally swelling up pridefully. "Glad you thought so. Maybe we could—"

She smiled. "Maybe we could."

He gave a weak sigh. "As much as I'd like to take you to breakfast, we had something come up kinda sudden that needs our attention over at the jail."

"Oh?"

"Some renegade was just brought in for bounty."

Kenitay. Leisha's pulse picked up.

"And that's Army business?"

"It is when the man he killed was a lieutenant at Fort Sill. Damn fine officer, too."

"And this fellow murdered him?"

"Slit his throat from ear to ear. Darn near took his head off. Most likely they'll be wanting him back in the territory. If he gets that far."

"How awful," she muttered, not having to pretend horror. "So will you be one of the men taking him back?"

"Don't know yet. The fellers we're supposed to escort

got in about an hour ago with a unit of men. Could be some of them will take the duty instead of me and Price."

"I hope so. I was looking forward to seeing you again." She managed not to give away her sudden jump of interest. Westfall was here in Shafter. He was early. She was so close to realizing her goal, and Kenitay now wasn't here to share in her success.

Johnny clearly chafed at doing his duty. "Tell you what. As soon as I find out what's what, I'll leave a message. Maybe we can have supper . . . or something."

"I'd like that, Johnny." She gave him a slight push. "You'd better go now."

"Yes, ma'am. I'll see you later."

And Leisha frowned pensively after him.

The blow took Kenitay on the chin, clacking his teeth together and knocking his head back with a cruel snap. It took a moment for him to blink his way back to a groggy awareness as he sagged against the bite of the ropes binding him to his chair.

"Where is it?" he was asked for the umpteenth time. "I know he must have told you. Talk and save yourself some of what we gave your daddy."

That brought Kenitay upright. He glared up through the eye that wasn't swollen shut and said, "I'm not telling you anything."

Another blow crashed into his cheek and bright flashes of color streaked across his vision. He let his head loll, letting them believe he was worse off than he actually was. Actually, he was pretty bad. He didn't think they'd broken anything inside yet but everything outside hurt like hell. He didn't resist when fingers meshed in his hair, dragging him up again.

"Tell us what we want to know. We're not interested in you. Could be we'll just let you walk out of here."

Kenitay gave a gurgling laugh. Sure they would. The sound turned into a grunt of pain as he took another in the ceaseless punishment to his midsection. He hung there against the ropes while blackness swirled, ready to welcome oblivion.

Warren Beech stepped back and rubbed his bloodied knuckles. "He's not going to tell us anything, Ross. Just as stubborn as his old man. Maybe he doesn't know."

"And maybe he's just not ready to say. You going to let him wear you down, Warren? Considering the stakes, I'm surprised you'd tire this easily."

Beech inhaled and let it out in resignation. "Still say he doesn't know anything but if you think I need the exercise, I can keep this up for a while." He flexed his fingers then closed them into a meaty fist. When he swung, it struck the side of Kenitay's head like a hammer, rocking the chair precariously up on two legs.

"Let's start again," Ross Westfall began patiently. "Where did your father tell you he hid it?" When there was no response, he signalled Beech, who sent another blow pounding into Kenitay's ribs.

"I'm sorry I'm late."

Corporal Wonderly slid into his chair in the hotel's dining room, looking spit-polished and painfully young. His eagerness gave Leisha a momentary twinge of guilt but it wasn't enough to force a change in her plans.

"That's all right, Johnny," she simpered prettily. "I haven't been waiting long."

"I wish I could say a few minutes didn't matter but truth is, they do. I'll be heading to Austin on the train first thing in the morning."

"You're leaving already? But I thought you were going to be here another day at least while these men you're guarding made some cattle deals or something."

"Seems they took care of their business this morning so there's no reason to stay on." He was flattered by her look of distress and possessed himself of her hand. "I tell you what. If you can find yourself a pretty dress, I can show you quite a night of it. These here fancy fellers are throwing a big wingding later on tonight and we've been told we can partake in the dancing and such. Could be a lot of fun and then maybe after . . ."

But Leisha didn't hear the tinge of hope in his voice. She was thinking Westfall would be hers for the taking. Tonight. If she could manage to coax him away from his guards, she'd have him packed on a horse and headed for Blue Creek before anyone was the wiser. There was just one more loose end.

"So what happened with that criminal? The one you thought you might have to take back to Fort Sill."

"They took him out in a prison wagon a couple of hours ago heading for the law and the rails in Presidio. Wouldn't give that fellow any odds of surviving the trip."

Though no sign of it registered upon her face, Leisha was giddy with panic inside. The sensation just kept getting bigger and bigger until her trembling worked its way to the outside and she had to grip her hands in her lap to keep them from shaking visibly.

"Johnny, could you excuse me a minute?"

He bolted up to catch her chair and ease it out for her. He was blushing. "Why, sure. Do you want me to order for us?"

"Something from the bar for now. Maybe a nice bottle of wine. I do so like wine."

His eyes glimmered. "Maybe champagne?"

She made an excited little sound and pinched his arm. "I won't be long."

She could feel his gaze follow her to the door of the dining room. It was a struggle to keep her steps slow and even. The moment she was clear, she bolted upstairs to her room and went to dash cold water on her face. Then she sank down on the edge of the bed, her palms rubbing absently over the still-rumpled sheets.

What was she going to do?

Westfall was here. She might not get another chance at him. In Austin, she'd be out of her element. It had to be now. It had to be tonight.

But if she stayed and went after Westfall, Kenitay could be dead by morning.

That wasn't her fault, she rationalized angrily. She didn't make the situation he was trapped in. It wasn't up to her to get him out of it. What was she thinking of? Freeing a murderer? With her firm belief in the law and in what was right?

*I love you, Leisha.*

So he promised not to complicate her life. What a liar he was!

How could she believe that if he hadn't been truthful about anything else? Had he said the words just to make her want to help him out of a tough spot? She wished she knew more about men—what she did know, didn't lend to trust. What she knew of Kenitay came from memories of a ten-year-old boy. He hadn't been willing to share anything about the man he'd become. Was that because there was nothing good to share? Because he was a renegade on the run? A murderer and maybe even worse?

Had he come home to West Texas after such a long absence to play upon the affection of a family he shunned? To cover up his real intentions? Which were—what?

She'd come to Shafter for Westfall. The last task she'd set upon had ended in failure, with her father and brother taking care of what she'd left undone. She had to complete this mission. Once she made a gift of Westfall to her father, she wouldn't have to struggle for his respect. She'd prove to him—and to herself—that she was of equal worth in this male-dominated world and with that acceptance would come respect and independence. Then she'd have everything she'd ever wanted.

Westfall was her ticket to the future.

*I love you, Leisha.*

"I don't believe you," she cried to the empty room as her hands balled the sheets into shaking fists.

The prison wagon was a lumbering conveyance without the slightest luxury. It was sheer torture to ride either inside or up top, the only difference being those up top weren't looking through bars or wearing leg irons.

Kenitay spent the first half-hour of the ride flat on his stomach, too hurt to move or care about anything. Finally, the notion that this might be his last chance to get a good look at his homeland forced him to drag himself up from where his blood was clotting on the floorboards beneath his nose and mouth. He slumped back against the bars, barely able to hold himself upright, while the jolts of the wagon brought a banging misery to his head. There wasn't much he could see. His left eye was swollen shut and things were pretty foggy out of his right. But what he couldn't see, he could imagine.

How he loved this land of mountains and plains. How he wished he could have spent his remaining years lost in the middle of it where a man could pretend no civilization existed over the next rise and he could feel free instead of just dreaming of freedom. He'd had such a brief taste of it, a tease of that independence he'd longed for during his lengthy incarceration. And he'd found something else just as precious, a woman worth surrendering up part of that personal freedom.

Now, if his days stretched out beyond the sudden jerk at the end of a rope, he'd never see his beloved Texas again. He'd never see the sky except through the vertical interruption of bars. And he'd never know how good it

might have been with Leisha Bass had he had enough
time to tame her.

"Hey, Zeke, what's that up yonder in the road?" the
man riding shotgun up top called out.

"I don't see nothing."

"Right there. You blind, old man? Looks to be someone
what got throwed from a horse."

The rhythmic jouncing of the wagon eased and when
it came to a stop, Kenitay allowed himself to topple over
onto his side to enjoy a few minutes of peaceful rest. He'd
just closed his eyes, readying to let go of consciousness,
when he heard the outrider climb down and cry, "Zeke,
c'mere! This you gots to see. It's a woman!"

"Now what in tarnation would a woman be doing way
out here in the middle of all this? Is she shot?"

"Don't look to be. Just knocked cold. Bring me down
that water jug."

The wagon rocked as the driver jumped off.

Then Kenitay heard a growl that was more devil than
angel but it sounded like heaven to him.

"Don't you boys so much as twitch. I'd hate to blow
you in half."

Kenitay smiled and pushed himself upright in time to
see his two jailers marched around the side of the wagon
with their hands in the air. Leisha was striding behind
them, her carbine held at ready.

"One of you open that box and let him out."

"Don't know if he can climb out on his own. He's in
a pretty bad way."

Leisha didn't look. "Kenitay, can you move?"

"I'll manage."

"Slide on out so these two can share your accommodations."

She heard the rattling of irons and a low, reluctant groan.
Still she didn't take her eyes off her prisoners. "Change
places with him. And get those irons off."

"We don't got the key."

"Climb in there and get all the way back."

When they scrambled to obey, Leisha snatched a glance at the man she'd risked so much to rescue.

"Oh, God. Did they do this to you?"

"No."

"Spread your feet so I can notch those leg irons."

"Don't miss and hit anything I'm fond of."

She squeezed off a round and the chain snapped apart like two pieces of a startled snake. "Can you ride?"

"Upright or facedown, anything's better than sitting in here."

He tumbled out of the back of the wagon, unable to catch himself, and ended up on his hands and knees with his face in the dirt. Leisha shut and locked the wagon door before she paid him any mind. She bent to loop an arm through his, hauling hard to get him on his feet. He was still cuffed but it was growing too dark to make such a delicate shot. They'd have to wait.

"What about us? You can't just leave us out here."

"Someone will come looking for you by morning. Until then, make yourselves at home."

She steered Kenitay over to the extra horse she had tied out of view and helped boost him into the saddle. She didn't want to think about how bad he looked or how a rapid ride might worsen his injuries. It couldn't matter now.

"Can you hang on?"

"Don't worry about me."

But she was worried. He was sitting sloppy, unable to handle the reins. "Just hang onto the horn and I'll lead you." He didn't argue. That scared her.

They rode until darkness grew too complete to continue. Kenitay did as he promised and hung on but the moment she reined in to set up their camp, he spilled down to Texas ground and lay unmoving. Leisha tended the horses, staking them out to munch bunch grass. Then she came to kneel beside him. There was little she could do at the moment except let him rest.

"I must be crazy," she muttered.

With a blanket from her saddle pack, she nudged in close to the unconscious man and draped the scratchy wool over both of them. She shut her eyes, refusing to think about the chance she'd missed, refusing to question the decision she'd made. There would be time to face those consequences later.

And when she eased her arm over the hard curve of his rib cage and felt the comforting rhythm of his heartbeats, she didn't doubt the wisdom of what she'd done.

Kenitay felt like he'd been dragged behind a runaway horse through the better part of Texas. The last thing he wanted to do was wake and face the agony living in every part of him. The idea of moving made him groan even before he started to open his eyes.

It was morning. A searingly blue sky formed an infinite canopy overhead, edging out the pinks of daybreak. For a moment, he was confused—about the place, about the pain. And then he managed to angle his head slightly to see Leisha squatted down on her heels a few feet away. She was regarding him with the same impassive stare an Apache used with a captive he planned on roasting. It wasn't a welcoming sight. Did she ask him how he felt? Did she spend even a second seeing to his comfort? Not Leisha. The first thing she did when she saw he was alive and awake was fire a demand at him in a growly, no-nonsense voice.

"You got some serious explaining to do, mister."

# Thirteen

Before he would answer, Kenitay dragged himself upright and extended his shackled wrists. Leisha studied the bonds coolly and said, "I don't think so. At least, not yet."

"Why? Are you planning to turn me in for the reward like your cousin did?"

His tone riled her just as his refusal to give thanks had. "I just might. I'm dealing with a murderer, after all."

"And you're the woman who sprung that murderer from the law," he pointed out unnecessarily. "Why? They'll be looking for you now, too."

"They won't find us. I've already gone back over our tracks. None they have could follow them." She got a sudden, unpleasant vision of her father and brother tracking her through West Texas. "Besides, I haven't turned you loose yet."

"Why?" he repeated.

"Because I don't trust you."

"I meant, why did you come after me?"

"Because I didn't think the odds of seeing justice done was very good. I'm taking you back to Terlingua."

That got a reaction. A spasm of anguish passed over his face and she wondered if he was thinking about his family there and how it would hurt them to see him in chains. His expression grew stony and his voice was like steel. "What difference does it make where they hang me?"

"Then, you did kill that man."

"Does it matter?"

"It matters to me."

"And if I did, you take me home in irons and turn me over to the law for hanging."

"I'll take you to Jack and see what he and my father can do to help you."

"Why would they bother?" he sneered.

She shook her head a bit sadly. "You've been away too long. You've forgotten what family is for."

He laughed bitterly. "And when they find out this latest bit of news, they're going to wish I'd really died at Fort Apache." Then his tone lowered so suddenly it took her by surprise. "Don't take me back there, Leisha. I couldn't bear to see the shame in their eyes."

"My family won't turn its back on you in disgrace. We've weathered worse by pulling together. You don't trust us at all, do you?"

He lifted his chained hands. "About as much as you trust me."

"I don't know you. I know nothing of the years that shaped the man you are. My father saw shadows on your soul. I see them in your eyes. You come to us wrapped up in lies—"

"And you would have received me with open arms had I come right out and said I had a price on my head. I can see that'd make great table conversation with a Texas Ranger, a bounty hunter, and a sheriff sitting down with me at dinner. I don't think so, Leisha. Like you said, thirteen years is a long time and they have no reason to believe in me."

"They might if you'd tried the truth, if you'd given them a chance instead of running off to make things worse. Now, hold still. I want to clean you up a bit."

She laid her carbine down safely out of his reach, then wet her kerchief from her canteen and touched it to the split of skin at the corner of his mouth. He sat stoically, staring straight ahead.

"Who did this? Beating up on prisoners isn't exactly Army policy."

"Beech and Westfall."

She paused, then continued to wash away the crusted blood. "Why? Was it something you said?"

"Something I wouldn't say."

He winced as she blotted the edge of his swollen eye and she was quick to murmur, "Sorry. I think your nose might be broken."

"Leave it. It's the only part of me that doesn't hurt."

He closed his sore eyes and let her bathe them with the cool water. It was a minor relief compared to his major misery but even that much was a blessing. And so was the knowledge that she was here, that she had risked so much to free him. No matter what she might say, no matter how hard her tone, she'd come for him when all she'd claimed to want was heading in the other direction. When forced to choose, she'd chosen him. It made him want to do something for her in exchange. But what could he offer, bound by shackles and by a past he could not escape? What could he give her that would have any meaning, that would reflect all that she was to him?

She continued her questions, unaware of the turn of his thoughts toward a more personal theme. "What did they want to find out from you?"

When he said nothing, Leisha sat back on her heels and waited until he looked at her. She scowled.

"It doesn't concern you, Leisha." How to explain without giving away all. "It's a trust given to me by my father."

"There's that word *trust* again."

His swollen jaw firmed and he went to staring straight

ahead again. She glared at him and dabbed at the contusion on his chin. When he sucked a harsh breath, she muttered, "Sorry," again but she didn't sound like she meant it quite so much this time.

She was leaning over him to examine the knot Jed's rifle butt had put on the side of his head. Her fingers were sliding gently through his hair to lift it out of the way when he told her very quietly, "It was an accident, Leisha. I didn't mean to kill him."

She was about to ask how one could accidentally slit a man's throat when he turned his head slightly and they were face to face, only inches apart. She could have fallen right into the green of his beseeching stare. Her gaze fluttered downward, fixing upon the sculpted lines of his mouth unintentionally. Then all she could think about was kissing him.

She cleared her throat roughly in an attempt to escape the treacherous softening of female spirit. "Let me take a look at your ribs. Anything broken?" She started to unbutton his shirt.

"No," he murmured, leaning down slightly to nuzzle at her hair.

Angry because her fingers had grown suddenly clumsy, Leisha jerked the sweat and blood-stained cotton from the waistband of his denims, then regretted it when he gasped. With greater care, she parted the shirt to expose the colorful wealth of bruising upon his chest and middle. Then she was the one who gasped. How horribly they had hurt him! Her hand trembled as it touched one of the purplish crescents. His skin quivered beneath the spread of her fingertips and his breathing gave a slight hitch as it brushed soft and warm along her cheek.

"This looks awful," she cried in distress. "Are you sure nothing's—"

Her words broke off as his fingers cupped beneath her

chin, lifting her head. The sight of tears in her eyes almost undid him.

"Nothing," he repeated softly, "except my heart."

Leisha closed her eyes and leaned into the gentle possession of his kiss.

"Thank you," he whispered against her lips.

"For the kiss?"

"For my life."

And right then, it was all worth it to Leisha—the risk, the possible consequences, the unanswered questions. It didn't matter what he'd done, what he was running from or heading for. All that mattered was the sudden warmth spreading through her on hurried little beats of expectation.

"I'm afraid that poor life's not worth much right now."

"If it were possible, I would pledge it to you." His voice was a low rumble of sincerity.

She took a shaky breath and tried to laugh. "What would I do with it?"

"Whatever you like." His eyes were open, a brilliant emerald color and full of glittering promise as he teased more kisses along her jaw and down her neck. "I have committed my future to my father's memory but for now, I am yours."

A slight tremor passed through Leisha, a combination of warm lips moving upon sensitive skin and hot suggestion taking over weakening will. "Mine," she mused as her hands came up to hold his head and her torso arched to greet the brush of his mouth at the moist vee of her shirt opening.

Kenitay straightened suddenly so that they were eye to eye. His gaze was intense, compelling, as he said, "Let me give what you wanted from me the other night. Let me return your power and your pride. Let me do this for you, Leisha. You've given me my freedom. Let me restore yours."

"H-how would you do that?"

He took her hand between his and pressed it palm down over his heart. "Feel the power you have over me. Use it to conquer your fear and be strong again."

His silken words produced a quiver of hope to war with her nervousness and doubt. He was moving her hand over the contours of his chest in slow revolutions. It was undeniably exciting. Yet the same hard strength that fascinated, frightened as well. She tried to pull her hand away but he held it a tender captive.

"Trust me, Leisha."

She blurted out the first thing that came to mind in panicked objection. "But you're hurt."

"My pain is fleeting and will heal with time. Will yours?"

Her own heart started beating faster in a flustered mix of expectation and alarm. Her gaze tore from his and flew about them anxiously. "Are you suggesting we make love—right here? Right now?" They were in a small shelter of rocks upon warm Texas ground beneath a sky cleared of its first hazy pastels. It wasn't exactly open territory. But it wasn't the private bedroom of the Claymore, either.

"Don't look around for problems. Look to me for answers."

She looked and her gaze was wide and wild. "Kenitay . . ."

"Don't be afraid of me."

"I-I'm not. I'm afraid for you. You're hurt. You can't possibly—"

He shifted her hand down to cup the hard ridge of him straining against denim. He felt her shock, her fright, but he wouldn't let her pull away.

"Power is found in knowledge, Leisha," came his persuasive croon. "Learn what you need to know to put fear in its proper place. Let me be your instrument of strength."

He felt curiosity stir in her as her fingertips stroked the length of him. He released her gradually, gratified when she didn't immediately jerk away. His hands rose to frame her face. He could sense her tension, her wariness, her need to trust. So he made it all sound very sensible, very non-threatening in hopes it would calm her troubled spirit.

"I owe you, Leisha. Take this one thing from me. It's the only gift I have to give. I cannot remain in debt to you and retain my pride. You sacrificed much to save me and now it's my turn to rescue you. Don't be a hostage to this fear that was so unfairly forced upon you. Use me to find your strength and I will consider it a debt paid. I don't want to leave you until we're even."

"Leave me?"

"I can't stay, Leisha. Now you know why. This time, right now, is all I can promise you. We may never see each other again."

She stared at him, her expression impassive, her eyes huge pools of blue.

"Let me leave with my conscience clear. No strings, no ties, just a fair exchange."

And then to thoroughly destroy the image of a safe barter, he kissed her. It wasn't the uninvolved kiss of a man set on settling an obligation. It was the searing, spearing union of a man hungry to the depths of his soul, hungry for her. And Leisha's will shattered.

He lay back on the hard ground, bringing her down with him, over him. There, he continued to kiss her, hard and deep, slow and soft until her mind was numb and her chest was aching.

Somewhere in that urgent exchange, the control shifted from him to her. He became more passive, forcing her to be the aggressor. She didn't disappoint either of them. She used her kisses to express all the anxiety she'd felt when he was arrested, all her dismay when she'd seen him locked up like a battered animal, all the wondrous emotion that sprang to life at his claim of *I love you*. He hadn't said it again. She didn't need to hear it now. All she needed was the eager flame in her blood and his willingness to let her have her way.

She still had her hand upon him. He'd grown even fuller, throbbing encouragingly beneath her touch. *Hers*. She phrased that cautiously within her mind as her palm began to move slowly, tentatively. His strength was tempting, so tempting, Her fingertips lingered on the fastening to his jeans, riding the accelerating rock of his abdomen. An instrument of strength, he'd said. A tool of pain and control, she knew. And she hesitated, easing her hand away from the threat he presented.

Gently, he took up her uncertain hand and lifted it to cup the contour of his bruised face. He pushed into that reluctantly offered well, kissing the swell of her palm, laving her thumb with the rasp of his tongue, coaxing her with the languid downward drift of his eyelids and the nudge of his cheek to continue to touch him. She leaned down to sample his mouth with a light, sweeping pressure.

"Don't be afraid of me, Leisha. I would never hurt you. Confront your fears and turn them to your use."

When she went still, his eyes opened. He could read apprehension in her gaze but there was also desire and determination. He could see her want of him, her need to know him. She was a brave one, a woman with a warrior's heart. His smile was small and confident.

"I trust you." It was an odd thing for him to say but as he displayed his shackled hands, then lifted them above his head to leave himself helpless and exposed, he could see by the change in her expression that it was the right thing. He saw a sudden influx of cautious power as he gave himself over into her hands. And his boldness was returned.

Her palms glided over his chest, a soft skim of skin on skin that wouldn't wake any distress from his sundry bruises. The movement grew more and more complex with purpose, surveying the curve of his ribs, charting the hard swell of his pectorals, thumbing his brown nipples until they beaded as tightly as her own. They roamed admiringly over his abdomen, intrigued by the tough terrain. A man's terrain. Hard, strong, yet yielding now to her exploration. Her fingers sieved through the furring on his taut belly and tucked under the band of his pants. He drew in a deep drought of air to give her more leeway.

Kenitay almost groaned aloud at the first shy brush of her fingertips. He'd been ready for this . . . forever! But Leisha hadn't been. She was inching out into new and, to her, dangerous territory, gathering the courage to proceed from a cruelly damaged soul. And he would not let his over-anxiousness interfere. He forced slow, steady breaths from a chest congested with anticipation. He struggled to control the tension shaking through his system. He closed his eyes and braced his forearm across them. He would think of something else, something distracting. He tried to herd his mind into considering how he was going to escape capture by the Army. But just then, she captured him with the warm gloving of her hand. His teeth ground and he moaned in impatience. He tried to turn his attention to the problem of his freedom but suddenly she was fumbling with buttons, freeing him from imprisoning denim. His heels burrowed down into sandy Texas soil.

Then nothing in his experience could match the exquisite torture of her touch. The scrape of her fingernails on his sensitive underside. The teasing stroke from smooth tip to nested root. The light fondling that had tension shaking through him like a relentless fever. His breath chugged in short, explosive bursts, quickening with a mounting desperation. His blood was thick and hot, pounding within the cradle of her hand. It was hell to lie still, harder to resist the need to manage his own passions.

Just when he thought he couldn't endure another second, the torment ended.

His body had begun to loosen into shivers of relief when he felt the brush of her bare thigh as Leisha moved to straddle his hips.

She saw the surprise in his eyes when they sprang open. That off-balanced startlement was just the encouragement she needed. With her knees hugged tight against his ribs to keep them from shaking, she bent to take his lips with her own. It was an aggressive claim, sheer bravado, because she was so scared her mind was nearly numb with it. But her body was hot—hot and ready for him—and that urgent desire goaded her on beyond the panicked warnings her past experience was flinging at her. She moved against him, acquainting herself with the way his hardness fit the groove of her femininity. The moment was tense and tantalizing. Then he gave an involuntary shudder beneath her. A slight thing but enough to thrust her back on her guard.

*Don't move. Don't move,* her subconscious willed of him and at the same time, she could feel him relax, reducing the threat but not the tension. She stayed where she was, crouched over him, the rush of her breathing had her still-covered breasts grazing his chest in a rapid rhythm.

"Leisha, look at me," he coaxed in a husky whisper. "Look at me." He moved his hand up slowly and used his first two fingers to draw a connecting line between his eyes and hers and back again. "Focus here. Right here."

She obeyed, concentrating on the rich green fire of his gaze, allowing her confidence to build, her control to return. He lifted his hands, spreading his fingers wide, inviting hers to spear between them and take them down to the ground above his head. She was stretched out over his inert form in a dominant pose. It was a position proving not her strength but his submission and the one bolstered the other.

"Focus, Leisha," he reminded her with a compelling quiet. "Don't look away from me."

And she fixed upon his bright stare as she eased back until she could feel him pressing stiff and bold against her moist center. Her courage faltered.

"Kiss me," came Kenitay's gruff command and when she did, she found his mouth so hot, so voracious, her own desires spiked to new heights. She was panting, ready, trembling with anticipation and reluctance. Finally, she let the instinct of passion guide her, sliding her back and down upon him in one liquid move. The sensation stunned her, the sense of fullness and heat so massive, so overwhelming. So glorious. Time stopped.

She heard Kenitay's soft gasp as his lips parted and his eyes rolled, flickered, and lost their own focus for a long moment. His fingers clenched around hers, clutching fiercely, working in jerky spasms, then finally relaxing into faint tremors. He wet his lips. His smile was small and dazed.

"Beautiful," he told her hoarsely. "God, you're beautiful."

She'd needed to hear his hushed reverence, needed to see the smoky look that clouded the brilliance of his gaze. "So are you," she whispered against his mouth. Then she began to move.

They were slow, small lifts at first, cautious, experimental, testing the perimeters of how he fit inside her. He was big, stretching her into snug conformance, but there was no discomfort, no pain. Only that amazing sense of fullness. And warmth. Heat pulsed from within, friction igniting streaks of fire. The faster she moved, the hotter it blazed. She ceased to think of the man below her, concentrating upon the mysterious energy building inside. Power like she'd never felt before. Hers to control and claim. Sensation sparked like flint striking steel, flaring up so suddenly, it scorched her senses, shaking her control all to hell and tearing a cry from her that was wild and freeing.

Leisha lost track of time in the wonderfully weak aftermath. She came around slowly, stirring from where she'd sprawled out across Kenitay's chest. She straightened slowly, aware that he was still firm as a post inside her and that his breathing was nowhere near as calm as hers. His eyes where closed in a face etched sharp with tension. But as he promised, he hadn't moved, he hadn't tried to force his own pleasure upon her. And she could feel the cost of that control in the way he was trembling beneath her.

Her kiss took him by surprise. His eyes flew open at her sudden, savage taking, then drifted shut again as her tongue teased and flirted with his. Then the sense of play was gone. Her thrusts into his mouth were deep and strong and the movement of her hips over his was just as vigorous, quickening his breaths until he was blowing them back into her with a gusty force and she was swallowing down his muffled groan.

The world around them was still and warm. Kenitay had no desire to stir. He'd no idea muscle and bone could dissolve so completely. He was light-headed, his mind dizzy, his thoughts giddy. It was like being drunk. Leisha Bass had intoxicated him into a helpless stupor. He felt her lips brush over his and made a vague effort to respond. He felt her fingers slip from his and had no strength to hold her. A protesting moan rumbled from him when she lifted up and off him. He let himself drift for a timeless moment. Then came the cool command of her voice.

"Don't move.

His eyes blinked open to the incredulous sight of her standing over him with her carbine. He sucked a quick breath just as she fired. His hands jerked apart as her bullet snapped the chain binding them together. He sat up, instinctively rubbing his wrists beneath the metal bracelets.

"Let's get a move on," Leisha said brusquely as she bent down to snag up her saddle. She was fully dressed and the set of her expression was all business. Kenitay watched her for a moment, too confused to know how to react. She glanced at him impatiently. "Are you planning to wait until the wagon shows up to give you a ride?"

"No." He got up awkwardly, favoring his bruised ribs, and hastily restored order to his clothes. He didn't understand. She was treating him as though nothing had happened between them. "Leisha?"

When she didn't turn, he strode to her and caught her arm, bringing her around to face him. Her head reared back, her eyes going dangerously narrow. She went stiff when he embraced her. He had to anchor her with a hand in her hair so he could kiss her. Her lips were thin, resisting his efforts until he pulled back, bewildered.

"What's wrong?"

"Nothing's wrong," she declared coolly. "It's time to go."

He didn't move so she had to pry herself from his grip. Then came her crisp summation.

"No strings. No ties. Remember?" She pushed away from him with a gruff, "Let's ride."

# Fourteen

That's what he'd said.

But he hadn't meant a word of it.

However, this wasn't the time to argue what he had or hadn't said, what he had or hadn't meant. Trouble was coming after them and he wasn't eager to be caught.

The minute he swung up into the saddle and reined his horse around, Leisha was there to grab on to the leads.

"Where are you going?"

"Back to town to pick up their trail."

Leisha stared, incredulously. "You can't go back there."

He ignored her. "I want you to go back home. This has gotten too dangerous for game-playing."

"What?"

He tried to haul back on the reins but she had a tight hold on them. "It's going to come down to some mean business from here on out. I don't want you tangled up in it."

"It's my business, too. And since when does what you want matter to me?"

He took a deep breath. "Leisha, I don't want to argue with you."

"Fine. There's nothing to argue about."

"Go home!"

"Go to hell!"

They glared at one another for a long moment, then Kenitay tried a reasonable approach.

"Leisha, I don't want you to get hurt."

She laughed tightly. "I'm not the one who's all busted up and needed to be sprung from a prison van."

Kenitay clenched his teeth. "You are the most maddening woman."

"If you wanted a docile female, you should have kissed my sister when we were children." Haughtily, she turned to step up into her saddle.

"I tried to."

His words made her pause. She twisted to stare at him in disbelief. He'd been interested in Becca, too? Her heart filled with a huge, unreasonable ache.

Then he grinned. "She slapped me."

Shooting daggers with her glare, Leisha kicked her horse into a gallop.

"Hey, you're going the wrong way!"

"I know where they're going," she called back over her shoulder. "You can follow me or you can find your own way."

Kenitay scowled at her back. Then a small, reluctant smile shaped his lips and he rode after her.


They crossed the rail line close to noon. That's when Kenitay reined, calling, "Where are you going?" He wasn't a fool. She was headed back toward the Chisos.

"I thought you trusted me," she chided with a toss of her blond head.

His gaze followed the rails in one direction, then the other. "What's on your mind, *silah?*"

"A plan. You can come with me or go your own way. It doesn't matter to me."

He frowned darkly. "What's your way?"

"I'm going home."

He was afraid that's what she was going to say. "But not to stay."

"Not to stay."

"I can't go with you."

"I'm not asking you to. I guess this is good-bye then."

And she said it so nonchalantly, he could have cheerfully knocked her off her horse and strangled her. But he was still all warmed up from making love with her—and that was the problem. It wasn't common sense that was leading him after her. It was something else altogether.

"What's at Blue Creek?" he demanded in surly humor.

"I need to pick up some things and send a telegram."

"To who?"

"My cousin."

She had a lot of cousins. The ones in the East, he knew nothing about. Jack and Sarah's brother, Sid, was the only one he knew of in Texas but he couldn't remember where he was living.

"What for?"

"Part of my plan." She grinned at him so smugly, he growled in frustration. "You don't have to come along."

"Then why don't you just tell me where I can find them?"

She gave him that bland Bass smile and rode on without a word, knowing he'd follow. They continued on in silence until they reached a small watering hole in the early afternoon hours. It was shaded by steep outcroppings of rock rising up on either side. The horses needed a chance to drink and rest and so did they.

Kenitay eased down out of the saddle, his forearm hugging to his ribs. He still looked as though someone had done a mean two-step on his face but he was moving better, without the obvious signs of distress. Still Leisha worried. As angry as she was, she couldn't stand the thought of him in pain.

*No strings. No ties.*

How could he say that to her on the heels of *I love you?* Was it just the physical release he'd wanted all

along? Hadn't he ever cared? What a fool she was for
wanting to believe him, even now. If he wanted his freedom so damned bad, why didn't he just ride off? She'd
all but pushed him away from her yet he stayed close,
refusing to act with the independence he claimed he
needed. Well, she had needs, too. She needed to know
where he stood. She needed to know why he'd give her
such a precious gift then tell her it was meaningless. She
needed to prove she was just as strong, just as capable of
being on her own as he was. She had to be tough enough
to protect her heart from the tenderness he'd shown her
and from the pain of losing him. She just wasn't sure that
was possible anymore.

She would not cling to him. She would not force any
promises because of what had happened between them.
Not if he didn't mean them. And obviously he didn't since
he was so anxious to leave her behind.

She watched him kneel down stiffly at the water's edge
to scoop up handfuls to drink. She approached cautiously
and squatted down at his side to drink from the well of
her palm. She could feel his gaze but didn't acknowledge
it. She didn't want to argue with him. But arguing wasn't
what he had on his mind.

Leisha gave a start as his fingers eased around the curve
of her jaw. He said her name in a low, seductive tone and
turned her head toward him. She went rigid, not in fear of
him but for fear of what she might give away. His gaze
detailed her face, searching and apparently not finding what
he wanted to see for he began to frown.

Then suddenly he surged to his feet, tense and wary,
his gaze scanning the valley ahead. Leisha rose beside
him, alerted by his manner. A lone rider appeared, coming
out of the sun.

"Give me your hand piece," Kenitay urged as he tried
to sweep her behind him with his arm so she'd be out of

harm's way. She'd already drawn the revolver and was maneuvering back into position at his side.

"I'm as good a shot as you are," she told him tersely, already bracing her feet in case she had to prove it. "And I've killed a man, too."

They stood together, waiting for the threat to materialize. Then Leisha gave a soft cry of relief, reholstering her gun.

"It's Jack."

Kenitay felt no such relief. If Jack Bass had come calling, he had a pretty good idea what was behind the visit.

The pale-eyed Ranger captain rode with his rifle resting atop his thigh in a deceivingly easy position. He directed his mount into the shallows of the watering hole, splashing across it at a slow, deliberate pace. There was no telling what was on his mind with the way his hat tipped forward to shade his expression.

"Long way from home, Ranger Jack," Kenitay said after Jack had drawn his horse up to stand belly-deep and muzzle down in the water.

Jack wasted no time with pleasantries. He pulled the "WANTED" dodger from his jacket. "Explain this to me."

Kenitay didn't need to look at it. "Did you come to take me in?"

"I came to ask if you were guilty."

"Does Mama know?"

Jack shook his head. "I wanted to take it up with you first."

Kenitay glanced in Leisha's direction. "Does her daddy know?"

"If he did, things wouldn't be near as civilized. Billy brought this to me. Far as I know, that's as far as it goes. Leisha, what are you doing here?"

"Nothing," Kenitay began.

She squared her stance and was quick to interrupt. "I broke him out of the prison wagon."

Kenitay uttered a fierce curse. "Don't you know when to keep your mouth shut?"

"So I guess you'll just have to take me in, too, Jack. And that'll put Daddy in a real charitable mood with you."

"Stay outta this, Leisha. I'm not taking you in for anything." He paused. "You didn't hurt anyone, did you?"

"I shot them down, skinned them out, and left them to dry in the sun," she remarked with a smooth drawl.

"Leisha! She did no such thing! Nobody got hurt, honest to God!"

Jack squinted, studying Kenitay's face. "Except you, from the looks of it. Who worked you over, son?"

"It doesn't matter."

"It matters to me."

"I'm taking care of it. Or are you taking me in to hang?"

"You haven't answered my question yet." Jack sat back in the saddle with that look of infinite patience, never once expecting the answer he would hear.

"I'm guilty."

Jack squeezed his eyes shut and let his hat tip down to shield his face. He muttered a soft oath and sat straight again. "Then I guess I'm going to have to take you back."

Kenitay took a step backward. "And let them hang me in front of my mama, her knowing that you were the one who brought me in? She'd never forgive you for it. I can't let you take me."

"Don't make no trouble, son."

He retreated another step. "She'll never forgive you." He didn't say it as a threat but rather as a soft beseechment. "I won't let you do it. She loves you."

"It's my job. I'm a Ranger. Emily knows that. I'll do everything I can for you. Everything."

"Then let me go."

"I can't." His rifle came up slowly into play. "Don't make me hurt you."

And on the sidelines, forgotten, Leisha knew a terrible indecision. She couldn't let Jack take Kenitay back to hang, nor could she allow her cousin to shoot him down. She eased her Colt out and leveled it. "Jack, you're not taking him in."

Both men were startled by the cold cut of her voice and glanced her way in surprise. Neither looked pleased to see a gun.

"Leisha, don't," Kenitay cautioned. He was eyeballing the distance to his horse, weighing the odds of Jack actually shooting him. He'd never met a more honorable man, a man more sworn to do his duty to the badge he wore. He'd shoot, all right. Not to kill, but to stop him.

"Put it down, Leisha," Jack ordered. "Don't get involved in this any more than you already are."

"You put it down, Jack."

"Can't do that," he told her solemnly.

She thumbed back the hammer. "Get on your horse, Kenitay. I'll see he doesn't move to stop you."

Kenitay hesitated. All his self-preserving instincts cried, *Go, run.* But he looked up at Jack, at the man he'd loved like a father, and he saw the determination in his gaze. Jack wasn't going to let him run. And he looked at Leisha, whose expression was just as fixed. If she fired on a Texas Ranger, she was going to jail. She'd already broken him out of custody. How much closer could he allow her to come to a noose of her own?

But if Jack took him back, he was going to hang and his father would go unavenged.

He took another slow step toward his horse.

Leisha widened her stance and steadied her hand. Her outward appearance didn't betray her inner panic. *Put it down, Jack. Please don't make me do this.* He was sitting at an angle to her. It was going to be hard not to hit anything vital. She wouldn't think of sitting down to supper with him and his family. Jack, her father's favorite, a man of unswerving decency. She wouldn't even consider what her father would say about her actions of the past twenty-four hours. Her head told her she was doing wrong things, her heart said they were justified.

*Jack, please!*

Kenitay took another step and began reaching for the trailing reins to his mount. His eyes never left Jack. He could see the anguish pulling through the other's expression at the same time he lifted his rifle. The reins brushed Kenitay's fingers and he gathered them up. Tension had grown so thick among the three of them, the outside world ceased to exist.

Until a sudden shrill cry sounded and Eenah launched himself from the rocks bordering the drinking hole. Sunlight glinted off the blade in his hand as his arm caught Jack around the neck and his momentum carried them both down into the water.

Kenitay lost the reins and all thoughts of escape. "No!" The cry tore from him as he raced into water that was already turning red where Jack's hat floated on the surface. He grabbed Eenah's hand as it whipped overhead and he wrestled the other brave off balance, throwing him backward into the shallows. "Stop! He's my father!"

Raw sounds ripped through him as he fished in the water with his hands, finally snagging Jack's roundabout jacket and hauling him up, limp and heavy. He didn't hear the single word he was sobbing over and over in despair. It would have surprised him for it was one he'd never used before. It was *Daddy*.

Kenitay backed out of the water, dragging Jack with him. He slipped on the muddy bank, falling hard, pulling Jack's motionless form up into his lap. There was blood on his hands.

"Leisha, help me!"

And she was there taking charge, pushing him out of the way when he was blinded by his own tears. She

stripped down Jack's coat and tore open his shirt, searching out the source of his bleeding while Eenah came up
out of the water, drying his blade and restoring it to its
sheath.

"I thought he was going to shoot you," the Apache
claimed stoically. "I did not know who he was."

Kenitay gave him a vague stare, unable to say anything.
Then he looked back to Leisha's bowed head, his panic
cresting. "How bad is it? Leisha?"

She lifted her head, her wide blue gaze softening. "He's
all right. Just nicked him there along the ribs under his
arm. Find me something I can use to bind him up."

He sat for a moment, too weak with relief to move. A
huge pain welled up inside, choking him. What if he'd
been the cause of Jack's death? How could he have stood
losing the other man who'd meant the most to him? It
was then he had an idea of how Jack had felt carrying
his own small jacket back to his mother with the news
that he was dead. The feeling around his heart was dark
as death itself.

Eenah stepped forward to offer his shirt for Leisha's
use. She stared up at him suspiciously before taking the
garment and ripping it into long strips. "Where did you
come from?"

"I, too, had been following the prison wagon. I thought
it best to wait and be sure of my welcome."

Leisha stared at him, hot color flooding up at what his
words inferred. How much had he seen? Had he been
watching her and Kenitay while they . . . while they made
love? Her gaze turned icy to combat the surge of embarrassment. He was the one who should be shamed, sneaking around, watching what he had no business watching.
She went back to binding up Jack's wound. Her hands
were shaking.

Jack moaned softly, coming around.

Eenah gave him a hard look, then said, "I will scout

around and make sure he was alone." Then he disappeared back into the rocks.

"Jack?" Leisha called gently, brushing his wet hair aside with a stroke of her palm. His eyes flickered open, dazed at first, then sharpening with remembrance. He tried to sit up and groaned, clutching at his side. "It's all right. Don't try to move. It's just a flesh wound but it probably needs some stitching. I'm fresh out of needles and thread." She forced a smile, hoping to lighten the situation. Jack closed his eyes, lying back to gather his strength.

Kenitay edged up beside him. He reached out hesitantly, catching his hand back in uncertainty, then touching his fingertips to his stepfather's cheek. Jack looked up at him, his expression somber and closed down tight.

"I'm sorry," Kenitay told him. "He thought you were my enemy. He was wrong, wasn't he?"

Jack wet his lips and winced as he elbowed up into a half-reclined position. "Don't run. If you do, you won't be able to stop. I don't want to sit home with your mama waiting to hear that some bounty man cashed you for the reward."

"I'm sorry," Kenitay said again. "I can't go back with you. There's something I must do first."

"Kenitay?" Jack hesitated, his expression working in distress. "Was it self-defense?"

"No." Kenitay ducked his head, wishing he could have reassured him of his innocence. "It was an accident."

"If you went back and explained—"

He shook his head and stood. "It wasn't my wish to dishonor you with what I've done." He went to Jack's horse and drew his spare carbine from its boot. He shucked out the shells and gave the rifle a toss into the water. "Leisha, take his sidearms and empty them."

Jack sat unmoving as she did so.

Kenitay tossed her a length of rope. "Tie his hands behind him. Make the bonds loose enough so that he can work them free. I don't want him right behind us on the trail."

"Give me your hands, Jack," she asked softly. He put them behind him, grimacing slightly in discomfort as she wrapped them and tied a slack knot. "You should be able to wiggle free in about a half hour. Don't try too hard or you'll start in bleeding again." Her hands kneaded his broad shoulders restlessly then she bent to press a quick kiss upon his cheek. "I'm sorry."

"Leisha," he spoke up urgently. "Don't ride out with him. Wait here with me."

She paused, casting a look at Kenitay, who had already swung up on his horse. Their exchange was wordless and intense. Then he said, "Stay."

Leisha picked up Jack's damp hat and affixed it on his head to shade him from the glaring sun. "Get stitches," she reminded him then she climbed aboard her own mount.

Kenitay regarded her and her decision impassively, then said to Jack, "Don't follow us."

"If not me, it'll be someone else. You'd be better off with me."

"We'll take our chances," he replied. Then he kicked up his horse, cantering through the pool to throw up great sprays of water in his wake.

"I'm sorry, Jack," Leisha said again. Then she, too, galloped off, leaving him bound uncomfortably by duty.

Eenah joined them as soon as they cleared the canyon, falling in beside Kenitay and wisely remaining silent. He didn't mention why he'd made no attempt to spring Kenitay from his captors, nor did his friend demand an accounting. But Leisha was wondering. She didn't trust the enigmatic brave and she told herself it was more than their rivalry over Kenitay and the man's arrogant Apache opinion that she should be at home tending woman's work.

She told herself it wasn't because his presence put a wedge between her and the man who rode between them.

Kenitay hadn't so much as glanced at her. If he objected to her company, he kept it to himself. Perhaps because he knew it would do no good. His gaze was fixed straight ahead and his concentration seemed focused inward. She knew he was thinking about his family in Terlingua so she didn't intrude upon the privacy of his thoughts. She didn't envy him the heartache.

They set up camp for the night near the Packsaddle Mountains. They'd make Blue Creek in time for breakfast. Over a dinner of mule deer that Eenah provided, Leisha laid out her plan to the two impassive Apaches.

"Beech and Westfall are on their way to Austin. They left by train yesterday morning so there's no way to intercept them. The only chance we'll have is to catch them in Austin."

"How do we get them there?" Kenitay asked, poking at the fire with a sharp stick. Embers danced up on the wafting current of heat, brilliant dots of light reflecting hotly in his gaze. "Don't you think folks would look at us kinda funny there in the big city?"

"Exactly. I'd thought of that."

"And?"

"You can trust me."

Both men frowned.

"I think we should leave her and strike out on our own," Eenah murmured to Kenitay in their own tongue.

"Try it and see how far you'll get," she answered in the same guttural tones.

Eenah looked surprised at her fluent response. He'd forgotten whose daughter she was. Then he scowled and stared sullenly out into the darkness.

Kenitay held to his smile and asked, "How do we get close to them? You said they were under special guard."

"That's where we rely on the fond memories Corporal Wonderly carries of our night together."

From across the fire, Kenitay's gaze sparked hotter than the flames. His bruised jaw squared up into a belligerent angle but he said nothing for a time. Then he told her, "I don't want you going in after them alone."

"I won't be. This time, you're going with me."

His black brows arched skeptically.

"As my cousin," she concluded, "Ken Bass."

By morning, their plan had been agreed upon. Eenah shaded off, heading north to where he'd wait for their return at Persimmon Gap, while Kenitay and Leisha rode on toward Blue Creek. She could tell by the set of his face that he had strong reservations, especially over that single word, *trust,* but he had no ideas of his own that would get him past Bureau security and he could feel time closing in. He never actually looked over his shoulder to see if Jack was there but Leisha knew by the stiff way he sat his saddle, he was expecting him at any moment. Personally, she didn't think Jack would be in hot pursuit. He was a methodical man, not given to impulse. He would tend his wounds and plot his course carefully. Then some day, when they were least expecting it, they'd look up and he'd be there. It was inevitable. And she wasn't looking forward to it, either.

They rode up to the Bass ranch off the plains, scattering Amanda's prize brood mares from their lazy graze among the lush grasses of the creek bed. There was even greater doubt in Kenitay's expression as they approached the big West Texas mansion but Leisha didn't share his fears. If Billy had gone to Jack first, she could bet the information had gone no farther. So unless they ran into Billy Cooper, no one would know she was riding with an escaped criminal.

That knowledge suddenly sat ill with her. She was bringing an escaped criminal to her family's door where she meant to stealthily extract their aid. She'd never expected things to take such a twisted path when she'd started out for vengeance in her father's name. But there was no use crying over it at this late date.

Becca was the first to see them. She cheerfully waved her big straw sunbonnet from the porch, her face all smiles.

As they pulled in their winded horses and readied to dismount, another figure joined her in the cooler shadows.

Harmon was home.

# Fifteen

" 'Morning," Harm called with a bland smile. "Step on down. Coffee's fresh and breakfast is just about ready."

"When did you get in, Daddy?" Leisha began cautiously.

"Last night." He didn't volunteer anything more as they both slid down and approached the porch. "Becca, why don't you take Kenitay inside and set him a place. I want to make some talk with your sister."

Kenitay hesitated, a fact Harm couldn't help but notice. He lingered at Leisha's side, curling his hand around the bend of her elbow in a silent gesture of support. She glanced up with a fixed smile. Sheer bravado, he was sure.

"Go ahead. I'll be right in."

He stepped back with obvious reluctance and went up to Becca, who was waiting to capture his arm and tow him inside. Then it was just father and daughter.

"How was your trip?" Leisha began on neutral ground.

"Dropped off a pair of those robbers in town. You can stop in and identify 'em if you like but they were pretty forthcoming with their confessions."

Leisha froze up, trying to give nothing away, just as he gave nothing away. "Did you talk to Billy?"

"For a bit."

"He have anything interesting to say?"

"Not much. Just that Jack was out looking for the boy." He waited.

"He found us."

"And?"

"What?"

"Did he come back with you?"

"No. He was kinda tied up with some other things."

Just then Rand became her unwitting savior as he strode out of the house to exclaim warmly, "Hey, sis." He jogged down the steps and shocked Leisha speechless by sweeping her up in a tight hug. They'd never had such a familiar exchange between them and she was rigid with surprise. He leaned in close, whispering, "He didn't hear it from me. Watch yourself." Then he let her loose and stepped away.

Harm was watching them narrowly. "Randall, why don't you—"

"Tend the horses," Rand finished for him. "Yessir, Daddy." He gathered up the reins and gave Kenitay's mount a critical eye. "Where'd he get this nag? Mama'd have a fit if anyone thought it was one of hers." He made a smoochy sound and coaxed the animals into following him down to the barn. Leisha watched him go, then looked back up at her father apprehensively.

"Kinda a long trip to town just to do a little banking, don't you think?" Harm drawled casually. There was nothing casual in the cut of his stare.

"Becca said she'd tell Mama—"

"She told your mama you were stopping in to see Sarah. Funny thing. Sarah never saw hide nor hair of you."

Leisha tried to keep her composure. "It's not Becca's fault. I asked her to—"

"Lie to your mama for you? I don't hold with lying, little girl. You do your own if you've a mind to, but don't drag your sister into it."

"I'm sorry."

He cut right to it. "Where you been?"

"Out." Steel sparked on steel as their gazes tangled.

"After that boy?"

"Yes." It wasn't really a lie.

"Guess you're gonna tell me that's none of my business."

"No, it's not."

He gave a curt nod. "Guess you'd be right."

Leisha blinked, her argument skewed by his concession. She watched him come down off the porch with his soft Apache step, waiting while he came up beside her so that they were shoulder to shoulder, her looking up at the house, him out at the barn. She could feel him building to something and she knew she didn't want to hear it.

"Those two fellas Rand and me brought in had a lot to say."

She stiffened her spine. "Oh?"

"I was wondering why your mama and me didn't hear it from you first."

"Because there was nothing you could do to change what happened, Daddy." Her tone was so gritty and hard he cast a sidelong glance at her.

"That the only reason?"

The firm line of her jaw quivered and she began to blink rapidly. "Did you say anything to Mama?"

"No. Is there a reason I shouldn't?"

"Please don't tell her, Daddy." Her voice was soft and frail. "I don't want her to be ashamed of me."

He was silent for a long moment. "Ashamed?" His arm reached out, cinching her up against him. He planted his hand on the back of her head, holding her tight in the curve of his shoulder. He kissed her temple, hard. And when he spoke, his voice was low and angry sounding. "Where did you get such a crazy idea? Ashamed? Of you? No, *shijii,* you got that all wrong."

Her hands knotted up in the front of his shirt, clutching desperately. "I'm sorry, Daddy."

His eyes squeezed shut and he pressed his face into her

hair. "No, little girl, I'm the one who's sorry. What can I do for you now?"

"Just this."

So he continued to hold her. "Kenitay was with you?" he asked after a time.

"He came up on us after—after I'd killed Collier."

"And he took care of you?"

She nodded. "He sent the other three packing and brought me home. I don't remember it. None of it. I couldn't take care of myself. That was a lie, too."

"Shhh." His embrace tightened. "You did fine, little girl, just fine."

She took a few quick breaths, then something else sunk in. "There were *three* others. You just brought in two."

"The third one wasn't anxious to come back with us. We planted him there."

"You killed him?"

"No. Randall did."

She drew back, eyes wide and amazed. "Rand did?"

Harm cleared his throat and looked incredibly uncomfortable. His gaze skated away from hers. "Are you—are you all right?"

"What do you mean, Daddy?"

"Did he—? Are you—?" He gave a soft curse at his own clumsiness. Then he met her eyes directly. "Are you with child?"

She blinked and blushed hot. "N-no." She swallowed and took a bracing breath. "You don't have to worry about that."

"Are you sure? You'd tell us, wouldn't you? Leisha, don't be afraid—"

"I'm not. And I'm not. Okay?"

He stroked her cheek with a gentle hand. "Okay." He glanced toward the house. "I smell biscuits burning. Breakfast must be ready."

"Daddy?"

"What?"

Her arms went around his neck, squeezing tight. Then she let go and hurried up into the house. Harm watched her go, his look so bittersweet it would have broken her heart to see it. Then Rand came up behind him, slipping a hand over his shoulder.

"Smells like Mama burnt the biscuits again."

Harm took a deep breath. "I'm beginning to like them that way." He put his arm around his son and they both went in to breakfast.

When the dishes were cleared away and the day's routine took over, Kenitay and Leisha were left adrift in the parlor. Seeing his uneasiness, Leisha came to loop her arm through his in much the same way as Becca had earlier. Only her gesture was much more possessive.

"The sooner we bring it up, the better."

"They're not going to go for it, Leisha."

"You don't know that. It's hard to tell how my father is going to take things, but Mama is pretty reasonable."

"This has got nothing to do with being reasonable. It's got to do with them being parents. They'd be crazy to let you run off with me."

There was a subtle throat-clearing. They looked up in alarm to see Amanda at the doorway. She observed their stricken expressions with a cool demeanor.

"I'm not sure I was supposed to hear that but since I have, you'd better tell me everything before I let your father shoot Kenitay out of his socks and I lock you in your room until you're thirty."

"Mama—"

"Don't 'Mama' me. Talk fast and make it good."

They exchanged uncertain looks. Kenitay shrugged and Leisha grabbed for breath before launching into it. "Mama, we got into some trouble and need your help."

Amanda's gaze went round and immediately dropped to her daughter's midsection. Leisha gasped.

"No! Not that!"

Amanda sighed with relief.

"Where's Daddy?"

"He and Randall rode out to round up some of the horses. I've got a buyer coming for them this afternoon. Should we wait for him?"

"No. Maybe it would be better if we told you and you talked to him." For all her complaining about it, Leisha was suddenly able to see the value of her mother's control over her father. Running it through Amanda was an automatic defuser.

What she didn't understand was that it wasn't the words she spoke but rather the way she and Kenitay acted in each other's behalf that sold Amanda. She listened intently and observed the soundless signals passed between the two young people: Leisha's gaze canted up to his in a meaningful slide; he'd touch his fingertips to the back of her arm or lightly ease them along her shoulder. Those were the little things that made her assure them of her support.

Her husband may have been the famous tracker but she knew how to read the signs of two people in love.

And she was happily working on a plan of her own when Harm came up behind her in the kitchen to take her in the curl of his arm and press a warm kiss to the side of her neck. She allowed herself a moment to savor the sensual enjoyment his nearness always created—the pleasure of his touch and the excitement of bringing something so wild and dangerous to heel. She reached back to hold his dark head, letting her body relax invitingly against him. She felt his surprise; he was very good at interpreting signals, too, and she smiled as he reached back with his foot to toe the door closed.

She revolved within his embrace, meeting his kiss with open-mouthed encouragement, moaning when his hands came up to wrap themselves in her hair, pulling it free of the coil she'd woven it into. He was rough and she responded with an eager passion until they were both panting and more riled than the time or place would warrant.

"Is this leading somewhere?" he murmured into her hurried kisses.

"Oh, Harmon, I hope so," she groaned as his face pressed into the scented valley of her breasts. Her eyes slid shut and for a moment she forgot herself in a daze of bliss.

"You'd best be deciding if you're gonna make lunch or make love 'cause I'm getting mighty hungry."

She grabbed for breath and remembered her purpose. "Harmon, I need to talk to you for a minute."

He straightened slowly, his gaze cool and cautious. "Is that what this is about? You wanting something?"

She gave him a sly smile as her palms moved up and down his chest. "You know what this is about, Harmon Bass, and it has nothing to do with anything other than the fact that I'd take you down to the floor right here and now if we didn't have a houseful of kids."

His gaze grew all smoky. "When are those kids gonna move out, anyway? Seems like we been tripping over family since the day we met."

"If you recall, we made most of this particular family."

"I been gone awhile and I find myself forgetting just how we accomplished that. Care to remind me?"

"Right here on the floor?" Her smile was sassy and sultry.

"It would serve you right." He caught her wrist and gave a tug. "Come upstairs with me."

"What about lunch?" It was a halfhearted protest.

"We raised a resourceful batch of kids. They won't starve. But I might." He tugged harder and she came up against the hardness of him. "Can we have this talk horizontally?"

"I love talking to you, Harmon. You've got such a way with words."

"It's my poetic soul."

And a half-hour later, when they'd exhausted all the aspects of their non-verbal conversation and Amanda was cozied up in the curl of his arm, Harm murmured, "You was saying?"

"What?" Her eyes were warm and dreamy.

"You had something on your mind downstairs."

Her smile spread lazily. "Yes, I did and you didn't disappoint me."

He grinned, then chided, "Ammy, that's not what I meant."

"Oh, you didn't mean it? Felt like you meant it to me."

He rolled his eyes. "You make me crazy. Talk."

"You've got to promise you won't get all blustery."

"I never do!"

"Promise, Harmon."

"Humph." He closed his eyes in feigned insult.

"What would you think of Kenitay as a son-in-law?" Amanda waited for the explosion.

"Nice choice," was all Harm would say.

"What?"

"We're talking Leisha, not Becca, right?"

"Right."

"Then I've got no problems with it."

"Well," Amanda ventured, "there might be a problem."

Harm waited for her to go on, then finally opened his eyes. "How big a problem?"

"Big."

"And what's the nature of this big problem? Got something to do with the mess someone made out of his face?"

She drew complex patterns on his bare chest with her fingertip. "It seems Kenitay's got himself into a little trouble with the law."

"Mind being a bit more specific, Ammy?"

"Well, I don't know all the specifics, exactly. Leisha wants to take him to see Sid in Austin for some help."

"What kind of help can't they get here, from us?"

"Harmon, you and Jack and Billy might know the law but Sid knows how to get around it. That's what lawyers are for."

"Funny, I thought they were supposed to uphold the law."

"Well, that, too."

"Back to this little trouble."

"She wants to get Sid's advice on how to get around it legally."

"Is it something that can be fixed?"

"That's the impression I got."

He mulled that over for a moment and Amanda waited, not knowing which way he was going to go with it. "Did you actually hear the word *marriage* mentioned or were wedding bells just ringing up here?" He tapped her temple.

"They're in love with each other, Harmon. One naturally follows the other."

"Not necessarily."

"It will in this case. It did with us."

"Well, you were kinda rabid on the subject as I recall."

"Me?"

"Ammy, you chased me all over Texas."

"You were the one on your knees!"

He blushed at the remembrance and grumbled, "I think we're getting off track here. This ain't about us. Them two don't look to be the marrying kind. I can't see them settling down to throw a batch of kids anytime soon."

"Well, they'd better start thinking in that direction."

Harm came up on his elbow about to bluster. "Something you're not telling me, Amanda?"

She was quick to soothe his ruffled paternal instincts. "No, not that I know of. I'm just saying all the signs are there and you know how one thing leads to— Well, let's just say, I'd rather they went about things in the right order."

"Like us?" Harm drawled.

She jabbed him in the ribs.

"So, you want me to get out my carbine and ask him what his intentions are toward my little girl?"

"Harmon, don't you dare!"

"Worked with Billy and Sarah."

She had to admit that was true. "But Sarah was ready and Billy needed to be convinced. Leisha and Kenitay are another matter. I think a trip to Austin together could have them looking at each other in a whole different light."

"Think I ought to ride along?"

"That's the last thing I'm thinking!"

He looked thoughtful for a moment, then his hand eased around the curve of one plump breast. "That'd be one down and two to go. Then we can roll around on the kitchen floor any time we want to."

"So things are all right with you, then?" There was no disguising the relief in Amanda's voice. Or the way she was arching into the cup of his palm.

"As far as things go, yes. But something tells me there's a lot more they're not saying." He was quiet and moody all of a sudden and Amanda was worried.

"You're going to say no then?"

"Don't see it would do much good if I did. Damn stubborn girl. Must get that from you. No, I think we should let them go. He'll take care of her and she'll watch his back. I trust them to see to each other. I just don't trust what they're not saying, is all."

There was a bang on their bedroom door.

"Mama, we gonna get lunch anytime soon?"

"Randall Bass, you know where the kitchen is!"

"Yeah, I know. Seems like you forgot, though." Then they heard the clump of his boots on the stairs.

Amanda smiled grimly. "That's gonna be the hard one to get rid of. No woman in her right mind would put up with that kind of male guff."

Harm grinned. "You did."

It was a tense meal with Harm purposely not responding to covert looks from his daughter. Leisha's anxious gaze darted from his lowered head to her mother's reassuring smile and she was left to guess what had transpired between them. They'd held their discussion upstairs. That was always a good sign. Harm hadn't shot Kenitay yet. That was another.

Finally, saying only that he was taking a string of horses into town to sell, Harm pushed back from the table, bent to kiss his wife, and was gone with little more than a nod to the rest of them.

"Well?" Leisha demanded of her mother. "What did he say?"

"If you're going to Austin, we're going to have to do something about the way you look."

Leisha was immediately suspicious. "I suppose you're talking *dress*."

"I'm talking several changes if you want to fit in unnoticed in Austin. It's a city of some sophistication. You can't go in looking like a savage off the plains, even if this is Texas." Since Kenitay looked more receptive, she started with him. "Let's get you looking more like a Ken Bass."

A while later, he wasn't looking at all pleased. Nor was he looking like Kenitay, son of Kodene. He was sitting in a chair in the Basses' kitchen with a towel draped around his neck and a pile of black hair feathered upon the floor around his feet. He put a hand to his newly shorn head, feeling a stir of alarm as his fingers slid through the short locks. It was bad luck to cut one's hair except at the death of a family member. His own had been growing since he'd been old enough to shun the mission schools. He felt unsettled and unmanned, as if he were sitting there naked for Amanda's close inspection.

"These will have to go, too."

He flinched when Amanda reached for his earrings. They were turquoise and white shell beads given to him by his people's shaman when his ears had been pierced as a child so that he might listen better and learn well. In his mind, they were protective amulets, just the thing needed to combat the bad omen of cutting his hair.

"No."

Amanda withdrew the gesture. She was familiar with the tone of that growly voice. When Harm used it, it meant *no.* "I guess we can leave them for now. But they won't match a dinner coat."

About that time, they heard Leisha and Becca coming downstairs. They paused in the dining room. Becca was goading her sister on.

"Go on. You look fine."

"I look ridiculous."

"Show them."

"No." There was that same growly tone.

Becca sighed with aggravation. "Mama, could you come here a minute? We need your opinion on something."

Amanda stepped into the room and was stunned by the change in her daughter. She was used to seeing the feminine side in Becca. The same look on Leisha was an intriguing mix of bronzed skin and hard eyes surrounded by layers of softness. When she glanced up at Kenitay, who'd come to stand at her shoulder, Amanda saw the same glaze of helplessness and appreciation in his eyes that she'd seen in Harm's on the day he'd first told her he loved her.

Becca had worked wonders in at least outwardly civilizing her sister. Leisha's heavy blond hair had been loosely drawn up over her ears and draped over a rounded frame at the back of her head to give an illusion of fullness where it was tucked into a bun. The slender grace of her throat was hugged by the high-standing collar of the mauve and silver taffeta day dress Becca had lent her. Huge puffed sleeves gathered at the elbow and buttoned snugly from there to her wrists, where the skirt fell straight in front and was drawn in precise pleating in the back.

Kenitay was struck dumb. He'd never seen anything so lovely. It was Leisha, but then again, it wasn't. The challenge in her eyes was the same but there was no similarity in the rest of her subtly female form. Until his gaze ran the full distance from stylishly coiffed hair to the gentle bell of her skirt. The curled-up toes of her Apache moccasins peeped incongruously from beneath the sweeping hem. That made him smile.

"You wouldn't smirk if you could see how *you* look," Leisha snapped.

His hand rose self-consciously to his nearly bare head.

Amanda shook her head. "Child, you've a lot to learn about accepting compliments from a man."

"He wasn't complimenting me, Mama. He was laughing at me," she grumbled in her own defense.

"If you can't tell the difference, we've got more work ahead of us than I anticipated."

Leisha stared at her blankly. What more could there possibly be to this humiliating process? She gritted her teeth as her mother started down a horrifying list.

"First, there's learning how to walk; then, what to say when introduced, how to flirt—in a refined manner, of course—how to dance."

Kenitay was looking for a place to slide through the floorboards.

"Well, I'll be," Randall Bass exclaimed from the hall.

He glanced behind him, then back at the four of them in the parlor. "Am I in the right house?"

A low growl rumbled in Leisha's throat as her brother sauntered in to give her a thorough up-and-down examination.

"Why, if you ain't as pretty as a picture postcard."

"Randall," his mother chastened gently. "You aren't helping matters."

Rand took a step closer and reached out to fluff the fullness of her skirt. "Where you hiding your carbine?"

"If I weren't a lady, I'd show you," his sister drawled with a lethal sweetness.

He grinned. "Didn't know you was a lady, Sis."

Amanda stepped neatly between the two of them, averting bloodshed in her formal room. "Randall, you know how to dance, don't you?"

"Sure, Mama."

"Jessie Cooper taught him last Fourth of July," Becca volunteered.

"That's not all she taught him," Leisha muttered, earning her brother's dark scowl.

"How would you know? You were busy learning how to drink whiskey outta the bottle behind the barn with Jed."

Ignoring that, Amanda said, "Let's see if you learned anything of value, Randall. You can help me teach your sister how to dance."

"Becca already knows how t—" Then his eyes went round and he stared at Leisha. He laughed. "Mama, ain't nobody that good a teacher."

If she'd been reluctant before, now Leisha was positively adamant. "I don't need to learn how to dance."

"Yes, you do, if you're going to blend in when you get to Austin," Amanda insisted. "Sid may want to introduce you to some influential people and you'd better know how to handle yourself in something other than a knife fight."

With that firm statement, she strode to her fancy phonograph and gave it a furious cranking. "Randall, you and Becca take a few turns to show her how it's done."

When the scratchy melody started up, Rand bowed elegantly and Becca responded with a pretty curtsy. They waltzed together about the parlor while Leisha and Kenitay watched with obvious misgivings.

"See? Very easy. The man leads, the woman follows."

Leisha made a disgruntled noise.

"Now, you try it."

Leisha was naturally graceful but with the unfamiliar weight of fabric dragging around her legs and her brother's pushing and pulling, she found herself stumbling awkwardly all over his feet.

"Mama, she won't let me lead."

"Because I can't see where you're going!"

"Leisha," their mother admonished. "You have to trust your brother."

"It's like trying to wrangle a mule," Rand grumbled, wiggling his abused toes.

"Here," Becca offered, stepping in behind her sister and placing her hands over Leisha's. "Try again."

When Rand moved, Becca responded, guiding Leisha in between them.

"Wonderful," Amanda praised. "That's it. Feel the rhythm of the music." She canted a glance at Kenitay, who was very still and trying to be unobtrusive. She caught his arm. "Now, you try."

He looked as though she'd suggested that he shoot himself.

Rand stepped back and Leisha stood there waiting, her features hot with discomfort, her empty arms an unwitting enticement. Kenitay paused long enough to shove the metal bracelets farther up on his forearms under his sleeves. He took a breath and went to stand in Rand's stead. Becca placed Leisha's hand into one of his and put his other on her trim waist before guiding Leisha's other to his shoulder. They stood toe-to-toe, looking grim as Amanda started the music up again.

After a few disastrous turns, it was obvious Kenitay couldn't lead and Leisha wouldn't follow.

"Oh, hell," Rand grumbled, stepping up to shadow Kenitay. "Like this, you big buffalo."

Kenitay started to turn in insult but Becca had a hold of him. She began to count out loud. "One-two-three. Lead off on the right. Come on. Don't look at your feet. Look at your partner."

Rand kicked the back of his ankle to get him moving on the right foot then banged his knees into the backs of Kenitay's with each step to push him forward.

"Ain't this fun," the youngest Bass taunted. " 'Course, it makes a big difference when it's not your sisters. Hike her in close there, Kenny. She's not contagious." And he bumped the stiff Apache forward until he and Leisha were brushing one another.

Then something miraculous happened.

Leisha's gaze rose, so deep and blue. And Kenitay stopped thinking about his feet and about the ridiculousness of moving about the Basses' parlor in a clumsy foursome. He heard the tempo of the music and matched it to Rand's movements. Leisha followed, light and effortless in his arms.

Smiling, Becca let go and faded back, letting her sister continue unaided. Kenitay wasn't quite sure when Rand was no longer guiding his steps—he was following something else altogether.

Then the music stopped and they stopped, lost in one another's gaze, each reluctant to surrender the other until Amanda said, "Well done. You move together quite naturally."

They were thinking about another kind of dance, one that was primal and not fit for the parlor.

"Shall we try it again?"

*Oh, yes,* thought Leisha.

*Soon,* was the smoky agreement in Kenitay's gaze.

And then the mood was broken by the sound of company coming.

All glanced to the doorway to see a stunned Harmon and a smiling Emily.

And behind them was Jack.

# *Sixteen*

Kenitay and Leisha stepped away from one another, seeing their ruination in the set of Jack Bass's features. He was grim-faced and pale, his arm in a homemade sling. For a moment, everything was still as one question hung in desperate balance.

What had Jack told them?

Then Emily broke the silence. She crossed the room in a flutter of concern, her work-worn hands coming up to cradle her son's battered face. She didn't waste words.

"Are you all right?"

His hands came up to lay big and warm over hers. "I'm fine, Mama."

"Harmon said you were in some kind of trouble and that you were going to Austin to see Sidney. I brought you some of Jack's things to wear. You're about the same size. And some money for the train ticket. I didn't know if you had any."

He had to look away. Love for her rose large enough to choke him. "Thank you, Mama," he murmured in a raspy voice. Then he looked cautiously to Jack, who was stoic enough to do his Apache uncle proud.

"Jack, what happened to you?" Amanda wanted to know. Beside her, Leisha caught her breath.

Jack glanced down at the sling and said with a casual drawl, "Ran into a little unexpected trouble. Got caught with my guard down. Nothing that a few stitches couldn't take care of." Then he looked at Leisha and she fought not to cringe beneath his straight-on stare. *Now,* she thought in dreadful anticipation. Now he would tell them all of her part in it, that she'd been ready to blow a hole in him while helping a fugitive escape justice.

But Jack was finished talking. When he looked away from her, Leisha realized he wasn't going to tell anyone what had happened on the trail.

At least, not now.

"Well, if we're going to have company for supper, I'd better be getting something started," Amanda stated.

"I'll give you a hand," Emily offered, earning Harm and Rand's silent word of thanks. The difference in culinary talent between Amanda and Emily was wrestling with hard tack compared to feasting on the gourmet.

Kenitay retained his mother's hand for a moment longer, pressing a soft kiss to her palm. "I love you, Mama," he told her in a low voice. "I'm sorry for what I said before."

She came up to kiss his cheek, unspoken forgiveness welling up in her green eyes before she followed Amanda into the kitchen.

Feeling conspicuous, Leisha took the opportunity to mutter that she needed to change her clothes. As she hurried for the hall, her father caught her up with an arm about her waist.

"You look beautiful, *shijii.*" Then his tender gaze grew teasing. "Where are you hiding your carbine?"

She pushed away with a scowl and ran straight into Jack. She stared up at him, unable to think of what to say. What could she say to someone she'd held a gun on, someone who was family and well loved and respected, whom she'd been measuring as to where to best place a bullet?

Jack gave her no chance to come up with anything. He stepped back, giving her plenty of room to pass. As if she was someone he didn't want to get too close to. As if she was someone he couldn't trust.

She rushed up the stairs as fast as she could with both her skirt and her heart dragging.

Jack turned his attention back to Kenitay and the two of them exchanged a long look.

"We need to talk," Jack said at last.

Kenitay nodded.

"Come on outside."

Kenitay went with him unquestioningly until their silent walk led them down toward the barn. "Where are we going?" Was Jack taking him in to the Terlingua jail?

"Thought you might like to get rid of your jewelry." Jack slipped his finger under Kenitay's cuff, tugging on his wrist shackle. He made no further comment so Kenitay remained silent as well.

The barn held the warm, familiar scents of grain and animals. Bound like one of them, Kenitay followed his stepfather back to the tack room where he searched for and found a chisel and hammer.

"Bare those bracelets."

Kenitay did so, stretching his forearm out atop one of the feed barrels, bracing it while Jack fit the chisel and began to pound on the clasp, using his good arm. The metal wasn't as strong as Jack's determination and after several good swings, it snapped apart. Kenitay offered up the other one. As Jack hammered, Kenitay watched him, drowning in his sense of shame and longing.

"I didn't mean to involve any of you."

Jack didn't look up. "You wearing leg irons, too?"

Kenitay rubbed his freed wrists, then brought one of his feet up onto the barrel. He'd tucked the piece of broken chain down into his boot to keep the iron cuff out of sight. Jack started beating on the metal with hard, fierce swings. Working out his anger.

"What are you planning to do?" Kenitay asked quietly.

"I don't know. Depends on what you're planning to do. Harmon said you were going to Austin for legal help. That true?"

"It was Leisha's idea."

"She's full of ideas lately. Quick-thinking girl. Just like her daddy. Too bad she didn't inherit Harmon's sense of honor."

"That's not true."

Kenitay's defensive growl brought Jack's gaze up in a curious study. "Well, I can't say I like having one of the family so willing to shoot me down. Makes me ornery."

"She was doing it for me."

He gave Kenitay another penetrating look. "I take it Harm doesn't know what you're wanted for?"

He ducked his head. "No."

"He's not going to like you leading his daughter into trouble."

"Nobody has to lead Leisha into trouble. She just jumps right into it on her own. I didn't ask for her help."

"You didn't ask for mine, either." The leg iron broke apart and Jack cast it to the floor. "Other one."

Kenitay balanced himself and waited for Jack to start swinging. The need to say something in his own defense rose sudden and strong. He wanted Jack to understand, even if he couldn't accept. "That soldier at the fort—I hit him and he went down. He must have hit his head. I never meant him any serious harm. I was just trying to get away." The explanation was issued in a hush of regret.

Jack glanced up, his expression still somber.

"It was run or hang. I didn't have any other choice. No one there was going to listen to me. I was running for my life anyway."

"What do you mean, running for your life?"

Kenitay looked long and hard into the pale-eyed Texan's gaze, trying to decide how much to tell him. "The men who did this to my face—it wasn't the first time they were heavy-handed with me. They're the ones who killed my father."

"What are their names?" There was a quiet chill in Jack's voice.

Kenitay didn't answer him directly. "That's why I have to go to Austin. I need them to tell their part in it. I need to make them pay for killing my father. Let me do that and I'll come back here and turn myself in to you."

Jack stared at him, trying to read what was in his soul.

"You don't trust me, do you? You think I'm going to run far and fast the minute you turn me loose. Does my word mean anything?"

"You're asking me to go against everything I promised to stand for when I took an oath to the State of Texas."

Kenitay hid his disappointment behind an impenetrable mask. Thirteen years had put too wide a gap between them, no matter how much their hearts might want to close the distance. He couldn't blame Jack. "I knew it was too much to ask." His gaze dipped covertly to the gun on Jack's hip. He could have it in his hand in an instant, snag a horse and be gone. A good Apache knew it was best to pick one's battleground. Running was sometimes the best choice. Then, like Jack had said, he'd never be able to stop. He'd have no home to come to.

Unbidden came the memory of a young Texas Ranger surrendering himself to the Apache lance that almost killed him so that a half-breed boy could be returned to his mother. He remembered his first meeting with the men of Jack's Ranger unit and the way one of them had asked who the Apache brat belonged to. And the way Jack held him tight and proud and claimed him as his own.

And then came the image of Leisha looking up into his eyes, her beauty dazzling him with the promise of future passion. But what kind of future could he give her? All he had ahead of him was a debt to be paid at the price of his own freedom. There was no way around it. No way

to be a part of this family again. Knowing that caused a
surge of melancholy to smother all hope of his own hap-
piness. The die was cast and he could but follow. He
couldn't ask Jack to compromise his honor or Leisha to
risk her heart unwisely. Not on him. Because there was
no chance of a return.

Jack startled him by fitting his palm to a bruised brown
cheek. Kenitay met his somber stare almost in a panic.
Seeing his confusion, Jack spoke softly.

"I look at you and I see your mama. You've got her
courage and heart. I see your daddy, too. We were about
as far from seeing things square as two men can get, but
I respected him and I knew him as a man of his word. I
told him I'd see you raised as I'd raise my own and I
gave a scared little boy my word that he could trust me
to be fair and to love him. I've never thought of you as
anything but a son. What kind of man would I be if I
didn't take your word now?"

Kenitay tried to speak but words failed him.

"You go on and get done what needs doing. If you
need any help, you ask for it. And you come home to
your mama and me."


Jack and Emily left right after the evening meal. Emily
clung tight to her son until her husband had to nudge her
gently and tell her it was time to go. She stood on the
shadow-darkened porch with Kenitay's face framed by her
hands, studying him so intently it was as if she was en-
graving the sight upon her heart. And he returned the look
just as intensely. She said his name and it was as soothing
and gentle as a mother's caress and she followed it with
the command that he take care. He promised he would
and he told her again that he loved her.

For Jack, there was a firm handshake and a meaningful
non-verbal exchange.

Then Kenitay watched them go, not knowing if he would ever see them again. And he wondered if he would ever get over the ache of losing them a second time as he turned from family to the hard path he had to travel.

The moon was full overhead, casting Jack's profile in soft, silvery lines. Emily had been watching him for some time in silence—then she could stand the suspense no longer.

"Jack, what's wrong?"

"What makes you think—"

"Jack."

He sighed heavily, wondering why he'd tried to hide it. He'd never been able to hide anything from her. "Em, it's more than a little trouble. He's wanted by the government."

He heard her quiet gasp. "For what?"

"For murder, Em. I'm sorry."

She uttered a fearful oath and clutched at his arm. "Why didn't you say something?"

"I'm saying it now."

"When did you find all this out?"

"That night Billy stopped over. He'd come across a poster on him. Em, I don't know what to do. I love that boy. I love you. If doing my job means hurting my family, I'm thinking maybe it's time to turn in my star."

She was silent for a moment. She knew what Jack's work meant to him. And she knew his fierce devotion to his family. It wasn't easy to advise him so she didn't. "Did Kenitay ask you to turn your back on your duty?"

"He asked me to trust him. He's got business to take care of, then he promised to turn himself in to me to see he gets treated squarely. Emily, he's half Apache. He killed an army officer. The circumstances aren't going to matter much. He won't be treated fairly any place I take him."

Emily shut her eyes tight. She'd asked next to nothing from him in all the years they'd been married. His love and protection had always been enough. Until now. "Jack, don't let them hang him."

"I'm thinking that money we've been setting aside could get him to California."

Emily was trembling with relief and leaned into the curl of his arm. "I love you, Jack."

He replied in kind but his heart was hollow. True, they wouldn't be turning Kenitay over to be hanged but they were losing him just the same. And the cost of his continued freedom was the honor Jack set such store in.

But if Kenitay kept his word and returned, that pride was a small price to pay.

Weary in body and spirit, Leisha took a long, hot bath and aspired to nothing beyond a good twelve hours of undisturbed sleep. She turned into her bedroom, still toweldrying her hair, and stopped on the threshold, surprised to see her brother seated on the foot of her bed. She could never remember a time when he'd trespassed into her private space and was both curious and cautious.

"Rand. Did you want something?"

He looked up and there was something she couldn't recognize churning behind his familiar features. He regarded her with an uneasy glance, his eyes quickly shifting elsewhere in a nervous survey of her austere room.

"I was wondering how things went with Daddy," he asked at last.

"Fine."

His gaze came up again, still uncomfortable but lingering longer with purpose. "And how are things with you?"

"Why all the sudden concern with my business?"

He didn't reply right away, then came up off the bed

in hurried agitation, blurting out, "You're right. It's none of mine."

Something in his manner made her reach out to place her hand upon his chest, stopping him from passing her by. She could feel his rapid respiration beneath the press of her palm.

"Are you all right?"

He wouldn't look at her. "Sure. Why wouldn't I be?"

Why wasn't he?

Then, suddenly, she figured it out.

"Daddy said you killed one of those men."

"Yeah, I did," he claimed as if it was no big deal. But she felt the shock of horror shiver through him telling her it was. "Blew his face clean off." He studied the toes of his boots, blinking hard. "Then I went and chucked my breakfast right in front of Daddy. You would have gotten a good laugh out of it."

"No, I wouldn't have."

Her tone was so uncommonly gentle, he flickered a look up at her. His eyes shimmered, all quicksilver. "I thought—oh, never mind."

Her hand rose to cup the back of his head. "You thought what?"

"I thought I'd feel good about it. You know. I wanted to feel good about it. He didn't deserve no mercy from me, not after— But I feel so bad inside. I can't close my eyes—"

Leisha drew him into a loose embrace, awash with empathic misery. "I know." Sometimes she forgot he was only eighteen, still an idealistic boy. And this was the kind of thing that would shape the kind of man he became. They hadn't been close as brother and sister. She'd spent most of her years wishing he'd fall off the face of West Texas. But he was her brother and sharing his pain kindled a fierce tenderness inside her that could only be love. And she wished she could take his hurt away.

He rested his head upon her shoulder, embarrassed by

the tears he couldn't seem to stop. "I let Daddy down. And I let you down. I'm sorry. You should have been his son. I'm not as tough as you are or as hard as he expects me to be."

She took no pleasure in his confession. She wasn't so tough. And she knew exactly how he was feeling. She didn't know how to ease his pain. She couldn't even take care of her own.

"I'd like to tell you it gets easier to live with but I don't know that it does. All I can say is that I'm proud of you."

He laughed hoarsely. "Sure you are. Me blubbering all over you like a baby." He leaned away, eyes averted while he wiped them on his sleeve.

Leisha angled his chin with her hand so that he met her sober gaze. "You took a stand for my honor and I will never forget that."

He stared back, wordlessly, for a long moment. Then he said, "I'd do it again."

And he would. Despite the awful aftermath, he would do the same thing all over again. Seeing that in his eyes, Leisha leaned forward to brush the lightest of kisses against his temple.

"I don't really hate you, you know."

He mustered up a reasonable reproduction of his cocky smile. "I know. But thanks for telling me."

"*Tough* is getting the job done whether you like it or not," she told him. "*Hard* is living with it afterward. I guess that makes us both pretty tough and hard."

"Guess it does."

"Now, get out of here. Close your eyes and sleep well."

"Maybe." Maybe now he could.


Kenitay couldn't sleep.

The big frame house was quiet around him with only the

tug of the dry Texas breeze at his window curtains to echo his restlessness. His soul was all stirred up with conflicting loyalties. There were no solutions to the ache of unrealized longing in his heart. He couldn't stay and yet, once he left, he knew he couldn't return. His path was one of retribution, not self-fulfillment. He would gain nothing except the gratification of revenge. It had been easy to promise Jack that he'd surrender himself when all was done. There wasn't a whisper of belief in heart or mind that he would survive what he planned. He was already as good as dead, a ghost out to avenge a spiritless people. He'd accepted that when he claimed the right of vengeance as a son. He'd lived so long without hope, the future held no sense of expectation or reward.

Until Leisha.

That was the hell of it. With little trouble, he could imagine himself wed to her, filling her with his children, surrounded by the close-knit Bass clan for a safe and satisfying forever. He could imagine it but he couldn't have it. Not if he walked the path honor demanded. Not with the soul of the man he'd killed in Oklahoma damning his days and limiting his tomorrows. Consequence was going to catch him. *When* was the only variable. He hadn't asked for help because there was no help to be had. He was walking in a doomed man's shoes and no matter how uncomfortable the fit, he was committed to the journey.

It did no good to stay and dream of what could never be. He'd never be a Bass. He was the son of Kodene, once-proud Apache warrior and now, restless spirit. To pretend beyond that was no good for him or any of those around him. To linger would mean more pain to those he loved and would only make the parting harder. He couldn't stay within these walls acting out a lie. He wasn't going to Austin to clear his name. And he wasn't coming back.

He was going to kill the two men who dishonored his father's soul.

He would travel light and quick with nothing but his purpose fixed in his mind. And when they were both dead, nothing else mattered. It was a path he'd walk alone to its necessarily brutal end. There was no future for him beyond the completion of his task. He had no fancy plan in mind beyond using his passable white looks to get him close enough to exact the fatal deed. He spent no time considering a route of escape or a way to cover his tracks. There was no reason to.

Taking only the roll of clothing and the money for the train ticket his mother brought him, Kenitay slipped out into the hall and started toward the stairs. He knew he had to keep going, but his footsteps slowed and finally stopped outside Leisha's door. It was madness, what he was thinking. It was futile, what he was wishing. But he couldn't resist one last chance to soak up the sight of her—his glorious warrior love.

She was stretched out on her stomach beneath the drape of a single sheet. Her blond hair was loose, covering her pillow in a silken cascade of gold. Sleek shoulders and the long, supple line of her back were bared to his view. She was naked.

Again, it was madness that drew him to her bedside and had him sinking down upon it. His fingertips drew a sensuous line down the curve of her spine as he bent to whisper her name.

She came awake with a wildcat's instincts. With one lethal move, she'd rolled to face him and whipped her blade up flush to his throat. Why was he surprised that she slept with it under her pillow in her own home? He didn't move, waiting for her violent reaction to ebb as recognition sank in.

"What are you—" she began in a surly growl. He swallowed up the rest of it with the crush of his mouth over hers. He heard the clank of her knife hitting the floor and then her fingers speared up into his fresh-cut hair. He was very aware that she was unclothed except for the tangle of the sheet about her hips. She seemed to forget that as she tugged him down over her, matching his kisses with a breathless urgency.

"I shouldn't be here," he moaned against her yielding lips.

"Don't go," she panted in reply.

"Leisha—"

"Make love to me." She had his hands and was fitting them to her yearning breasts.

"No ties."

"No strings." Then she groaned softly in delight as he buffed her pebble-hard nipples with his mouth and began a vigorous suction. She strained up against him, her body shuddering in anticipation. "Love me." It was a plea.

"I love you." It was a pledge.

They were distracted during the time it took to rid him of his clothing, then he was sliding over her, a thrilling friction of flesh on flesh. She wanted him. She'd said so. Yet when he used his palms to push her thighs apart, he could feel the tension gathering along the slim length of her legs. She was still responding wildly to his kisses yet this lower part of her was bracing as if preparing for an assault.

She was still afraid. Not of him but of this. Tenderness played in torment against his need and in the end, his love for her won out. He coaxed her with long, lavish kisses, keeping his weight suspended upon his forearms even though the effort cost his healing ribs dearly. He didn't want her to feel trapped beneath his weight. He couldn't bear to think of her as vulnerable and in pain. Again, he told her he loved her and this time, she seemed to believe him, for her legs parted sweetly and the pressure of her palms upon his hips urged him down into that hot, inviting valley where pleasure pulsed when flesh joined flesh. He eased in slowly and when he could go no farther, she whispered his name. He wondered if she knew how that quiet cry conquered the last of his reserves.

He began to move, a slow plunging that had him on the ragged edge of control. Her hands stroked over him in restless abandon, alternately hugging, kneading, clawing at him until she was writhing, moaning softly. Remembering where they were, he covered her mouth with his to quiet her cries, tasting her pleasure in each anxious breath, savoring her satisfaction in each shivery little sigh, drinking down her ecstasy as it burst through her.

And then his own completion was upon him, shattering all thoughts of gentleness or restraint. He lunged against her, then relaxed into the wonderful weightlessness that followed.

She held him atop her without complaint while he recovered his senses. Her hands were still, one on the small of his back, one on the back of his head, holding him tight against her. It was one of the few moments of complete bliss he could ever remember.

And probably the last he would ever have.

Leisha never wanted the moment to end. Hers was a delicious sense of surrender and strength all in one. What she had with Kenitay was power—power over fear, power over doubt. The power of love. He'd said he loved her and though she'd yet to say the same out loud, her heart was murmuring it in every lazy beat. She loved everything about him: his fierce pride, his darkly handsome looks, the hard perfection of his body, the tenderness of his touch. She couldn't have found a man to suit her better but having found him, she wasn't sure what she should do with him. Clandestine passion was fabulous but fleeting. She wasn't sure what she wanted beyond that. She didn't know if there was anything more he could give.

She didn't fool herself. He was a man of secrets, a man on a mission. He'd given her no assurances of a future, no reason to think they'd be sharing one together. No strings.

No ties. Did that mean no tomorrows? She didn't want it to mean that. Holding him close, feeling his weight, enveloped by his love, she didn't want to give him up.

And she was still holding him tight as dreamy thoughts of the future became peaceful slumber.


It was still dark when Leisha woke from a particularly titillating dream. With a smile she stretched her body, arching along the empty sheets.

Empty sheets.

Her eyes flashed open, then quickly glanced around the room. She was alone. Kenitay had left her, probably to return to his own bed. They were under her parents' roof, after all.

She lay musing in wondrous lassitude when she became aware of other sounds. Sounds from outside. Sounds of someone riding out in a hurry.

Leisha came up off her bed in a panic, snatching up her trousers and wiggling into her shirt. She padded on bared feet down the hall, then cautiously opened Kenitay's door.

The room was empty, his bed not slept in, his belongings gone.

And as she stood staring at the vacant space, its meaning became clear.

Kenitay had left without her.

# Seventeen

Leisha had a deeper, darker curse for each succeeding step leading down to the first story of her parents' home. She stomped across the parquet floor, shoving cartridges into her gun, imagining where on Kenitay's treacherous form she was going to place each one. By the time she'd reached the front door, she'd pretty much limited the target area to just below his belt.

She was about to step outside when she was distracted by a soft sound from the back of the house. It was a low, moaning cry, steeped in pain and anguish. After casting a hesitant glance out into the night, she was drawn back toward the kitchen where the lamentations seemed to originate.

There was no light on and Leisha paused for a long moment, trying to get her bearings. She waited in silence until the noises started up again—soft, snuffling sounds like a child in terrible pain. Coming from under the table?

She bent down to peer into that small, dark space, seeing denimed knees updrawn and a dark head bowed between them.

"Randall?"

She reached out a tentative hand, touching his bare back. Instead of smooth skin, she could feel the hard ridges of massive scarring.

"Daddy?"

He lifted his head. Pale moonlight glimmered in the

trails of dampness marking his cheeks but she could see nothing of his expression.

"Are you all right?"

"Have to get out," he panted in a low, panicky voice. "Can't find my way out."

"Out where? Daddy, you're not making sense. What's wrong?"

"Can't breathe in here. Can't get out."

"You want to go outside? Here, take my hands." When hers brushed lightly over the backs of his, he seized them in a grip that was damp-palmed and desperate. "Come on, Daddy. It's all right. Just follow me."

She eased back and he scooched out from under the table like something wild and wary. His hold on her was hurtful. The soft sob of his breathing was upsetting. She knew he was prone to violent nightmares. She could remember his horrible cries making her cower in her bed when she was little. But that was a long time ago. And her mother was always there to calmly assure her that everything was fine. Everything was far from fine now.

"Let me go get Mama," she soothed, trying to slip her hands free of his. He hung on tighter, grinding bone and making her wince.

"Mama's dead," he whimpered forlornly. Leisha felt a chill drip down her spine. "They killed her. Don't put me in with her. It's dark in there and I can't see. I can't keep her warm."

My God, what was he talking about?

"Daddy, Mama's upstairs. I'll get her for you."

His hands clutched fiercely. "No, don't leave me. Don't leave me." His breathing was fast and hoarse and impossibly agitated.

"I won't leave you. What can I do?"

"Where am I?"

"In the kitchen."

"I don't know this place. I don't know you."

"Daddy, it's Leisha!"

"Where's Becky? I need to find Becky."

Leisha went very still, tears welling up in her eyes. "Aunt Becky died almost fourteen years ago. Don't you remember?"

He gave an agonized cry. "They killed her? No! Becky?" He staggered up to his feet, reeling drunkenly, banging against the table, fending off Leisha's supporting hands. "Becky, don't leave me! Don't leave me here!"

Lamplight flooded in, warm and radiant, from the hall. They both turned toward it. Amanda stood on the threshold in her silk wrapper. She didn't look shocked or the least bit distressed as she came across the room.

"Harmon, it's all right."

"Ammy?" He reached out for her and she stepped in to fill his anxious arms. He hugged her close, weeping awfully. "Ammy, they killed my mama."

"I know. I know, Harmon."

"And Becky. Becky, too."

"Shhh."

"I wasn't there to save them. I wasn't there. They won't forgive me. They'll never forgive me! I wasn't there when they needed me."

"That's not true. You know it's not true," Amanda crooned gently, rocking him the way she'd rocked Rand when he was little.

"I don't know where I am. I couldn't find my way out."

"You're safe. The door's right there. See it? I'm here now. I won't leave you."

There was no sound but his soft sobbing. Leisha stood apart from them, frightened and dismayed. And marveling at her mother for her tremendous calm.

"Ammy?"

"What is it, Harmon?" she murmured as she stroked his damp hair.

"I can't go back. Don't let me go back."

"I won't."

"I don't want to see those things anymore. I don't want to hear them or see them. Make it stop. Ammy, make it stop."

"I wish I could."

"Let me go after him. It'll stop when he's dead." His tone sharpened, becoming razor-edged and deadly. Leisha understood at once. He was talking about Westfall. "It'll stop when I've killed him."

"That won't stop it, Harmon. That's not the way."

"I don't know any other way. Ammy, please! Release me from my vow. Let me put my nightmares to an end. Let me put my soul to rest."

"I'm sorry. Harmon, I love you. I love you." She continued to hold him while he cried desolately, like a child lost, like a soul torn a asunder.

And then nothing mattered to Leisha except finding Westfall and putting her father's anguished spirit at ease.

She left before dawn, penning a brief note for her family to say she and Kenitay were headed for Austin. She didn't mention they weren't traveling together.

By daybreak, she was in Terlingua to pick up supplies, wire Sid, and withdraw the rest of her reward money. She was in a hurry and in no mood to wait the extra hours for the bank to open. There was only one way she knew of to rush the process.

She found Billy Cooper snoring at his desk, his back room filled with rowdies sleeping off their wildness of the night before.

"Hey, Leisha," he mumbled groggily. "What can I do for you?"

"Another favor?

"What is it this time?"

"I need to get my money out of the bank."

"You askin' me to rob it for you? Not exactly my line of work anymore."

"I just want you to wake up Mr. Forester and ask him to open early."

"Oh, hell, is that all?"

"Billy, please! Have I ever asked anything of you before?"

"Lately, yes." But he was dragging himself up out of his chair, stretching his long legs. And to the prisoners in the back, he called, "Don't you boys go anywhere now, you hear?"

Abe Forester, the bank president, was less thrilled to cooperate than Billy had been. But once the lanky blond sheriff reminded him of a certain banker's wild son he'd let off when he was caught lighting firecrackers under the church pews, Forester grumbled but complied. Money in hand, Leisha was about to head for the telegraph office when Billy stopped her.

"Leisha, you haven't seen Jed lately, have you?"

She paused, reading the worry on his handsome face. For all his worthlessness, Jed Cooper had found a tender-hearted champion in his uncle. Jed didn't deserve any special favors from her—but Billy did.

"No, can't say that I have, Billy. You misplace him?"

"He's been gone a couple of days. Probably nothing."

"You're probably right. Don't fret. He'll remember the way home when he's out of money."

Billy smiled, relieved, and wished her well before returning to the jailhouse and the rest of his sleep.

Cursing Jed Cooper and Kenitay and the whole complex business, Leisha stalked down the walk to finish her business in Terlingua.

She lit out in good time, riding hard and fast to Marathon where she would hop the Southern Pacific. She couldn't catch up to Kenitay but she would be right behind him.

And hopefully she'd be on hand before he stepped in to go against their deal.

There wasn't much in the world that intimidated Kenitay. But standing at the threshold of the plush dining room in his stepfather's stiff suit, looking out over a sea of starched linen, glimmering crystal, and polished silver while the elite of Austin sat to dinner, he was filled with apprehension. He'd never mingled with the high circles of white society and barely remembered the rudiments of West Texas table manners his mother taught him as a boy. He felt an uncomfortable stir of panic and was considering a cowardly retreat when a smooth voice spoke at his elbow, startling him.

"Will you be dining alone this evening, sir?"

He glanced at the pasty-faced gentleman in his shiny suit and couldn't think of anything to say. He saw the man's look of surprise that was quickly masked by well-trained politeness and wondered what the little fellow was staring at in such dismay. Hadn't he ever seen a black eye and a few bruises before?

Then, a hand tucked into the bend of his elbow and the woman who nudged up beside him murmured, "We'll be dining together."

The edge of Leisha Bass's smile could have cut brick. Her fingers clamped down on his arm like a vise, holding him still when he would have taken a step back in sheer astonishment.

To the maitre d', she purred, "Someplace private, if you please. My cousin and I have much to talk about, don't we, Kenny, dear?"

"I'll see what I have available, madame. One moment."

The minute he turned away, Leisha's hand flashed up toward Kenitay's head. He started to flinch but she was faster, catching first one earring then the other and plucking them from his ears. He'd forgotten about them in his haste. She stuffed them in her handbag with a curt, "They don't match the suit."

"Right this way, if you please," instructed the elegant little man who, with his armful of leatherbound menus, began winding through the row of crisply dressed tables.

Kenitay balked.

Leisha looked up at him, her lovely features warming with a sweet smile. Between clenched teeth, she hissed, "Walk with me, you sonofabitch, or I'll drag you."

He walked.

They were taken to a secluded table tucked back in the shadowed bow of one of the hotel's large side windows. Leisha stood next to her chair, waiting. Kenitay stood next to her, waiting. She slid a pointed glance from the back of the chair to him, her impatience obvious. He blinked, uncertain.

"Allow me, madame," the headwaiter cooed. He drew back her seat and she settled with a sigh of scarlet silk and a softly murmured, "Thank you." Then he put his hand on the back of Kenitay's chair. Green eyes narrowed fiercely and he growled, "I can sit myself down."

The little fellow took a hop back, his eyes rounding with alarm. "Very good, sir," he stammered. "Your server will be right with you."

Leisha shook out her napkin and proclaimed without looking at him, "You have the sophistication of a goat. Whatever made you think you could handle this alone?"

Kenitay glowered at her and snapped, "This from Miss Suddenly Prim and Proper."

"Just because I chose to ignore the rules didn't mean I was ignorant of them." She'd learned by watching Becca, half in disgust, half in envy. But she wouldn't tell him that.

His surprise was slowly fading. His gaze moved over her in a leisurely appreciation. It was a dangerous look, all heat and smoke and the suggestion of a slow-burning fire.

"You're very beautiful."

His husky rumble woke a shiver of response and that provoked a different sort of reaction. Fury. How dare he think he could placate her with a smoldery stare and a slick compliment? She glared at him.

"We won't discuss what you are."

"Leisha—"

"Don't talk, just listen. It'll be the way I say from now on. You shut up and try not to draw any attention to us. We'll dine like two civilized relatives and when Beech and Westfall show up for supper, you'll point them out to me. Then you're out of here before you ruin everything. Is that understood?"

His discolored jaw gripped tight and he had no reply.

Their waiter appeared to take their order. Leisha gave hers, then turned to Kenitay. His impassive features never altered.

"Why don't you order for me, cousin," he drawled. "You've so much more practiced as the sophisticate. I don't want to embarrass you by making the wrong choice."

"You already made the wrong choice, Kenny." Her eyes glittered above a harmless smile. Then to the waiter, she said, "He'll have the same."

Then silence fell between them. He was studying the parade of tableware as if it was a battlefield. She felt charitable enough to growl, "Start from the outside and work your way in."

His gaze flickered up and for a moment, his uneasiness plain. Just when she began to feel some sympathy for him, he said, "I'll just use my fingers. That way I won't have to worry about using the wrong fork by mistake."

"Put your dish on the floor and eat on all fours if it makes you more comfortable. Just watch for our two friends."

Again, the chill silence.

Finally, the tension got the best of him. "I'd like to explain—"

"Don't try," Leisha interrupted. "It doesn't matter now, anyway. We're both here. We'll both get what we want and then I hope I won't ever have to see you again." She held his gaze unwaveringly. If she'd hoped to shame him, she was mistaken. He never so much as blinked.

Then, his gaze shifted and a sense of distilled violence was palpable in his mood. It was the kind of rage that simmered when held for too long.

"Are they here?"

Eyes like chips of emerald tracked their passage across the dining room. "The big man with the beard—that's Westfall. Beech is behind him, the one with the bruised knuckles."

Leisha understood. Beech was the one who'd beaten him. A cold, unreasonable fury got hold of her as she casually dropped her napkin off her lap, then bent to retrieve it. As she did, she looked behind her, finding and imprinting the two men on her memory. She straightened and looked back at Kenitay. He was sitting as if sculpted from stone. She could only guess what worked behind his impassive stare.

"You'd better go before they catch sight of you," she suggested. "I'm going to see if I can get close."

"What about my dinner?"

"I'll bring it up to you. Then you can eat with your toes if you like."

His smile was small and an obvious effort. He didn't want to leave. She didn't flatter herself by thinking it was because he was worried about her. He didn't trust her any more than she trusted him. Which was fine.

"Wait for me in your room. I'll be there in a few minutes." Then her tone sharpened. "Stop staring at them before you burn a hole in the back of their heads."

"An amusing thought." But he pushed back from the table to oblige her. "Don't try anything foolish."

"Like leaving without you?"

He didn't respond to her sarcasm. "They're dangerous men, Leisha. You don't know how dangerous."

"And they don't know me, either. It's time we got acquainted."

It was an hour later when she tapped on his door. It jerked open before her hand had a chance to leave the wood.

"Where have you been? You said a few minutes."

Leisha eyed him severely and waited until he backed up, giving her room to enter. "I ate my dinner first. I see you got yours all right. I told the waiter you'd fallen suddenly ill."

Kenitay cast a glance at his untouched tray. Food was the last thing on his mind. "What about Westfall and Beech?" he demanded as he closed the door behind her.

Leisha felt immediately overwhelmed by him. His travel clothes were tossed haphazardly about the room. The bedcovers bore the impression of his body where he'd lain waiting for her while his expensive meal got cold. Her gaze lingered on that bed a second too long for she jumped uneasily when he came up close behind her.

"Well?"

"Guarded better than the Crown Jewels," she told him crisply, sidling away from the foot of the bed to stand by the open window. "I walked by the table and bumped into Beech's shoulder and had five burly fellows on their feet ready to pat me down for weapons."

"Not Army?"

"No. These were private hire. I'll do some more checking and find out what happened to the soldiers they were assigned. Maybe they use them only for public appearances."

"Maybe."

Kenitay paced. His expression was closed down tight around his agitation, like a hunter anxious for the right time to make a move. Leisha watched him, appreciating his frustration. And the fluid way he stalked the small room. She was getting used to the way he looked in short hair but when she'd seen him in the dining room in his pressed suit, she'd hardly known him. Except for the earrings, he could have passed for the son of some wealthy Austin diplomat. His green eyes gleamed against his bronzed skin, emphasizing his mother's lineage rather than his father's. His looks were breathtaking. She'd been aware of the way the eyes of the other women in the room followed him. And she hadn't liked it. It made her remember how good he was at kissing and how much experience he must have had to get that good at it.

With unfamiliar jealousy growling through her, she vowed to remember how he'd left her without a word. It couldn't matter to her what he'd done or with whom. She had her own priorities and he wasn't one of them. They were using each other and that meant not attaching more emotion to it than that. But the more she lingered in his room, so close to that man-rumpled bed, the more she wanted to be used by him again.

"I'm meeting with Sid for breakfast. You should probably go with me. For appearances."

He gave her a brief look. "Fine." Then his attention returned to her for a longer, more thorough study. It was time to leave.

"I'd better get to my room."

"Which one is it?"

Her eyes narrowed warily. "Next door."

He started to smile, just a slight bend of his chiseled mouth. "Neighbors. That's nice.

"Cousins," she reminded him curtly. "Cousins who stick to their own rooms."

"Kissing cousins?"

"No."

She was still smarting over his abandonment and damned if she'd let him know how it had devastated her. She'd believed one lie too many from his lips to want to be led on by another one. *I love you.* Why had she listened?

"Good night. I'll meet you downstairs at eight."

She reached for the doorknob and found his palm pressed flat above it, holding the door shut. She could feel him, big and bold, behind her, close but not touching. Anger and apprehension leapt. And so did a spark of anticipation. She stuck with anger. It was safer.

"I'm going now."

"Wouldn't it be more efficient if we shared one room and could leave together in the morning?" She felt the warm brush of his breath as his mouth hovered near her temple.

She turned toward him, not in acceptance as he'd hoped, but to slam her palms against his chest and shove hard. He stumbled back, surprised.

"I'm here about business, nothing more. If you come into my room, I'll shoot first and ask why later. Have I made myself real clear?"

"Clear as crystal." He rubbed his sore ribs while regarding her impassively. "I'll see you downstairs at eight."

And she walked out, slamming his door behind her.

It was no better than he deserved, Kenitay knew, and probably the smartest thing for both of them. He knew he'd taken a big chunk out of her pride by leaving the way he had. He should have known she'd come after him with blood in her eye. Maybe he was hoping she would, even as he'd ridden away. They did make a good partnership. He couldn't name a single man who could think as fast and move as quick. Except maybe Harmon. And Leisha was definitely easier on the eye.

*Yusn,* what a gorgeous woman, all done up behind her sophisticated war paint and ready to do battle. And that dress . . . as fiery as his passion for her. He'd wanted to touch her, to mold that flame and coax it to burn brighter. What man would not be moved by the challenge of a woman both aloof and alluring? What man, indeed?

Frowning to himself, he settled on the edge of his bed and picked up his fork. The meal was cold but he didn't care. He was hungry so he ate. It was no good dwelling on Leisha. When he'd ridden from her at Blue Creek, that had put an end to any hope he'd held. She'd never forgive him. If he opened the door to her room, he'd no doubt at all that she'd bust a cap on him. And he couldn't afford to be distracted with his purpose so nearly served. His thoughts were captivated by images of revenge and that was enough to supply the necessary heat the food was lacking.

His vengeance was at hand and his woman was at his side. What more could he wish for?

Then he glanced at the barren width of his bed and sighed. That was too much.

# Eighteen

Sid Bass was the epitome of the city he resided in. Austin represented the fast-changing face of Texas as it moved toward the next century—moving fast and efficiently by train, not horse. It was urban and industrial with its straight streets and rectangular blocks, carefully designed for rapid expansion in three directions where it butted up against the Colorado. Elegant public buildings had long since replaced its first log structures and now that the frontier had stretched to its limits, Austin stood proud in the center of a great state, living grandly off its government. And so was Sid.

He was five years into a successful law practice, driven by a profitable marriage to a wealthy politician's daughter. His home wasn't elaborate by Texas standards but it was in the prestigious section of the city surrounded by parks and boulevards. He was like everything around him: neat, clean, regimented, and eager to expand. And since the last time Leisha had seen him, what had expanded the most was his waistline. She wondered if he remembered how to sit a horse.

He greeted them at the door with unrestrained hugs, right out where the world could see them, and Leisha liked him better for that. His wife waited until they were safely inside, where those passing by couldn't see the way she offered an alabaster cheek to her two country cousins.

Leisha had only met Judith Bass once. They'd come out

to visit several years back and Judith had seemed overwhelmed by the crudeness and dust and heat. And by her husband's uncivilized family. But her proper clothes never lost their starch . . . and neither had Judith. Here, in the polished interior of her home, she was as austere as the marble floors and as cold as the crystals dripping overhead.

"How divine of you to pay us a call," she cooed, giving Leisha a critical once-over. "A pity it can't be of long duration." Apparently, Leisha's grey wrinkled silk passed inspection, for Judith turned to regard Kenitay with another frosty smile. "And Ken, how well you look. The time you spent in the East has done wonders."

Kenitay smiled thinly. "Yes. Those were enlightening years, Cousin Judith."

"Why, one would hardly guess that you were part—"

"Indian?" he supplied smoothly.

Her expression grew rigid. "Yes."

"No more than they would looking at Sid, here."

She glanced at her portly husband in alarm as if trying to discern how apparent his mixed past was to the casual eye. She needn't have worried. Sid had his mother's black hair and dark eyes but that was the only tie he had to her people. He was balding and bespectacled at a mere thirty-two and no more savage looking than any of their influential friends who dined on rich foods and imported wines. He was as tame as a pedigreed lapdog and just as harmless. Which was exactly what she wanted in a husband.

"Of course, you'll want to see the sights while you're here," she prattled on politely. "And I'll arrange a small dinner party to introduce you to our friends. We'll have to go shopping first and get you something—presentable for society."

"She looks fine in what she brought," Kenitay interjected as he watched Leisha pale in discomfort.

"Yes, of course," Judith drawled. "For West Texas. But this is the state capital."

Kenitay was about to shove those snobby words down her throat when Leisha said docilely, "I'd be most grateful for your opinions, Cousin Judith. I fear we're woefully behind times in the Bend. Perhaps you could help me better my wardrobe after breakfast while the men discuss their business. I'm sure we'd be bored silly by their stuffy talk."

She smiled beseechingly while Kenitay stared at her in open-mouthed disbelief. The Leisha he knew would have gutted anyone who criticized her or her homeland. Could it be she was intimidated by these opulent surroundings and by Sid's imperious wife? He couldn't believe that. But there was definitely something behind her meek mood and he was determined to find out what it was.

His confusion grew over breakfast, where Judith lorded her refined superiority and Leisha bent before it with baffling humility. By the time the dishes were cleared and their hostess went up to change into suitable morning attire, Kenitay pulled Leisha aside, seething because of the insults she'd swallowed.

"Why are you letting that she-dog treat you so disrespectfully? Fifty of her would not be worth one of you!"

Leisha looked up at him in surprise. Then the pleasure of his words warmed through her. Fifty to one. Those were impressive odds. She gave him a cunning smile. "I thought it better if I had the she-dog off sniffing around another trail while you talked to Sid. I don't think you'd find her very responsive to anything you have to say."

Comprehension dawned and he had to applaud her ingenuity. By playing upon the woman's vanity, she could be easily controlled. Still, Kenitay didn't like it. "The sacrifice of pride is too much, Leisha. I don't see how talking to Sid is going to—"

He stopped talking as Sid approached. He put a hand

on Kenitay's arm. "I've got some coffee waiting in my study. None of that watered-down brew Judith serves at the table but good horseshoe-floating coffee the way Uncle Harm taught me to make it."

"I thought you'd forgotten those things," Kenitay said with cool reserve.

Sid smiled. "Those are the only things worth remembering, Kenitay. Or is it Ken now?" He eyed the short hair and stiff suit in uncertainty.

"Kenitay," he corrected.

"Good. Fine name. Come on. We'll sit and talk a spell. Leisha, don't let my wife spend all my money."

Bemused, Kenitay followed his cousin into a dark paneled room where the scent of fresh-ground beans scorched the nose. The walls were lined with more books than Kenitay could have read in a lifetime. He was staring at them in awe when Sid motioned to a deep, brass-studded leather chair. He went to pour a couple of big cups of steaming coffee while Kenitay settled into it.

"Jack tells me you're up to your ears in trouble with the government or the law or both."

Kenitay took the cup he was given, startled by the way Sid cut right to it. He stared down into the dark brew and murmured, "I don't see how you can be of any help."

"Well, we won't know that until you tell me what's got my brother in such a lather. I know Jack. It takes a lot to push him into a panic. And nothing riles him like the thought of those he loves being in danger. What can I do for you that he can't?"

"Nothing. I was wrong to come here and waste your time."

"It's my time and I'll decide if it's wasted. You want to knock that proud Apache chip off your shoulder and tell me what's got a noose around your neck?"

Kenitay's gaze flew up. He wasn't sure if he should be

angry or apologetic. He didn't know what to make of Sid Bass and his bewildered stare conveyed that.

Sid laughed. "Son, don't let all this fool you. I was raised in West Texas. I might look all sissified and soft but I haven't forgotten how to be patient and stalk. Harmon taught me that. He told me looks were deceiving and the best offense came when an enemy wasn't prepared. My daddy instilled a love of the law into us. Jack lives and breathes it to the letter. But Harmon showed me that laws aren't always fair to everyone and sometimes you have to know how to bend them to see justice done. I'm damned good at bending the rules if it's right. You're family, Kenitay, and there isn't a stronger recommendation in the world to me. Now you can tell me what's on your mind and I can do my best to help or we can sit back and drink this coffee while we wait for the ladies to get back and you can go on your way. It's up to you."

Kenitay regarded him for a long, silent moment, seeing the shrewdness and strength he'd missed before. Jack may have had the brawn and bravery, but here were the brains of the Bass family.

"What I tell you can go no farther."

"Between you, me, and God and we can try excluding Him, if you'd rather. Only I've found He can be pretty handy to have on your side. You talk, I'll listen."

For the next two hours, Kenitay talked. Sid took notes and interrupted on occasion with a brief question. By the time the harsh coffee was gone, Kenitay had emptied his soul, spilling everything, even the things he'd told no one else, because something in Sid Bass's demeanor made him believe he might have a future after all.

The two women returned well past the luncheon hour, laden with parcels. The smile on Leisha's face was definitely affixed by willpower as Judith chattered happily about their day.

"You'll never guess who we bumped into," she gushed to a tolerant Sid. "Ethel Powell's boy, Farley. He was quite smitten with our Leisha and all but begged permission to court her. Oh, my dear, your mother would be positively beaming. She's of such fine stock herself, you know, and I'm sure wants only the best for you. I'll never know how she could have settled for—" Judith broke off with uncommon self-restraint. "Well, anyway, it would be quite a coup for this family to mingle with the Powells. It wouldn't do your career any harm either, Sidney."

"Yes, dear," he murmured in a placating tone until she turned toward the stairs. Then he rolled his eyes heavenward as she ascended. To Leisha, he muttered, "Farley Powell is the product of centuries of inbreeding. He gambles, he cheats his friends, and he beats his dog. Wonderful stock indeed. Your mother would most likely shoot him before weakening the line. I think you'd do better looking closer to home." His gaze shifted subtly to where Kenitay was standing. "We'll see you this evening, then?"

"I wouldn't want to keep Farley waiting," Leisha drawled.

Kenitay clenched his teeth, saying nothing, until the two of them were in a carriage headed back to their hotel.

"How did your meeting with Sid go?"

"He's a very smart man."

Leisha cast a hopeful look up at him. "Did he think he could keep you off a gallows?"

"Let's say he gave me plenty to think about."

"And?"

"I'm going to do some thinking." He eyed Leisha for a moment. "And how did your day go with the she-dog?"

"If it weren't for Sid, I'd have had her hair after the first five minutes. I spent the whole morning listening to her defame my family. She thinks my father is a heathen and that my mother is a fool for staying with him. The fact that they love one another and have been happy for almost twenty-four years is nothing compared to the pollution of my mother's breeding stock, is the way she put it. And I think she was trying to be tactful. I'd like to bury her up to her neck near an ant hole."

Kenitay chuckled and wrapped a supportive arm about her shoulders. She let him hug her up close in sympathy, then lingered against him, her eyes shut as his lips pressed to her brow and his cheek rubbed the crown of her head. It wasn't until she heard the sigh of her own breath, that she levered away in denial of the desires that quickened in an instant. His touch did that to her. It was an unconscious thing. An uncontrollable thing. But it could and would be resisted. Because she didn't have time to drag her heart around after a man like Kenitay who would only hurt her in the end.

"I'm going to see if I can find Corporal Wonderly." Did she imagine it or did Kenitay's every muscle tense at the mention of the soldier's name? "He'll know when we can arrange to get close to the others."

"And how close do you plan to get to find these things out?"

"As close as I have to."

She heard the unmistakable sounds of his knuckles popping.

Leisha didn't have to look long or hard.

When they returned to the hotel, a half-dozen soldiers were milling about the lobby. Johnny Wonderly was among them.

His face lit up like a Chinese lantern when he saw her. He broke away from the others and approached with a rapid stride, slowing only when he saw Kenitay at her side. He gave the other man a speculative stare, gauging him for competition as he swept off his hat before Leisha.

"Miss Bass, this is a mighty nice surprise."

"Why, Johnny Wonderly! Indeed it is!" She leaned forward to squeeze his arm, moistening her lips suggestively. He simmered, her behavior in Shafter instantly forgotten. "I've been thinking about you," she whispered in a husky aside. She could fairly hear his seams groaning.

"What are you doing here in Austin? If this ain't the best kind of coincidence."

"I'm visiting family. And, of course, I knew you'd be here." That last was softly purred and his lust responded with a roar.

The young corporal's gaze lingered on Kenitay. Noticing his curiosity, Leisha waved a dismissing hand. "Oh, Johnny, this is my cousin, Ken Bass. He's traveling as my escort as a favor to my father. We grew up together and have been best friends, oh, forever."

Wonderly grinned gratefully and extended his hand. "Mr. Bass. Pleased to meetcha."

Kenitay looked at the outstretched hand, then slowly placed his within it for a warm jostling. In his best Texas drawl, he lied, "The pleasure's mine. Now maybe I won't have to spend all my time chaperoning my cousin and can get to some manly amusements."

Johnny smiled wider. "Why, it'd be a privilege to take her off your hands."

"As long as that's all you're taking off her."

Leisha glared around at him then smiled at the blushing soldier. "Kenny takes his job too seriously. When can we get together?"

"I'd be right happy to take you out to dinner."

"We have plans," Kenitay growled.

Again, Leisha skewered him with a look before crooning, "But I have time to meet you beforehand—over a glass of wine, maybe?"

"Which room are you in?"

"She'll meet you in the dining room at six." That stated, Kenitay gripped her arm and towed her away like a truculent mule. She shook him off the moment they were out of sight.

"What do you think you're doing? You almost ruined everything."

"I hope so," he muttered under his breath.

"What?"

"I'm supposed to be your chaperone. Should I have tossed you two in bed together?"

That bit of logic did make sense so Leisha calmed herself and marched with him to their adjoining rooms. He paused with her before her door to say he'd pick her up in the dining room at seven. That would give her an hour to wheedle information out of Wonderly in a very public place. He could handle that.

At least he thought so until he came downstairs at the appointed time and they were nowhere in sight. Muttering an Apache curse, he stalked between the rows of elegant diners to the little maitre d' he'd intimidated the night before. The poor fellow nearly fainted at the sight of his dark expression.

"The woman I was with last night, have you—? Never mind."

Out on the torch-lit terrace, he caught a glimpse of scarlet tassels and blond hair. He strode through the open doors with a fierce purpose. Until Leisha turned on the handsome young soldier's arm. She was laughing over something he'd said to her. And she was so beautiful, Kenitay's heart staggered to a stop.

"Oh, Kenny, there you are. Am I late? I was having such a good time, I forgot to check my watch."

"We don't want to keep the family waiting," came his quiet reply.

Leisha gave him a suspicious look, then turned her cud-

dly attention to the young corporal. "Johnny, thank you
for being such fun. I hope we can find the time to get
together again before I have to leave." Her fingertips
stroked up and down his blue coat. Kenitay's gaze followed the movement.

"I'll see what I can do about tomorrow night."

"You do that." She stretched up to press a lingering
kiss upon his lips. Then she hurried after Kenitay, who
was already striding back through the dining room.

He said nothing to her as they settled side by side in
the carriage Sid sent to fetch them. His gaze was focused
straight ahead. He didn't ask what she'd learned from
Wonderly so she volunteered the information.

"He's getting me invited to a society ball tomorrow night.
Beech and Westfall will be there. It may be our only opportunity to get close to them."

"I'm sure you'll make the most of it," he commented
softly.

"Yes. I will. What's wrong with you?"

"Nothing."

She didn't believe him but she thought it wiser not to
pry for more.

Judith had arranged a sparkling dinner party for them,
complete with Farley Powell and his filthy rich family.
Leisha found herself sitting next to the leering Farley while
Kenitay sat across from them, his expression inscrutable.
He would smile on occasion when the pretty Miss Powell
would whisper something, then touch his arm. Leisha sat
glaring knife-points at the vapid beauty while at the same
time admiring much the same scenery as that silly miss.
The bold, broad sweep of Kenitay's cheekbones. The green
glitter of his eyes. The sensual bow of his mouth. Knowing
how much more there was to him than this quiet gentleman
buttoned up in proper broadcloth, Leisha smoldered helplessly through the remaining course of the meal, fending
off Farley's hands that tended to roam to her thigh. She

wondered if it would be proper manners to stab him with her fork.

Leisha was relieved when she was able to escape her table companion at the meal's end but had to groan when Judith announced they were adjourning to the music room where the young Miss Powell would favor them with her operatic favorites. On their way out of the dining room, she felt the heat of a broad palm curving snug about her waist. She didn't need to look up to know it was Kenitay. She'd dreamed of that burn through sleek silken fabric ever since she'd first laid eyes upon the dress in a Terlingua window. It was a possessive hold, yet open enough to allow her freedom of movement. As the others filed dutifully toward the music room down another of the endless halls in Sid's home, Leisha lagged back, letting the others enter the room before them.

Then, without a word, she angled Kenitay up against the embossed wallcovering and rose up to take his mouth with a scalding kiss. It was a fleeting flare of passion, a single deep plunge of her tongue and crushing of her lips over his. *Mine,* was the searing impression it left upon his mouth. Then she stepped away and disappeared after the others, leaving him to sag against the wall, too dazed and desire-drugged by her impulse to move.

Several minutes went by and Kenitay managed to quiet the catapulting thrusts of his heart and calm the stiff upward thrust of his manhood. The first warbling notes came from inside the music room just as Sid emerged.

"Kenitay? Are you alright?"

He grabbed for a shaky breath. "Sid, we need to talk."

"All right."

"What must I do to stay out of prison?"

# Nineteen

It was a long, torturous evening. It seemed Miss Powell had memorized every aria and could render them all with the same ear-piercing tremolo. Leisha sat smiling grimly, thinking it would have made an effective Apache war cry. The enemy would have fled in droves.

Beside her, Farley Powell was determined to wiggle over onto her chair. He was leaning against her arm, his thigh pressed tight against hers. It was an annoying heat, unwelcome and encroaching. But as everyone's attention was centered on his sister, he must have felt free to impose his on Leisha. She felt his moist breath rush against the curve of her ear and that was quite enough. With a purposeful move, she scooted her chair to the left and when the gap opened, Farley found himself without purchase. His fall was loud and ungentlemanly.

"Oh, dear!" she cried in mock dismay. "Mr. Powell, are you all right?"

Floundering on the floor between the two chairs, Farley flushed a hot crimson.

"Could it be you were overcome by the sweetness of your sister's voice?" Leisha asked with feigned innocence. It took all her control not to smirk as Farley's humiliated father and mother hoisted him from his ungainly position.

And that pretty much concluded the night's entertainment.

Leisha was acutely aware that Kenitay had not joined

them. She was wondering morosely if it was the music or
her unplanned passion that kept him away. It was a foolish
move on her part, breaking all the ground rules she'd
posted about the perimeters of her heart. They weren't
supposed to be involved yet she couldn't seem to let him
go. *Free to pursue gentlemanly entertainments,* he'd told
Johnny Wonderly. That had sparked great distress within
her. The thought of him with another woman was the cru-
elest kind of torture. Then when the vapid Miss Powell
devoured him along with her veal, her rationality had
flown.

She wanted him.

And she didn't want to share.

He'd said all sorts of pretty things to her in the past in
order to satisfy his desires. They hadn't meant anything;
just ways to coax her into his arms. If a man felt no
compunction about seducing for pleasure's sake, why
should she? What was wrong with enjoying each other
without ties, without strings? It wasn't as if either of them
could claim innocence or demand commitment. They were
two strong people, already committed to their goals. Why
not indulge their passions in the process?

She was telling herself these things despite a firm conviction inbred from birth that the pleasures she was seeking were meant for a marriage bed.

But Kenitay had made it very clear that he offered no
future. And the idea of a marriage bed held little lure without him in it. Not that she was considering a lifetime with
him. So what did it matter? She had no purity to protect.
That had already been stolen. She wasn't interested in an
alliance with someone like Farley Powell to become breeding stock in much the same way as her mother's purebred
mares. Why not make the most of her opportunities before
they were gone? She didn't fool herself into believing there
would ever be another to stir her blood once Kenitay was

gone. He was the one—the kindred of her soul. And she would not forgo this chance to have him.

He and Sid were concluding what looked to be a serious conversation in her cousin's study. Judith wasn't pleased.

"Sidney, you've been ignoring our guests. The Powells are about to leave and you've said scarcely more than two words to them."

"I'm sure you've filled in for me, my dear. Kenitay and I have been taking care of some important matters."

"Ken," she corrected with a glance over her shoulder to see if her pristine company heard the offensive name.

"Kenitay," Sid persisted. "He's half Apache, Judith, and that is his name."

"Shhh! Sidney, for heaven's sake!"

His eyes narrowed behind the steel rims of his glasses. "I am not ashamed of where my family comes from."

"You should be," she hissed while Leisha and Kenitay stood uncomfortably off to one side. "I haven't worked so hard to let a savage past interfere with what I've planned for your future."

"No? My dear, if you're making plans for me, shouldn't you consult me first?"

She blinked. "But I thought that was all settled. That you'd be going on Daddy's staff—"

"That's what you've decided. I've decided to continue in private practice awhile longer. I mean to look into the reservation problem in Oklahoma. I think it's time my mother's people were allowed to come home."

Judith was gasping for breath, her features apoplectic. "You will do no such thing. I forbid it. You will forget this nonsense at once."

"No."

There it was, that flat, immovable Bass "no."

Then Sid smiled at his cousins and murmured, "Judith, you're being rude to our guests."

* * *

The ride back to the hotel was silent. Kenitay was brooding over whatever he and Sid had been discussing and Leisha was chafing with impatience. Her gaze traveled over him in fascination, lingering over his mouth, his hands, his sturdy thighs. A potent feeling rose strong and hot inside her. Lust, she called it, because to name it anything else would have been too dangerous. He stared ahead, unaware of her scrutiny, of her increasing arousal and she wondered how best to let him know of it. He was too clever not to question a direct invitation. He would want to know why her sudden change of heart after her earlier rejection. She didn't want to spend time arguing or convincing. She wanted to spend it experiencing.

His body gave a sudden jerk of surprise when she fastened her lips to the strong channel of his throat. She heard the break in his breathing pattern and felt his rapid swallowing. He went tense with suspicion and his hands came up to catch her shoulders, ready to push her away. She chose that moment to ease her hand into his lap to begin a firm kneading. It only took a few seconds for his hands to fall helplessly to the cushions and his head dropped back as her mouth caressed his neck.

She overcame his thoughts of resistance with the sheer force of her sensuality. Without a sound, he leaned back into the seat of their secluded coach, his eyes closing, willing to let her have her way but far from a passive victim. When her mouth moved to his, he opened the way to a hot, enticing dance of passion, meeting the thrust of her tongue with his own, bathing it with his and drawing upon it until she moaned aloud in frustration. It wasn't enough.

He'd risen bold and hard within the curl of her palm and her fingers worked with blind inexperience against the fastenings of his trousers. He was moved to aid her, guiding her hand in next to his pulsing heat. Her touch wasn't gentle or revering. It was insistent, demanding a response with each hard squeeze and provoking stroke. He wasn't thinking about protesting or questioning her intentions. He wasn't capable of thinking at all. Just as she intended.

He groaned into her greedy kisses and when she left his mouth, he panted raggedly as the heavy ache she was invoking grew too fierce to ignore. He was trying to decide what to do about it when she lowered her head down to his lap. The first touch of her kiss jolted through him, followed by the slow swirl of her tongue to quicken a shuddering paradise.

He made a sound. It wasn't a word, it wasn't anything beyond an expression of surprise and shock and sensation. He was beyond coherency. His hands tangled in her hair, alternately trying to pull her away and press her down in blissful confusion as her mouth drew upon him in the same tugging manner he'd used to torment her during their kiss. He couldn't hold on to the violent pleasure she was determined to wring from him. His feet came up to press against the wall of the carriage, bracing for a convulsive conclusion that burst with his hoarse cry and an immediate flood of relief.

He slumped in the seat, panting unevenly, mind numb, senses fluttering wildly. He stroked her hair with hands that shook. At first he assumed the shuddering that overcame him was from sheer delight but then realized it was the carriage coming to a stop outside their hotel.

Leisha rose to slide a kiss across his lips.

"The ride was too short," came her purring complaint as his eyes returned to a bleary focus. She was smiling with a purely predatory promise. "We can travel the rest of the way up in my room."

What could he say? That he hadn't enjoyed the trip thus far?

As he walked on incredibly weak legs through the hotel lobby at her side, she looked so elegant, so much a lady that he had to wonder: who was that wildcat driving him crazy moments before? Her small hand was tucked demurely at his elbow. As she asked for two separate keys at the desk, her gaze slid up to his with the expression of an angel. It was all he could do to keep from pressing a kiss upon her sweet lips right then and there. Except they were playing roles and as her cousin, he would raise more than a few eyebrows with such a display. So he had no choice but to stand at rigid attention while she flirted with the desk clerk and pretended he was no more than a bothersome chaperone. Until they got upstairs and paused outside her door. She fit the key, pushed him inside, and was fast upon his mouth as she shut the door behind them.

Her hands roamed restlessly over his face and shoulders. She pressed his mouth open to delve deeply inside, stroking wetly along its roof, over his tongue, across his teeth. Her manner was aggressive, with a singleness of purpose, as if they were involved in a contest she was determined to win. By then, he found himself fully recovered from the carriage ride, his body eager to pursue what her kisses initiated—but his mind was suddenly and maddeningly clear. He was abruptly thinking of the way she'd stroked Johnny Wonderly's coat to gain his mindless devotion. He was thinking about the first time she'd turned to him with urgent appeals for him to make love to her. Then, he had her by the forearms, holding hard, prying her away. Her eyes gleamed. Her lips were parted with an eagerness for more.

"What's this about, Leisha?" he demanded with a husky cynicism. "You don't do anything without a reason."

Her eyelids fell to a sultry half-mast from beneath which passion glittered like hot, jewels. "I want you. Isn't that reason enough?"

Knowing her as he did, it shouldn't have been but he

wasn't exactly in a clear-thinking frame of mind. He was drawn back to her willing lips, again and again.

"Take off your clothes," she murmured into his kiss. "I want to see you."

Part of him reacted with shock. For all his experience, he was still a fairly modest man, as were all Apaches. But another part of him responded to the hoarse urgency in her voice and had him tearing at his shirt collar. She was kissing and touching each portion he bared, worshipping him with an unashamed appreciation until he stood sleek and bronze before her. Her palms rubbed up from the flat of his belly over the swell of his chest to fan along his shoulders. Her gaze was heated and admiring.

"You've kept yourself well as a warrior while in captivity. You're very strong. Very beautiful." She moved closer so her face nuzzled against the center of his chest. She sighed deeply, inhaling his scent. Her praise was an aphrodisiac because he knew she'd never said them to another.

His hands moved up the front of her gown, seeking the small fastenings. He paused. "I would see you the same way."

She nodded, still pressed against him.

He worked down the interminable row of buttons, until fabric parted and finally fell away, slipping to her waist. She wore nothing else.

"Your cousin Judith would be shocked," he murmured as his hands skimmed over smooth skin. He felt her smile.

"This was for you, not her."

Nothing she could have said could have packed a harder punch. She'd anticipated this. She'd wanted him, not just on a whim but enough to plan it out with care. He lifted her and the heavy gown pooled upon the floor as he carried her to her bed and laid her down upon it. Even as he sank into her upraised arms, her legs were twining about his waist, drawing him in tighter with their supple strength. She was aggressive, bold in her desire, but it didn't matter to him as it might have with some who thought a female was meant to be the passive partner. Because her boldness belied an absence of fear, a trust in him, a confidence in herself, and that made for a perfect moment in his mind. There was no reason to hold back. With one swift move, he was sheathed inside her.

"Make it a long ride," she challenged breathlessly against his ear. "Make me yours and yours alone."

And so he would, with hard, fevered thrusts that had her arching up for more, crying out in soft little pleas until her body spasmed around his, guiding him to spectacular fulfillment.

He sank down into the covers, kissing her gently about the face and throat and breasts. She shifted languidly beneath him, holding his head, her eyes closed. She was so beautiful; she'd given herself so completely, he wanted to weep with the fullness of his love for her.

"I don't want to leave you, Leisha." He meant *forever.*

"Then stay." She meant *for now.* Then she shifted so they were side by side and she nestled in against him with soft little purring sounds of contentment. He was lost.

"I love you, Leisha."

But she was already asleep.

Kenitay didn't sleep. He was awake all night considering the options Sid had given him. There were no easy choices, no one route. But when he looked down at the woman tucked around him like a sleek mountain cat, he knew where his priorities lay.

Maybe his father wouldn't have understood. He was a full-blooded Apache to whom honor meant all.

But Jack would agree. And so would Harm. And Billy. They were men who knew what it meant to find a soulmate. They knew what it meant to sacrifice pride for love. To this point, all his hardships had been forced upon him.

He'd never had to make a conscious sacrifice. He'd just gone in the direction he'd been pushed in.

Now, he had a choice. He remembered hearing Harm describe what he felt for Amanda. He'd said he'd die for her, he'd go down on his knees for her when he'd bow to no man or god. Because she was everything. And now Kenitay knew what that meant. Leisha was his everything. He'd tried so desperately to push her away because he'd always known there would come a time when he could no longer let her go. That time was now.

He finally drifted off into a light sleep toward dawn, only to be reawakened by the gliding tease of Leisha's fingertips, swirling over his abdomen, playing about his navel. He was instantly alert, firm and straight, pulsing eagerly in anticipation of her touch.

Without so much as a *good morning,* she slid over him, engulfing him with her snug heat, accepting him again and again without reservation, until their hard, driving motion had them gasping in unison, straining for the reward they both knew awaited. With Kenitay's hands on her hips to command the rhythm, the goal grew nearer. He lifted his upper body to fasten upon the taut peak of one breast, sucking hard, biting down without gentleness and she went wild above him, her body bucking, dissolving into a series of frantic quakes that pulled him over the edge of expectation into ecstasy.

After that, she stretched out over him, sighing lazily as he tried to prevent his total collapse. He needed to talk to her and he couldn't afford to let this companionable time between them pass. He had to tell her of the difficult decisions he'd made during the course of the night, decisions that would effect their future together, their lives as one.

"Leisha?"

"Hmmm?" She stirred languidly and started to nibble at his collarbone. He put a hand to her head, meaning to nudge her away but ended up petting the tumble of her golden hair instead.

"Leisha, I've been thinking about what Sid had to say."

She was licking along the side of his neck, working her way up to his earlobe where she tugged with her sharp little teeth and got his toes curling.

"Leisha—"

"And?" she prompted before sucking at the angle of his jaw.

"And I think we ought to go home today."

She stiffened as she considered his words. "What?"

"I want to take you back to Blue Creek. There are some things I need to say to your father and to mine."

She rose slowly, her elbows braced upon his chest, and stared down into his face warily. "What are you talking about?"

"I think we should leave now before—"

"Before what?"

"While there's still a chance to turn things around."

Her eyes narrowed and he could see the rapid turn of her thoughts behind them. And, as he should have guessed, she arrived at all the wrong conclusions.

"*Cabron!* You think because I asked you to my bed that I've given you any control over me?"

"That's not—"

"No, it's not. And it never will be! How dare you! How dare you think I'd give up my right to vengeance just because I enjoy you in bed. I'm not going all soft and silly and foolishly female so you can play the strong man and put me in my place. I wanted you, you wanted me. Beyond that, there's nothing but business. That hasn't changed, Kenitay, and it won't, so don't try to push me aside just because we've shared the same sheets. I would never ask you to surrender your honor for my sake, so don't you think I'd be willing to give up mine just because you think I'm not strong enough to uphold it."

"Leisha, listen to me—"

She pushed his hands aside, her fury massing into an intolerable ache. "Did you think by sweet-talking me you could discard me and get on with your manly business? Think again. I've come this far to see a job done and I'm not abandoning it just because you think I make a better bedmate than trailmate. I didn't make love with you because I needed anything from you. I wanted you, plain and simple. No strings, no ties. Remember? Now, bedtime's over and it's time to get back to work and I don't want to hear any more about going home or giving up. I'm not going home without Westfall and you're not going to get in my way."

He was motionless for the longest time, an opaque mist clouding the expression in his eyes. All the hope, the love, the willingness to surrender everything for her sake dimmed in response to her reaction. She didn't love him. She hadn't come to him out of the same need for oneness that moved his soul. She couldn't have put it plainer had she cut his heart in two. Her very determination to see her plan through shamed him for his readiness to surrender his own. She was twice the Apache he was—he who had denied his heritage for fear of losing his comfortable life amongst the enemies of his people. He who was ready to forfeit his father's spirit for his own personal desires. Leisha restored his priorities by her refusal to be lured from hers. Very quietly, humbled by her strength, he told her, "I won't get in your way, Leisha."

"Good," she declared with a savage finality. "Get up. We have things to do."

They didn't speak as they dressed. The sense of intimacy between them was gone and the tension that replaced it didn't invite any sentiment. Leisha stole a glance at Kenitay. His hard-set features gave nothing away. If he was angry with her for standing up to him, he didn't show it. He didn't show anything.

"I'm going to meet with Wonderly this morning and

get details about when and where this party is tonight. Then we can go there and get the lay of the land. That is, if you still plan to help me."

She waited for his reply. Finally he said, "I said I would and I will. An honorable man keeps his word."

Something was very wrong. She could sense it the way a coyote could sense a snare even when it couldn't understand the consequences of stepping in it. She'd already stepped in and the consequences were coming. She just didn't know what they were.

"Kenitay, what else did Sid suggest you do?"

He gave her another long, emotionless look. "It doesn't matter now." Then he left the room to return to his own.

Leisha closed her eyes and exhaled harshly. Damn him. Why could she never read what was on his mind?

And why was it so difficult to play by his rules?

After that morning, things went almost too fast. Johnny Wonderly confirmed the location of the society affair. It was in an Austin municipal building, not a private home as Leisha had hoped. The young corporal glumly informed her that he was not allowed to attend so she was left to her own devices to find a way into the invitation-only event.

And that's when she thought of Farley Powell.

A few words to her ambitious cousin Judith and Farley was calling on her for lunch. Through clenched teeth she smiled and endured his flirtations, secretly hoping Kenitay would arrive to rescue her. He didn't. She had no idea where he was but Johnny watched the two of them from a distance with a hangdog look that Leisha couldn't afford to console.

"Buy you a beer?"

Johnny looked up from his empty glass to see Leisha's swarthy cousin Ken at his elbow. "Sure. Why not?"

"No duty this afternoon?"

"I asked to have it off, hoping—well, hoping I'd have something better to do than hang around in the bar."

Kenitay made a sound of sympathy. He knew the feeling. He ordered drinks for the both of them. "I wouldn't worry about it."

"About what?"

"That fancy fellow she's with."

"Oh?" He gave Kenitay a curious look. "Why's that?"

"She's not interested in him. She's just looking for an introduction to that shindig tonight. I pity the poor fellow if he tries something with her."

Johnny's eyes narrowed. "Why?"

" 'Cause of who her daddy is. Harmon Bass, you know."

"So she said."

"Well, if you know anything about Harm, you know he's not a very forgiving fellow. I heard the last gent who tried to compromise her disappeared right out of his bed one night. They identified the pieces they found out on the desert by a belt buckle he'd been wearing. 'Course, no one could prove it was Harmon but I've never known a man who could fillet a fellow as fast when he's motivated. He told me to keep an eye on her whilst she's in Austin and to do what he'd do should the need arise."

Wonderly was positively pasty-faced as Kenitay hoisted his beer and drank deep. His voice shook slightly as he claimed, "Me and your cousin are nothing but friends, you know."

Kenitay smiled blandly. "That's what she said, too. Guess I'll have to believe you."

" 'Sides, I won't have time to pay her no more visits what with that Indian agent Beech heading out this morning."

Kenitay stiffened, keeping his composure by sheer will alone. "You don't say."

"Yep. Got some message and lit out like his tail was afire."

"He say where he was going?"

"Some border town name of Terlingua."

# *Twenty*

Leisha looked up into her dressing mirror and gasped in surprise. She'd been struggling to get into her evening gown and hadn't heard Kenitay enter her room. He was standing at her back, his impassive stare meeting hers in the glass.

"Beech is gone."

"What?" She turned toward him so quickly, the front of her gown fell away. His gaze never lowered to the faint wrap of fine linen that remained. "What do you mean, *gone?*"

"He left for Terlingua this morning. Alone."

She cursed softly, a frown knitting her brow. "Why? Why would he suddenly go there?"

Kenitay didn't express his opinion. He had no foundation to base it on and no reason to think it true.

Beech was going there to find *him*.

He'd been very careful never to forge a link between himself and the Basses, at least not in his later years at Fort Sill. He went by his single name only and claimed only Kodene as kin. Beech would have no reason to suspect the Basses of complicity. In their clever game of cat and mouse, the line had blurred between who was after whom and he didn't like the idea of being pursued so close to home.

Nor did he like the tingle of anxiety creeping along his spine at the thought of his past haunting his family.

"What matters is he's gone."

"But Westfall is still here," she reminded him. "And he's the one I'm after."

She turned back to the mirror and rearranged the bodice of her dress. It was a low-necked creation Judith had chosen—a cream-colored silk striped with thin bands of pale turquoise, black and silver-grey satin. Pearls were draped at the neckline to emphasize the curve of her breasts and were stitched in a vee to the snug waist. Fabric gathered in the back to fall in a heavy train. For the life of her, she couldn't get the hooks together to close up the bodice back. A light sheen of perspiration shone on her skin after many minutes of frustrated tugging. She went still as Kenitay's hands settled upon her bared shoulders.

"You're supposed to have a corset under this."

"I don't need a corset," she snapped. "Besides, what do you know about what goes on under a lady's clothes?"

"Probably a lot more than you do. Stand still. I'll hook you up."

She stood but she couldn't make herself be still. Her bosom heaved with agitation, knowing he was probably right. She gasped as he yanked on the sides of the bodice, bringing them together so he could start with the hooks at the small of her back. For a man with such large hands, he was remarkably dexterous. Or experienced.

"Deep breath," he instructed. "Don't let it out."

"You're not saddling a mule," she wheezed in protest.

"That so? Hold that breath in or I'm going to have to put my boot to your ribs."

She sucked in an indignant hiss as he finished up the hooks and smoothed his palms down the tight hug of silk and satin. She had no breath left with which to protest when his hands lingered at the smallest part of her waist. Their heat was suggestive of the night they'd spent together and she found herself standing with her eyes closed, her lips softly parted as she recalled the nuances of his touch.

Seeing her flushed and expectant expression in the glass gave Kenitay a sharp twinge of regret. He let her go and stepped back.

"There. Make sure it doesn't pop open and put out Farley's eye when he tries to take it off you."

Leisha's eyes sprang open, dazed at first then darkening. "Farley Powell is just a tool to get me what I want. The only way he'll ever put his hands on me is if I'm unconscious."

Her words made him frown. *A tool.* Is that how she saw him, as well?

"I can't breathe in this thing," she complained in annoyance.

"You're not supposed to be running a race. You're supposed to be dainty and demure, all faint and fluttery."

She cursed him in vivid Apache and he couldn't help but smile. Farley Powell would lose more than an eye if he tried to tamper with this warrior woman. *His* warrior woman, his heart corrected seditiously.

She froze when his fingertips rested on either side of her gracefully sloped neck.

"Leisha," he began in a somber tone. "I would ask one thing of you. I want you to consider it, not as an insult but because it makes sense."

She waited. She could tell by his hesitation that she wasn't going to like it.

"Leisha, let me be the one to take Westfall. If you're suspected of kidnapping a man of his stature, you will have no future. I have none to risk. Sometimes it takes more strength to walk away. I think that's what you should do now. I'll see Westfall meets a proper justice."

"That's what you think."

"Yes."

"No."

He bowed his head briefly, inhaling deeply to continue the argument. She was quick to cut him off.

"You do what you must to regain your father's honor and I will do what I must for mine."

"This is for Harmon?"

"This vengeance is mine. You cannot carry it out in my name. That's not the Apache way. My father's way."

"Do you think your father expects you to sacrifice your life for him?"

"Isn't that what yours did?"

"My case is different."

"Why? Because you're a man?"

"No. Because my father is dead!"

"And so is my father's peace of mind. There's nothing I would not do to restore that to him. We've had this discussion before. Nothing has changed. It would be best if you rode out after Beech and left Westfall to me. Unless you don't think I can handle it."

"I know you can handle it. All too well."

Suddenly she took no satisfaction in his praise. What was this terrible attachment she felt? It couldn't be love, not anymore, not when she knew the futility of it. To sever the ties, to push him away, she made her words gruff and cold. Words that would end what might have begun on that bed of mutual bliss.

"Go. I don't need you anymore."

She expected an angry, typically male response. She could have dismissed that with ease. But he wouldn't leave her with even the slightest sense of victory.

His hand curved around to catch her chin, compelling her head to turn up to him at an awkward angle. His kiss was soft and slow and so heart-stoppingly gentle she was close to swooning when he moved away, whispering, "I wish I could say the same."

And then he was gone and it was too late to take back the words she didn't mean.

* * *

The room was big and hot and crowded with the peacocks of Austin. From somewhere on the fringe of the seething mass, music played, a tune that couldn't compete with the loud laughter and boisterous voices.

Farley's grip on her arm was viselike, tucking her in against his side like a possession to be shown and admired but not touched by any other. His attention dragged her down as heavily as the train of her dress. Leisha paid no mind to it as her gaze searched the swirl of faces for one in particular. She blocked everything else from her thoughts, refusing to dwell upon the heartache of Kenitay's leaving: When she'd turned her key in at the desk, she'd been told he'd checked out. He was off in pursuit of his own destiny and she was after hers. She'd always known they would separate but that hadn't given her the wisdom to guard against the pain of losing him again—a fact brought closer to home as Farley moved her about the dance floor. There was no magic in his arms. Only Kenitay could make her float to the strains of a waltz. With the eager Mr. Powell, she was stumbling.

After she stomped over his feet for the ninth time, Farley lost interest in dancing and suggested they take a spin through the moonlight. She was about to make another suggestion with the back of her hand when she caught sight of a bearded face.

Westfall.

"Farley, be a dear and fetch me some punch while I go freshen up. Then we'll see about that walk." She blinked her lashes with expectation and could see him quivering all over with unbridled lust. It was all she could do to contain her disgust until he was out of sight. Then her focus was all business as she made her approach.

"Excuse me, sir. Is your name Westfall?"

Dark, suspicious eyes were cast down at her. "Ma'am? I don't believe we've been introduced."

Leisha took a quick breath and clutched at his arm,

giving him an unobstructed view of her bosom as she leaned against him. "I must have a moment of your time. Alone."

He was glancing around, seeking his personal guards. "Ma'am, I don't think—"

"Please. It's vital." She pressed even closer. "It's about something I overheard at the hotel where I'm staying. You're in danger, sir. I would not make up such a tale."

"Let me get my—"

"No. Just you. I must speak to you alone. It's about a man, an . . . *Indian.* I heard him making threats."

Westfall gave her his full attention. "He's here?" he said with a mixture of apprehension and anticipation. "Where?"

"I can show you. Please. You must come now before I'm missed."

She made her tone frantic to urge him to move before he had a chance to think it out. Then she was tugging on his arm, rushing him through the crowd and away from the watchful eyes paid to keep him in their sight. Away from the safety of the crowd and out into the cooler night air.

Once outside, he balked. "Just where are you taking me, ma'am?"

"Right over there where we can have a word in private." She towed him toward the dim alleyway. "I can't risk being seen. It would ruin my family and I refuse to be endangered by what I know. Please, hurry."

As he walked with her, Leisha's thoughts settled into a cold, dark pattern of intent. Her father would have recognized it. He'd taught it to her—in actions, in words—that sizzle of deadly passion divorced from reason or sentiment. A lesson learned well.

The moment they turned off into the shadows, she reached down into the bodice of her dress where she'd torn a small hole between the silk and its inner lining. A hole large enough to sheath her knife against the boning stays.

Westfall went rigid as the blade nudged beneath his ribcage. "What do you want? My money?" he growled in disgust, angry at being taken in by her act, worried that he was so far away from those he'd paid to protect him.

"I want your soul."

It was then that the true depth of his peril sank in.

"Quickly, move to the end of the alley. I have a carriage there. Make a sound and I'll put a hole in you that the best surgeons in Austin couldn't stitch back together."

He started to walk—a slow, tense step that warned he might be thinking foolish thoughts. Still, his sudden action took her by surprise. His elbow flashed back, catching her in the nose, blinding her with tears of pain. He jerked free and ran toward the end of the alley. Cursing softly, she went after him. She hadn't planned on a footrace when she put on the bulky evening gown. The snug bodice wouldn't allow a decent breath and the heavy skirt hampered her.

He was going to get away.

Then a dark shape stepped into the open, blocking the end of the alley and Westfall's escape. As the big man skidded to a halt, Leisha overtook him, hooking him around the neck with her arm and bulldogging him to the ground. Kenitay was immediately crouched beside her, wedging his Colt up under Westfall's chin. He'd thumbed back the hammer before Leisha realized he had every intention of firing.

"No!" She grabbed his hand and wrestled the gun off target. "I need him alive!"

Seeing a chance to slip them while they struggled with each other, Westfall rolled and scrambled for freedom. With a snarl, Leisha was on his back, driving him down to his hands and knees and pounding his face into the pavement. There was a sound of rending fabric as her bodice tore beneath the arms. He gave a grunt of pain and she hoped it hurt every bit as much as her own face did.

"You're not going anywhere except to hell when I decide it's time," she seethed.

"What's going on here?"

"Soldier, these two are trying to abduct me!" Westfall cried. "Shoot them!"

Leisha looked up into the startled eyes of Johnny Wonderly.

"What are you waiting for?" Westfall was shouting. "Shoot them!"

But the young corporal continued to hesitate, the muzzle of his rifle drooping in indecision. That was all it took for Kenitay to bring his pistol to bear.

"Don't!" Leisha cried, pushing down the barrel of the .45 with her hand. Kenitay glared at her, his eyes hot and full of deadly purpose. "Don't," she repeated with a quiet authority. And he backed down. She turned her attention to the confused soldier. "Johnny, turn your back and let us go."

"I can't do that."

"Then you're going to have to kill us both and I don't think you can do that, either."

His hands were shaking as duty and devotion warred in his expression. "Tell me what's going on."

"This man is a murderer and worse. I'm taking him with me to see justice done."

"Then you're the ones he was afraid of." He began to comprehend that and other things. The fact that Leisha had used him was foremost among them. He lifted the rifle. "Get up off him."

Leisha stood slowly, never lessening her hold on Westfall's shirt collar.

"What happened to your face?" Johnny's voice had gone suddenly soft.

"He hit me."

In that instant Kenitay lunged forward, gripping the rifle, wrenching it from the corporal's unprepared hands.

He brought the stock up beneath his chin with a stunning force and Johnny went down without a sound.

"He'll wake up with a good lump and an excuse to save himself from court martial. Come on, Leisha. Let's go."

"I've got a carriage waiting to take us to the train."

From behind them came the sound of anxious voices. One of them called out Westfall's name.

"Here!"

Leisha struck him, silencing any further outcry by stuffing her tiny evening purse in his mouth.

But the alarm had already gone out. Footsteps sounded in the alley, running toward them.

"Come on!" Kenitay urged. "Forget the carriage. I have horses."

"But all my things are on the train."

"We can hop it somewhere else. They'll expect us to board here. The station will be watched. Come on!"

Dragging the struggling Westfall between them, they hurried down one of the side alleys that opened on a dim back street. Two horses were tethered there. Apparently, Kenitay had no plans to bring Westfall out alive and now he was a definite liability. To make him easier to handle, Kenitay struck him in the temple with the butt of his revolver, then loaded his slack form up onto one of the horses.

Leisha was trying to mount the other one but the sheer weight and bulk of her gown made stepping up into the stirrup impossible.

"Let me." Kenitay caught the back of her dress and yanked hard, tearing the skirt from the bodice with one pull. She stepped out of the pooling fabric in her frilled petticoat and was swiftly in the saddle. With an impulse just as quick, she bent, catching Kenitay behind the head to bring him up for the hard smash of her lips upon his.

"I'm glad to see you," was all she said, as she let him go and took up her reins.

He was smiling faintly as he vaulted up behind the limp burden occupying his saddle and guided his horse after hers.

They rode hard until the early morning, clearing the city and any further trouble there. Near a small sheltered stream, Kenitay reined in and tossed Westfall down from his saddle. He slid off, too, and before the dazed man could respond, Kenitay had bound him hand and foot. Then he looked to Leisha.

She was a mess. Her hair was down in a lopsided tangle, her face still bloodied. The bodice of her ruined gown was ripped open beneath the arms and her petticoat was a mat of wrinkles. She looked glorious to him. He put up his hands and she eased down into them without a fuss.

"I think your nose is broken."

"It feels like it," she mumbled.

"Come, sit. Let me see to it."

She sat and watched while he dipped his kerchief in the cool water. She bleated softly when he touched it to the swelling, then closed her eyes while he finished cleaning up her face. He studied her critically. His gaze suddenly fixed and he lifted a hank of her yellow hair away from one ear. She was wearing his shell and turquoise earrings, but they hadn't helped her learn to listen. He turned his attention back to her swelling face.

"I can set it now or you can get it rebroken later."

"Does it look that bad?"

"Do you want me to lie?"

She grimaced. "Set it now. It couldn't feel any worse."

She was wrong but managed to sit stoically for his manipulation. After he'd wiped her tears away and convinced her to lie back with the wet cloth over her throbbing nose, Kenitay was in no mood to listen to Westfall's threats.

"You won't get away with this."

"I'm not trying to."

"Killing me won't solve anything."

"I'm not the one you have to worry about."

Westfall considered Kenitay's words, then looked to Leisha. "What's her stake in this? I don't know her."

"Man like you makes a lot of enemies. Must be your sterling personality." He squatted down at the edge of the stream to bathe his face and dusty hair and drink from his palms. He could feel Westfall's hard eyes upon him and felt uncharitable enough to drawl, "You'd be better off with me. I'd planned to kill you quickly. I don't know what she has in mind."

"You taking orders from a woman?" Westfall sneered.

Kenitay glanced over his shoulder and smiled faintly. "From this one. For now."

The man snorted. "All that living tame must have softened up the man in you. Just like it did your daddy."

Kenitay's eyes glittered with a hard emerald brilliance. "I'd shut my mouth if I were you. I'd like nothing better than to spend a few hours rearranging your looks. And believe me, the kiss of my fists wouldn't be as sweet as your friend Beech's."

Leisha sat up. "How am I supposed to get any rest with all this yammering? We might as well ride if you have that much energy."

"How do you feel?" Kenitay asked.

"About as good as you looked when I broke you from that prison wagon. I'll survive."

"For now," Westfall interjected. "Until my men get a hold of you."

"Well, you won't be around to enjoy the show," she told him flatly.

"Just who the hell are you?"

"The name's Bass. That mean anything to you?"

"Bass, like the dime novel tracker?"

"The same." She waited but he said no more. "That all the name means to you?"

"Is it supposed to mean something more?"

She jumped up in angry agitation. "Let's go. I want to make the rail by tomorrow morning." She caught Kenitay eyeballing her. "What are you looking at?" She glanced down at her odd attire. "This is all the rage. My cousin Judith picked it out for me and she has impeccable taste."

"And I'm sure she'd love having you show up on her doorstep now."

Leisha grinned then grimaced, holding her sore nose. Black circles had already begun spreading under her eyes. "Let me have your shirt."

He lifted a dark brow.

She sighed impatiently. "Until I can come up with something else. This thing is strangling me." She took her knife and began cutting down from the rip under one arm. Afraid she'd nick herself, Kenitay stepped in.

"Here." He gripped the back and tore the fastenings open. Leisha drew a grateful breath and peeled it off. Then she wiggled out of her stiff petticoat. The gauzy linen of her combination drawers did little to hide the lushness of the body it was supposed to cover. Kenitay was quick to shed his shirt and draped it around her. His reaction to the tantalizing glimpse he'd had was devastating.

"We'll have to find you some clothes. You can't board a train looking like this."

She raised her eyes with mock innocence. "You don't like the way I look?"

There was a brief hot flare in his eyes. "Let's just say your cousin wouldn't approve—not of the attire and definitely not of what I'm thinking."

Imagining what moved in his mind had her senses sizzling.

Since Westfall was able to sit a saddle and the economics of two men on one horse was a waste of horse, Kenitay rode behind Leisha with their prisoner bound and trailing behind them on the other. Kenitay's thighs were comfortably framing hers and his hand rested easy on the flat of her belly. There was nothing easy about the flutter his touch woke beneath that casual press of palm.

After they'd gone several miles, she asked, "I thought you were going after Beech. What made you change your mind?"

"Your dress."

"What?"

"I told you it wasn't made for running," came his wry observation.

"So you didn't think I could do it on my own, is that it?"

"Is that what I said?"

She clamped her jaw tight. It was what he'd meant. And he was right. If he hadn't shown up, Westfall would have escaped. She hadn't planned it well. Again, she had overestimated her abilities and Kenitay had proved them lacking. She didn't know why he chose not to lord it over her. He had every right. She'd failed to hang onto Westfall and she'd weakened when it came to Johnny Wonderly. Kenitay would have killed him without hesitation, without remorse, but she couldn't bear the thought of his death on her hands. And she'd endangered them with her reluctance. Perhaps that's why her father had passed over her in favor of Rand. He'd known she lacked the cold edge of fortitude to do what had to be done.

She would show him he was wrong when she brought Westfall to his door.

"What's your daddy's beef with me, girl? I don't recall ever meeting Harm Bass."

"It was a long time ago, when he was a boy. He remembers you real well."

Westfall was silent for a long moment, then he asked

tensely, "What does your daddy look like? Blond, like you?"

"No. He takes after his mother's people. He's an Apache in all but his blue eyes."

Another long pause. "Did he live with his mama and a sister?" There was a tremor in his voice.

Leisha turned in the saddle so she could see his face when she answered. "Yes."

And Westfall went pale as milk as the ghosts of his past rose up before him.

# Twenty-one

By nightfall, Leisha was bobbing in the saddle, depending almost totally upon the support of Kenitay's arms to keep her upright. Her mind was sluggish with fatigue and her face ached miserably. It was a relief when he finally reined in and said, "We'll make camp here."

After binding Westfall securely to a tree, Kenitay went out in search of supper. Leisha made a small fire and regarded their captive over it.

"Why did your heavy-handed partner leave for Terlingua in such a hurry?"

Flat black eyes stared at her across the flames.

She prodded the fire with a slender stick until the end grew hot and glowing. Then she lifted it out and blew on the tip. "I could make you tell me," she said almost conversationally.

"What happened between me and your daddy, that was a long time ago," he began earnestly. "I'm a different man now. I have a family."

"So does he but the shadow of your debt hangs over it."

"So you plan to murder me, is that it? You think that will change anything that happened? It won't make anything different for your daddy or me but your life will never be the same. You'll be wanted as a kidnapper and killer. You'll be on the run till the day you die or they catch you. Is that what you want? A pretty young thing like you? The breed, I can understand him. He's working on hate and greed, but you, what are you getting out of this? Is the boy making it worth your while?"

Leisha scowled at him. "I don't know what you're talking about. This has nothing to do with Kenitay."

Westfall laughed harshly. "Sure. I suppose all that money means nothing to you at all."

"Money?"

"What do you think he's doing it for? Honor?" Another rough laugh. "Honor is the first thing bred out of them on the reservation. After a few years there, they're no better than dogs fighting over what's left on the carcass. Why do you think he killed that soldier in Fort Sill? Because after all those years he got tired of living with the rest of his people? No. He got wind of an easy way and went after it. Your friend's no noble savage. He's just as greedy as the rest of us. He's not tracking us down because of what we did to his father. He wants us dead because we know too much about his business and he doesn't want to share. You might want to remember that, missy. His kind don't trust nobody and they don't share what's theirs if they can kill and have it all."

Just then, the sound of Kenitay's soft step shut him up, but his words were a torment to Leisha. What money? More secrets? She looked up as Kenitay approached the fire. He had a pair of rabbits ready for roasting and was quick about setting them over the fire on a makeshift rack of sticks. Uneven firelight bronzed the angles of his face, giving them a sharp and, yes, a noble cast. Leisha watched him, wondering how much he wasn't telling her. Were Westfall's words true or just an attempt to push a wedge of distrust between the two of them. If it was, it was working.

"We'll catch the train in the morning and ride it to Marathon," Kenitay was saying.

"What then?" Leisha asked with a soft note of suspicion.

"Just what we planned. Eenah will meet us at the Gap and we'll head for Blue Creek."

"And then?"

"You'll have what you want and I'll go after what I want."

"Beech."

"Yes."

"Then what?"

He stared at her, not understanding the question.

"Then what will you do? Your debt to your father will be paid."

He looked at her through carefully guarded eyes. It wouldn't do for her to see the hope simmering there. "That depends."

"On what?"

"On a lot of things."

"Is getting caught one of them?"

He made an affirmative sound.

"Will you make a run for the border or head West to California?"

"I haven't decided." In truth, he didn't want to run anywhere. He knew where his home was and that's where he wanted to stay. But the events of the last twenty-four hours had made that likelihood a distant dream. "And what about you?"

"Me?"

"Where will you run?"

She looked at him blankly.

"Leisha, the entire U.S. Army will be on you as soon as that soldier comes around and tells what he saw. You knew that, didn't you? You knew there'd be no going home the minute you went ahead with your plan to get him?" He jerked his head toward their prisoner.

She stared at Kenitay so long and intensely, he could see that she had never thought it out the way he had. She had considered the immediate, not the long range. And now the magnitude struck and struck hard.

No going home. No going back to a normal life. No family to surround and protect her. Just an empty road ahead and constant danger.

The shadow of fear came into her eyes, but she never let it surface.

"I guess I could always go with you."

It was a huge assumption spoken so casually Kenitay was stunned. Didn't she know she was handing him his dearest dream with that offhand remark? Everything he wanted—under the worst possible circumstances. Why hadn't she been willing to go with him before she effectively ruined their chance to have a future? As it was, she was accepting him only as a last resort. Knowing that made him irritable as all hell.

"If your father doesn't skin me for letting you get into this trouble," he growled.

"Letting me? I don't recall you *letting* me do anything. My choices were my own—they had nothing to do with you."

"I'm well aware of that," he snapped. He knew he didn't figure importantly in her plans. She'd made that painfully clear. "But Harmon might not see it that way."

The rabbits were sizzling and golden brown. Kenitay handed one of the sticks to Leisha and began to tear into the other himself.

"What about me?"

He regarded Westfall with a narrowed gaze. "You can live off your arrogance. I was told that many times on the reservation when my belly was so empty it roared. See if those words give you any comfort." He continued eating. When he'd chewed the rabbit down to little more than gristle and bone, he tossed the carcass at Westfall's feet, watching grimly as the man, in his expensive evening wear, scrambled to get his hands on it. Hunger knew no pride. Another hard lesson he'd learned long ago.

A chill settled in with the evening hours and soon Leisha was shivering. She drew the folds of Kenitay's shirt closer about her and tucked up next to the ineffective fire in her next-to-non-existent underclothes. She watched as Kenitay spread one of the saddle blankets upon the hard ground. Glazed by firelight, his torso was a tempting ripple of strength—dark skin over hard muscle. Desire stirred, warming the way the fire never could.

"We'll share these," he was saying as he shook out the other blanket. "It'll be warmer that way."

A practical solution that woke all sorts of emotions. Leisha didn't want to think about lying in his arms and yet, she couldn't resist the suggestion. She joined him on the scratchy wool without comment, putting her back to him and letting him wrap his big, hard body around her. There was heat and there was longing aplenty.

Who was this man, she wondered as she hugged one strong arm to her breast. Was he an honorable man driven by a noble code or the greedy deceiver Westfall described? He hadn't been truthful with her. She'd known that from the start but what was the reason behind his silence? Was it pride or was it cunning?

In the deep-starred quiet, she considered all that she'd done. She'd broken a wanted criminal from the clutches of the government. She'd aided that same fugitive in a cross-country trek to abduct a man with murder in mind. At Kenitay's side, she'd gone across the grain of everything her family stood for. She couldn't pretend it was just for the sake of her father's sanity. It was also because Kenitay had said he loved her. Was that loyalty or extreme foolishness on her part? Not knowing made for an uneasy slumber.

And then she awoke to a cool dawn to find him gone. He'd built up the fire and tucked the blanket in around her. Westfall was still asleep in the awkward constraints of his tether. One of the horses was gone. That Kenitay would leave her made no sense so she fought down her initial panic and began a restless wait. Sure enough, before a half hour had passed and the sun was beginning to warm, she heard the sound of a single horse approaching.

"Why didn't you wake me?" she accused as Kenitay swung down.

"You needed the rest and I needed to do some raiding." He extended an armload of booty, not volunteering its source. She found a woman's calico dress and frilly sunbonnet, some smoked meat and crusty bread for their breakfast. One didn't question a warrior's gifts so she took the clothes, returned his shirt, and was quick to dress under his silent scrutiny.

They arrived to meet the train, using the money from the sale of their horses to purchase Kenitay's ticket. Leisha had already bought one for herself and Westfall and still had them in her mangled evening bag. They didn't board together. Leisha sat in a forward seat, her features shielded by the bonnet amid a batch of crying children and harried Texas prairie mothers. Kenitay settled in the center of the car with Westfall bound and gagged beside him, using their very visibility to hide them. When curious looks turned his way, he grinned and drawled in his Texas best, "Takin' this here embezzler back to stand for his crimes. Workin' for my daddy—maybe you heard of him, Cap'n Jack Bass of the Rangers outta Terlingua? The gag? Well, that's to protect the ladies' ears. He's got a real bad mouth on him."

And in her forward seat, Leisha smiled and leaned back to enjoy the ride.


The three of them left the train at Marathon. Leisha claimed her baggage, expecting to be asked about her part in Westfall's abduction at any minute but everything was quiet at the station. She quickly abandoned the calico in favor of her buckskins and joined Kenitay at the livery where he was picking up four horses. They loaded the still-trussed Indian agent into his saddle and headed down out of Marathon, leading him and the fourth pack animal across the dust of West Texas into the Bend. Leisha asked about the extra horse but Kenitay didn't answer.

Eenah met them, joining the trio like a silent shadow in the waning afternoon light. He had a black glare for Westfall and asked no questions.

"Beech left early for Terlingua," Kenitay explained in thick Apache gutturals. "We weren't able to catch him. By traveling fast cross-country, we should be able to arrive ahead of him."

"What is his business there?"

"The same as ours, I would guess, so we must be careful to catch him before he catches us."

"Then what?" Leisha asked.

The two men looked at her impassively and she thought they wouldn't answer. Then Kenitay replied, "We take the vengeance that is rightfully ours."

They didn't need to draw her a picture. They were going to kill him horribly in the way of the Apache.

Probably the same way her father would see to Westfall.

And suddenly that impending savagery began to prey upon her. She'd considered herself toughened to the way of life her father and his people led. But hearing about it and being a part of it were two very different things. She'd never had to experience the brutality that hardened men into unfeeling instruments of revenge. She understood that drive, that instinctive quest, but it wasn't bred in her. She'd been raised in the comfort of a West Texas mansion, her imagination fed with stories of great deeds of courage and nobility. But faced with the same test, her convictions wavered. She had killed in her own defense and the act haunted her nightly. How could she justify in her own heart and mind that this was retribution and not just plain murder? She had to find a way or be forced to accept the fact that the two men she loved most in the world were no better than cold-blooded killers.

But Leisha was a realist. She knew she'd come too far to back away from distress. She knew she had to go forward with what she'd so blindly begun. It was too late to wonder if it was the right thing. It was done. She would not weaken before Kenitay and his Apache companion. Such indecision would shame her after demanding to be treated as an equal.

After all, Kenitay had given her every opportunity to relinquish her right to revenge. And she'd declined with haughty Bass pride.

And now she was condoning murder and would spend the rest of her life on the run regretting it.

They camped on the northwest slope of the Chisos where the winds blew soft and cool and whispered of centuries past, where the landscape was painted so vividly in strokes of red, yellow, and purple it almost hurt the eye to gaze upon it in the fiery pre-twilight hour. To Leisha, these things meant home and a huge melancholy wedged up around her heart as she stood alone in the disappearing daylight gazing off over the distant foothills.

"You haven't had much to say today."

She started as Kenitay came to stand beside her. She glanced up at him to see his expression shadowed with the same depth of moody mystery that cloaked the high peaks above them.

"I'm not much inclined toward talk."

"It's this place, *silah*. You can feel the restless spirits on such a night as this, all those souls torn from this life by violence."

"Will ours wander here someday?"

"Maybe. Unless we got real smart and got ourselves

married, raised a batch of kids, and died with smiles on our faces in our own bed."

Leisha went very still. It was a long moment before she dared look up at him again. He was gazing at the far hills, a slight smile softening the chiseled angles of his mouth. What was he suggesting? She found her pulse was pounding like crazy.

Then he sighed. "Of course those dreams aren't for us. We've been restless spirits since the day we were born, haven't we, *shijii?*" He said that so sadly as if he wished it wasn't true. She didn't know what to say so she stayed silent. He took her lack of response for agreement and let his arm ease about her shoulders, drawing her in against his side. She allowed herself to be led, then was seduced by his strength into wrapping her arms around his waist with her head leaning upon his chest.

They stood like that for some time, absorbed in one another and in the fanciful glimpse of what might have been if they'd been other than who they were. Then Kenitay kissed the crown of her head and held her away.

"I've got to head out for a while. Eenah's riding into Terlingua to see if Beech is there yet. You keep an eye on Westfall whilst I'm gone."

"Where—?"

But he placed his forefinger to her lips then leaned down to replace it with his mouth. It was a brief gesture, too quick to bring passion, too sweet to discourage emotion.

"I don't want you to worry, Leisha. Everything will turn out all right for you. I promise." Then his hand stroked over her hair and he left her there in a fluster of bittersweet longing.

She didn't realize until later that she hadn't corrected him for his patronizing attitude. Deep down inside, she was hoping he was right.

He didn't return to their camp until close to dawn.

Leisha had been dozing fitfully, listening for him as slumber played in and out of her consciousness. She was glad for Eenah's absence, never feeling quite comfortable beneath his inscrutable stare. After tomorrow, he would be Kenitay's worry, not hers any longer. She would have enough worries of her own, despite the promise she'd been given.

She had almost dropped off when Kenitay rode in quietly, leading the extra horse. She could tell from the way it moved that the animal was loaded down.

She didn't betray her wakefulness, watching through slitted eyes as Kenitay tied up both horses, then checked briefly on Westfall's bonds before stretching out on his own blanket. He was asleep instantly.

Leisha waited as long, tense minutes passed and the sounds of his slumber deepened. Then she crept from her blanket to where Kenitay had tethered the fourth horse. There was only a sliver of a moon overhead but she hoped it would be enough to reveal the secrets he'd bundled on that packhorse's back.

Working silently, she loosened the ropes that crisscrossed the canvas covering, then tugged up one of the edges. Several bulky leather pouches were lashed down beneath it. She felt one of them. Whatever was in them was heavy and unyielding. Like rock.

Like bars of gold.

The fortune Westfall had told her about.

The fortune Kenitay was keeping all to himself.


They were up early, readying to ride into Blue Creek. Kenitay made no mention of the packhorse, as if by his silence, she wouldn't notice it. Leisha noticed plenty. Like the way he kicked out their fire almost reluctantly and jerked Westfall to his feet with angry abruptness. It was the first time she'd seen their prisoner shaken from his

stoicism since that moment in the alley when she was sure
Kenitay was going to blow the man's head off. He had
no words to spare her as they mounted up and headed
along the foothills to the place she knew as home.

They came up on the big West Texas mansion. There,
Kenitay found his voice as he reached out to snag her
reins, pulling her up.

"Leisha, are you sure you want to do this?"

She gave him a frigid look to mask her own mounting
apprehension. "Of course I'm sure. Let go."

"You could be making a big mistake."

"Well, that's none of your concern, is it?"

He let go, mirroring her hard expression. "I guess not."

She urged her horse ahead at a brisk gait, drawing upon
that energy to bolster her own mood. She'd done it. She'd
gone after Westfall in the name of her father and was
bringing the man back. She was returning home in tri-
umph to earn her father's respect. And that's all she'd ever
wanted, for him to see her as a competent equal. The price
of that success wasn't important, not compared to the acceptance she'd always longed for. By the time she reined
up before the wraparound front porch, she was flushed
with the pride of her accomplishment and eager for his
reaction.

She swung down while Kenitay remained seated, holding Westfall's reins. In two quick strides, she'd topped the
porch.

"Daddy?"

Harm met her at the door, his features pulling with
concern when he got a look at her black-ringed eyes and
swollen nose.

*"Shijii,* what happened? Are you all right?"

She brushed off his worry with a wave. "It's nothing."
Taking hold of his arm, she tugged him from the house.
"Come see what I've brought you."

He smiled, bemused by her excitement, and allowed

himself to be led to the steps where he got his first look at the two riders in the yard. He nodded to Kenitay then turned his gaze to the second man. Then he stared for a long, disbelieving moment.

"For you," Leisha claimed.

# Twenty-two

Leisha had expected it to be an emotional moment but she was unprepared for the feelings it brought forth from her father's soul.

Harm made a soft sound, a raw pull of air tangled around a tremendous pain. His eyes had gone round and blank with shock as he stared up at the man who'd helped tear his childhood from him. There was no doubt that Westfall remembered him. He sat like a man doomed, seeing a fierce Apache boy in the man on the stairs next to his hard-jawed daughter. He was expecting to die at any instant.

But Harm took a step back. His voice was a whisper. "What's he doing here?"

Leisha gave him a grim smile. "I brought him for you, Daddy. I tracked him down and convinced him to come make amends for the past."

"Harmon?" Amanda came up behind him, feeling the tension jumping through him when she placed her hands upon his arms. "What's going on?" She looked to her daughter, stunned by her ferocious expression. She'd seen the look before, on the face of a wild half-breed man as he roasted his victim over a smoldering fire. Seeing it on Leisha put a terrible fear in her. "What have you done?"

Leisha gestured grandly to the trussed-up man. "Westfall. You wouldn't let Daddy go after him to exact his revenge so I brought him here." Then she waited, all sharp, deadly anticipation.

But that proud look collapsed in confusion when Harm turned away and silently strode inside. Then there was just her mother to face.

Amanda was livid.

"How could you do such a thing to him? How could you push all the horrible things he's suffered back into his face just to feed your vanity?"

While Leisha gaped, Amanda whirled and followed her husband into the house.

What had gone so wrong? Leisha didn't understand it. Hurting her father was the last thing she'd intended. She hadn't done it for herself, she'd done it for him.

Or had she?

Upset and uncertain, she turned to the two on horseback with a shaky false composure. Kenitay regarded her levelly without a trace of "I told you so." She was supremely grateful that he'd allow her to keep face.

"I'll see to the horses," he offered. "And secure him in the barn."

Leisha nodded, unable to trust her voice just then.

As they headed across the yard, Westfall sighed in relief. It was a short-lived sense of security.

"I wouldn't get to feeling too comfortable if I were you," Kenitay drawled without looking at him. "You still have me to deal with."

Harm was standing at the windows in their bedroom, his palms and forehead pressed against the glass. Amanda approached with a mix of caution and care. She could only guess what the confrontation with his nightmare had done to the tenuous balance of his mental state. He flinched at her light touch, then gathered her arms about himself in a tight wrap.

"I'm all right, Ammy."

He didn't sound it.

"She just surprised me is all. One helluva surprise." What started as a laugh suddenly fractured in a big way. "Dear God, Ammy, what kind of monster do my children think I am?" He brought her hands up to the dampness on his cheek. "She brought that man here the way a cat brings a dead bird to the door, then drops it and waits for praise. What does she expect me to do with him? Just step right up and cut out his heart right on my own doorstep?"

Amanda leaned into him, pressing her lips to the nape of his neck before murmuring gently, "There was a time when you might have done just that."

"I'm not that man anymore!" He turned to meet her gaze somewhat desperately. "Ammy, I'm not that man." He waited anxiously for her to support him.

She stroked his face and smiled. "No, you're not that man."

"I changed for you and our kids. I've worked so hard to put what I was behind me. I wanted to become something you could all be proud of. Was I wrong? Is it something I can't escape? Have I walked so long in darkness that I can't separate it from the light I feel with you?" A terrible, stricken look came over him. "Amanda, when I saw him there on that horse, a part of me went crazy enough to want to pull him down and kill him as horribly as I could. Seeing him brought back the way my mama looked after they'd used her up and killed her, the way I found Becky with those two who made off with her for Mexico, half-naked with a rope around her neck tying her to the saddle like an animal. It brought back the sound of their screaming and all the times I wanted to but couldn't." The back of his head thudded against the windowpane and his eyes screwed up tightly as if he was still struggling to close it out. "I wanted to make him pay for those things."

"What stopped you?"

He opened his eyes. They glittered like the surface of Blue Creek on a cloudless summer day. "The look on Leisha's face. It was like a reflection of my soul and it scared me so bad, the hate was shocked right out of me."

Amanda made a sympathetic sound and drew his dark head down to her shoulder where she held him and kissed his brow tenderly. "She doesn't understand, Harmon. She doesn't know the truth."

"She learned it from me, Ammy. I didn't mean for her to pick up on the darkness of my past. I wanted her—I wanted all our children to be strong and secure and capable of seeing to themselves."

"And they are. You did a good job with them. You're a good man, Harmon Bass. I've always known that."

He shook his head. "I'm not so good, Ammy. What I am is smart. Smart enough to hang on to the best thing a man could ever wish for." He straightened and slid his palms up to capture her face between them. "You are the good in me, you and those children we were blessed with. If I ever thought for a minute that I'd bring you to regret the day you said 'I do'—"

"I don't. I never have. I never will." That was said with such firm conviction, he had to smile.

"Sometimes I wonder which one of us is the craziest, little girl."

"I don't mind being crazy as long as I can howl at the moon with you."

Their kiss was long and intense.

"So," Amanda murmured as she rubbed her cheek against his much darker one, "what are we going to do with him?"

"Well, I sure as hell don't plan on asking him to sit down with us at supper." Then Harm's smile spread slow and thin. "Unless we make it a good old-fashioned Apache barbecue."

"I don't think so, Harmon." But she smiled back because he was feeling strong enough to joke about it. Even if the joke was more than a little grisly. It was typical Harmon humor. "He can stay tied up in the barn until we come up with something."

Harm's features sobered. "What are we going to do with Leisha?"

"I'll talk to her. Our woman-to-woman talk is long overdue and I'd just as soon have everything settled before Randall and Becca get back from town."

"I'll see our guest is comfortable."

"Be a good host, Harmon."

"Aren't I always?" He gave her his best smile and started from the room. After a second's thought, Amanda caught his hand and held it tightly.

"Harmon, whatever you decide to do with him will be all right with me. He doesn't deserve your mercy."

Harm stared at her for a long moment, overwhelmed by her devotion. Then he said simply, "I want to do the right thing."


Leisha was on the front porch, pacing like something wild and caged. Her expression was closed down tight but there was a frantic brilliance to her gaze, betraying her agitation. She came to a stop when she saw her mother. Arrogance firmed up her posture.

"I suppose you're going to tell me what a wrong and terrible thing I did."

It was a struggle for Amanda not to react to the belligerence in her daughter's tone but rather to the fright deep inside. She came calmly out onto the porch and Leisha was instantly wary. They regarded each other for a long moment, almost as combatants searching out weaknesses. Then Amanda spoke up with a careful neutrality.

"It was wrong and it was foolish and probably something I would have done at your age."

Leisha narrowed her eyes, waiting for the rest.

"But it was also one of the most courageous and caring things I've ever seen."

Leisha's caution didn't lessen. "Then why are you so angry with me?"

"Because I've worked for years to turn your father away from his past and I won't allow you to resurrect it."

"You just don't understand the Apache way," Leisha accused with a haughty tilt of her chin.

Amanda gave her a weary smile and sighed. "Leisha, there's very little about the Apaches that I don't understand. I have the utmost respect for their ways even if they are not my own. But this isn't about being an Apache."

Leisha wasn't listening. "If you loved him as much as you love your own comfort, you wouldn't have held him back."

Amanda shook her head in exasperation. "If I valued my comfort, I wouldn't be living out here where I have to shake the dust off my clothes before getting dressed each morning. I'd be living in a posh apartment in New York City in the care of a dozen servants. There's nothing comfortable or safe about this life or the man I married, but I stay because I do care about him. I understand what he needs. He needs me to keep him looking ahead instead of back. He needs me to be strong when he's weak. Harmon says an Apache man calls his mate 'the one with whom he goes about.' I'm that someone and there's nothing I would not do for him."

"Except let him do what he must as a man."

"I'm not stopping him, Leisha. He could walk any path he chooses and I'd still take him back. He knows that. I knew the kind of man your father was when I married him but we made an agreement then: he'd give me all the love and security he could and I'd be the anchor that keeps him civilized and sane. Those terms have served us very well over the years."

"You make him weak with your demands."

"No. I make him a stronger, better man by standing behind him. That's what a woman does for the man she loves. It's every bit as important as standing beside him in a fight. I can see you don't believe me. You think if I loved him, I'd goad him into going down to the barn to slice that man to pieces. If I thought murder would brighten the darkness in his heart, I'd go down there myself and help."

Leisha blinked at the savageness of her mother's tone.

"No one hurts what's mine," Amanda continued with conviction. "Harmon is mine. By bringing that man here, you hurt him and I won't stand for it. By strutting around like someone who's too good to listen to what anyone else has to say, you hurt him and that's going to stop, too. We raised you to be strong, not ruthless. We raised you to be clever, not cunning. We want you to be independent, not self-centered. You want to do something to please your father? Love him. You want him to be proud of you? Make the best life for yourself that you can. That's it. That's all he wants. He doesn't want to see his mistakes in you. You're breaking his heart, Leisha, and if *you* cared, you'd let him bury his past and get on with your own future."

Leisha stood stiffly while her mother embraced her with a sudden, surprising tenderness.

"I'll take care of Harmon," she confided. "You find a man of your own that will mean more to you than your life. And then love him. Stand behind him, beside him, or in front of him, wherever he needs you to be. Then you'll realize it's not a weakness not to want to be alone."

Then she stroked her daughter's hair and returned to the house, leaving Leisha to consider her words and the confusion in her own heart.

And in those quiet, soul-searching moments, she discovered one undeniable truth: she'd already found the man for her, the man who meant more to her than life, but his

interest was in the now, not in the later. He was packing
24-carat secrets he didn't care to share and rode with the
shadow of a noose over his head.

So any way she looked at it, she was going to be alone.


"Making our visitor comfortable?"

Kenitay looked to Harm with a thin smile. "As comfortable as he deserves." He'd bound Westfall to one of
the stall doors with his hands wedged up high behind his
back.

"I think we both know what he deserves."

Kenitay scooted over on the bale he was perched upon
so Harm could take a seat beside him. The Texas tracker
was glaring a hole through their prisoner but his outward
expression was admirably controlled. Westfall was well
aware of the look even though he was too far away to
hear their words. His expression said he was sure they
were plotting his murder.

"What do you plan to do with him?" Kenitay asked at
last.

"I suppose I should do something since my daughter
went through all the trouble to round him up and bring
him to me gift wrapped. What do you think I should do
with him?"

"If you kill him, Leisha will be accountable."

"And that bothers you, does it?"

"Doesn't it bother you? She stole him out of a party
full of Austin bigwigs, had him at knifepoint in front of
the U.S. Army, and carted him across half of Texas tied
up like a Christmas turkey."

Harm smiled. "Resourceful little girl."

"She's in a helluva lot of trouble because of you!"

"Because of me? I suppose breaking a murderer out of
a prison wagon wouldn't count for anything against her."
Seeing Kenitay's surprised look, he explained, "Jack's not

much of a liar. He came clean shortly after you left. I'd say if anyone was leading my little girl down a troubled path, it's you."

"I'm going to make amends for that."

Harm snorted. "How? By butchering this man's partner and going off on the run? You know she'll follow you."

"Why would she?"

"Because she's got more of her mama in her than she'll admit to."

"I haven't asked her to."

"Son, she won't wait for no invitation."

Kenitay looked worried. "I don't want her living on the run with me. That's no kind of life."

"I agree. I've been on that road before and it's no kind of place to take those you love."

He said it so matter-of-factly Kenitay never thought to protest. He didn't care if Harm knew he was in love with his daughter. But he would make it clear he was not going to be responsible for ruining her life.

"I guess the only thing to do is not to run."

Harm glanced at him with a modest amount of interest. "What are you planning to do?"

"I'm going to take care of my business and turn myself over to Jack."

"Now there's a noble sentiment that will be followed real quick by a hanging."

"What else can I do?" he asked in gruff agitation. "I've already killed one man. Another can't matter much. They can only hang me once and I'll have the satisfaction of knowing my father's spirit will be at rest."

Harm plucked a piece of straw from the bale and chewed the tip thoughtfully. "I knew your daddy. He was a proud man, a good warrior, a smart leader. He knew that sometimes when you're going for evens, settling for less than blood is the better deal. If he hadn't thought so, I wouldn't be here today and neither would Jack. Revenge doesn't have to be cut and dry, an eye for an eye. It's getting an acceptable payment for what you're owed. A fair trade. Do you understand?"

Kenitay scowled in Westfall's direction for a long moment, then glowered at Harm. "He killed my father. How can you ask me to settle for less than his life? You don't know—"

"He killed my mother."

Kenitay was taken aback. He could only stare, speechless, while Harm twirled the straw between his fingers with an eerie calm.

"Him and eight others paid a visit to our ranch when I was ten. They had orders to leave nothing standing but took their time doing it. Folks call Apaches savages but the things they did no decent Apache would have conceived of. They killed my mama—eventually, and they buried me with her, thinking they'd killed me, too. Then they burned down everything we had and took my sister, Jack's mama, with them, meaning to sell her below the border when they got tired of her. They should have made sure I was dead before they dropped me in that hole. I made sure they were when I caught up to them one by one."

Kenitay saw unimaginable horror flashing through the shadows in Harm's eyes. He knew his father's people respected, even feared, Harm Bass and now he could understand why. He was a man who understood going for evens without mercy.

"You killed them all?"

"Seven of them. One managed to acquit himself at the last minute by dying with honor at another's hand. Now, there's just him and the man responsible for it all."

"Does Leisha know all this?"

"I saw no reason to saddle her with my ghosts. How she found out about it, I don't know. Guess she figured I'd be so eager to claim his hair, I'd overlook what she risked to get him. I've never put a hand to any of my kids but if I thought it'd do any good, I'd beat her for making such a foolish sacrifice. I've tried to bury my past and I won't have her reviving or reliving it. A man can't live and be ruled by revenge and I decided long ago that nothing is worth losing family."

"So you're going to let him go?" The question was stark with amazement.

"I didn't say that. I just said mine doesn't have to be the hand that spills his blood. He's done murder twice and probably worse things in between. I'll let the law have him. We're almost at a new century. Man can't hang onto the old ways forever. Not if he wants to survive."

Kenitay was silent, pensive.

"I love my family," Harm concluded. "He's taken enough from me already. I won't give him more. I have to let go now or he'll have a hold on me forever. You think on that, Kenitay. It's surviving to fight another day. That's always been the secret to our people's existence. A foolish man holds his ground even when there's no chance of winning. A wise man quits and walks away, knowing he'll have another chance at another time when the odds are more in his favor. Would your father want you to follow a dead-end path or would he consider it a waste of his only son?"

"Sid gave me some options."

"Sid's a smart boy. You listen to him."

"He said if I turned myself in, he'd represent me. I'll still have to do some time for the killing of that soldier in Fort Sill."

"And you're wondering if a certain lady'd be willing to wait for you?"

Kenitay's gaze cut over to him briefly, steeped in hope and desperate for reassurance.

"Did you ask her to?"

"No. It's not much to offer a woman you want to marry."

"I think the hardest part's gonna fall on me. I'm the one who'll have to keep her from breaking you outta prison. She and her mama aren't known for their patience."

"I—I thought you'd be of a mind that she deserved better."

Harm chuckled. "If we got what we deserved, I surely wouldn't have what I've got now. Amanda's of the mind that Leisha's wild about you. I don't know where she gets these crazy notions but I've long since given up arguing with her. You make things right and me and her mama will help her pack her bags."

Kenitay met his eye squarely. "I'll make her a good husband."

"I know you will, son. Convincing her that she wants one is gonna be up to you."

They at side by side for a companionable minute, both toying with future plans they never expected to be making. Then Kenitay hopped off the bale.

"Harmon, there's one more thing I need to ask you. I think my father would approve of you being the one to handle it for him."

"I'd he honored to do what I can in your father's name."

"Over here."

Puzzled, Harm followed him to the distant stall where he'd stabled the packhorse. Kenitay burrowed down into the clean straw in the animal's manger and withdrew a heavy pouch. He tossed it to Harm, who groaned with the weight of it.

"What's this?"

"A lot of dreams."

Leisha was brooding on the porch steps when Kenitay emerged from the barn, leading his horse. Her thoughts came to a halt as she took in the sight of him. No other could send her heart off into such fluttery tangents or make her blood run like hot quicksilver. He moved with a strong masculine stride lightened with Apache grace. Confident. Exciting. Leisha was so caught up in the watching she almost missed the significance.

His horse was saddled and ready to ride.

Everything staggered to a stop inside her as that awareness settled deep. Emotion built in an instant to something so mighty it scared her.

"You're leaving," she stated with remarkable calm.

He drew up in front of her and nodded. "I have to."

"I guess this is it then. I want to thank you for all your help. I couldn't have—I couldn't have done it alone."

The formal tone of her voice brought a mask to his features. But his reply wasn't as detached. "It was a good partnership."

This time, she nodded. The swell of longing was almost intolerable. It plugged up around her heart, massing in her chest, clogging her throat when there were so many words she needed to say. Words like *Don't go!* Words like *I need you!* But she couldn't force them through that solid ache of misery. He was leaving to pursue his own path. His promise to her had been fulfilled and she had no right to demand more of him. He'd made it plain from the start that he had his own agenda. And there was no place in those plans for her.

No strings. No ties. They'd both agreed.

It was the hardest pledge she'd ever had to honor.

"Leisha, I've spoken with your father and he'll see that you're not held accountable for helping me to escape. As I promised, you have nothing to worry about. You can go on with your life here just as it was before."

Oh, what a grim prospect! She clenched her jaw tight so it wouldn't tremble and betray her. Then, when she could finally work her way around the paralysis freezing her heart and mind, she said, as normally as possible, "If I don't see you again, take care of yourself."

He frowned slightly. Had he been waiting to hear something else? "You do the same," he said at last. Then he turned and stepped up onto his horse and all her hopes rose with him, hanging there upon this one man who had never given her any reason to hold onto them. He'd said he loved her. More than once. Maybe he'd meant it. But if he had, wouldn't there have been more? Maybe not a firm offer of commitment—she wasn't naive enough to believe that possible, but maybe just a suggestion that he thought of the two of them as a pair. Something she could hang onto, something she could use to fill the gaping hole in her heart after he rode away.

She'd known all along it would end like this. All her efforts to prevent it had failed. He was leaving and she was never going to get over it. Never.

But she'd be damned if she'd let him know how long and hard she planned to cry after he rode out of the yard.

"Good-bye," she called. She even managed what he might have taken for a smile.

He gave her a brisk nod and hauled his horse around.

He'd gone halfway across the yard when her composure cracked.

My God, he was leaving! She might never see him again!

"Kenitay!"

The cry had sprung to her lips before she was aware of it. She stood on the steps, feeling the tears on her face, feeling the terrible burn in her heart, praying he hadn't heard her, that he wouldn't turn back.

But he did.

He sat his horse looking every inch the noble warrior ready to do battle. And the look he gave her was that of a conqueror who wasn't about to let her retreat.

"You're going to have to say it, Leisha."

His words made no sense at first. She stood staring at him, her vision blurred by tears. Say what? She started to shake her head, to claim she didn't understand.

But that wasn't true.

She did know what he was waiting to hear. And she was as surprised as he was when she spoke up loud and clear.

"I love you."

# Twenty-three

He rode back up to the porch and stared down at her. "What did you say?"

She squared off boldly because inside she was shaking all over. "I said I love you." There. She'd said it twice. Now he had to believe her.

Now he had to stay.

But instead of climbing down, he bent to sweep his arm around her waist, lifting her up to him, smashing his mouth down over hers. His power and possessiveness shocked her senses as her arms locked around his neck. The impact of his kiss raced all the way to her dangling toes. He was a starved man with his last meal and he meant to savor every morsel.

One kiss melted into the next. Leisha was responding with the same desperate passion, the same hungry urgency, a kettle too long at simmer finally coming to a boil. Relief came like an explosion, all hot and sizzling and moist. *Mine.*

He broke away and she found herself hanging limply against him, her face wet with tears, her mouth damp from his kisses. Prairie fires were cooler than the light in his eyes.

"The last thing in the world I want to do right now is ride out of here," he told her gruffly. "You know that, don't you?"

She nodded numbly.

"Tell me that you want me to come back."

"You'd better. 'Cause if I have to, I'll track you down and you know there's no place on earth you could hide from me."

He kissed her again, greedily, with a grinding pressure that was hurtful and heaven at the same time. "You'll wait for me," he murmured against her parted lips. It was a command. She never thought to object.

"Forever," she breathed back with a scorching intensity.

He set her down on the porch and wheeled his horse away, galloping from the yard without a backward glance while she stood there, weeping and watching him go.

And then she realized how light he was traveling.

He'd left the money behind!

She headed for the barn at a run, wiping her eyes and sniffing hard against the need to shed more tears. She skidded to a halt just inside the open door when she saw her father framed against the darker interior. She hesitated, swamped by remorse and not knowing how to get back onto familiar ground with him. Until he spread his hands wide and beckoned to her with the curl of his fingers. With a soft cry, she rushed to fill his arms. Here, too, was something that needed to be settled.

"I'm sorry, Daddy. Mama was right. I was only thinking of myself. I wanted to be important in your eyes."

"Hush now, little girl. Quit talking nonsense. You've always shone in my eyes. Always. I've always been proud of you for being so brave and smart and sure of yourself. And pretty, like your mama. I don't know where you got the idea that you had anything to prove to me or to yourself. You're as fine a piece of work as ever's been bred in West Texas." She clung to him in silence. "I thought there was an openness between us, *shijii*. When did that change?"

"The day you looked at me and saw a daughter instead of your firstborn."

"Oh." He shifted her slightly so her head was pillowed on his shoulder and he was petting her hair. "I was raised to believe there was a difference between a man and a woman. Different but equal, the way me and your mama are. The one's there to support the other, not to challenge, not to compete. It's a balance of strength, a harmony. If you thought I respected you less because of that pretty face, *shijii*, you couldn't be more wrong. I don't believe in holding to strict man-woman roles. If I did, I wouldn't have married your mama. She sure as hell isn't much on the domestic front but I don't trust anyone the way I trust her. She's the other half of the man I am. You've got her grit, little girl. I always knew there was nothing in this world you couldn't do if you set your mind to it. Because you're a Bass and you're the best of your mama and me. If I pulled away from you, it's because I was brought up to have a respect for women. I've never been one to be comfortable with displays, not even with my sister or my mama."

"You are with Sarah," she complained faintly.

Harm laughed. "Your cousin Sarah kinda overwhelms everyone. She'd never stand for me being shy around her. But that's the Apache way. Wait until you and Kenitay marry and he starts hedging about being in the same room with your mama. A son-in-law believes it's a sign of disrespect to be in the presence of his wife's mother. If you're planning on living under this roof, you'd better start talking to him now or you won't see hide nor hair of him later."

Leisha pulled back out of his arms to stare in bewilderment. "Marry Kenitay? What gave you that idea?"

"Your mama. She seems to think you're made to fit. I suggest you make sure that fit's permanent before you try it on too often."

Leisha blushed at his insinuation but cast up a questioning gaze that was unexpectedly soft and feminine. "And did Kenitay mention anything to you along those lines?"

"Could be he did. Why? You thinking serious thoughts about that boy?"

She didn't try to squirm her way around his teasing. "Very serious," was her forthright reply. Then there was no mistaking the troubled furrowing of her brow.

"But—?" Harm prompted gently.

"But he's got an awful lot of past behind him. A lot of it's not good, some of it illegal, and some of it he won't tell me."

"There ain't a man in West Texas without something in his history he's not proud of. It's how he lives with what he's done that makes the measure of the man. I think Kenitay will measure up just fine."

"But he's wanted for killing a man and he's going after another right now."

"He's going to send Billy out here to fetch Westfall and to pick up Beech in town. Between the two of us, I think we can come up with enough testimony to put them away for a long time."

Leisha digested this, a glint of hope growing stronger. "But I broke him out of a prison wagon and kidnapped Westfall right in front of an army corporal."

He brushed her hair back with the gentle stroke of his hand. His smile was wry. "Funny, I don't think those men with the prison wagon would keep their jobs long if they was to say one pretty little blond girl robbed them of their prisoner. I'm sure they've already reported it was the work of at least a gang of big, burly men. And as for your corporal, a Wonderly, is it?"

"How—?"

"I got this telegram addressed to you saying something like, 'I can't recall seeing who it was that took that BIA man in the alley but I'll never forget our night together in Shafter. My best to your cousin, Ken, and your daddy.' Something you want to tell me?" He arched a dark brow and waited.

Leisha laughed with relief, "It's a great story. Another time, all right?"

"All right."

Then her amusement faded. "Daddy, Kenitay's toting a whole lot of gold. I think he might have stolen it and that's why he's in trouble with the law."

"That what you think? Did you ask him about it?"

"Well, no . . ."

"I did." And he related the story as Kenitay had told it, of how Kodene and his band were raiding south of the border when they overtook a single rider carrying a big load of silver. This man, a government man, had stolen the bars from a burro caravan making its way back to Shafter from a smelter in Mexico. A nice, smooth inside job that didn't take into account a batch of raiding Apaches. It was right after that when the Mescalero joined up with Geronimo in Arizona.

"How did Kenitay end up with it?"

"Turns out when he and his daddy settled at Fort Sill, these two fellows who were partnered in that first robbery got wind that Kodene was there. They'd found out he had hidden the silver before heading off on the warpath in Arizona and they used their positions with the government to try to beat the whereabouts out of him."

"Beech and Westfall."

Harm nodded. "But they got a little too greedy and a little too carried away and Kodene died before telling them anything. That's when they figured he must have told someone where he'd hidden all that money."

"They thought he'd told Kenitay."

Harm nodded again. "They were leaning on him real hard for answers. That's when he jumped the reservation at Fort Sill."

Leisha looked grim. "And he slit that soldier's throat."

Harm shook his head. "Where did you hear that?"

"Corporal Wonderly told me. He wouldn't have any reason to make it up. Why?"

"Because Kenitay said he struck the soldier once and the man fell, hitting his head. He swears it was an accident and I believe him."

"Then if that's how it happened, Kenitay didn't kill him. Someone else did."

The moment the connotations sank in, Leisha was racing for her horse.

Jed Cooper squinted out into the light of day. His mood was worsened by the way the sunlight glanced off his blood-shot eyes and skewered right to where the pain was the most intense between his temples. He glowered over toward his uncle's office, hating the humbling to come. He was flat broke after the night's run of bad luck. The saloon whore he'd been shacked up with had his clothes out in the hall before he could drag himself up to break the bad news. Apparently, she wasn't much for charity. That left one alternative if he wanted a roof over his head.

The thought of crawling over to Billy galled him something fierce but he didn't dare show up without his invite. Sarah had lost patience with him long ago and would be all too happy to bar the door. If he was going to have a place to stay, he'd have to do the necessary whining. His fool uncle couldn't stand firm against a good sob story.

He was working up the stomach for it when he happened upon an inspiration in the form of Becca Bass. As his gaze followed the pretty blonde down the length of the opposite walk, a smile curled his lips. She was toting an armful of packages which meant she'd come to town with money. He tipped his hat down to shade his red-streaked eyes and trotted across the dusty street.

"Hey, there, Miss Becca. Lemme carry those for you."

Big brown eyes peered over the top box and he gave

her his most dashing grin. "Why, thank you, Jed. That would be nice of you."

He scooped off the top few parcels and tucked them carelessly under one arm and looped the other through Becca's. She looked slightly surprised by his gallantry and blushed bemusedly.

"Where you headed?"

"The buggy's right down there at the end of the walk."

"Going home so soon? I ain't seen much of you lately and was hoping—well, I was kinda hoping you'd feel sorry for me and keep me from purely perishing of loneliness." He grinned and she blushed hotter. Becca was a sweet thing—nothing like her sister.

"I couldn't have that on my conscience," she murmured with a mild smile. "I could probably use a bite of lunch."

He hung his head and scuffed the toes of his boots on the boardwalk. "I'd love to treat you but—" He sighed heavily and cast up a sly glance. "Well, you don't want to hear my sad story."

She was instantly all concern. "Why? What happened?"

"Oh, I got a little careless with my beers last night and some fellers rolled me for the twenty I was carrying when I left the saloon."

"That's terrible!"

"Yeah, and I don't dare tell Uncle Billy 'cause I promised him I wouldn't do no more serious drinking. He won't believe it was just a couple of beers. I wouldn't want him to think I went back on my word. Honest to God, Becca, I'm trying to make something of myself. I just don't get no breaks. I was supposed to pick up something for Jessie's birthday and I don't have so much as a penny. It's gonna break her heart when I show up empty-handed."

"How much do you need?"

"Oh, Becca, I couldn't take no money offa you!" He was fighting hard not to smile in his eagerness.

"Don't be silly, Jed. What's family for? How much?"

He was wetting his lips, getting ready to name a figure when Rand stepped up to relieve his sister of her packages.

"Ready to go, Becca?"

"In a minute, Randall." She was reaching for her bag and Rand made the connection between that gesture and the greedy anticipation on Jed Cooper's face. He put his hand over his sister's to still it.

"Now, Becca, don't go embarrassing Jed by tipping him for carrying your boxes."

She gave him a chastising look. "I wasn't doing any such thing. I was just making him a small loan so he could get something for his sister's birthday."

Rand's cool gaze cut over to Jed. "That so," he drawled. "Funny, I seem to recall Jessie's birthday being three months ago."

"I missed it," Jed growled, seeing his plan go all to hell.

"Well, then she won't mind waiting a few more days while you do some honest work to pay for something she'll appreciate all the more."

Jed glared wordlessly while Rand took Becca's packages from him.

"Randall—"

Rand smiled at his sister and urged, "Go on down and climb on into the buggy, Becca. I want to make a little talk with Jed."

She hesitated, looking from one to the other. Rand was smiling affably but Jed's expression was as sour as bad milk. "All right, Randall. It was good to see you again, Jed."

" 'Bye, Miss Becca."

The minute she was out of earshot, Rand turned to him, the smile still on his face. But the glitter in his eyes turned the gesture into something far from pleasant.

"You might fool my sister but I know a coyote in lamb's

wool when I see one and you're not fleecing one cent from her so you can lose it on a bad hand."

"You don't know what you're talking about, Bass."

"The hell I don't. Becca's a nice girl. She don't want to see what you really are but you got none of the rest of us fooled. You're bad news, Jed. Stay away from Becca."

"Oh, I get it. You can go banging my sister on the sheets at night but I can't say so much as howdy to yours in broad daylight. Don't you sneer at me like you was something special jus' 'cause your mama's rich. That's the only reason your half-breed daddy stays with her, you know. Makes him something of a whore, too, don't it?"

Jed never saw the blow coming. It laid him out flat on his back in the street with his senses spinning. By the time he pushed up on his elbows to rub the massive ache in his jaw, Rand was helping his perplexed sister into their buggy and was settling beside her to take up the reins. He never looked back.

Jed grumbled a curse for all the Basses and dragged himself to his feet, glaring at everyone who glanced his way. He stumbled on to the jail and was half-relieved to find Billy wasn't there. He drew his kerchief through the water basin and held it to the throbbing reminder of Rand Bass's right hook. With a groan of resignation, he dropped into Billy's chair and shut his eyes.

"Excuse me. Could you tell me where I might find the sheriff?"

"He ain't here," Jed growled.

"Have you any idea when he might return?"

"Who wants to know?"

"My name is Beech. I'm with the Bureau of Indian Affairs."

Jed's eyes opened slowly, glittering with speculation. "Yeah? Maybe I can help you."

"I'm looking for some information about a half-breed wanted for a killing at Fort Sill, Oklahoma."

"Green-eyed feller?"

"Yes. I hear he has some family nearby by the name of Bass."

"You won't find out nothing from the sheriff but could be I might have a thing or two to tell you. If the price is right." Jed rubbed his jaw and smiled despite the pain. "We can discuss it over a whiskey. Where are you staying?"

That afternoon, a plump and pretty Sarah Bass opened the door of the Terlingua jail just as Kenitay was getting ready to enter. She looked at him curiously for a moment, then with a squeal of recognition and delight, launched herself upon him to pepper his face with kisses. That brought Billy up out of his chair in a hurry but he relaxed as soon as he saw who it was.

"Lucky you're related," he drawled with a welcoming smile. "I don't take kindly to my wife kissing on anyone but family. Would have hated to shoot you off the porch."

Sarah stood down and linked her arm possessively through Kenitay's. Her expression was one of pure deviltry, "Why, Billy, you forgot to mention how handsome he grew up to be."

"Did I? Must have slipped my mind. Come on in, Kenny." He got up and came around his desk, seeing the hesitation in the other's face and the way he kept glancing at the badge pinned to Billy's shirtfront. His nervousness was understandable. Billy relieved it by stepping up and enfolding Kenitay in a huge, rib-creaking bear hug. "Damn, it's good to see you again."

Once the tension of Kenitay's surprise eased, Billy let him go, keeping a companionable arm about his shoulders. He pointed to his middle where he was wearing the snake-skin and leather tooled belt he'd been given at Christmas a lot of years ago. Kenitay had made it for him and it was one of his prize possessions. "Still fits. Ain't put on so much as an inch." He gave Sarah a nudge. "Unlike some folks."

Sarah's dark eyes narrowed fiercely. "You didn't make four kids, either, Billy Cooper."

"Why, darlin', that's not true. I was there, too. Remember?" His dimples grew provokingly.

Sarah gave him a sultry look but she wasn't ready to forgive him yet. "For all I know, you could have been out there reseeding West Texas with your eye for skinny women in fluffy petticoats and you'd look no worse for wear."

Billy grinned disarmingly. "Now, darlin', you know yours are the only petticoats I get into these days. Hell, you don't leave me with enough energy to look elsewhere."

"Not to mention I'd shoot you dead if I ever caught you."

Billy's smile never faltered. "There's that, too."

Listening to their banter woke Kenitay to a wonderful remembrance of happier times, times he'd give anything to have again.

"What can I do for you, Kenny? Just visitin' or somethin' on your mind?" Billy was still smiling, his arm remaining casually draped in a show of camaraderie but there was a sudden shrewd intensity to his dark-eyed gaze. Kenitay was reminded that this man, though family and friend, was still the law. And knew his history well.

"Business for now but I hope to get around to the visiting someday."

"I hope so, too," Billy said with a somber sigh. "Whatcha need? Whatever I can do. You know that."

Kenitay nodded, feeling a surge of emotion through his chest. How could he have forgotten how good these people were? Billy, Sarah, Harm and Amanda, Jack, people to whom family was all. And they still considered him family.

"I need you to swing by Harm's and pick up a fellow

named Westfall. The man's a murderer and a thief. Harm can explain the details better. His accomplice is here in town or soon will be. His name is Beech. They're both with the BIA out of Fort Sill. Watch out for them. They're full of surprises."

"All right. I'll round 'em up." Then Billy gave him a penetrating look. "Can they clear you?"

"No."

"Sorry to hear that."

Kenitay nodded. "I'll be over at my mama's . . . when you need to come get me. I won't run."

Billy rumpled his short hair with a fond touch. "I know. I'll give you as much time as I can."

"I'd appreciate it." He gave Sarah a faint smile and left them.

Feeling his remorse, Sarah tucked up against her husband's side, hugging him tight. His big hand was instantly in her hair, stroking, tangling, holding her to him as he bent to press his lips upon those dark locks. She rode out the tremendous swell of his next reluctant breath.

"It's gonna break my heart to lock him up in back."

"Do you have to?"

"There's no way around it, Sarah. He'll be safer in my keeping then if he was to run into someone after bounty. And it'll look better, him turning himself in. He's got more guts than I'd have. I'd have run like hell."

Her palm rubbed over his middle in a soothing gesture. "But you didn't," she reminded softly.

Billy smiled into her hair. No, he hadn't at that. "I had me something worth staying for." Then he got to thinking, remembering how Leisha had been asking after those same two fellows—Beech and Westfall. Maybe Jack's adopted son had found something worth staying for, too.

He gave his wife a nudge. "As much as I'd like to stand around dreaming about your petticoats, I got me some work to do. I'm gonna mosey on over to the hotel and see if they got a guest by the name of Beech." He checked his pistol chambers with a casual flick of the wrist. "Then I'll have to persuade him to change accommodations before I go riding out to Harm's. Baby, why don't you run on over to Calvin's and see if he's up to sitting with a prisoner?"

"I'd rather go to the hotel with you."

"Now, darlin', I ain't got time for that." He grinned, deliberately misinterpreting her offer because she had that dangerous look in her eye that often as not backfired on him.

But Sarah didn't take the bait. She strode to his desk and retrieved his extra .45 from the drawer. She spun the cylinder expertly with her thumb and stared up at him steadily. "You need someone to back you."

"That may be, but—"

"And I'm not planning on losing you any time soon."

"Well, now, you just stick with that plan. Let's you and me take a little walk across the street."

The front room of the hotel was quiet and shaded in the sleepy afternoon hour. Billy strolled up to the desk with Sarah following slightly behind him. The desk clerk met him with an amiable smile.

"Afternoon, Sheriff Cooper, ma'am. Do something for you?"

"Check your books and see if you got a Beech signed in, will you, Henry?"

"Name's familiar. Let me take a gander."

"He ain't here," said a voice behind them.

Billy and Sarah turned to see Jed slouched at one of the tables at the entrance to the bar area. He was already halfway through the bottle sitting on the tabletop. In front of him was a huge pile of silver coins.

"What are you talking about, Jed?" Billy demanded.

"Beech. If you're looking for him, you're too damn late. He's already gone."

Billy sauntered over with a deceptively easy amble. "Suppose you tell me what you know about it?"

"Why? So you can stick up for them no-account Basses again? I ain't telling you nothing." His bruised jaw squared up belligerently.

Billy did a mental calculation of the money on the table. "Where did you get all this?"

"From being smart enough to see to myself."

His uncle reached out for a handful of his shirtfront and hauled him up off his chair. "Be smart now and do some fast talking."

Seeing the no-nonsense glint in Billy's eyes and figuring it wouldn't make any difference anyway, Jed spilled the details of his meeting with Beech. The more he said, the darker Billy's expression grew. And the darker it got, the more Jed's bravado faltered.

"You sonofabitch," Billy said hoarsely when he'd concluded. "You greedy sonofabitch. Do you have any idea what you've done?"

Jed's chin came up a sullen notch. "I took care of myself, like I always done before you showed up to dish out charity."

"Charity? Is that what you call it? It's family. And you haven't got the slightest idea what I'm talking about, do you?"

"Sure I do. It's family when it comes to them. It's handouts when it's your own kin. I'm sick of getting their leftovers and if you was any kinda man, you would be, too."

Driven by a deep internal rage, Billy drew back his fist but the blow was never delivered. As Jed cringed in anticipation, the memory of his own father's brutal punishments restrained him. Angrily, he pulled his nephew into a hard embrace where Jed stood stiff and wary.

"I'm not gonna hit you. I can't teach you anything with the back of my hand but I thought you'd learned by now that I took you in because I loved you. You're my family, you and Jessie. I only wanted what was best for you. I wanted you to have things I never did. I wanted to give you a chance."

But Jed's rigid posture never relaxed and Billy could see he didn't—and never would—understand a word he was saying. It was the hardest thing he'd ever had to do—step back and let go. Jed was staring at him through hostile eyes.

"I don't want you to come around no more, Jed. I'm done with you." With one last look at him, Billy turned and walked away.

Jed glared after him, his lips curling back in surly contempt. And that's when Sarah's punch took him just below the ribs, knocking the breath out of him. With a rattle of surprise, he crashed back into his chair from the force of the blow.

"I didn't say *I* wouldn't hit you," she growled menacingly while he gasped for air. "I better not ever see you anywhere near any of mine." Her hand swiped across the table, sending Beech's blood money flying. Her disgust grew as Jed followed the flight of winking silver in obvious dismay. "Take your silver and run far and fast because if any harm comes to my family because of you, there won't be a place on earth you can hide. And you don't have Billy to cover for you anymore. Start running, you coyote."

Then Jed was off his chair, scooping up the coins as fast as he could, a wary eye on Sarah until she whirled and went after her husband to see if the damage could be repaired.

# Twenty-four

Jack climbed up on his porch, thumping the dust of a long ride from his hat and jeans. He could feel the dirt in every crease of his skin and his side felt like it was streaked with fire. He'd never wanted anything so much as a lengthy soak in a warm tub and the quiet of the peaceful evening hours with his wife pressed up beside him in their big, comfortable bed.

Until he stepped inside and saw Kenitay seated in the midst of his family. He knew right then that he wanted to hold to that image forever: the four of them there waiting for him to come home.

Kenitay rose to his feet. His gaze was riveted on Jack's face, searching for a sign that the Ranger was surprised to see him. There was no surprise. Just gladness.

"I'm here, like I promised."

"Never doubted that you would be, son." He looked Kenitay up and down, noting the short hair and lack of Apache adornment. It made him look more . . . civilized. "How'd things go for you in Austin? Get anything settled?"

"Some."

"And?"

"I told Billy he could come for me here. I wanted to spend some time with you . . . if that's all right."

Jack couldn't respond at first. A tremendous lump of sentiment filled his throat, growing that much worse when he intercepted Emily's pleading gaze. Her eyes were bright with unshed tears, begging that he do something so that she could keep her son with her. If only there was a way.

" 'Course it is," he rumbled at last. "This is your home. Always will be." He cleared his throat roughly so he could continue in a more normal voice. "Did you catch up to those fellows responsible for your daddy?"

"Harmon's holding one of them and Billy's gone to pick up the other. They'll stand for what they did to my father and for their other crimes. I'm satisfied. Harmon's taking care of some other things for me, but I'm still going to have to answer for that man at Fort Sill. Sid's pleading my case and I have confidence in him. He'll keep me off the gallows but I can't say I'm looking forward to spending my next few years in prison. Not after being in one for the last thirteen."

Emily had taken her son's hand and her tears were wetting the back of it. Jack couldn't stand seeing her in such pain.

"Kenitay, your mama and I have put some money aside and we'd like you to take it and head out while you can. Make a new life for yourself someplace, a good life."

Kenitay clearly didn't know what to say. He looked down at his mother's anxious features and then to the man to whom honor was all and he realized what a sacrifice they were willing to make for his sake. And it staggered him.

"I can't take your money."

"We want you to—"

"No, you don't understand. I don't want to run. My life is here. My family is here. I want to put down roots and be free to call someplace home. I'll never be able to do that with this thing hanging over my head. I'll do my time without complaint as long as I can come back here."

"You know you can," Jack whispered hoarsely.

"But there *is* something you can do for me."

Jack gulped down a steadying breath. "What's that?"

"Make your peace with Leisha. She's going to be my wife."

"Leisha Bass?" Carson yelped.

"Something wrong with that?" Kenitay asked his half-brother with a chill calm.

"No. No, of course not," he stammered defensively. "I jus' never thought of Leisha as the kind a woman a man would marry."

"Not just any man," Emily stated softly. She stood and put her arm around Kenitay, hearing an echo from her own past: a woman crying out that no man would ever want her after all she'd been through. And the answer given by a courageous young Ranger: *I do.* And he still did. She smiled at Jack, then up at her son. "Not just any man. The right one." She stretched up to kiss his swarthy cheek. "That's wonderful news, Kenitay. You two will be good for one another."

"She's said yes?" Katie wanted to know, excited at the prospect of a family wedding.

"Well, not yet, exactly. But she promised she'd wait."

But Leisha wasn't one for patience and before they'd even sat down to a family supper—their first together in thirteen years—she was at their door, her expression intense, her attention focused on Kenitay.

With a soft murmur of apology, Kenitay left the table and went to the door.

"Leisha, what—"

"How did you kill that man at Fort Sill?"

Her bluntness startled him. "What?" He glanced back at his family uncomfortably, confused by her sudden insistence. "I told you that already."

"No. You told me it was an accident. I want you to tell me the exact details."

"I can't see why this is important now."

What was important to him was the way his pulse had lunged into a full gallop at the sight of her. It was torture to stand so close without grabbing her up in his arms. But she was all business and there seemed to be no distracting her. Until he stroked his hand down the length of her arm and stepped closer so she could feel his heat. His gaze focused on the curve of her mouth, causing his own to moisten. Her lips parted and trembled slightly. Her blue eyes grew wide with awareness—helplessly, shamelessly aglow with the same longing twisting through him. She seemed to have forgotten what she'd come to say.

"Excuse us for a minute," she said to Jack and his family as she gripped Kenitay by the forearm and hauled him out onto the porch where cool shadows washed over them as hot passion rose like a tide.

Her hands were on his face, pulling him down for the ruthless plunder of her kiss. His fingers dove into her hair, raking through it, clenching heavy golden handfuls and holding hard so he could command the angle of her head. He turned her so her back was pressed to the adobe wall where it was still warmed from the heat of day. Then he moved against her in a purposeful seduction of the senses, courting her desires with the languid rock of his body. She moaned softly, deep in her throat, and her hands dropped to clutch at his hips, tugging at him, rubbing him suggestively into the willing arch of her own slender form until what they were building between them was in danger of becoming cataclysmic. The time and place weren't right for any further pursuit of pleasure but neither of them was willing to give up this desperate, to-the-limit tease. Their breathing had grown rough and ragged, their tongues continuing to mate with an almost fierce determination. Control teetered on the sharp edge of bliss.

Then, reminding himself of where they were, Kenitay forced his mouth away from the drugging power of hers to whisper against her satin-smooth cheek, "The thought of being away from you is tearing my soul in two. Tell me again that you love me."

"I do."

"Say the words."

"I love you." Her lips were a hot caress along his cheek and throat. "I love you and I want you and I'm not going to let you leave me. Maybe you won't have to. That's what I came to find out." Her sense of reason was ebbing back, along with the purpose of her ride. Then he turned his head to reclaim her mouth and awareness faded once more beneath the surge of urgent need.

They continued to kiss until they were starved for breath—and starved for what they couldn't explore on Jack's front porch. Leisha pulled back, gasping, struggling for command of her emotions.

"We have to talk."

"So talk," he murmured, sweeping his lips over the taut ridge of her cheekbone.

"I can't think with you this close," she protested weakly. She pushed against his chest but the minute he withdrew a little, she was grasping at him, drawing him back up against her.

"Do I fluster you, little warrior?" he crooned, nipping at her chin and lower lip while she moved upward, inviting more.

"Yes," she breathed through the glaze of her desire. Then she blinked and made a concentrated effort to force a separation. "Now, please, move away, This is important."

"How's this?" He took a step back but had captured her hands in his and was directing her palms over the intriguing terrain of his upper body. She followed the movement with her gaze as if mesmerized, then gave herself a visible shake.

"No." She jerked her hands free and clutched them together behind her back, to restrain herself as much as him. "Go over there until I can catch my breath."

Pleased by his effect on her, Kenitay edged backward until he came to the rail, putting the width of the porch between them. "Is this better?"

"Yes." Leisha was still gasping, She sagged back against the warm adobe, closing her eyes, but shutting off the sight of him did nothing to erase the way his presence continued to throb through her very being. She wet her lips and allowed a shudder of yearning to overtake her. Then she inhaled deeply to restore order to her fragmented thoughts so she could confront him once again.

He was leaning against the rail, his expression so male and smug and self-secure; her own pride had to provide the necessary stiffening of resolve.

"Tell me about Fort Sill."

His features smoothed into an impenetrable mask. "I'd spent the day as Beech and Westfall's guest while they tried to persuade me to betray my father's trust."

"They wanted you to tell them about the silver?"

He stared at her.

"My father told me. Go on."

So he told her of how they'd cuffed him to a chair and beaten him to near unconsciousness. When they saw they couldn't break his spirit, they were cautious enough to stop short of sending him the way his father had gone. Instead, they implied a threat. If he cared for his father's second wife and the children he'd borne with her, he would give careful thought to answering their questions. Who would care for them if he was dead? How would he endure the guilt of their fate upon his hands should something—*unexpected* befall them? Their words had sent a chill of terror through him. It was one thing to hold out against a personal pain and quite another to be the source of innocents' suffering. He'd confided his fears to his friend, Eenah—not the details but the concerns. And Eenah had bidden Kenitay to trust him.

"The next day when the soldier was taking me from my quarters for another interview with them, Eenah distracted him long enough for me to hit him." He paused, troubled by regret and tortured by the image. "I knocked him down and ran to where Eenah said he had horses waiting. I was weak from the beating I'd taken and Eenah said he would go back and tie the soldier so he couldn't spread the alarm and we would have time to escape. I waited and he returned to tell me the soldier was dead. He'd hit his head when he fell and the blow killed him. But who was going to believe me then? I'm not sure anyone will believe me now."

"Did you have a knife?"

"No. I had nothing with me."

"Then how do you explain that the cause of the soldier's death was a slashed throat?"

"What? But it wasn't."

"It was. Corporal Wonderly told me the man's throat was cut. You didn't kill him."

Kenitay made a soft sound of disbelief then looked to her, uncertain, as he replayed that moment over in his mind. "Eenah had a knife. But why would he go back and kill that man and let me believe that I had done it?"

"Maybe because he wanted to make sure you'd be desperate enough to run."

"Why?"

"So you'd lead him to the silver."

Kenitay shook his head. "No. That makes no sense. I know him. He has no lust for wealth. We are of the same people. He wouldn't have betrayed me for the money. Besides, I never told him about it."

"But Beech and Westfall knew."

Just as Eenah knew he had family in Terlingua. Had he somehow contacted Beech in Austin? Was that why he'd left in such an unexpected hurry? To lay a trap for him here? Kenitay's thoughts spun in that direction.

"And you think they paid him to aid in my escape so I'd take them to the silver?" Her brows rose, urging him to consider the possibility. Again, he shook his head, this time more emphatically. "No. I don't believe that. He hates the

White Eyes as much as my father did. He wouldn't have worked for them, not for money."

"Then why? Shall we go find him and ask?"

Before they could act upon her suggestion, the sound of rapidly approaching hoofbeats reached them. Too long a fugitive to do otherwise, Kenitay faded back into deeper shadows while Leisha stepped out to shield him. Jack and Emily came out, too, adding to the barrier. Jack had his pistol in hand, keeping it concealed behind him. He and Leisha exchanged quick looks. His small smile said all was forgiven between them as they stood braced for the possibility of some new danger.

"It's Billy," Emily announced with a sigh of relief. "And Sarah."

Jack tucked his revolver into his trouser band and came down off the porch to meet them, reaching up to swing his younger sister down. Billy clapped a hand on his shoulder in a brief greeting before coming up to speak with Kenitay. His features were grim.

"I went to the hotel and sure enough, there was a Beech registered."

Kenitay scanned his expression, hoping to hear good news.

"He'd already gone."

"Damn," moaned Leisha. She tucked up against Kenitay's side, banding his middle with a supportive arm. "We'll find him," she said with confidence. "And maybe we can kill two birds with one stone if they're together."

Not knowing who else they were referring to, Billy said, "Happens I know where Beech is going."

"Where?" Kenitay quickly demanded.

When Billy hesitated, Sarah came up to take his arm, hugging it tight. "He was asking questions around town about Kenitay," she told them. She heard Billy draw in a deep breath, getting ready to tell them of Jed's involvement. Knowing what such an admission would cost him, she neatly circumvented it. "He found out that Kenitay was part of our family."

Kenitay's worried gaze flew immediately to his mother. She shook her head.

"I haven't seen any strangers around. No one's been by here. I can't believe he'd have the gall to ride into a Ranger camp to do us any harm, even with the law on his side."

"The law's not on his side," Kenitay supplied. "Never has been. His kind make their own laws and he won't let anything stop him from getting what he wants."

"Well, he's not taking you," came Emily's flat summation.

"He's not after me." He quickly explained the significance of Kodene's stolen silver shipment.

"Give him the silver," was his mother's first reaction. "You weren't planning to keep it, were you? What do we care about money compared to the safety of this family?"

"That silver was the price of my father's life and could be the cost of my people's freedom. Sid thinks he can use it to buy lobbying power in Washington to bring the Apache home. General Crook was petitioning Congress for their return when he died. He still has a lot of support there. If it can help bring our people back where they belong, my father would consider it a sacrifice worthy of his life. I won't let these two murderers steal the future of the Apache the way they stole my father's and tried to take mine."

"He's right, Em." Jack surrounded his wife with a firm embrace. "We don't give in to the likes of them. Not ever. What say we ride on out to Harmon's to pick up his partner and see what we can convince him to tell us? If he knows any secrets, Uncle Harm can persuade him to spill them."

"Jack," Billy began uncomfortably, "that's what I was getting to."

"What?"

"That fellow, Beech. When he left town, he was trailing Randall and Becca. He's heading for Harm's."

"No!" Leisha screamed as she lunged to get to her horse. Kenitay caught her, subduing her with some difficulty. "Let me go! They have to be warned that he's coming," she cried.

"Leisha, *shijii*. He's already there."

That stark bit of logic undercut her purpose. With a soft moan of despair, she allowed Kenitay to enfold her in his arms where she clung, numb with anxiety.

"Carson, saddle up my horse."

"Yessir, Daddy." There was the sound of rapid footfalls as he ran through the house and out the back.

"Em, if we're not back by tomorrow morning, send for Corporal Ketchum and lay it all out for him. Have him bring a bunch of boys in a hurry. All right?"

"I will." Her gaze went between husband and son but, a true Ranger's wife, she kept her fears to herself. She brought Jack his gunbelt and slipped it about his waist, cinching it in, then hugging him just as tight for a long, wordless minute.

Sarah retrieved her revolver from where Billy had tucked it into his waistband. She had that stubborn Bass expression that never failed to alarm her husband.

"Sarah, I want you to head on home now." Billy placed his hand over the barrel of the pistol, but she met his gaze with a stare as hard as gun metal.

"I'm going with you," she said firmly.

"You've got family at home to see to," he coaxed gently.

"This is my family, too."

The sound of her gutsy voice brought Leisha's head around. How had she ever thought of Sarah Bass Cooper as docile and domestic? She stood up to her husband with a full-blown fierceness but Billy was smart enough to talk around a direct confrontation.

"Sarah, we don't know which of the Basses he's going

after. I want to know my four little kids are in good hands before I ride out. Will you see to them for me?"

She lowered the gun and wrapped her arms around him. "Don't bring me any bad news."

"I won't." He kissed the top of her head, squeezing her tight.

Carson jogged around front, leading Jack's horse. As Jack stepped away from Emily, she ordered, "Don't bring me home anything to mend."

"I'll try not to." He gave her a loving kiss and readied to ride out. Just then he caught sight of Leisha striding ahead at Kenitay's side. "Leisha, you'd better stay here with Emily."

Leisha stopped and leveled a withering stare at him—but before she could come to her own defense, Kenitay did it for her.

"She can hold her own, Daddy."

Whether it was his quiet claim or his use of the unfamiliar title, Jack was convinced. "All right." He stepped up onto his horse, charging Carson to take care of his mother and sister.

Kenitay gave Leisha a long look. "Ready?"

He was offering her a chance to travel at his side, as his partner, as his equal. The enormity of it shook through her as she whispered, "Yes."

"Leisha, you take care now," Emily called after her. "We have wedding plans to discuss."

Leisha stared back at her blankly. "What wedding?"

Kenitay grabbed her hand, dragging her after him with a gruff, "I'll explain later."

And as twilight settled in, still and gray, the four of them rode toward Blue Creek.

# Twenty-five

Amanda was in the side yard pinning up her clothes in the arid mid-afternoon breeze when she saw the buggy spin in at an unusually slow pace, considering that Rand was at the reins. She caught a glimpse of her daughter's pale hair and made a mental note to scold her for going out without a hat. It might not have been New York, where such things were only proper, but still she didn't care to have her daughter's fair skin the texture of Texas jerky before she found herself a good man.

"Randall, did you remember to check for mail?" she called out as she struggled to drape a heavy quilt over the high line. When there was no answer, she began to grumble to herself, wondering what had distracted him this time from doing what he'd been told. Probably some pretty piece of calico, she was thinking as she secured the damp linen and came around the curtain of wash. And drew up short.

Becca was in the front seat of the buggy but Rand wasn't at the reins. It was a man, someone she'd never seen. Amanda started forward, cursing the fact that she had only a handful of wooden clothespins instead of the comforting grip of her Winchester. The closer she came, the worse things got. Becca turned toward her, her face ashen and streaked with tears. There was a wildness to her eyes that bespoke of some terrible fright.

The man beside her had a revolver nudged in next to her rib cage.

"Mrs. Bass, sorry to drop in on you uninvited like this. The name's Warren Beech. That mean anything to you?"

Amanda kept her features carefully schooled. "No. What do you want, Mr. Beech?"

"A little conversation and maybe some coffee."

"And you need to do that at gunpoint?"

" 'Fraid so."

"M-Mama, he s-shot Randall."

That brought Amanda up to the buggy at a run. She could see one of Rand's well-worn boots propped up on the small bed of the buggy. She put a trembling hand on it when she came close enough to peer over the low box.

"Oh, God. Randall."

He was crumpled up at an awkward angle right where Beech had dumped him in the cramped space behind the seat. His face was averted but she couldn't look away from all the blood on his shirt. She started to reach out to him.

"Where's your husband, Mrs. Bass?"

"He's not here" she replied a bit too quickly as her hand paused on Rand's bent knee. He was so still.

"If he wasn't at home, you wouldn't be out here without a sidearm, now would you? Call him."

Amanda looked up him, defiance and fury glittering in her eyes. She flinched when Beech twisted his hand in her daughter's hair making Becca cry out in fear and pain.

"Call him," he repeated.

"Harmon!"

They could see the front door open but Harm didn't appear. Apparently he was taking stock of the situation.

"Mr. Bass," Beech called out in a loud voice. "Come quick. Your boy's been hurt." Then he jabbed Becca with the nose of the .45 and gave Amanda a warning look to keep her mouth shut.

Harm came down from the house at a run, skidding to a halt when Beech produced his pistol.

"That's fine right there. Put your hands out where I can see them. I don't want to put a hole in your pretty little girl to match the one your boy's sporting."

Harm moved cautiously into the open, his hands spread wide. His attention was focused on Amanda, seeing the distress and shock pinching her features.

"Ammy, is he all right?"

"I don't know, Harmon. It looks bad."

Harm's pale gaze shifted to Beech and fixed there as he started toward his wife, his hands still visible.

"Don't do anything stupid, Bass."

He crossed behind Amanda and moved to the other side of the wagon bed. "Rand?" he called softly. "Son? Can you hear me?" He put his fingertips to the side of the boy's neck, waiting for what seemed like forever. Then he glanced over at Amanda and nodded slightly. Their son was alive.

"The boy would probably be more comfortable up in the house. Why don't we move on up there," Beach suggested.

With a hoarse sob, Becca jumped down into her mother's arms and clung there weeping quietly while they both watched Harm lever Rand's slack figure from the buggy bed. They followed as he carried the still form draped along his shoulders up to the porch, all of them aware of Beech's pistol at their backs.

Harm eased Rand down on the parlor sofa and was immediately searching for the site of entry, finding it high in his right chest wall. There was no exit wound.

Amanda started for the hall.

"Whoa, there. Where do you think you're going?"

"For some sheets. We need to get the bleeding stopped."

"No." Beech used the pistol to wave her back to where

Harm was kneeling over their son. "Let him bleed. You'll be more inclined to talk with him ruining your nice furniture."

Harm's hand curved around the side of Rand's face and he leaned down so his cheek was pressed to the boy's damp brow. "Hold on, *shiye*. Hold on for me," he whispered intently. Then he straightened to confront the man with the gun. "What do you want from us? I don't know you."

"Maybe not, but that renegade running with your other daughter does. Where are they?"

"I don't know. They're not here."

"What about the silver?"

Harm never blinked. "I don't know anything about any silver. All I know is my boy could be dying."

"So could the rest of you, real soon if I don't hear what I want to hear. I know the two of them left Austin with my partner in tow. Westfall. That name mean anything?"

"No."

"They were headed here." He pointed his .45 at a quaking Becca and she cried out in panic.

"They were here this mornin', just the two of them," Harm told him. "They wanted some money. We gave them what we had on hand and they rode out. Toward the border, I think."

"You're a damn good liar, Bass."

They all looked to the hall toward the new voice. Ross Westfall stood there, rubbing his raw wrists.

"And you should have killed me while you had the chance."

Wondering how he'd managed to get loose, Harm smiled blandly. "My mistake. I won't make it again."

Beech passed the gun he'd taken from Rand to his partner. "You look like hell. I think your nose is broken."

"I was beginning to think you'd never find your way over here."

"Well, I'm here now so quit your complaining. Where's the breed?"

"He went for the law."

Beech cursed explicitly. "Then shouldn't you be out there keeping an eye out?"

"Got it covered."

"I'd think you boys would be in a hurry to light out before the law gets here," Harm drawled. Despite his calm manner, his fear was growing as Rand's blood began to drip on the parlor carpet.

"Not without the silver," Westfall stated. "We've gone through too much trouble to walk off without it now. We wait."

On the sofa, Rand moaned weakly. Amanda's gaze rose to her husband's, pleading that he think of something quick.

"No need to wait. I have what you want," Harm said softly.

Both men looked at him in disbelief.

"It's true," he continued. "Kenitay left it here for me to hide and that's just what I did."

"Okay, Bass, we're listening," Beech said.

"The money means nothing to me but they do." He gestured to his family. "You let them go and I'll take you to it."

"That'd be real obliging of you, Bass," Westfall snorted. "I think you'd be more inclined to speak the truth if we keep them right where they are."

Harm rose slowly and both men were instantly wary. They'd heard of his reputation as a merciless killer. "I'm not saying anything until they're gone. If they stay, you're going to kill them anyway. It's not worth my while to make you rich unless they ride out. My boy is dying, I'm not inclined to stand around arguing with you. They go now or you can go to hell poor men."

Beech and Westfall exchanged looks. They knew he was serious and they knew the law would be on them by morning. Westfall decided for them.

"Here's how it's going to be. One of 'em takes the boy out, the other stays here to make sure you stay cooperative."

"I'll stay." Amanda spoke up without hesitation, her eyes meeting those of her husband, willing him to agree. Without looking around, she said, "Becca, grab a sheet out of the linen cupboard. I want your brother bound up tight. He's lost too much blood already."

Becca hesitated only a second, then brushed between the two gunmen to see to her mother's bidding. Beech followed along behind her.

Within minutes, Rand's wound had been snugly dressed. Harm carried him gently down to the buggy, easing him into the back where Amanda covered him with a throw. She bent to kiss him, then turned to hug her daughter tight. Her eyes were swimming with emotion but her tone was firm. "Don't try to go easy. Get him to the doctor as fast as you can. And don't look back."

"All right, Mama," Becca whispered. Then she was wrapped up in her father's arms, trying to hang onto her tears. "Daddy—"

"You be brave, little girl. Randall's counting on you."

She leaned back, drawing a deep breath. There was a glimmer of her mother's grit in her eyes. "I'll see he makes it, Daddy."

"Good girl." He swung her up onto the buggy seat and slapped his palm down on the horse's rump, startling it into motion before anyone could change their mind. Then he crushed Amanda up to his chest as they watched their children go, knowing well it could be the last time they'd ever see them.

"All right, Bass, time's a-wastin'. Suppose you show us where you hid our property and we'll be on our way."

Harm gave Beech a long, piercing stare, his blue eyes cold as the sudden snap of a Norther. "I'll take him with me. And if you so much as breathe heavy on my wife whilst I'm gone, you'll be fertilizer for her flower garden."

Beech's expression didn't change. If he was in the least bit intimidated, he didn't show it. "With what you're going to bring us, I can buy myself a thousand willing women. I ain't interested in yours, but seeing as how she's important to you, you'd best do what you're told 'cause I won't blink an eye if it comes to killing her."

Harm eased his gaze downward until it met Amanda's. She gave him a tense smile, her dark eyes expressive pools of love and well-contained worry. Her fingertips brushed lightly along the line of his lower lip and followed the angle of his jaw. Her hand was shaking but her stare never wavered.

"You are my life," he told her softly, then drew her into one of his engulfing Apache embraces that surrounded and melded them into one. He could feel her heart beating at a frantic pace against him but the lips she pressed to his throat were warm. He nuzzled her hair, whispering, "Trust me, *shijii.*" He meant, *I love you. Don't do anything foolish.*

Amanda's fingers speared back into his black hair, holding his head hard while her other palm rubbed quickly, greedily up his arm and over his shoulder and chest, exulting in the familiar feel of him. "You be careful, Harmon," she charged with a fierce intensity. *Come back to me,* was what she didn't say aloud.

"C'mon, Bass," Westfall growled impatiently, motioning toward the corral with his pistol. "Warren will keep your little lady company while we go treasure hunting."

Harm took a step back but Amanda leaned after him, the movement too poignant for him to ignore. He seized her beloved face between his palms and claimed her softly parted lips with a deep, possessing kiss, one she would still feel for a good long time after he'd gone. Then he broke from her and without another glance, strode toward the horses.

Amanda watched him go, her eyes imprinting every detail upon heart and mind and soul. Then she turned to Beech with a narrow smile.

"I believe you said something about wanting coffee."

No words were exchanged as Harm led Westfall up into the Chisos foothills. None were needed. Harm didn't waste his breath with questions about what they planned to do with him and Amanda once the silver was recovered. He knew the odds weren't good for them to survive the night. Westfall was no fool. He was aware of the threat Harm would always be. And that left Amanda alone with the two of them, a situation Harm meant to prevent at all costs. His memory was too clear concerning Westfall's way of dealing with women. His wife wouldn't suffer the way his mother and sister had. Not if he had anything to say about it.

As they climbed, Harm emptied himself of all meaningful images: Amanda's closed eyes and freshly kissed lips; his son's still features; Becca's tear-streaked face; and Leisha's defiant glare. Other fleeting impressions came—those of his mother and sister at the mercy of Westfall and his friends. He suppressed those, too, wanting only calm to remain, an air of detachment that made him Apache, that made him dangerous. He wanted nothing to exist beyond the next few seconds, distilling sensation and energy until he was aware of the texture of the breeze and the scents it carried. Until he could feel Westfall sweating behind him in his nervousness and anticipation. Until nothing escaped his notice and all was in his control. He drew back on his reins.

"Here."

Westfall didn't move. He aimed his pistol at Harm's back. "Climb down real slow and fetch it for me."

Harm slithered off his horse and landed lightly, all coiled grace and wired readiness. "Right here behind these rocks."

"Whoa, now. I want to be able to see your hands." He nudged his horse ahead so he had a complete view of Harmon. "Okay. Go ahead."

Harm knelt down and pushed aside several good-sized rocks, uncovering the leather satchels. Westfall's mouth went dry with greed.

"All right now. Bring them to me. Slow and easy."

Draping the pouches over his forearm, Harm approached slowly, his gaze fixed on Westfall, his focus on the finger curved about the trigger. Westfall was going to kill him here. He knew it. He could feel it in the man's tension, could hear it in the way he'd begun to breathe faster. As soon as he passed the bags over, he'd be dead. He lifted them up gradually.

"Don't you think you should check inside to make sure it's what you had in mind before you shoot me?"

Westfall took the first satchel, weighing it in one hand. It was heavy enough but Bass could have filled it with rock for the same effect. He made a motion with his gun.

"Step on back a bit whilst I take look-see."

Harm retreated a few feet and waited, arms hanging easy, expression unreadable.

Balancing the pouch across one thigh so he could keep his pistol trained on Harm, Westfall loosened the strings of the bag and tossed them back. Then he risked a quick downward glance as he opened the satchel.

There was an explosion of movement and a fiery stab of pain. Westfall screamed and caught hold of the four-foot rattler that sprang out to latch itself through skin into tendon at the junction of his neck and shoulder. He was still screaming as he managed to tear it loose and fling it far away. Panting wildly, he quickly scanned the area.

Harm was gone. Only the other three pouches lay on the ground where he'd been standing.

"Bass, you son of a bitch!" he roared up at the mountains.

Panicked and dizzy with shock, he toppled down out of the saddle to retrieve the other bags. Using a stick and some tardy caution, he opened each one to free the surprise Harm had placed inside. Westfall noted grimly that each snake had had its warning rattles removed. And that had left them very annoyed. He flung the satchels across his saddle and crawled up after them while the diamondbacks disappeared into the tough Texas terrain as quickly and silently as Harm had. Westfall scanned the rocks as a superstitious shiver shook through him. The hills were full of ghosts and now Harm Bass was up there among them.

The buggy shot past them in the gathering shadows. Leisha got a glimpse of blond hair.

"Becca!"

Leisha wheeled her horse around and urged it after the near-runaway buggy. Finally, she was forced to grab onto the leads to pull the animal to a stop herself. Even then Becca was sitting rigid, the reins clutched in her hands, her eyes wide and glittery in the dimness.

"Becca, what on earth—"

"The man you're after," her sister gasped between fractured breaths. "He caught up to us on the way home. He s-shot Randall. I've got to get him to the doctor. Mama told me not to stop for anything." She was sobbing then, clearly out of control.

"Rand." Leisha kicked out of the saddle and slid down,

running to the back of the buggy as the three she was riding with circled around to pull up on either side.

"Is he all right?" Becca cried frantically. "I haven't dared look."

Blood gleamed black and for a moment, Leisha was too scared to look beyond it. Then her brother uttered a low groan and she bent down close to console him. When she touched his face, she found it cold and slick from shock.

"Rand? *Silah?* Randy, are you with me?" Her voice choked up with anxiety. She stroked his cheek until his eyelids fluttered and the fullness of the moon turned the blue of his eyes to silver.

"Leisha?" It was whispered as weak as his respiration.

"Shhh. It's all right. Everything's going to be all right."

His hand came up to grip hers. There was so little strength in his fingers. Silent tears started to course down her face. He gestured to them with his forefinger.

"Didn't know you cared."

"Oh, shut up, Rand," she muttered as she bent to kiss his cheek. She could feel him smile. "You're going to be all right."

He shook his head slowly. "I don't think so," he moaned softly. "Becca's trying to kill me with her driving."

Leisha laughed weakly and brushed her hand across his brow and down his face. "She's saving your miserable life, you fool."

He grabbed for a sudden gulp of air and his fingers twisted around hers. "He didn't give me no warning, Leisha. He just drew and fired." He started panting rapidly in agitation, his knees shifting restlessly. "Oh, God, it hurts."

Making soft, soothing sounds, Leisha bent to hold him, staying close until he quieted. When she straightened, his eyes had closed and his breathing had become almost too faint to detect. While she lifted his hand to her lips, then to her cheek, she could hear Becca making a rambling explanation in response to Jack's calm questioning. Very gently, she eased his hand down to rest upon a barely moving shirtfront and let go with extreme reluctance.

"Becca, you get going now. Don't spare that horse. Don't you let him die. He's the only brother we have."

She could see her sister's fair head bobbing, then she had to step back as the reins cracked down on the horse's back and the buggy continued on toward Terlingua.


The house was dark and silent against the backdrop of the Chisos. They sat their horses, each holding in their own fears of what they'd find.

"I'm going down," Kenitay announced.

"No," came a quiet challenge from Leisha. An odd intensity had taken over her features since she'd let go of her brother's hand, an eerie stillness that was so like her father's when he was obsessed with something, "I will. You're the one they want, not me. I know the house. I can slip in without them seeing me. You all wait here while I see what's what."

Jack and Billy looked like they might object but Kenitay was studying the set of her expression.

"Be careful."

She nodded and nudged her horse ahead.

She went in through the back, easing through familiar shadows without making a sound. The silence was overwhelming, putting Leisha even more on edge as she inched through the kitchen and into the dining room beyond. She could see a faint glow coming from the parlor—a single lamp burning low. She had no choice but to go forward, drawn to that light with pulse pounding.

The first thing she saw was Westfall stretched out on the sofa. His eyes were closed, he wasn't moving, There was blood on the floor but she couldn't see any on him.

Next to the sofa, her mother sat on a straight backed chair, the stiffness of her position conveying the fact that her hands were bound behind her. Her head was bowed so Leisha couldn't see her face.

"Mama?"

The piercing whisper brought her head up. Leisha caught back a gasp of dismay when she saw Amanda's split lip and swollen eye. Then all she felt was a cold fury toward whomever had hurt her family.

"No," Amanda whispered back. "Don't come any closer."

"Where's Daddy?"

Amanda nodded toward the window and the night beyond. "Go find him."

"I can't leave you here." She crept forward with a wary eye on the empty rooms as she crossed them. She gave Westfall another cautious look. "What happened to him?"

"Snake bite." Amanda smiled grimly. "Pity I don't know anything about drawing the poisons. I might have been able to save his life."

Leisha stared at her, surprised by the venomous quality of her words. Her mother knew all about snake bite. She'd saved Harm's life by drawing and sucking the deadly toxins from his leg before they were married. Leisha hadn't known her Eastern-bred mother had the toughness to sit and watch a man die. And it impressed the hell out of her.

"Where's the other one?"

"He went out looking for Harmon." Another tight smile. "He won't find him."

Leisha bent to work at the ropes knotted behind the chair. "We ran into Becca."

"And Randall?"

"He's in bad shape, Mama, but he's a Bass. He'll make it."

"We all will." The ropes gave and Amanda pulled her hands free. "Did you come here alone?"

"No. Jack, Billy, and Kenitay are waiting to hear from me."

There was a metallic click behind Leisha's head and she stiffened at the feel of a .45 bore and at the sound of Warren Beech's harsh drawl.

"Then let's invite them in, shall we?"

*Twenty-six*

A part of Kenitay went dead inside when he saw the lights blaze on inside the Basses' big house and Beech step out onto the front porch against that brightness with a gun at Leisha's head.

"C'mon in," the gunman called. "Time for a little Bass reunion. I know there's three of you so come in slow and I won't have to do anything drastic. Harm Bass, can you hear me? You might as well show yourself, too. Your little wife is beginning to miss you and it's wearing on her hard."

Jack uttered a soft, uncharacteristic curse and started down with Billy behind him. Kenitay hesitated only a moment, then followed. There was no sign of Harmon.

"C'mon in, boys. Leave your hardware on the porch. Step lively now. Let's get this done so I can be on my way."

Beech stepped back to allow them a fair distance to pass while he held Leisha in an iron-tight grasp. Her gaze touched on Kenitay's briefly—hers full of apology, his reassurance. When the three men entered the parlor, Beech ordered, "Mrs. Bass, if you'd be so kind as to secure them." He jabbed the gun barrel up under Leisha's chin. "Don't make me ask twice."

Wordlessly, Amanda took up the rope that had held her and began to wrap it about Billy's wrists, threading it over to Jack's, then Kenitay's. When it was done, Beech gave

Leisha a shove away from him. He gave Kenitay a hard look.

"Boy, you have caused me considerable difficulty."

"Glad to."

Beech smiled. "You might well have saved yourself the trouble. I got what I wanted anyway."

"You won't get far," Leisha promised.

"Just across the border and from there, it's South America. I'm going to live well to spite all of you."

Westfall murmured a raspy groan and dragged himself upright on the sofa. His shirt collar was torn open to reveal twin puncture wounds in the midst of a mass of discolored swelling that rose halfway up his neck. "Warren," he croaked, "I'm gonna need the buggy. I'm not gonna make it on horseback."

Beech pursed his lips sadly. "Ross, I'm sorry to say we've come to a parting of the ways. I can't let you slow me down. But you'll be glad to know I'll spend your half in your memory."

"You double-crossing—" He tried to stand but the effort was too much. He went down to his knees on the carpet where Rand's bloodstains added to the pattern.

"No honor among thieves," Billy interjected. "I could have told you that."

Beech laughed. "What does honor get you?" He nodded to Kenitay. "Where did it get your father? It got him dead. Things would have been so much easier if he'd just told us where he'd put our property. Didn't mean to kill him. It's just that he made me mad, interfering the way he did by stealing what was ours."

"Especially after you went through all the trouble to steal it in the first place."

Beech smiled at Jack. "That's right, Ranger. And it was such a sweet plan. We could have been rich young men. Guess I'll have to settle for wealth in my twilight years instead." His amiable look was gone. "Miss Bass, pick up those satchels."

Leisha moved cautiously to do as she was told. She was picking up the final one when Westfall grabbed onto it, hanging on tight.

"No! It's mine. Damn you, Warren. I earned it."

"Where you gonna spend it, Ross? You'll be in the grave before morning."

"And you'll be joining him there if you make so much as a move."

Harm stepped in from the shadows of the dining room, his sawed-off carbine fixed upon Beech's chest. Beech raised his hands slightly, losing none of his good humor.

"Ah, Mr. Bass. Nice of you to join us."

"Wouldn't be a good host if I didn't put in an appearance. My wife prefers me to be polite." He glanced at Amanda, his features tightening when he saw her face. "You all right, little girl?"

She nodded. "Now, I am."

"Which one of them was unlucky enough to hurt you?"

She glanced at Beech with a vengeful eye. Her other one was sealed shut from swelling.

"I thought I told you what would happen if you touched her. Guess you didn't believe me. I get kinda unfriendly when it comes to folks messing with my family. Ask your partner there how he's feeling." Harm glanced down at Westfall, who seemed to be having a very difficult time breathing. Harm shook his head in mock sympathy. "Ugly way to die, snake bite. But there are worse ways. Like what you planned for me all them years ago. Ammy, now that everyone's accounted for, cut them loose."

Kenitay frowned, pensively. "Not everyone," he began uneasily.

"I think he means me," came Eenah's soft words as he stepped up behind Harm. He'd been out skirting the night shadows since cutting Westfall loose in the barn. He'd followed Harm because there was no doubt in his mind that the small part-Apache tracker was the most dangerous among them. The one who would have to be dealt with first and finally before the others. As Harm turned toward him, there was a low blur of movement. With a gasp of surprise and impact, Harm went down bonelessly, sliding off the blade of Eenah's knife.

"Harmon!" Shrieking hysterically, Amanda dropped over him, using her body as a shield against further attack. Her hands and clothing were quick to take on a vivid crimson stain.

Shaking off her shock, Leisha lunged for the carbine beneath her father's still fingers. As she went down, Eenah caught her by the hair and hauled her up with the wrap of it around his fist. He laid the wet blade against her throat and all movement in the room stopped. It was silent except for Amanda's crazed sobbing. Kenitay took a rash step forward.

"Don't," his former trailmate warned. "I'll cut her throat."

"Like you did that soldier's at Fort Sill?"

"Just like that."

"Why?" Kenitay demanded, furious and frightened for the woman he loved. "For the money?"

Eenah spat on the floor next to Harm's immobile figure. "Money? Money means nothing."

Jack suddenly muttered in recognition. "I know you. You were the one at Fort Apache. The scout who brought me my son's coat and told me he was dead."

Eenah smiled savagely. "And the look on your face, it was worth spending the next thirteen years suffering from the white army's reward for loyalty. You don't remember me, do you? I was just a boy when your Rangers ambushed our camp. My mother was killed and my brother. Then when you came for Kodene's son, my father tried to avenge them and this one," he said as he kicked Harm, "this one slew him."

"Your father was Ahkochne." Jack pieced it together into one unpleasant picture, recalling well the warrior who'd nearly had his life on lance point, the Apache Harm had killed in a knife fight in his own front yard while trying to keep the Mescalero braves from reclaiming Kenitay and killing Jack. Kodene had kept things from going to a bloody hell from there.

"And now he will be avenged. I wanted you to suffer the loss of a son the way my father suffered. And that coyote, Kodene—I wanted him to pay as well for turning his back on my father when he would seek a justified vengeance. I joined the white man's army, wore his scout uniform to help find the dog where he lay in hiding. Only I was sent with the rest of the Apache on that train to Florida. Then I saw another chance for justice at Fort Sill. I told these two greedy white men about Kodene's silver. I promised to help them recover it if they would allow me to seek my enemies out and destroy them."

Beech grabbed up Harm's carbine. "You got what you wanted, now let's get the hell out of here." He snatched up the satchels, jerking the last one from his convulsing partner's hands. "I need you to lead me safely into Mexico."

"Not until I'm satisfied that it is finished." He gave Harm's body a nudge with his toe and Amanda lifted herself off him, her face and the front of her gown drenched in blood. Her features were contorted by grief.

"You killed my husband," came her raw wail of pain.

And Eenah nodded, grimly pleased. Leisha twisted wildly in his cruel hold and he wrenched her head back hard enough to make her grit her teeth against the pain. "Now," he said quietly, "there is just Kodene's son and the Ranger to settle with." He glared at Kenitay and Jack, hatred warping his expression with a chill malice.

"Come on. We got no time for this," Beech growled. "I ain't killing no Ranger. Borders mean nothing to those boys when you do one of their own. Leave 'em. They won't be able to track us until morning. By then we'll be out of their reach."

"We go." Eenah smiled narrowly, his black eyes glittering, "And I will take this one with me."

"No!" Kenitay chafed within his restraints. "Let her go. She isn't a part of this."

Eenah laughed. "You have too much white blood or you would see the beauty of my plan. She is the center of everything." He pulled Leisha backward as he began to withdraw. "I will avenge my mother's spirit upon her in the way of the Apache. And then when you, Kodene's son, come for me, I will kill you, too. Then you, Ranger, will have lost a son for good, just as I lost a brother."

He turned into the hall and Leisha cast one last look at Kenitay. The one thing that he would never forget was the courageousness of her expression and the love in that brief glance. Then she was gone.

"Warren, don't leave me here!" Westfall gurgled, stretching a twitching hand along the carpet. Beech stepped over it on his way to the door.

"And if we see anyone leave this house before we get up into the hills, we'll kill that pretty little girl on the spot."

With a bang of the front door, the two of them disappeared into the night with the silver and Leisha Bass.

There was a long beat of silence in the parlor, then a low groan sounded from beneath Amanda.

"Ammy, you can get off me now."

She slid back onto her knees and carefully helped Harm sit up.

Jack was gaping. "You're not dead!"

"Sorry to disappoint you," Harm panted softly as he held to Amanda with one arm and pressed his other palm to the wound in his side. He grimaced. "Pretty damned close to it. Would have been for real if Ammy hadn't convinced me to play possum." He kissed her temple and let her hug him fiercely for a long moment before murmuring, "Amanda, let them loose, then get me something to plug this hole up with."

She sat back with a shaky smile and put her hand to his face, leaving a red palm print. Then she stood and went to undo the ropes restraining the other three men. The instant he was freed, Kenitay broke for the door.

"Jack, grab him!" Harm shouted and Kenitay was pulled up short.

"Let me go! They have Leisha. You know what they're going to do to her! If they get into those hills, we'll never be able to track them."

"I can," Harm announced flatly. "Let 'em go, Kenitay. Let 'em get up into the hills where they'll think they're safe. Far as they know, the only man who could have tracked 'em is dead and gone. Keep 'em believing that."

Kenitay could see his reasoning but that didn't make it any easier to wait while Leisha was taken farther and farther out of his reach by two ruthless, vengeful men.

Within fifteen minutes, Harm was on his feet, leaning heavily upon Amanda. He'd seen to his own wound, proclaiming it nothing serious. That was belied by the amount of blood he'd lost, but he wouldn't hear any arguments. If he took the time to rest up properly, his daughter would be dead. It was that simple.

While giving orders, Jack kept a cautious eye on his uncle. "Kenitay, slip on down to the barn and saddle us up three good horses. Billy, stay here with Westfall. Keep him alive until Ketchum gets here with the rest of the unit. I want someone who isn't a Bass to hear him tell his story so we can clear Kenitay in court."

"I won't let the sonofabitch expire until he does right by us," Billy promised. He was somber-faced, wondering how much of this catastrophe was due to his misplaced trust in Jed. If Jack had asked him to escort Westfall personally into Hell, he would have done it without hesitation.

Amanda was helping Harm to the door. Only she was aware of how much the slightest effort cost him, but knowing him and knowing how much effect any argument would have, she kept silent. He'd sustained more than the nick he claimed. She could feel his agony in each breath he took but forced herself to be strong for him. She'd promised him that she always would be. When they got to the edge of the porch and Kenitay led the horses up from the barn, she turned to him. "You be careful."

He smiled faintly. "Yes, ma'am."

She touched his cheek and their gazes locked in deep communion. She broke it at last by saying, "I love you, Harmon."

He didn't reply but continued to smile at her until Jack brought his horse up close to the steps and gave him a boost. Amanda caught Jack's arm.

"You bring him home to me, Jack."

"I will."

"Bring them both home."

"I plan to."

Then she stepped back and let them ride out, holding everything inside until she was able to step into Billy's big embrace for a good, long cry.

The darkness in the rocky foothills was broken irregularly by bright strips of moonlight. Harm led the way, his elbow hooked around his saddlehorn so he could lean down along his mount's shoulder to study the ground.

It was slow going and to Kenitay, almost an agony. His heart was impatient. His mind was filled with the confusion of the past few hours. He hadn't killed the soldier

at Fort Sill. That meant the path to his future was free
but it was a path he didn't want to travel alone. His future
was up ahead, in the hands of a merciless enemy, an enemy he had brought to the bosom of his family. Tormented
by that, a darkness began to gather in his soul, a deep
throb of purpose that his would-be father-in-law would
have understood. At the center of that black pulse was a
single growing fury, an outrage at the thought of his loved
one in danger.

He had plans for Leisha Bass, hopes that spanned an
eternity, yet that could cruelly end in hours. He could
picture too clearly how she must be suffering from the
dread of what was to happen. It would be Collier all over
again—worse. He had to get to her, if not to stop it from
happening, then to console her in the terrible aftermath.
She was strong. He would help her find the strength to
go on. If he got to her in time.

The prospect of losing everything that mattered to him
made for a deadly accumulation of violent intent dwarfing
all his earlier motives of retribution. Those had called for
personal sacrifice. These were demanding a surrender of
all that he was—a difference in degree, the charge of duty
next to the commitment of his entire being. The difference
between paying for past sins and pursuing future promises.
And he wanted that future with Leisha with a dedication
of spirit, with a desperation of heart, and a determination
of mind.

It all hinged on a part-Apache tracker gleaning the impossible from the unyielding floor of West Texas.

And abruptly that one faint hope spilled out of the saddle, head first to the inhospitable soil.

"Uncle Harm!" Jack jumped from his saddle and knelt
beside the crumpled figure, easing him over onto his back.
"Oh, God, Harmon," he moaned as he lifted his hand so
the silver of moonlight could spill over it. His palm was
slick and dark. Harm tried to sit up but Jack was quick

to restrain him. "Easy, easy now. You're bleeding bad, Uncle Harm. This is crazy. You can't do this. You're all tore up inside."

Harm had him by the shoulder. "I taught you, Jack. Can you run this trail?"

"No." His voice was flat with regret.

Kenitay cursed softly. He'd been raised for most of his life as a reservation Indian, prevented from learning or practicing the basics of survival. He knew no way of helping Leisha, and knowing it was making him crazy.

Until Harm stated plain, "Then I'm gonna *have* to lead you. Let me up."

"No. I won't let you do this. You won't last another half hour, bleeding the way you are."

Harm lay back, breathing hard, trying to think through the slow-rising threat of unconsciousness. Jack hovered over him, his well-loved features drawn with worry. Then Kenitay was at his shoulder and the glitter of fire in his eyes brought inspiration.

"Have to stop the bleeding. Kenitay, you remember that trip to Study Butte?"

Kenitay frowned, searching back through distant memory to a time when he was maybe eight years old and Harm had taken him along on a horse-selling venture. But what had that to do with this? He scoured his sketchy recall of that trip, remembering a sudden storm, being thrown from his horse, and the graze of its hoof cutting a deep gash in his thigh . . . and what Harm had done to keep him from bleeding to death out in the middle of nowhere.

Kenitay put a hand to Harm's shoulder. "I'll see to it."

While Harm rested fitfully and Jack watched uneasily, Kenitay built a small fire, stoking it until the embers were hot. Then he stuck his knife blade into them and waited until the metal glowed.

"What the hell you got in mind, son?" Jack demanded.

"What needs to be done," was his terse answer.

Jack went pale with understanding even as he realized the necessity. He felt his uncle's life pulsing out against the palm he'd pressed to Harm's wound.

Kenitay picked up the knife, his features etched with somber concentration. "Lift him up, Daddy, and don't let him move."

Jack hauled him up and hugged him in tight as Kenitay laid bare the wound. Harm began to breathe in harsh gusts, bracing for what was to come. His head was on Jack's shoulder, his hands clenched on his nephew's upper arms.

"Talk to me, Jack," he panted softly. "Give my soul something to hang onto."

"I want you to think real hard on Randall in the back of that buggy." Jack felt Harm's fingers dig into the muscle of his arms. "And Leisha with that gun to her head. And Amanda waiting for you. Don't you let her down, Harmon." He nodded to Kenitay and there was the sudden, sickly sweet scent of searing flesh as the wound was swiftly cauterized. Harm's fingers bit deep and spasmed briefly, then he went completely lax in Jack's embrace. He hadn't made a sound so Jack did his crying for him.

*Amanda's counting on you. Don't let her down, Harmon.*

*Leisha's gonna be wondering what's keeping us.*

Those words made their way through the red haze of pain to draw Harm back up to a fragile awareness. His eyes blinked open. Faces, Jack's and Kenitay's, wheeled overhead like somber twin moons. He was lying on the hard Texas earth and he couldn't seem to remember why. Until his vision focused in and he caught the intensity of Kenitay's stare. Waiting. Asking.

"Uncle Harm, don't try to get up."

That was Jack—good, solid, sensible Jack.

"No use trying," Harm told him. "I couldn't if I wanted to." Then he put up his hand. "That's why I brought you along. Grab on, son, and get me up. We got things to do."

Her hands were bound behind her back. Another loop was tight about her neck, fastened to the saddlehorn so if she was foolish enough to try to jump, she'd strangle. A tenuous balance was kept by the pressure of her knees against horseflesh. Concentrating on staying upright was an ironic blessing. It kept her from dwelling on other things too deeply. Things like the life she might have led with Kenitay. Things like her mother sobbing over her father's body. Leisha closed her eyes briefly and swallowed down the pain. The time to mourn would come later, if ever. Now, she had to remain alert. Her father wouldn't have wanted her to surrender meekly to the fate the treacherous Eenah had in mind.

She opened her eyes and fixed a murderous stare on the back of her captor. *Run, coyote. See what good it does you.* Kenitay was coming. She had no doubts. Eenah could feel it, too, for though he never looked around, she could see the tension in the way he sat his saddle. She didn't mind the grueling travel. As long as they were moving, it postponed what the Apache had in store for her. She refused to feel afraid. She hoped he was very creative in his torture, for the longer he kept her lingering, the closer Kenitay would be to rescuing her. Emily had mentioned marriage and she was not about to die before exploring that possibility with the man she loved. She wasn't going to let him slip out of his promises that easily.

She glared holes in Eenah's back. *Run, you coward. When my father catches up to you—* Her heart snagged on that unfinished threat. Because her father wasn't coming. And the sorrow surged up too thick to be denied. Anguished tears skewed her sight. She couldn't wipe them away so she blinked furiously to clear them from her eyes.

"How much farther to the border?" Beech's voice betrayed his anxiousness. He was riding in the rear and Leisha could hear his saddle leather creaking as he frequently checked the trail behind them.

"A few hours," Eenah called back calmly. "You worry like an old woman."

"Well, this old woman wants to live long enough to spend every ounce of this silver."

Eenah snorted. "There are things more important than money."

"Not that I've found," Beech retorted wryly.

"When we reach the Rio Grande, you can cross alone. I will wait to make sure we have no followers."

Leisha sat straighter. She knew what that meant. Beech would ride off and Eenah would set up camp and entertain himself by torturing her while waiting for Kenitay. *Do your worst, you cabron. I can take it. Just leave me my last breath so I might share it with the man I love.*

Dawn came with a subtle lifting of shadow, layer by layer, into softer shades of gray. They'd come to a cleft in the escarpment surrounding the Chisos Basin. From that window in the rock wall, daylight would bring a spectacular westward vista across the hot plains to Terlingua. From the south rim platform, the vast domain of basins, solitary mesas, distant mountains, and the blue thread of the Rio Grande led into Mexico.

Warren Beech sighed. He was seeing the realization of a dream.

"What a view," he murmured, relaxing for the first time into a smile.

Until a low drawl intruded upon his pleasure.

"Enjoy it, 'cause the next one you get will be of Hell."

# *Twenty-seven*

"Daddy!"

Leisha twisted wildly in the saddle, needing visual proof of what she had just heard. She got a fleeting glimpse of Harm Bass against the brightening sky, her mother's Winchester cradled in his arms. Beech cried out as if he'd seen a ghost but Eenah, who had every right to be superstitious in these surroundings, had no doubt he was facing a flesh and blood threat. He grabbed for the carbine he'd stolen from Harm. And Leisha knew in an instant that she could not allow the Apache a chance to try for her father's life a second time.

Recklessly, she drove her heels into her mount's ribs. It lunged forward, crashing into the back of Eenah's horse, throwing his aim off. While the animal surged beneath her, Leisha clung frantically with her knees to hang on. She felt the horse stumble and the rope's sharp pull, snapping taut around her neck. She managed a choked-off cry as the animal went down with her still clinging to its back like a panther. The impact jogged her senses loose as a terrible pain shot through her hip and she lost her grip on the saddle. The horse thrashed. Then came the sudden terror that the frightened animal would regain its footing, breaking her neck in the process.

A large hand caught at her shirtfront. She looked up in panic, eyes fastening on a glint of metal. A star and the word "RANGER."

"Jack!"

He cut the rope with a quick pull and she collapsed against him while he severed the bonds behind her back. Then she was hugging him, her mind numb with relief. Jack was here. Her father was alive! And Kenitay . . .

Leisha's head shot up and she looked around frantically. Beech had wheeled his horse away and was pounding back the way they'd come. There was no sign of Harm. Eenah's horse stood with an empty saddle.

Then she heard a footstep and a shadow blocked her view. With a gasp, she looked straight up at the same time Kenitay came down to claim her. It was little more than the rough slant of his mouth over hers, bruising in intensity, aggressive in its hunger. But she opened to that brief possession, responding with a bold, instinctive need only to be left gasping and dazed when he moved away. He cupped her cheek, his thumb wiping away her tears even as more followed in an unbidden deluge.

"Take care of her for me, Daddy," Kenitay ordered crisply. "There's something I have to ask her as soon as this is done."

She stared after him, breathless, never thinking to protest about being ordered to the sidelines.

Panic made Warren Beech careless. He forced his mount down a narrow path not fit for the fleetest antelope. He was looking back over his shoulder when the world seemed to fall out from under him. His horse went down, flinging him free to roll, unhurt, up ahead. He staggered to his feet and paused in indecision. A thick copse of piñon pine was just yards away. They would hide him in their dense branches. Then his gaze touched upon the pouches of silver strapped to the writhing animal's back. Abandoning freedom for wealth, he limped back to the horse and bent to pull the ties loose. And he stiffened at the unmistakable feel of a rifle bore at the base of his skull.

"I told you not to touch my wife."

With a desperate cry, Beech lunged for the rifle in his saddle scabbard. And the roar of eternity was the next thing he heard.

Kenitay slipped along the rocks like the skimming shadow of a hunting hawk. He moved quickly and with care, refusing to give in to anger, for that would have led to recklessness. He had too much to look forward to to risk a moment of rash behavior. He wasn't thinking about retribution or revenge. All he wanted was a finish to it, so he could go on to Leisha. He hadn't started the blood feud between two families. But he would end it here for the sake of all who survived.

There was an ominous rattle of stones and he drew up, casting his attention upward in time to intercept Eenah's leap. He caught the other brave by the forearms and they both tumbled together off the rocky path, plunging, rolling through the juniper and mesquite while grappling for an advantage. They exchanged several brutal body blows, grunting with the impact but oblivious to the pain. Eenah surged up, struggling for the proper purchase on the loose rock so he could squeeze off a decent shot from his hastily drawn sidearm. Kenitay plowed into him, his head ramming into Eenah's mid-section, and over they went again, pistols flying, both sliding even farther down the rough embankment.

Stopping short of killing his opponent had never occurred to Kenitay. What Eenah had done deserved death and that was his intention as he managed to wrestle his own knife free as they skidded the last few feet down to the original path where Jack and Leisha waited. He landed a stunning blow to Eenah's temple and while the Apache groggily tried to shake off his dizziness, Kenitay gained his footing and stood braced above him, gasping for breath.

Seeing the hopelessness of his situation, Eenah chose to surrender the fight. Under Kenitay's wary watch, he got to his knees and stared up fearlessly at his foe. Then with a defiant Apache dignity, he tore open his shirt, exposing his chest and neck to Kenitay's blade. With a stony determination, Kenitay took a step toward him, knife ready.

"Kenitay," Jack called with a tone of authority. "It's over. Let the law have him."

Kenitay hesitated. Eenah was glaring up at him, daring him to end it in the manner of their people. His black eyes glittered but his features were stoic and resigned.

"What do you wait for?" he taunted. "Too white to act as a man?"

Kenitay's hand tightened on the grip of his blade but he wouldn't be goaded. "You would have served your family better by looking ahead to the salvation of our people instead of back upon the futility of revenge. You've dishonored them with your actions and I will not honor you with a warrior's death. You can rot in the white man's prison. It's what you deserve." And he stepped back, disgusted by the single-minded hate he saw in the other's eyes, shaken by how close he'd come to becoming just what he saw before him. And would have become if it hadn't been for Leisha.

Thinking of her brought an instant of distraction as he glanced her way. That was all it took for Eenah to gain his feet and to lunge, with hidden knife drawn, in search of a vital spot. Kenitay heard Leisha's cry of warning a fraction too late to respond. He was wide open and vulnerable to Eenah's retribution. And then there was a boom from overhead and Eenah was flung backward, a bright flower of crimson blooming across his chest. Kenitay looked up in surprise to where Harm stood, lowering his rifle.

"Son," he drawled out wearily, "I've learned the hard way that there are those you never leave alive."

As Harm came skidding down off the rocks on his boot heels, Leisha raced to him, catching him up in a squeezing embrace, her tears falling all over his face.

"Oh, Daddy, I thought he'd killed you!"

Harm leaned into her with a faint smile, then murmured, "Turn me loose, little girl, before you finish the job for him. 'Sides, I don't think it's your daddy you want to be hugging on right now, is it?"

Leisha smashed a quick kiss to his cheek then turned, drew a quick breath, and went with measured dignity to where Kenitay was waiting. They toed off and studied one another without expression.

"What did you want to ask me?" she demanded with a lift of her head.

He cupped that arrogant Bass chin in his palm. "It's not a sign of weakness for a woman to let a man take care of her. Marry me, Leisha."

She frowned slightly, pondering the question. "I don't need you to take care of me," she declared proudly and Kenitay knew a humbling moment. Before he could recover, she flashed him a small smile and continued. "But I have heard that marriage can be like a partnership, the way it is with my mother and father and yours. If that's the kind of arrangement you're interested in . . . then the answer is yes."

Harm gave a sigh of relief as Kenitay swept his daughter up for a long, lusty kiss. He supposed that meant the boy was agreeable. Smart man. He was still smiling as the sight of the two of them began to waver and fade before a sudden, creeping darkness. He was aware of a numbing chill seeping through his limbs, a cold that settled in his chest and made it impossible to draw his next breath.

"Jack . . ."

His knees gave but he never felt Jack's arm cinch up beneath his. He kept falling farther and farther down into darkness. It wasn't an unpleasant sensation.

*Uncle Harm? Harmon! Oh, God—*

*Daddy? Daddy?*

The sound of their voices drifted, floating up and away from him. He could feel Jack's hand gripping his, holding on tight, pulling him back but he was too tired to follow. His fingers opened, sliding free. Falling.

There was something else. Something he almost forgot. He fought briefly, just long enough to get it said.

"Tell Ammy I love her."

And those were his last words.

"Mama, it's time. Everybody's waiting downstairs."

Amanda wiped her red-rimmed eyes and glanced up at her son. His black suit brought out the swarthy coloring of his skin and against it, his blue eyes glimmered, jewel-like. In that moment, he looked so much like his father, she almost started crying again. But she'd promised she wouldn't in front of family so she forced a weak smile and reached up for his good hand. His other was still tucked into a sling.

"How does everything look?" she asked in a faltering voice.

"All fine and fussy," Rand assured her with a thin smile. "Just the kinda thing Daddy would have hated. Good thing he can't see it. I'm about ready to keel over from the smell of all them flowers you had brought in. Everybody's all gussied up and looking about as uncomfortable as I feel."

He tugged at the top button of his shirt until Amanda slapped at his hand and curled his fingers back over her forearm. She took a deep breath and held tight to his arm.

"Let's go before I get all weepy again." She glanced

over at Leisha, who was still standing by the windows looking out. "Are you going to be all right?"

Leisha nodded, but she looked pale and her blue eyes were enormous. "I just need a minute alone to—to gather up my courage."

"Do you want Randall to come back up for you?"

"No. I'll be fine. I'll be down in a minute."

Amanda gave her a bolstering smile and nodded to her son.

The parlor was full of family and friends, all of them turning when Rand and Amanda stepped in from the hall. They lined either side of the room with an open aisle down the center. At the far end was the same aged preacher who'd married Amanda Duncan to Harmon Bass a lifetime ago. Amanda felt her tears start up again remembering the circumstances. Harm had shaken her out of bed and had dragged her into Cal and Elena's living room. She'd been in her nightgown! She glanced to her left and saw Elena and Cal, arm in arm. Elena's eyes were all misty, too, remembering just as she was.

She walked at Rand's side, nodding to those she passed: friends from town; Rangers from Terlingua and Ysleta who'd ridden with Harm and Jack; Sarah and Billy with their brood between them; Jessie with her face freshly scrubbed and a secret smile for Rand; and Jed, conspicuously missing. Sid was there with his prissy wife, Judith. Some fresh-faced boy in an army uniform sat looking awkward. Leisha had told her his name but she'd forgotten. Johnny something. Jack and Emily, her eyes as suspiciously swollen as her own, were the last ones she saw. She smiled at them all because she'd promised Harm she wouldn't cry. She just hadn't known how hard it was going to be to keep that promise.

Upstairs, Leisha made a few last adjustments to her gown and tried to square up her composure as well. The dress fit funny, too snug across the chest where its hateful stays poked and prodded. She was half-tempted to take it off when a soft drawl from the door stopped her.

"*Shijii,* you look like an angel."

She turned, stern-looking instead of pleased by the praise. "Daddy, what are you doing out of bed? If Mama sees you up, she'll shoot you!"

Harm gave her one of his rare wide smiles. "Did you think I'd let someone else give my little girl away?" Then she was in his arms, hugging him carefully, mindful of the heavy yards of tape wound around his middle. "It'd take more than your mama's threats to keep me from walking you on my arm."

"I love you, Daddy." Then she leaned back with a saucy frown. "But don't you think you ought to be wearing more than your long underwear and bandages?"

He grinned back. "It's not like I could ask your mama to help me get dressed. Give me a hand, little girl, and promise you won't let me fall down in front of everybody."

"We'll hold each other up, Daddy."

Amanda heard a murmur ripple through the gathering. She hurriedly dried her eyes again, then looked up in surprise as Rand slid in on the other side of her.

"Where's your sister?" she whispered in confusion.

"She replaced me at the last minute." He took her arm, smiling smugly to himself.

Frowning slightly, Amanda turned to see father and daughter coming toward her. Looking heartbreakingly handsome in his dark suit, Harm was pale and moving so slow she knew he had to be hurting, but his smile was wide and proud as he led his oldest child up to where the preacher waited. He took Leisha's hand and pressed it into Kenitay's, curling their fingers together.

"Take care of each other," he told them firmly. Then

he eased in next to Amanda, smiling rather sheepishly in the face of her surprise. She stared at him for a long moment, then sighed as she glanced down and saw he was barefooted.

"Harmon Bass, you make me crazy," she whispered, then put her arm around him to hold him up while they heard their daughter's vows.

The minute Kenitay's hand engulfed hers, all Leisha's nervousness fled. She forgot about the wicked jabbing of her bodice stays and the overpowering smell of all the flowers her mother had insisted upon. Though Becca and Carson and the preacher surrounded them, she was aware of no one but the man beside her. Lost in the deep green mystery of his eyes and thrilled by what his small smile insinuated, she almost forgot to listen to the words, even though she was wearing Kenitay's spirit earrings so she could learn to listen better. They were just words, after all, and she didn't need words to tell her they were joined in heart and soul any more than she needed the feel of warm gold sliding over her knuckle to tell her they were bound, one to the other. She'd known that from their first kiss, so when all the words were said and he took her in his arms for a long, lingering kiss, it was not a beginning but rather a continuation of what she'd always realized. This man was her man.

It had just taken her Bass pride a helluva long time to admit it.

After all the congratulations were said, the imported champagne appreciated, her father had been toted back to bed by Jack and Billy and a scolding Amanda, and the company had gone home and the house was settled into the cool quiet of a Texas evening, Leisha prepared to lead her new husband up to her room for the long-anticipated wedding night.

But Kenitay had other ideas.

He had her hand tight in his, pulling her toward the

front door. Her first instinct was to balk and demand an explanation. Then she heard the whisper of her mother's advice: *sometimes it is best to follow.*

So she did.

Kenitay paused long enough to snatch up one of her mama's fancy crocheted coverups from the back of the sofa. Then before she could question him, he hoisted her up in his arms to carry her, all bundled up in miles of wedding lace and satin, out into the hall, down the stairs, and out into the starry night. By then, she was smiling. Her arms curled around his neck and she nibbled tiny kisses along his jaw. He walked faster, carrying her away from the house, down to where Blue Creek meandered indifferently.

"What if my family gets to wondering what happened to us?" she murmured coyly, teasing his necktie loose.

"Let them wonder."

He set her down on the cool, dark bank and at once, she rose up against him, pressing her tongue between his lips. Then came her husky whisper. "Get me out of this dress before I strangle."

She put her back to him, presenting him with more than twenty tiny buttons. He started down them obligingly enough but when the creamy satin parted, revealing inch after inch of bare skin, his patience fled.

"What have you got on under this dress?"

Leisha glanced over her shoulder, her blue eyes smoky. "Stockings."

He had ten more buttons to go but his fingers wouldn't cooperate. Finally, in frustration, he caught the separate sides in either hand and pulled the rest of it open for a tantalizing view of his wife's smooth back from nape to the cleft of her buttocks. He leaned against her, his mouth scorching that sleek skin until she moaned in anticipation.

His palms brushed the heavy beaded sleeves from the caps of her shoulders, sending the gown to the bunch grass with a sigh. She turned to him, wearing nothing but pale stockings, his wedding band, and dangling earrings. And an expectant smile.

Kenitay tossed the coverlet over the sandy ground, then tossed her down atop it and became her covering. And became as fierce and fiery a lover as she could ever wish for as she sent her cries of pleasure up to an uncaring sky.

Then when she was tucked all smug and sated against his chest and they could think of things beyond the immediate, Kenitay rumbled, "We'll buy land. Lots of it so we can surround ourselves and our children with freedom." Like her part-Apache father, he was quite practical when it came to matters of the home, which were, after all, a woman's domain. Though marriage gave him control of the vast fortune she inherited upon saying her vows, he had no interest in it. Theirs was a partnership.

She smiled up at the dark, starry canopy overhead. "Yes."

"Do you have a problem with honeymooning in Austin?"

"Why there?"

"Because Sid wants to start petitioning the government and he wants me to advise him. It'll mean some traveling, probably to Washington and Fort Sill. Will you go with me?"

"We don't stay with Sid," came her firm warning.

He smiled. "No."

She raked her fingers through his short locks. "That'll mean wearing your hair like this and acting civilized."

"You can teach me."

She smiled wider. "Who'll teach me?"

"Then we won't be civilized. I married you for who you are. I don't want that to change."

She reached to draw out one of the turquoise and shell earrings she wore and slipped it through the hole in his ear. It hung down, grazing his swarthy cheek as he came up on his elbow above her. It gave him a wild look, a dangerous air. She liked it. "Then wear that so that we might always hear what the other has to say."

And under the clear Texas sky, they spent the rest of the evening communicating silently in the way of lovers, building a partnership that would endure for an eternity.